PRAISE FOR
THE SUSPECT

"Barton is a stunning storyteller. Her career as a journalist has helped make this story terrifyingly real. Every turn of the plot feels authentic and very scary." —*Library Journal* (starred review)

"Expertly written. . . . Barton's characterizations are exceptional." —*The Washington Post*

"Barton's Kate Waters is the real deal . . . [*The Suspect*] is a great binge-read." —*The Globe and Mail*

"Barton's classic use of short chapters and multiple narratives keeps the reader on edge. . . . Barton's skill in weaving both unexpected [and] believable twists and turns right up to the final page is commendable." —*USA Today* (3½ out of 4 stars)

"Barton is a veritable master of complex mysteries." —PopSugar

"An edge-of-your-seat suspense novel about a parent's worst nightmare." —*Glamour*

"Using her exceptional storytelling skills and her keen insight into the minds of each of her characters—from the many shades of grief the parents go through to the fear and loneliness the teens feel, alone and abroad for the first time in their lives—Barton creates a twisty mystery that packs a serious emotional punch." —Bustle

"The razor-sharp thriller *The Suspect* reaffirms the reputation of Fiona Barton as an author who combines propulsive narrative with subtle, insightful commentary on the universal stories of family, identity, and loss. Perhaps this is one reason many critics are comparing her to the likes of Tana French, Louise Penny, Megan Abbott, and Paula Hawkins. . . . A well-crafted commercial thriller." —Mystery Tribune

"A stunning triumph of suspense and pacing certain to solidify [Barton's] hold on the psychological thriller genre . . . a thriller that breaks the mold . . . *The Suspect* tugs at our heartstrings, even as it leaves us gasping."

—*The Providence Journal*

PRAISE FOR

THE CHILD

"Tense, tantalizing, and ultimately very satisfying . . . definitely one of the year's must-reads."

—Lee Child

"An engrossing, irresistible story about the coming to light of a long-buried secret, and an absolutely fabulous read—I loved it!"

—Shari Lapena, author of *The Couple Next Door*

"Another winner . . . a truly engaging tale. Those who enjoyed *The Widow* will discover that Barton has only gotten better."

—The Associated Press

"Nonstop action."

—NPR

"Barton knows what we're afraid of—our inability to protect society's most vulnerable members from harm—and she's not afraid to plunge us headfirst into the abyss, for all the right reasons."

—*Toronto Star*

"Fiona Barton has masterfully delivered again . . . so much perfect suspense. . . . Barton tells the child's story as only she can—brilliantly."

—*Fort Worth Star-Telegram*

"A novel that is both fast-paced and thought-provoking, it keeps the reader guessing right to the end."

—*USA Today*

"A lightning-paced, twisty story with an ending so surprising you might have to read it twice."

—*Good Housekeeping*

"Startling twists—and a stunning, emotionally satisfying conclusion."
—*Publishers Weekly* (starred review)

PRAISE FOR
THE WIDOW

"If you liked *Gone Girl* and *The Girl on the Train*, you might want to pick up *The Widow* by Fiona Barton. Engrossing. Suspenseful."
—Stephen King

"Both a taut reconstruction of a crime and a ruthless examination of marriage . . . a smartly crafted, compulsively readable tale."
—*Entertainment Weekly*

"Barton has written a compelling book inside a horrible crime. While it could be devoured in one heart-stopping gulp, this is a book best savoured slowly, with the time to luxuriate in the myriad carefully placed details— even act so automatic as picking up a piece of litter will eventually have a major impact later in the saga."
—*Maclean's*

"[Barton] delivers the goods. . . . Richly character-driven in a way that is both satisfying and engrossing."
—*The Washington Post*

"[A] twisty tale . . . with a mesmerizing if unreliable narrator . . . that will blow your mind."
—*O, The Oprah Magazine*

"Barton's writing is compelling and top-notch."
—The Associated Press

"A twisted psychological thriller you'll have trouble putting down."
—*People*

"[Jean is] a fascinating puzzle. . . . Barton knows how to ramp up tension."

ALSO BY FIONA BARTON

THE WIDOW
THE CHILD

THE SUSPECT

FIONA BARTON

PENGUIN

an imprint of Penguin Canada, a division of Penguin Random House Canada Limited

Penguin Canada
320 Front Street West, Suite 1400, Toronto, Ontario M5V 3B6, Canada

First published in Penguin paperback by Penguin Canada, 2019. Simultaneously published in the
United States by BERKLEY, an imprint of Penguin Random House LLC, New York.

Published in this edition, 2020

1   2   3   4   5   6   7   8   9   10

Library and Archives Canada Cataloguing in Publication

Barton, Fiona, author
The suspect / Fiona Barton.

Originally published: Toronto: Penguin Canada, 2019.
ISBN 978-0-14-319778-2 (softcover)

I. Title.

PR6102.A7839S87 2020   823'.92   C2018-905418-2

Cover image: © Alamy and Shutterstock
Cover design by R.Shailer/TW
Book design by Kristin del Rosario

Printed and bound in the United States of America

www.penguinrandomhouse.ca

Penguin
Random House
PENGUIN CANADA

For Beatrice, Arthur, Jemima, Olive, and Isabelle

Never let the truth get in the way of a good story.

UNKNOWN

PART ONE

THE JOB

ONE

The Reporter

The call comes at three a.m. The jagged ring of the bedside telephone tearing a hole in our sleep.

I reach out a hand to silence it.

"Hello," I whisper.

Static whispers back to me. I press the phone harder to my ear.

"Who is this?"

I feel Steve roll over to face me, but he doesn't speak.

The hissing static fades and I hear a voice.

"Hello. Hello," it says, searching for me.

I pull myself up and switch on the light. Steve groans and rubs his eyes.

"Kate? What's going on?" he says.

"Who is this?" I repeat. But I know.

"Jake?"

"Mum," the voice says, the word distorted by distance—*or drink, perhaps*, I think uncharitably.

"Sorry I missed your birthday," it says.

The line fizzes again and he's gone.

I look at Steve.

"Was it him?" he asks.

I nod. "He's sorry he missed my birthday . . ."

It's the first time in seven months that he's phoned. There've been three e-mails, but our eldest son told us early on that he wouldn't be contactable by phone. Said he was freeing himself of all the stress that constant calls would bring. He'd stay in touch with us.

When he last rang, it was Christmas morning. We'd hoped he would be there with us, pulling crackers and making his lethal mulled wine. We'd suggested and then pleaded by e-mail, even buying a plane ticket when he seemed to weaken. But Jake had stayed away, managing only a ten-minute call on the day. Steve had answered the phone and spoken to him first while I hovered beside him; then he'd asked to speak to his little brother, Freddie, and finally to his mother.

I'd hugged the phone, as if I could feel the heft and warmth of him, and tried to listen, not talk. But he'd remained distant as the seconds counted down in a phone booth somewhere and I'd found myself turning inquisitor.

"So, where are you now, love?"

"Here." He'd laughed.

"Still in Phuket?"

"Yes, yes."

"And are you working?"

"Yeah, sure. Doing this and that."

"But what about money?"

"I'm managing, Mum. Don't worry about me. I'm fine."

"Well, as long as you are happy," I'd heard myself say. The coward's way out.

"Yes, I am."

After I'd put the phone down, Freddie had put a glass of prosecco in my hand and kissed my cheek.

"Come on, Mum. He's fine. Having a brilliant time lying around in the sun while we're sitting here in the slush and rain."

But I'd known deep down he wasn't fine. His voice had become wary. And that nervy laugh. He didn't sound like my Jake anymore.

TWO

The Mother

Lesley searched the inbox again. Just in case she'd missed it. She knew she hadn't, but to stop looking would mean they had to act. They'd agreed. Malcolm stood behind her, watching her every move. She could feel the tension radiating off him.

"Anything?" he asked.

"No."

"I'm ringing the police."

She nodded. They'd never had to ring the police before in all their married life. The police belonged to another world—the world they saw on television or in the papers. Not theirs. She was shaking as Malcolm picked up the phone. She wanted to tell him to wait. To give it another day. Not to start this. Not to bring this into their home.

"Mal," she said, but he looked at her as he dialed, silencing her. She could hear the hum of the fridge and a car passing by outside. Life going on.

"Hello. I'd like to report my daughter missing," she heard him say. That life was over.

"A week. We haven't heard from her or the friend she's with for almost a week," he said. "Her A Level results came out yesterday, but she still hasn't been in touch.

"She's Alexandra O'Connor.

"Eighteen. Her birthday was in May."

Icing that cake, Lesley thought. *Didn't look anything like Ed Sheeran apart from the red hair, but Alex had loved it.*

She tuned back in to hear her husband apologizing.

"Sorry, I thought I said. She's in Thailand, backpacking with her friend Rosie Shaw. Her last text message said they were still in Bangkok."

It took another twenty minutes for Malcolm to explain the situation, give his details, and listen to the advice. When he put the phone down he rubbed his eyes and kept his hands there for a moment.

"What? What did they say?" Lesley said, the panic making her voice loud and unlike her usual tone. "Who did you talk to? Tell me!"

Her husband jerked his head up and looked at her as if to reassure himself this was his wife, shrieking in their kitchen.

"They took down all the details, love. You heard me. I spoke to a woman officer. I wrote it on a bit of paper." He reached over to the counter and picked up a Post-it note.

"Here, look."

Lesley brushed it aside so it floated to the tiled floor.

"Never mind that. What did this woman say? What are they going to do to find Alex and Rosie?"

Malcolm stooped to pick up the piece of paper and put it back on the counter. Lesley wanted to hit him.

"Malcolm!"

"Sorry, love, but we are going to need this." He spoke slowly, as if she were an elderly relative. "She said she's going to pass on the details to Interpol and we should ring the British embassy in Bangkok. That's what they advise. But she said this happens a lot, young people going traveling and forgetting to contact their parents. She said it was early days and that we should try not to worry."

"So she thinks it's going to be all right?" Lesley willed him to say yes or nod. *Let it be all right . . .*

Malcolm shook his head. "She doesn't know, love. We've to ring her if Alex gets in touch—or if she doesn't in another week."

"She will, won't she?"

Malcolm pulled her to him. "Of course she will. She'll want to know her A Level results. Tomorrow or the next day. She'll turn up, like a bad penny."

Lesley wiped her eyes with a paper towel and tried to look hopeful.

"I'd better ring Jenny back," she said, grateful there was something practical to be done. "I told her I would as soon as we'd spoken to the police. She got a bit funny about it yesterday."

"I think she's as frantic as we are. Rosie's her only one. And Jenny's on her own."

"Okay. What are you doing?"

Malcolm was tapping at the keyboard of the laptop. "The police want a photo. I said I'd send one. Then I'll find the number for the embassy."

Lesley looked over his shoulder. He'd picked the selfie Alex had sent of her and Rosie in a tuk-tuk on the day they arrived, grinning madly, their surroundings a blur.

"At least they're together," Lesley said and wept, her head on her arms on the kitchen table.

BANGKOK DAY 1
(SUNDAY, JULY 27, 2014)

Her fingers danced over the keypad of her phone as she posted the selfie of her standing in front of Suvarnabhumi Airport with tired eyes and a silly grin on her face. She'd planned this photo on the plane. She knew what it would look like but she hadn't factored in the noise and heat as the terminal doors slid open. The heat had shaken her physically. She'd known it would be hot—Google had told her—but not like this. It was wet on her face and she could taste it on her tongue. She put her backpack down carefully, trapping it with her feet to keep it safe, and stretched her arms above her head, feeling the first buzz of freedom.

Alex had looked forward to this for a year, fantasizing about places, people, adventures, while she stacked shelves and pulled pints to earn the money.

She'd looked forward to everything about it, starting with the flight—she'd always loved the sensation of suddenly rushing down the runway toward something new. And she'd felt the same thrill as the engines revved high at the start of this, her first long haul taking her across the world. But the sensation had worn off quickly. It was eleven hours sitting in a middle seat, trying not to touch the arms of people hidden like corpses under thin blankets.

Rosie had had three glasses of wine with her hideous airline meal—"The chicken or the pasta?"—and Alex had warned her she'd get dehydrated. Her friend had rolled her eyes and made a big show of flirting with the man in the next seat before falling asleep and snoring gently. Alex had tried to sleep, too, squirming in her narrow seat to find a comfortable position, pulling up her blanket and uncovering her feet, fidgeting with her safety belt to stop it digging into her hip. In the end she'd sat in the dark and watched films on the tiny rectangle in front of her until her eyes stung.

When the lights came back on an hour before landing, she'd unbuckled and gone to the toilet. Her face in the mirror looked weird. Eyes red-rimmed and mouth slack with sleep deprivation. She'd yawned at herself and, suddenly panicky, wrestled with the unfamiliar door to get out.

There'd been a boy standing waiting when she burst out. She'd laughed at herself—"They're a real nightmare to unlock, aren't they?"

He'd smiled shyly back and let her past.

And now she was here. Bangkok. She picked up her backpack and swung it heavily onto her shoulder and staggered slightly, dizzy from the sudden movement. She felt stiff and spacey, as if her feet didn't quite touch the ground.

Strangers were asking her to come with them. Small men with wide smiles and insistent hands.

"You need a taxi?"

"I know good guesthouse."

"You want to see temple?"

She stood, the choices drumming on her skull. It was five a.m., dark, hot, and she wanted to lie down somewhere.

Come on, Alex—let's go, she told herself. *Where's Rosie?*

Her friend had wandered off, looking for something for her headache.

"You shouldn't have had all that wine on the plane. Didn't you bring any paracetamol?" Alex had said, reaching to unzip the side pocket of her bag.

"No," Rosie had snapped and marched off.

Alex hoped it was going to be all right. Anyway, it was too late for doubts. They were here. And it was brilliant. Well, it would be.

THREE

The Detective

FRIDAY, AUGUST 15, 2014

DS Zara Salmond was treading so lightly around DI Bob Sparkes that morning, it felt like he was being stalked. Her presence was always just out of sight, but she couldn't have been more intrusive if she'd been holding up a neon sign reading "The Boss's Wife Is Dying."

Eileen's cancer had come back two months ago, blowing new holes in her, murdering her slowly. "We can beat this," he'd told her after the latest results came back. "We've done it once; we can do it again."

The kids had cried with him at home, away from their mother. Now everyone was being strong for one another, the effort exhausting. It was all he could do to get out of bed some mornings.

Work had been fantastic, his bosses urging him to take as much time off as he needed, but Sparkes could not settle at the hospital or at home. He needed something in his life that was not about cancer. He needed to pretend that a normal life was possible, for Eileen's sake and to distract his aching heart.

But he had clearly forgotten to brief DS Salmond.

He knew she was keeping the rabble in the incident room from his door out of kindness, but Sparkes lost it when he overheard his detective sergeant telling a colleague, "You'll have to come back later. He's not having a good day." He could picture her caring look and shouted, "Salmond, get in here."

When she put her neatly groomed head round the door, he wiped the smile off her face.

"You are getting right up my nose, Salmond. Stop telling people to leave me alone. Go and do something useful. I feel as if I am being quarantined."

The DS tried to laugh it off, but Bob knew he'd been too rough. He stood to stop her leaving.

"Sorry. It's just, when you are talking about me, you sound as if you are dealing with a jumper on a bridge. I'm all right."

"Okay, boss. Point taken. I'll leave you to it. I've got reports to finish."

"Tell me what you are up to." He pointed to a chair.

Salmond sat and crossed her arms. *Still defensive,* Bob thought.

"Come on, Zara. Remind me."

"Well, I'm chasing up the final results on the drugs bust out at Portsmouth."

"It's a bit slow, isn't it?"

"Yes. Well, people have been off for the summer holidays."

"Anything to worry about?"

"No, all looks tidy. Oh, and we've had a report of two girls from Winchester going missing."

"Missing? How old?" he said, immediately on full alert. "When did this come in? Why didn't you tell me straightaway?"

"They're eighteen and missing in Thailand."

"Ah," Sparkes muttered, his mind slipping away to the meeting with Eileen's consultant later.

"Bit off our patch, but I'm up for it if you want to send . . ." DS Salmond said, a shade louder to show she'd noticed his eyes glazing over.

"In your dreams, Zara. Anyway, you've just been away."

"Hardly a holiday, boss. When Neil said Turkey, I thought sun loungers. We spent most of the time looking at ancient latrines for his Year Ten's project. In one-hundred-four-degree heat."

"Latrines? Excellent. Any photos?"

Salmond laughed. "Neil's got loads. I'll ask him to send you a se-
lection."

"Yeah, no hurry. What about these girls, then?"

"It's only been a week but the parents are twitchy. Girls are away for
the first time and didn't ring for their A Level results yesterday. The dad
of one of them phoned it in this morning and I'm passing on the details
to Interpol, but my bet is they'll be on a beach somewhere. Lucky them."

"Yes, lucky them. Well, let me know any updates. The media will
be all over this if it develops—you'd better brief the press office."

And he winked to let her know they were all right.

"Quick update, sir," Salmond said twenty minutes later. "The press
office was briefed about the backpackers and there's a Facebook
campaign already running—the family are doing it."

Sparkes pulled a face.

"It's a good idea, sir. That's where kids who might be sitting in a
bar next to Alex and Rosie will be looking."

"Yes, them and every weirdo and glory seeker on the planet, offering fake sympathy and sightings just to be part of the drama. And
then there'll be the trolls, blaming the parents for letting their kids go
traveling, calling the girls sluts and whores. God, who opened the
microphone to people like them? At least before social media you
didn't have to hear this stuff. They could sit in the snug of their local
pub or their front room and spout their bile."

"Anyway . . ." Salmond said. "Moving on . . ."

"Yes, let's."

Sparkes was looking at reports on-screen, his head elsewhere.

He leaned back, stretched out his arms to touch the computer,
and then took them over his head, making his back click. There was a

metallic taste in his mouth and he could no longer get out of his chair without an involuntary groan. He felt old. Really old.

Eileen had said he needed more sleep that morning when he'd gone in to see her, but he'd waved her concerns away. "I'm fine, love. Why are we talking about me? Let's concentrate on you and getting rid of this stupid infection."

She'd lain back on her pillow. "I am trying, Bob."

He tried to focus on the words on his screen, but his head was full of the growing fragility in his wife's eyes. They were sinking into her head, away from him. It was as if she were being hollowed out. He flexed and clenched his fingers.

Not now. Can't think about it now. It'll be all right.

He tapped the touch pad to awaken his screen and a photo appeared. DS Salmond had uploaded images of the missing girls and the link to the Facebook page the O'Connors had set up.

Sparkes looked at their faces and sighed. He clicked and began reading, starting with Alex's last Facebook post and e-mail home on Saturday, August 9.

Alex O'Connor . . . is planning to celebrate (🤞!) her A Level results with her bezzy in Ko Phi Phi, "gazing out at monolithic rocks in an azure blue sea" according to Lonely Planet . . .

FROM: Alexinnit96@yahoo.co.uk
TO: lesandmaloconnor@gmail.com
SUBJECT: Results

Hi Mum and Dad,

Still in Bangkok—so much to see, we've decided to stay longer—but planning to move on in time for the results! Everything crossed that I get into Warwick. Will ring like we said about 12noon your time (1800 here) to open the envelope together. Like the Oscars! Text me if the post arrives earlier!! Love you, Alex xx

> Ps Seeing elephants tomorrow. Another bucket list item
> ticked off . . .

The SOS was then sounded by Alex O'Connor's brother, quietly at first. More of a nudge, really.

> Hi Alex. Haven't heard from you for a few days. Where are
> you now?
>
> We can't get through on your phone. Mum's a bit worried. Can
> you message us.
>
> Alex?
>
> Alex??
>
> FFS ALEX. CALL!!!!!

The capitalized scream marked the tipping point when the gentle reminders became a full-throated roar of panic.

> It's been 4 days since anyone saw my sister and her friend.
> Please keep sharing and posting.
>
> It's been 5 days.
>
> 6 days.

And the "community" had kicked in:

> Let your families know you are OK, Alex and Rosie.
> Please.
>
> Was that you I bought a drink for last night in Oxxi's Place?
> Ring your parents.
>
> They just want to know U R safe.
>
> Don't be so selfish. Contact your family.

The parents will give them such a rocket when they turn up, he thought. *Causing all this fuss. Bet they wish they'd never agreed to let them go.*

He'd never had to struggle with such a decision. His children hadn't been the adventurous sort. He couldn't even remember discussing gap years with them. His son, Jim, had been set on going to university and getting on with his career in accountancy, and his daughter, Sam, had already fallen in love, so she wasn't going anywhere.

Wonder if their lives would have turned out differently if they'd gone to Thailand, he mused, idly scrolling back through the messages. Kate Waters's son had gone. She'd confided in Sparkes when she and he last met to discuss a case. He didn't normally get into personal stuff with reporters, but Kate had clearly needed to talk, and had told him about the silences from Jake stretching into months. And how she secretly worried he was struggling but didn't want to admit it to her husband.

Sparkes hadn't liked to say his secret worry about his son was that he was getting old before his time. He was only in his thirties, but his hair was thinning and he wore slippers in the house.

"They've got oak flooring," Eileen had said when he'd mentioned it. "He's fine."

But he was never going to go to a Full Moon Party.

Perhaps they'd got off lightly. He flicked back to look at the laughing faces of the missing girls. Fresh faces. Lost children.

Where were they? He'd ring Kate later and tell her about the story. Get things moving.

FOUR

The Reporter
FRIDAY, AUGUST 15, 2014

Joe Jackson is sitting in my chair to watch the newsroom television and I swat him as I pass, catching his shoulder.

"Oy, Jackson! Out!"

He grins up at me and pushes back from the desk, freewheeling out of my way, and I see Jake in my head, messing around, hair in his eyes, teasing me.

"Get on with your work," I growl.

"I'm making calls." He shows me his mobile as proof, jumps up, and pulls my chair back into position. "Nothing much to tell, yet. I've got a bit of time before the Sunday-for-Monday news meeting. I hope Terry doesn't call it early."

As if by magic, the news editor appears from the Goldfish Bowl, his glass-walled cubicle of an office.

"He's bugged our desks, hasn't he?" Joe murmurs, and I nod.

"What are you whispering about?" Terry shouts across. "It'd better be a story. Your hit rate is a joke, Jackson."

As the youngest staff reporter in the newsroom, Joe Jackson is an easy target for so-called banter. Bullying, if we're being honest. Joe and I had had a prickly start when he'd been assigned to me for work experience—I told Terry I didn't have time to run the office crèche, but the editor had insisted—and he's grown on me. I know the other reporters call him my "office son" or "the chief reporter's bitch," but I ignore it. I hope he does, too. I keep telling him they'll get bored and find another game.

"Here, put this up to Terry," I say, slipping a cutting across the desk. "It's got follow-up written all over it."

"Thanks. I owe you another one."

"Put it on the slate. Now make a call on it so you'll sound like you know what you're talking about."

I flick a quick look at Terry. He's heard it all. He hears everything. He pulls a face. "Soft touch," it says. I shrug back and pick up my phone to avoid talking to him.

I scroll through the contacts, looking for a likely target, and stop at DI Bob Sparkes. I see his name most days—I've filed him under his first name to keep him near the top of the list. But today I don't go past. I press it. I need a friendly voice this morning. And he might have a story.

Bob Sparkes and I have enjoyed—or maybe he'd say endured—the sort of forced intimacy that working on difficult cases brings. It's a reality of life that detectives and reporters find themselves knocking on the same doors in search of the facts and cooped up in the same pubs, courtrooms, and canteens.

For some officers, reporters are a cross to bear and they make us sweat for every piece of information, but Sparkes is a generous copper. He knows what we need to tell the story and is usually happy to oblige. He doesn't play games.

"Suits all of us to work together," he said once. "The police get the publicity they need for the investigation—and some recognition for the work done—and you get your story."

And he deserves the recognition. He works his socks off to get a result.

I've seen him do it. Eight years ago, in the Bella Elliott case, he spent every waking hour looking for the missing toddler, thinking about her. He said he dreamed about her, too. And even in cases he wasn't running, he's acted as my touchstone. When I was trying to find the identity of a baby whose remains had been found on a London building site in 2012, he'd been there on the end of a phone. He didn't have to do it, but I'd relied on him for grown-up advice when I got too involved. Too close to see what was in front of me.

It's not exactly Holmes and Watson, but we rub along.

Of course, it means that he knows far too much about me. I know I overshare sometimes, telling him my private thoughts and domestic problems, but I trust him.

The phone rings. "Kate!" the voice says sharply, startling me.

"Good grief, Bob—have you been issued with new psychic powers? I was just about to ring you."

"Ha! Must have been thinking about each other at the same moment."

I can feel myself blushing. *For Christ's sake, get a grip, woman!*

"Thinking about me? In a good way? Or cursing me?"

"In a good way, Kate," he replies evenly. He doesn't do flirting. Never been a swordsman.

I try not to smile—he'll hear it in my voice.

"Go on, then. What were you thinking?"

"I've got an inquiry that you might be able to help with. Two teen-age girl backpackers in Thailand have been reported missing by their families. They haven't been in touch for a week, so it's early days, but they missed getting their exam results yesterday and their parents are very anxious. My sergeant thinks they'll probably turn up with a hang-over, but a story might winkle them out of whichever bar they're sit-ting in. Anyway, I thought of you. And Jake."

Bob Sparkes knows about Jake. How he dropped out of university and about the row it had caused—I'd told him after the result in the Building Site Baby case, when we'd had a quiet drink to decompress. He's got adult kids, too. He knows how god-awful being a parent is sometimes and he listens carefully. He always listens well, Bob. A trained ear. But he hasn't told me about Eileen's illness. I found out about the cancer from another copper. I was shocked—more that Bob hadn't confided in me than by the cancer, if I'm honest. I've tried to prompt him to tell me since then, mentioning Steve and his work in oncology a couple of times. But Sparkes has never taken the bait.

"Sure. How old are the girls? Are there photos? Where are they from? Can I speak to the parents?"

"Good grief, Kate. Slow down. You're like a greyhound out of the traps. They're eighteen and from Winchester. Look, I'll send you the details as soon as we get off the phone."

"Great. Are you putting it all round?" I have to ask.

"Yes, the press office is writing something to put on the tape at the moment."

"Any chance you could give me a couple of hours' head start, Bob?"

There's a pause. I wait him out.

"Go on, then," he says. "It's hardly breaking news. I'll ask them to hold on to it until after lunch."

"Brilliant. Thanks, Bob."

"Anyway, how is Jake?"

I've forgotten my son, pushed past him in the rush to write about someone else's child. *What sort of mother are you?*

"Er, not sure. He rang in the middle of the night a few weeks ago—first call for months—but it sounded like it was from some jungle outpost and I lost the line."

"What a shame. Still, he did call."

"Yes, he did. I have to be grateful for that, I suppose."

"The parents of Alex O'Connor and Rosie Shaw would be, Kate."

I can hear the edge of censure in his voice and try not to react. I scribble down the names.

"Yes, well . . . okay, send the missing girls' stuff as soon as you can—I'm sure I can get it in the paper. There's nothing else happening. And, Bob, thanks for holding it. I appreciate it."

I open my laptop to wait for his e-mail. My inbox has filled again. It's been only half an hour since I weeded through the overnight mass mailings, but there are a dozen new PR puffs for television shows and celebrities selling ghosted memoirs with promises of "amazing revelations."

"I don't know why I'm getting so much showbiz dross," I regularly grumble to Joe. But actually I do. My name has joined a list of journos who write the celeb stories. I'm a marked woman. I used to be a serious reporter, whatever that means these days.

I spent yesterday afternoon writing a "heartwarming"—in my head I am raking the air with ironic quotation marks—picture story about a dog adopting ducklings.

"It probably ate them after the photographer left," I'd told Steve when I'd got home. "God, I hate August. Bloody Silly Season. We are in a news-free zone, scratching around for stories when the whole country has gone on holiday. The editor gave me back one of my old spreads this afternoon. He must have stashed it in his bottom drawer in the New Year. Told me to dust it off so he could put it in the paper. I had to make sure no one in it had died in the meantime."

Steve had poured me another glass of sauvignon blanc and clinked glasses in sympathy.

. . .

I deleted the offending e-mails without opening, my eye automatically on alert for jakeinparadise2012@hotmail.com.

His e-mails are never in answer to my or Steve's regular messages. When they arrive, they're short and to the point—two or three sentences, more a telegram than a letter—telling us he's still alive and, clearly, not thinking about us. We still pore over them, looking for meaning in every word.

It's been two years since he embarked on his journey "to find himself" in Southeast Asia. He should have been studying for his bar exams this year. He'd been doing so well at university before . . . We'd dreamed of him becoming a barrister. We were excited for him. I suppose, looking back, maybe we were more excited than he was. But he always did relaxed and cool. Used to drive me mad. He was a lucky boy—bright and lucky—but he wasn't grateful. He had it too easy, maybe. He'd never had to struggle to get top grades, as his little brother had. It was Freddie we worried about. Steve and I tried to hide it from him. We kept our agonized discussions about his future for after he'd gone to bed. Poor Freddie. Always in Jake's shadow at school. Then, out of the blue, Jake had come home and casually announced he'd jacked in his degree and was going traveling.

He'd said he was thinking about joining a turtle conservancy project in Phuket and there'd been an almighty row.

I'd raged at him that he was ruining his life, and we were barely speaking when he left for Thailand.

We didn't hear from him for the first month, and Steve had blamed me. "He thinks you are still angry," he'd said.

"I am still angry," I'd snapped back.

"You need to be careful, Kate, or you'll lose him."

I'd wanted to shout: "How do you lose a son? He's been part of me for twenty-two years. I will always be his mother." But I kept it to myself. I hid the hurt and pretended to be indifferent to his silence. But fear had taken root inside me, creating lurid images of him dying in a motorbike crash or being brutally mugged.

Being a reporter means I know that these things happen to people like us.

FIVE

The Reporter

FRIDAY, AUGUST 15, 2014

It's been five minutes and no e-mail. I sit fidgeting with my phone, trying to decide whether to ring Bob Sparkes back and ask when he's going to push the send button. He'll hate that, but he said he'd do it immediately. I put the phone down. I'll have a look myself. Everything's on the net. And when I type in the names, the missing girls are there.

Bingo. But a blog. I hate blogs.

"Blah blah blah dressed up as journalism," I'd told Joe once, my guard down.

"God, you sound like my mum," he'd said. His mother, a recently "retired" editor, had been widely mocked among the wicked press as a Fleet Street dinosaur. That'd shut me up. I wasn't about to be kicked into the long grass with her.

The blogger is another backpacker sounding the alarm and urging Alex and Rosie to get in touch with their families.

I wonder how many of the thousands of teenagers who set off for a gap year go missing. Must be fewer now everyone has a smartphone and Wi-Fi. But still.

I stare at the screen. My heartbeat feels like it is bruising my ribs. My child is missing, too. At home, we all pretend that it's all fine; he's an adult, living his own life, making his own choices. But we don't even know which country he's in, really. I've googled the price of plane tickets for Thailand so many times. *Just looking,* I tell myself. And I've secretly e-mailed dozens of conservation projects in Phuket over the last two years, asking for him, but Jake hasn't registered with any of them. He could be anywhere, but I've kept it to myself. No point worrying Steve. Sometimes I wonder if he's done the same thing and is keeping it secret from me.

I write Jake an e-mail straightaway.

> Hi, Just wondering where you are and what you
> are doing. Thanks for ringing the other night—it was
> lovely to hear your voice. We miss you. Freddie finally
> passed his driving test!!! Let me know when you pick
> this up, mx

I don't know when he'll get it but it's out there when he next logs in.

"Kate," Joe's saying, "Kate! I asked where you found this cutting. Please, Terry's about to call the meeting."

"What? Can't you look online? Think it was one of the Sunday magazines. Is it on shiny paper? Oh, say the *Sunday Express*. No one ever reads it."

"Are you coming in?"

"What time is it in Bangkok, Joe?"

"Er, afternoon or evening, I think. They're ahead of us, aren't they? Why?"

But I'm already dialing the *Post*'s Southeast Asia correspondent and waving Joe away.

"I'll be in in a minute. Just need to check something."

Don Richards answers on the first ring.

"Yes," he barks, daring the caller to carry on disturbing him.

"Don? It's Kate Waters. On the *Post*."

The voice softens to gruff. "Ah, the lovely Kate. How are you? Christ, when did I last see you? Must be ten years ago, when you came to cover the tsunami. That was a hell of a story, wasn't it? Paid for my new bungalow."

I grit my teeth. Don's sensitivity button was disabled a long time ago—"Living out here does it to you," he'd confessed back then, when we were both drunk and exhausted after weeks of horrifying sights and testimonies.

"It blunts you. I've become some terrible old colonial cliché." I'd bought us another beer and steered him back to his glory days.

"God, is it ten years, already?" I say. "We must be getting old, Don. Look, I know you're busy, so I'll keep it short. I wondered if you were working on two missing British girls, Alex O'Connor and Rosie Shaw?"

"Well, the backpack network is talking about them. But this happens all the time—the embassy here gets one or two reported every day. Bloody thoughtless teenagers. The families have been trying to make contact for a week, apparently, but kids drift through. They meet someone in a bar, hear about a new place, and go. These girls are probably shacked up with some boys and having too good a time to tell anyone. Anyway, why are you asking? Are you being sent on it?"

I smile. Don can smell the money.

"Can't see them sending me this early, but I'm going to talk to Terry about it—could be a good story. Every parent's nightmare with kids all heading off on their gap years at the moment. And there's nothing else happening here."

"I'll send you some copy. You will put me down for a credit, won't you?"

The cry of the lesser spotted freelance: "Giss'a credit."

"'Course, Don. Send over what you've got and I'll put a payment through. Have you spoken to the families? I'm going to give them a call."

"Only via Facebook posts. The O'Connors from Winchester are making the most noise."

Terry's head appears round the door of the meeting room.

"Get your arse in here, Kate. You're the chief reporter. Set an example, for goodness' sake."

https://www.facebook.com/alexoconnor.333

Alex O'Connor

July 27 at 0830

. . . is staying in the penthouse of Bates Motel. YOLO

She and Rosie had fallen out of the 551 bus in the city center at a vast roundabout straddling what looked like the M3. The girls from the plane, who knew what they were doing, had somehow got off before them without Alex noticing. It was the driver who'd told them they'd reached their stop.

"Democracy Monument," he'd said. "Khao San Road."

Standing beside four lanes of traffic, Alex felt any remnant of elation die in her stomach. This wasn't what she'd been expecting. She'd seen pictures of the old town and this wasn't it. Where were the narrow streets and alleys? Rosie was looking at her expectantly.

"Where's our hotel?" she'd said.

"Hostel," Alex had corrected, looking at page one of the itinerary on her phone. "It's the Green Paradise and it is only fifteen minutes' walk from here, according to this."

"But which way?"

She hadn't been sure and was too tired to think sensibly. She'd planned to find the way on her phone, but she'd forgotten to buy a Thai SIM card at the airport. She'd headed off, trying to look as if she knew what she was doing, and her friend followed.

"This way," she'd said, muttering, "I think," as insurance.

It wasn't. And no one seemed to understand when she asked and showed them the hostel name.

"This is a nightmare," Rosie had said, and Alex had quickened her pace to get out of earshot.

When they finally fell upon Khao San Road, shop fronts were opening down alleyways; pans of water were coming to the boil on wood fires and gas stoves; child-size green and red plastic stools were scattered outside, ready for the first sitting of the day. But there was still no sign of their hostel.

Rosie's sulk was turning to loud despair when Alex spotted Mama's Paradise Bar and Guesthouse down a side road.

"This was on my list as well," she lied. *Well, it's got "Paradise" in the name.* "Let's forget the other one and ask here."

"Right," Rosie said.

"It looks okay," Alex said as they peered into the gloom beyond the bar front.

She and Rosie had been given a room on the top floor.

An astonishing figure in a flowing caftan and platinum blond wig had towered over them with a wide smile. "I am Mama," she said. "This is my place. I will put you in private room on second floor." It sounded as if it was the royal suite.

It wasn't. It was like a flophouse. Not that she'd ever been in one, but Alex had read *Down and Out in Paris and London* for A Level and imagined the room would fit Orwell's brief.

They'd trudged with their backpacks up dark concrete stairs, Alex first, clutching the key like a lucky charm while faces appeared and disappeared above them in the stairwell. The room number had been painted on the wall in black paint, and when she opened the door the vinegary stench of old trainers pushed past them into the corridor.

"Seriously?" Rosie had said.

"It's cheap," Alex had snapped, too tired for the row brewing. "It's a hundred and fifty baht a night. Three quid. We can't expect much more. And we're not staying long."

"I guess not."

"It'll be an experience," Alex had said.

"Yes."

"And someone must have recommended it online for me to put it on my list."

"Who? Someone with a sense of humor? And no sense of smell . . ."

"It's not that bad," Alex had said weakly, taking in the full horror. "And we won't be spending much time in it."

"That's lucky," Rosie had muttered, looking pointedly at the cream-colored walls, smeared with squashed mosquitoes. Alex went to close the thin curtains at the window looking out onto the corridor. They gaped. There weren't enough hooks.

It was certainly no-frills. Their room contained a fan, a single plastic chair, and a small double bed. The sheet bore the marks of generations of sweating tourists, the central dip in the mattress darker than the rest of the material.

"Love the pillows," Rosie had said, still not moving from the doorway. Ghostly imprints of cartoon kittens stared out, their giant, once-appealing eyes barely visible after hundreds of washes.

"Come on," Alex had muttered. "Which side do you want?" She

hadn't counted on sharing a bed and knew from the plane that Rosie snored.

"The side furthest from the mosquito graveyard," Rosie had said, her voice sullen. "I hope you don't snore . . ."

She'd plonked her bag down and sat heavily on the bed. Alex had done the same. At that moment, she'd wanted more than anything to go home.

"I'm going to have a shower." She'd fought the tremor in her voice and begun rummaging in her things for a toothbrush and soap.

Rosie had widened her eyes. "God knows what that will be like. Cockroach city."

"I've never seen a cockroach," Alex had said. "Another first."

They'd suddenly realized two Thai women were in the corridor outside, peeping through the gap in the curtains, watching their every move.

"The shower?" Alex had opened the door and mimed rain over her head.

They'd pointed wordlessly down the corridor.

The girls had edged past them and inspected a tiny room with a tiled floor, a drain hole, and a sputtering head. Limp, faded towels hung on a hook. "Okay, I'm going in," Alex had said in a comedy American accent. "If I'm not back in five minutes, call a plumber."

And Rosie had laughed.

Thank God for that, Alex had thought.

Later, when they were sitting at the guesthouse bar with their hair still wet, Mama emerged from the gloom at the back. Rosie nudged Alex.

"She could play for the England rugby team."

Mama gave them a look and Alex worried that she'd heard, but she carried on sweeping up the rubbish in front of her property.

"Dirty people," she hissed at a passerby who spat out his chewing gum, and her lipstick left a red slick on her teeth.

It was probably still early for the traveler crowd, only just midday, and hangovers of every shade of gray showed on the faces of those who'd made it out of bed. A boy their age walked past wearing just a pair of shorts. Thin, thin. Greenish skin and old eyes, dragging on a cigarette as if it were his last breath.

Alex was about to say how ill he looked, but Rosie chirped up.

"Looks like people are having a good time."

SIX

The Reporter

FRIDAY, AUGUST 15, 2014

It hasn't taken much persuading for Terry to buy into the story. The news list is cigarette-paper thin—"I see you've decided to create a wish list this morning, Mr. News Editor. I can't see an actual story on this," the Editor, Simon Pearson, had shouted from his office door, waving the offending document in his hand. Terry had grinned as if it were a joke. But we all knew he'd get a kicking when the door closed.

He puts a brave face on it when he emerges, but his news list is screwed up in a ball in one fist.

"We're splashing on the missing girls," he says as if it were his idea.

"It's a bit soft for the front, Terry," I say. *It is.* *"Girls Fail to E-mail Parents While on Holiday" is hardly a headline.*

"Then give it a kick up the arse, Kate. It's the only story I've got today."

I watch as he barricades himself in his cubicle and sits, staring into space. I wonder how long he'll go on, taking the flak twelve hours a day. He always says he loves it—loves the buzz, the being at the center of things—but he looks more like a victim of domestic violence every day.

I'd better make the story work.

Malcolm O'Connor answers on the first ring.

He must be sitting beside the phone.

"Hello, Mr. O'Connor? I am so sorry to disturb you but I'm ringing about your daughter, Alex. I'm a reporter for the *Daily Post* and I want to help you find her."

I try to picture the man on the other end of the line. Middle-aged, thinning hair? Desperate, anyway. I'd hoped to get the mother. Women are so much easier to talk to about grief, emotions, loss. Blokes, even fathers, struggle to find the words. And putting on a brave face sounds so cold in print.

There is silence on the line.

"Mr. O'Connor?"

"Sorry, yes. I think you'd better talk to my wife."

There's the sound of voices in another room and the rustle of movement before the phone is picked up.

"Hello, who is this?"

"Kate Waters, Mrs. O'Connor. I was just telling your husband that I work for the *Daily Post* and I want to help you find Alex."

"The *Post*? It's not the one we read but . . . have you heard anything? What have you been told? You must know more than us. You're a reporter."

"I probably know as much as you, Mrs. O'Connor. *Less, if I'm honest.* I'm talking to Hampshire Police and our correspondent in Bangkok but there isn't much information yet. Why don't you tell me what you've heard?"

"Just that they've notified Interpol and we've spoken to the embassy in Bangkok. They all say we have to wait. I don't know how much longer we can do that." Her voice is slipping and I know she's about to break down.

"Using Facebook is a great idea," I say, steering her away from tears. I need her to talk, not cry. "You must be reaching thousands of backpackers and tourists over there."

"So my son, Dan, tells me," she says wearily. "I only signed up for Facebook when Alex went off. She said there'd be photos for me to look at. We'd be able to see what she was up to. But there's been nothing for a week now. Nobody has heard from her. Nobody knows anything. We waited. We thought she'd probably gone on a trip for a couple of days, but we'd arranged for her to ring yesterday for her results. Her A Levels. She was desperate to know if she'd got into university. And if she didn't have the right grades, she knew she'd have to ring round to find another place."

"Yes, I remember that," I say. Jake had sailed into his first choice, but there'd been a day of agonizing telephone calls for Freddie, me standing beside him in the school hall, willing him on with smiles and nods to bear the humiliation of rejection. In the end he took the offer of a media studies course in Birmingham. It wouldn't have been my choice—three years pretending to be a journalist and building up a huge debt—but I was too exhausted by the process to fight about it. He's enjoying it, he says.

"What about Rosie?" I ask.

"No, nothing from her either. But it was usually Alex who did the messages. Rosie was a bit less . . . you know."

"Yes, I've got one like that. Look, could I come and see you, Lesley? Is it okay if I call you Lesley? To talk to you properly. It's hard on the phone, isn't it? I could drive down now if you like."

There's a pause and I can hear Lesley O'Connor whispering to her husband: "She wants to come and see us."

I can't hear the reply, but seconds later Lesley says, "Okay. Have you got our address?"

Mick Murray drives. He prefers it that way. "I've got all my camera gear in the boot—it's simpler if we take my car. And you're a shit driver."

I get into the passenger seat, edging empty Coke bottles and evidence of ancient takeaways to the side of the footwell with my shoe, and try not to notice the overflowing ashtray. But he sees me looking.

"Sorry, haven't had it valeted this week."

"This week! This century, more like. There are Big Mac boxes older than my kids in here."

"Bit of a dumpster, but it's home." He laughs, lighting a ciggie.

"Anyway . . . Terry is determined to splash the story. It's a bit thin, if you ask me, but it is August."

"Picture desk is desperate, too. We'll make it work. They're pretty girls—there are a couple of photos of them in front of a temple on the brother's appeal page, but there's security on the girls' Facebook accounts."

"Hopefully the mum and dad will let us have more. Poor things. They sound like nice people. It'll be a decent talk."

Mick nods and throws his cigarette butt out of the window and fishes another one out of the packet on the dashboard. He lights it and inhales deeply.

"Bloody hell, Mick, open a window. I'm smoking that cigarette for you."

He laughs, making himself cough as if he's dying. "You reformed smokers are the worst. Enjoy it. It's a free one . . ."

I open my window and think about the interview.

We pull up outside the address, one of a terrace of redbrick houses on the outskirts of the affluent market town, and as I get out of the car, my phone rings. It's Steve but the rumble of the traffic makes it hard to hear him.

"Sorry, love, I'm standing on a pavement about to do an interview. Can we talk about this later?"

"Just wanted to remind you about tonight. We're meeting Henry and Deepika for tapas. Remember?" he shouts.

"Yes, yes." I'd forgotten. Steve would say it was deliberate but I've got a lot on my mind. And I can't stand Henry. He may be one of

Steve's fellow consultants but he's also an arse. He's a man who thinks it's funny to put his wife down in company and then crow, "I'm joking!" when people look uncomfortable. Deepika, a partner in a law firm, appears not to mind. She laughs along when he calls her "She Who Must Be Obeyed" and says his marriage is like a life sentence, but it sticks in my craw.

The last time he did it, I ordered another glass of wine despite Steve giving me the "You've had enough" look.

"Tell him if he channels a Neanderthal tonight, I'll ram a scorched Padrón pepper up his nose," I shout back.

"Katie, you will behave, won't you?" Steve laughs but I can hear the tension in his voice.

"Might. Love you, bye."

"Who are you going to assault with a chili?" Mick says, shouldering his bag of cameras.

"None of your business. Come on, let's get on with it."

SEVEN

The Reporter
FRIDAY, AUGUST 15, 2014

The O'Connors' front room is an assault course of furniture and knickknacks and I have to negotiate an upholstered footstool, a large, trembling orchid, and a sharp-cornered coffee table to reach the armchair indicated by Lesley. Another woman is sitting on the sofa with a mug of tea already in her hand.

"This is Rosie's mum, Jenny. We rang her to let her know you were coming and she wanted to be here," Lesley says quickly.

But you don't seem keen on the idea, I think. *Wonder why.*

Jenny nods at me wordlessly and takes a sip of tea.

"Hello, Mrs. Shaw. I'm Kate and this is Mick, my—" Mick cuts me off with a look.

"I'm the photographer working with Kate on the story," he says.

He's become increasingly annoyed if I forget myself and call him "my photographer."

"I'm not your fucking monkey," he hisses, and I'm sure Lesley O'Connor hears. She pretends not to notice.

"Tea?" She speaks into the sudden silence. I nod gratefully.

"Two more teas, Malcolm," she calls through the door. Lesley's about the same age as me, early fifties, I'd guess. She's wearing supermarket-mum jeans, sandals the color of sticking plasters, and a long T-shirt. No makeup. No earrings. Just her.

I unbutton the jacket of my suit and quickly slip it off. I don't want to look like an official.

"Lesley," I start, but she breaks in with, "Did you find us all right?" *She's putting off the evil moment. Of having to talk about it.*

"Fine. No problems. Thank you so much for seeing us."

I lean forward in my chair to make eye contact.

"Why don't you tell me about Alex, Lesley? She must have been so excited about going on this trip."

Lesley gives me a grateful smile. Remembering the happy times before this last week is where she wants to be.

"She was. They both were, weren't they, Jenny?"

Jenny Shaw doesn't look up from her mug of tea. And I feel the tension in the room ratchet up a notch. But Lesley carries on, apparently oblivious.

"She couldn't talk about anything else. She was going with her best friend, Mags, to begin with, but that all fell through and Rosie stepped in. Alex spent hours on the Internet, looking at the islands, how to get there— you know, bus routes, ferries—and where to stay. She had it all planned. They were going for three months and then they'd see, they said. They thought they might go on to Australia if they could find some work."

"It was quite a trip, then. Had they been traveling before?"

"No," Jenny Shaw says. Her first word.

"No, that's right," Lesley adds quickly. "First time away from home like this for both of them. But they are sensible girls and they had everything planned. Alex did a spreadsheet."

I hear what sounds like a snort from Jenny Shaw. "Sorry, Jenny, I missed that."

"I didn't say anything."

"Jenny's very upset," Lesley offers. "We all are."

Malcolm O'Connor puts down the tray he's dressed with milk jug, sugar bowl, chocolate digestives, and a teapot with cozy. *Standards not being allowed to slip,* I note.

"We are, yes," he says, sitting down between his wife and Jenny.

"We need to find them," Lesley says and takes her husband's hand. "We are desperate. Not sleeping, imagining the worst."

"Why did you sound the alarm, Lesley? Had Alex said something to worry you?"

"No. Nothing like that. That's just it. They were having a great time. But we've heard nothing for days. There was an arrangement for the girls to contact us every other day. Facebook, a text, or an e-mail if they had time. And their A Level results came out yesterday. I haven't opened the envelope yet because we wanted to do it with Alex. She knew it was August the fourteenth—she e-mailed to say what time she'd ring. She knew we'd be waiting to hear from her, didn't she, Mal?"

He nods and lets go of her hand to pour the tea.

"Would it be possible to see the e-mails, Lesley? I'd like to use some of the girls' own words if I can."

"Why?" Jenny says.

To make the story sing is not what they will want to hear.

"To give them a voice in the story," I say instead. "It is about them, after all."

She looks dubious so I move on. "Who have you spoken to in Thailand, Lesley?"

"We've been in touch with the embassy out there. They've been very nice but they say it's early days. That this happens a lot. They had more than four hundred tourists reported missing last year. That people turn up again quickly. That we shouldn't panic. And we're trying not to."

Lesley gulps the last word of the sentence and stops. I keep eye contact, nodding encouragement, and she takes a breath and goes on.

"She'd have been in touch. Alex is a lovely girl. She wouldn't want us to suffer like this. We know she'd booked a hostel in Bangkok—the Green Paradise Guesthouse—but when we rang they said she hadn't turned up. We don't know which one she went to—she called it Bates Motel on Facebook, like it was a joke. I didn't know they'd changed hostels—she didn't mention it when she phoned the first time—there was so much else to talk about. She was buzzing with it all. So excited. They were loving Bangkok. And she told us all about the temples and the new friends she was making. Then nothing. No one has heard from her. None of her friends—we've rung them all. Her phone is switched off. We just don't know."

Malcolm puts his arm round her. Jenny Shaw looks completely isolated, perched at the end of the sofa, and I reach over and touch her arm to bring her into the interview.

"What about you, Jenny? How are you and your husband coping?"

"Ex-husband."

Shit. "Right, sorry. It must be a very difficult time for you."

Jenny Shaw takes a deep breath. She looks so brittle she might break at any moment.

"Yes," she says. "Very difficult. She is my only one. She shouldn't even be in Thailand. She should be starting her course. A degree in midwifery. But she decided to defer for a year."

"To go traveling?" I prompt.

"Yes. Well, it was Alex's idea, but she persuaded Rosie to go."

Lesley shoots her what looks like a warning glance.

"They're best friends, then?" I plow on into troubled waters.

"Not really. They've only known each other a couple of years, since we moved in down the road. We've had to downsize since the divorce."

I nod sympathetically. "That must have been tough."

"We managed," Jenny says tartly. "I was very surprised when Rosie said she wanted to go. The girls went to the same sixth-form school but they didn't spend that much time together. And they'll be going to different universities when they come back."

There is a beat of silence in the room. *When.*

"Did Rosie do well on her exams?" I say.

"I haven't opened the results either but I'm sure she'll have done fine."

"What sort of girl is Rosie?"

"She's a bright girl." Jenny's voice is getting tighter and she sounds breathless. "But she's young and sometimes can get caught up in things. Not bad things but just lately, she gets an idea in her head and you can't shift it."

"Like going traveling?"

"Yes. Like going traveling. I thought she should start her degree like she'd planned. But she wouldn't listen and then her father loaned her the money so she could go."

She speaks carefully, checking each statement with a small, self-referential nod. She reminds me of a bird in a cage. That bobbing movement of the head.

"Is your husband—sorry, ex-husband—involved in the campaign to find her?"

"No. His new wife needs him at home. She's had a baby."

The subtext of blame and a family reconfigured by divorce go unspoken. For the moment. But I can feel it simmering and I wonder how long it will be before it boils over.

Won't be long if Rosie isn't found. Jenny will need someone to point the finger at.

"The police say the girls might have gone on a trip for a few days where there's no Wi-Fi or phone signal," Malcolm O'Connor says and shakes his head.

Lesley looks at her husband. "Why does everyone keep saying that? We think they were still in Bangkok when they last messaged. Alex said she'd booked a thing to see some elephants last Sunday. They were having a wonderful time."

She stops. The past tense has slipped past her guard.

"I'm so frightened we've lost her. I keep thinking about her at the airport, waving to us from the security queue. Off on her big adventure."

Tears slide down her face, dripping off her chin onto her husband's bare arm.

"Sorry," she mutters, wiping them away with her sleeve, and makes to get up.

"Give yourself a moment, Lesley," I say quietly, fishing a tissue out of my bag. "Of course you're frightened. What parent wouldn't be? Have you got a picture of them at the airport?"

Jenny gets up and squeezes past their knees. She's crying, too.

"I need a minute," she says.

"Oh, Jenny, stay," Lesley says, sobbing, but her neighbor disappears into the hall. She turns to me: "We feel so out of control. You will help us, won't you?"

I go and sit beside her and squeeze her hand. "Of course I will. I'll write a story as soon as we have finished talking, to keep people looking. The *Post* is read online all over the world."

Lesley looks suddenly wary. *She's just remembered I'm a reporter.*

"What will you write?"

"That you are desperate to find Alex and Rosie and frightened for them. I'll write about the girls and the last information you have about their movements. We'll need photographs of them—and you. We want other parents to understand what you are going through."

"Well, if you think it will do some good." Lesley falters. Jenny has reappeared, standing in the doorway and dabbing at her eyes.

"What do you think, Jenny?" Lesley says.

Jenny stares at the carpet.

"Okay," she says.

BANGKOK DAY 2
(MONDAY, JULY 28, 2014)

She'd been about to cancel the whole trip a month ago when her best friend, Mags, dropped out. It'd been the day they'd been due to buy the plane tickets and Mags had turned up at the house to tell her she'd changed her mind. She just didn't have enough money; she was so sorry. Alex had been too stunned to have a row. Afterward, she wondered if her friend had ever really intended to go.

And then Rosie had begged to come with her. Alex had been amazed. For a start, they weren't really *friends* friends. They hadn't grown up together like her and Mags. Rosie had moved into Alex's street only at the start of sixth form, and they were doing different subjects. It had been Alex's mum who'd suggested she walk with Rosie to school at the beginning of their first term and introduce her to her friends, that kind of thing.

"She's new, Alex. Be nice."

The first time they'd met had been when Rosie and her mum—no dad—had come round for an excruciating welcome lunch.

Alex had opened the door to the guests. The girl on the doorstep was smaller than her, had a perky blond ponytail and a short flowery playsuit and high wedges to match. Alex had tugged her Hogwarts T-shirt out of her jeans self-consciously and waved her in.

"Didn't realize we were dressing up," she'd muttered to her mother as they processed into the living room.

They'd had an awkward "What subjects are you taking for A Level?" moment before her mum called them in to eat. Rosie had brightened when Dan, Alex's big brother, appeared, and she'd taken the chair beside him at the table, monopolizing him with her dimples and big-eyed questions. Alex had slumped into moody silence. They'd endured the meal until after the apple charlotte—"Lesley's signature dish," her dad had announced, and Alex had wanted to die. If that wasn't bad enough, the parental one-upmanship had swiftly followed.

"Rosie is going to study midwifery at university," her mother, Jenny, had said. "It's what she's always wanted to do. She'll need good grades to do it, but she's very bright."

Alex's mum had put on her tight smile and said, "That sounds lovely. Alex wants to do an academic subject—don't you, love?"

The girls had risen as one and headed for the patio.

"Sorry about that. She goes on a bit about the nursing thing," Rosie had said. "I'm not sure I'll get the grades, but she's desperate for me to do it."

"Mine's as bad." Alex had smiled. "Tiger mothers, eh?"

It had felt like a bonding moment, but somehow they hadn't been able to build on it. Alex had never been sure why. Normally, she was the go-to person for problems and advice in her group. The Head Girl, her friends joked. But, on their walks to school, when Alex had tried, chatting about books she'd read (Rosie read only assigned books and

Heat magazine) and films she wanted to see (brainless rom-coms were her new friend's pick), it turned out she was all about boys. That's all. She wanted boys to look at her, tell her she was pretty, admire her outfit. She didn't give a stuff about anything else. Alex had tried some "me, toos," telling Rosie about a boy she was seeing, and there was a spark of interest. It became their default subject, and when Alex broke up with him, she'd cried a bit and Rosie had given her a tissue and said she'd get over him. But the truth was that they never got beyond the social-media-chatter stage.

"We're like Facebook friends," she'd told her mother, who looked blank. "We talk but don't really connect."

"Right," her mum had said. "Well, you tried."

At the start of the winter term, when Rosie had begun taking the bus to class—"It's cold and I get an extra twenty minutes in bed"— Alex had shrugged and left her to it. They still stopped to say hello when they ran into each other—and had gone to each other's birthday parties—but Alex had long been relieved of big-sister duties.

So when she'd found Rosie waiting for her outside school the day after Mags's bombshell, Alex hadn't come close to guessing what was coming.

"I hear you've been let down, Alex," Rosie had blurted without preamble. "Everyone was talking about it at lunch. I'm really sorry."

"Thanks, Rosie," Alex had said, genuinely touched. "I'm not sure what I'm going to do, really. My mum doesn't want me to go on my own . . ."

"Well, can I come instead? Please? Thailand sounds fantastic," Rosie had said, slipping her arm through Alex's.

"You? You want to come?"

"Yes. It'd be brilliant."

"It's really lovely of you to offer," Alex had said carefully, too stunned to trust her answers. "I thought you were going straight to uni . . ."

"I was, but I've changed my mind."

"Oh, I didn't know."

"No one does. You're the first person I've told."

"Okay . . . Well, can we talk about it in the morning? I've got a student council meeting now."

"'Course. Not sure I'll be able to sleep, though."

Rosie had walked away, singing.

Alex hadn't slept much either as she wrestled with the idea of three months with Rosie. She'd had misgivings. Of course she had. What would they talk about on twelve-hour bus journeys? Would Rosie get homesick as soon as they arrived? Would she leave her stranded? But she'd bundled up her worries and closed a door on them at three a.m.

The truth was she would have grabbed at any lifeline to save her beloved trip. Later that morning when she saw Rosie waiting at the end of the road, she'd shouted, *"Yes!"* and run to hug her.

Rosie had hugged her back, trembling with excitement, and said, "Thank you. You've saved my life."

Alex had had no idea what that was about but stuffed it in the misgivings cupboard. She didn't want anything to spoil the moment and Rosie didn't mention it again. She talked at hyperspeed all the way to school about what they were going to do. What should she pack? Would they see elephants?

The euphoria had carried them through the squally days that followed. Alex had tried to tell herself they were minor hiccups, but there'd been a couple of terrible rows. More than a couple, if Alex was honest. The main problem was that Rosie hadn't told her mum about taking a year off and there'd been screaming matches between them that had spilled into a very difficult meeting with Alex's parents; it emerged that Rosie couldn't afford to pay for the flights and had no money for the trip. There'd been a desperate forty-eight hours when the trip was off until Rosie suddenly announced she'd come up with the cash. Her dad had given her money.

"He didn't have much of a choice, really." She'd laughed.

"What do you mean?" Alex asked.

"I told him he owed me something for the way he's behaved. He does."

Alex was too relieved to ask further questions. "That's great, Rosie," she'd said.

But news of her dad's "interference" had caused a new round of rows between Rosie and her mum. The constant highs and lows had been exhausting.

However, getting her own way with her parents seemed to have given Rosie new confidence. She had sat and nodded her little blond head when Alex first outlined the plans she had spent months making with Mags. "It all sounds magical," she'd said.

Now she had her own ideas.

"Bloody hell, not another temple," she'd said, laughing, when she reviewed her copy of the neatly typed "A & R's Final Itinerary" as they waited to board the plane. "Have you got a thing about monks?" Alex had laughed, but Rosie hadn't let it go; she'd pressed her case, wheedling and chipping away at Alex's cultural agenda. Rosie no longer wanted a magical experience. She wanted to party.

They'd worked it out. Most of it, anyway.

EIGHT

The Reporter

I'm late and I see them sitting at a table outside the restaurant. Henry's looking at his watch. *Sod him.*

I wave to them and mime an apology, lifting my hands in defeat. It'll have to do.

The men stand when I march up, and I kiss everyone.

"Have you ordered?"

"We were waiting for you, Katie," Steve says meaningfully.

"Right, sorry. I'm not that late, am I?"

"No. What do you want to drink?"

I'm in trouble.

I look to see what the others are having. The boys are sharing a bottle of red and Deepika picks up her glass of fizzy water. "Having an alcohol-free week," she explains righteously.

"Glass of white wine, please," I say. "Make it a large one. I've had quite a day."

Deepika smiles sympathetically. "Big news story, Kate?"

"Biggish. Two missing girls in Thailand. I've been interviewing the parents down in Winchester."

"Isn't Jake in Thailand?" she asks, dipping her breadstick in some tapenade.

"Yes, that's right," I say and turn to see where my wine is.

Henry and Steve are talking shop, moaning about the latest cuts at the hospital, and I try to steer Deepika away from my boy.

"This is nice, isn't it?" I say, and even I can hear the insincerity in my voice. "We haven't seen you for ages. What have you been up to?"

I tune out as she tells me about a complicated corporate case and problems with noisy neighbors, and I think about Lesley and Jenny, sitting in their separate houses, dealing with the fear that their girls may be in danger.

I've written the story as hard as I can, packing official comments and previous missing backpacker stories around the families' emotional quotes, but it's the selfie of the girls laughing in a tuk-tuk under the headline "The Lost Girls" that will clutch at other parents' hearts and stomachs.

I crumble my breadstick between my fingers and fight the ache in my own stomach.

Henry has moved on to politics when the waiter finally brings my glass. I try not to throw it down my throat, but Henry notices my first big gulp.

"Thirsty, Kate?" He laughs his rugger-bugger laugh and Steve puts his hand on my knee under the table to still me.

"A bit," I say. "What are we eating?"

Later, when we've grazed through plates of prawns, chicken lollipops, and squid, Henry turns his wine-glazed eyes on me.

"See more of your lot have been arrested for hacking," he says, picking a shred of lettuce out of his teeth.

"Hmm," I say, pretending to chew. Steve's hand is back on my knee and I move my leg away from him.

"Don't know why they bothered to hack into answerphones," Henry continues. "All reporters just make it up anyway. Don't they?"

"Henry!" Deepika chides, but she's smiling. Complicit. And something shifts in me.

"I'm a reporter, Henry," I say, and Steve lifts his finger to signal to the waiter for the bill.

"Yes, you are," Henry slurs and laughs.

"And I have never made anything up."

"Right," he says and raises an eyebrow at his wife.

"Are you calling me a liar?" I say, my voice getting quieter so he has to lean forward to hear me.

"Come on, Katie," Steve says. "Henry's just teasing. Here's the bill."

"Only teasing, Katie." Henry giggles as Steve thrusts his credit card into the machine and punches in his code.

"She's feisty, isn't she? I like that in a woman," he tells Steve and is suddenly wearing Deepika's fizzy water, a slice of lime sliding down his face.

Steve hustles me away from the table, miming to the dripping Henry that I've had too much to drink.

When we get to the taxi rank, I start laughing. He tries hard not to, but in the end, we are both holding each other up.

"His face," I say. And we're off again.

"I'll ring him later to apologize. I'll say you were drunk," he says in the taxi home.

"You will not!" I say.

"I've got to work with the man, Kate."

"Oh, do what you have to do, but I'm never going for dinner with them again."

"I doubt they'd risk it."

"Well, he said he liked feisty girls. He might fancy a return match."

BANGKOK DAY 2
(MONDAY, JULY 28, 2014)

FROM: Alexinnit96@gmail.com
TO: Magsishot@hotmail.co.uk
SUBJECT: ARRIVED!!!

Hi, Mags,

Well we're here!

It is HOT! But it's great. I went out with Rosie and two lads from the hostel to celebrate our first night. One's English and the other is an Aussie. Shaun. He wanted to show us the sights before he headed off to Ko Tao. We were giggling like little kids getting into our first tuk-tuk, posting loads of selfies and clinging onto the chrome rails and screaming. It was MAD driving—like a computer game and no safety belts. A x

"I'm in the dorm room with four others," Shaun had said when he appeared, barely awake. "Bunks are half the usual rate. D'you want a look?"

He opened the door to show them. The grilles on the windows were patched with T-shirts and boxer shorts tucked into the holes. "Instead of curtains," he explained.

The room was lined with metal-frame bunks, and a sea of everyone's belongings had washed into the corners. There was another lad asleep on one of the thin mattresses, lying on his stomach with a pillow over his head.

"This is cozy. A boy nest . . ." Rosie had said, the beer making her lighter and louder.

Shaun had laughed with her. "Only one more night. Then the beach."

He was going to Ko Tao on the bus and ferry. "Nine hours, so I can catch up on sleep."

"Have you booked a hostel?" Alex had asked, the disaster over finding a bed for the night still hovering over her.

"No. Maybe I'll kip on the beach. If you're in paradise, you don't care where you sleep."

"Yeah," Rosie had said, as if she knew.

You've only been in the country for five hours, Alex had thought. *And this is supposed to be paradise.* She looked up at the guesthouse sign, nestling in a clot of thick power cables. *More like Bates Motel.*

She'd scream-laughed along with Rosie when they'd got into their first tuk-tuk, but it kind of went downhill after that. It turned into a bar crawl with plastic buckets of vodka and Red Bull and straws. It tasted disgusting and Alex ordered a Coke.

By the time they pulled up outside Nana Plaza at one in the morning, Alex had had enough. The sign on the towering building screamed, "The World's Largest Adult Playground," and Shaun had grinned and shouted, "Ready for this?"

"Ready for anything," Rosie had yelled back.

Alex had hesitated. "I'm a bit jet-lagged. I might go back to the guesthouse," she'd muttered. But the others didn't hear her over the music. So she'd followed.

Try everything once, Mum always says, she told herself. *But I think she meant sprouts, not ladyboys.*

It was a bit sleazy and sad inside. There were girls their age banging their pelvises against each other, touching tongues, and smearing themselves in foam, while tourists and leering men watched.

"I thought we were going to a club," Alex had hissed to Rosie, who was pawing at Shaun as she tried not to fall over.

"We are. Shaun says there are thirty of them here. It's mega, isn't it?"

"Are they all like this?" Alex had said, waving a vague hand at a bar called Spanky's with its promises of "girl shower action."

"Probably." She'd laughed, her ankles buckling. "Can you imagine what my mum would say if she could see us?"

"No," Alex had said. But she could.

Perhaps I should have had more to drink, she'd thought. *So I wouldn't have to care what Jenny Shaw would say. Let alone my mum.*

"Well, I'm not going to stay long. It's all a bit sleazy, isn't it?" she'd said.

Rosie had turned away from her.

An hour of topless twerking later, Alex had announced loudly that she was going back to the guesthouse. The clincher had been when Shaun drunkenly tried to snog her.

"Come back with me, Rosie," she had shouted above the music for the third time.

"I'm not going home, Alex. I'm having a great time. Shaun's lovely, isn't he?" Rosie had slurred up close, hot vodka breath making her face wet. "See you in paradise . . ."

I n the tuk-tuk back to Mama's, Alex wrestled with the guilt of leaving Rosie. She'd failed the mum test on the first night.

What sort of a friend am I?

NINE

The Mother

SATURDAY, AUGUST 16, 2014

She'd got a photo of Alex from the shelving unit and put her on the table while she drank her first cup of coffee of the day. "Hello, my lovely," she'd said, like she'd said every morning of her child's life.

Malcolm had gone out to get the newspaper. They'd both told work they wouldn't be in. They'd seen Kate Waters's story online, on their son Dan's laptop, but they wanted it in their hands. They needed something solid they could hold and keep. Everything else was shifting under their feet or happening in cyberspace, wherever that was.

When he got back, they sat with Alex's photo and read the story again. "It's like it's happening to someone else," she said.

"I know, love. But this should help, shouldn't it? Kate's done it really well. People will really start looking, won't they?"

"Danny says there are loads more messages on the Facebook page. People getting in touch."

"But what are they saying?"

"That they are sorry for us, mainly. I want the police, not kids in swimsuits, to look for them."

"I know, love, but they say there's nothing to indicate the girls are in trouble."

"Then why haven't they fucking well been in touch?" Lesley screamed, the F word ricocheting off the units of their neat little kitchen. She wanted to shake someone. Wanted to hear their teeth rattle.

Malcolm stood up quickly, almost knocking over his chair, and backed away from her.

"Lesley, for God's sake, calm down," he shouted back. "Danny will hear you."

He was frightened of her; she could see it in his eyes. She was frightened, too. She didn't recognize this woman who was screaming like a fishwife and banging the table with her fists. She couldn't imagine what her colleagues at St. John's Primary School would say. She was the one who always calmed everything down when things got heated, the one who everyone expected to talk sense. But she couldn't help herself.

She burst into noisy sobs. "I just want someone to do something. To find her," she howled.

"We both do, Lesley," Malcolm said but didn't move from the safety of his side of the table. "I'll make you a cup of tea."

"I don't want a fucking cup of tea," she shouted as she ran from the room.

TEN

The Reporter

The *Herald* has splashed on an exclusive interview with Rosie's dad and I can hear the sound of Terry grinding his teeth somewhere in Surbiton as I scroll through our rival's story on my phone.

As if summoned by my thought, he rings.

"Why didn't we have this?"

I mime to Steve that it's a work call and go into the kitchen so I don't disturb his Saturday morning ritual of newspapers and coffee. I also don't want him to hear. He takes it very personally if the desk is difficult with me. As if it's him being bollocked.

"I hate seeing you upset by them," he always says.

"Water off a duck's back," I say, but he stays grumpy—much longer than I do—and I end up having to soothe *his* hurt feelings. So I try to keep any trouble away from him.

I prefer a public slanging match in front of the whole newsroom.

"This is very much second best, Terry," I say, switching on the kettle. "We've got a fantastic in with the mothers. If we'd run this, we'd have lost Jenny Shaw. She's a difficult woman, very prickly, but I'm starting to get past that. And she hates her ex—he left her and gave Rosie the money to go—and don't get her started on Imogen, his new partner. If we'd done this interview, she would never speak to me again. It was a no-brainer."

There is a pause at the other end of the line.

"And that picture . . ." I say, letting Terry look at the photo of Mike Shaw with his arm round his new wife, holding a picture of his missing daughter.

"She's had her hair and makeup done," I say. "Not exactly the grieving stepmother. And there are no new lines in what the dad says. He knows nothing. He's been off the scene for five years. We've got tons more. The mothers are the main event."

"Okay, okay. But make sure Rosie's mother knows we made the choice to stick with her. We need her to ourselves."

"Will do. Are you off to wheel a trolley round Sainsbury's now?"

"Bugger off. Speak later."

Job done.

I phone Jenny and she starts shouting immediately.

"Have you seen the *Herald*? Have you? It's a disgrace."

I can't get a word in so let her vent her years of fury on the saintly looking Imogen.

"Why have they used her picture? What has she got to do with this? His bit on the side. Did you know she worked for him? A temp in the office. What a cliché. Left us for her with her sixty words a minute and push-up bras. After twenty years of marriage."

"Jenny," I try softly. "I know how upset you are. Don't let this make it worse. We both know she looks ridiculous, dolled up like that for the cameras when your daughter is missing."

Jenny snorts. It's what she wants to hear.

"You're right. I hope people will see her—and him—for what they are. Self-centered. This is all about them. Mike barely mentions Rosie. It's all about how he feels. Bastard."

"Quite. Look, Jenny, I just wanted you to know that it's you the *Post* wants to help."

"Right. Yes. I'm definitely not speaking to that rag the *Herald*."

Result. But don't crow. I need a new line.

"Anyway, how are you doing? Apart from this, I mean. Did you manage to get some sleep last night? Have you heard anything new?"

"I haven't been off the phone all morning. First Mike's mother bleating on about her bank making a mistake. I cut her off when Lesley's number came up on my mobile. There are more possible sightings that have been posted on the Internet. But they don't really sound like our girls."

"I've seen them, too, Jenny. But, like you say, there's nothing that springs out. Did you see the one that said two girls—one blond and one dark like Rosie and Alex—were in a café talking about catching a bus to Laos? Says the blond girl had a tattoo of a gecko on her shoulder."

"Rosie hasn't got a tattoo. I said no. So common and a health risk."

She might have had one done without telling you, I think. *You're not there to say no anymore.*

I make Steve another coffee and update the online story to include the tattoo sighting.

I decide to send Don to visit tattoo parlors and bus companies with photos of the girls, but he laughs when I ring him. "I'll have a go, but there are too many for me to make much of a dent. Usual day rate?"

"And any luck with Bates Motel?" I ask.

"Have you ever been to Bangkok, Kate? There's a chain of them here. You wouldn't keep a dog in some of the rooms."

"Oh, get on with it. Call me before you go to bed."

She rang the number she had for Mike Shaw. She had to. *Cover all the bases.*

BANGKOK DAY 7
(SATURDAY, AUGUST 2, 2014)

FROM: Alexinnit96@gmail.com
TO: Magsishot@hotmail.co.uk
SUBJECT: ROSIE!

Hi Mags,

I'm a bit worried about R. She's hooked up with two Dutch boys in the dorm now Shaun has gone. And Rosie's completely out of it tonight. Can't get any sense out of her. She's just sitting there, panting, and her eyes are all glazed and scary. God knows what she's taken. I asked Lars—one of the boys—but he just laughed. Said she was fine, he'd taken something, too. I'm putting her to bed and I'll try to talk to her about it in the morning.

She's gone a bit mad since we got here. She's working her way through the bars down Khao San Road so I have to listen to her stories of setting her hair on fire with Flaming Sambucas (is that how you spell it?) and Ping-Pong balls being shot out of fannies. FFS. Not sure which one R is sleeping with, Lars or Diederik? Or both? I think she's on a mission to work her way through the inmates!

She's definitely not interested in seeing the real
Bangkok. She says nothing is real here. It's all fake. It's
all about having fun. That's why she loves it. And I'm
just jealous. As if . . .

I'm trying to ignore it and have a good time but it's hard
sometimes. What are you up to? Have you decided if
you're going to school in October? E-mail soon and tell
me everything. Better go and see where Rosie is. I
thought we'd be doing things together but it isn't
working out like that. I can hear you saying told you so.
Should have listened, shouldn't I? Too late now. It'll be
all right, A x

Mags had tried to warn her when she found out Rosie was to be
her substitute.

"Are you sure, Alex? Do you even know anything about her?"

"Of course I do," Alex had snapped. "It'll be fine. And it's not as if
it'll be just us. We'll be meeting people all the time." She'd wanted to
add, "And this is all your fault," but couldn't face any more of Mags's
guilty tears.

"Well, they say you don't know someone until you have been on
holiday with them."

"Thanks, Mags. Not helpful."

But Mags had been right.

Alex was trying to tune Rosie out and watching huge storm clouds
roll up from behind the tower blocks. And when the daily rains
crashed onto the roofs, she buried herself away in dog-eared books left
by other travelers and she posted on Facebook. She wrote funny stories
about monks watching soap operas on their phones in the temples,
and how the local stallholders set up a tent of umbrellas and slipped
shower caps over their hair to keep dry in the epic downpours.

She read them out to Rosie to begin with but stopped after she announced she was "so over temples." She'd been to a couple on the second day, but that had been her limit, apparently. "Been there, done that, and I don't want to hear another chanting monk again in my life," she told everyone in the bar.

"No offense," she'd added for the benefit of the listening Mama, who'd bared her teeth in a dead-eyed smile and continued to stare at the girls from behind the bar, unnerving Alex. But Rosie didn't seem to notice.

She was too busy telling everyone in the bar she wanted a tattoo. A big one of a gecko like Lars had.

ELEVEN

The Detective

SATURDAY, AUGUST 16, 2014

Sparkes was on the phone to the hospital when Salmond appeared at his office door in a running outfit, exuding health and efficiency.

He waved her away, mouthing, "Busy," and she jogged out.

"Bloody hell, Eileen," he said down the phone, "I thought I'd have a bit of peace and quiet coming in at the weekend, but Zara's in and looks like she's on another get-fit kick. Don't think I can bear her lectures."

His wife laughed. "She'll have you in Lycra before you know it. I'm going to have a little sleep now. This morphine is marvelous."

"I'll be in later. Love you."

She snorted. "Bugger off and catch some criminals."

Salmond had showered and changed into her work clothes by the time she reappeared, a freshly tied damp bun pulling on the fine hairs at her temples.

"Didn't know you'd be in today, sir. I'm catching up on some revision for my exams. But I thought you'd like to know we've had a call from Rosie Shaw's granny," she said.

"Oh yes. Has she heard from her?"

"No, but she's reporting a theft from her bank account."

Sparkes sat back in his chair.

"Go on."

"She's not sure exactly how much has gone, but she thinks it's around two thousand. Well, she's got a load of accounts for different bits of her finances—stocks and shares, dividends, all that. She only realized there was a problem when her bank manager rang her."

"What? She didn't notice that two grand had gone?" Bob said. "Eileen would know if fifty quid disappeared." *That used to be Eileen's department,* but he wondered when she'd last looked. "And do they still have bank managers? Thought it was all call centers now . . ."

"Well, that's what she called him. The bloke who rang, whoever he was, said she was overdrawn without an arrangement. First time in her life, she says."

"And?"

"She thinks someone has taken money from her account without her knowing."

Sparkes sighed. Old people and money. His father had banked his life savings in his chest of drawers. When he died, he and his brother had found hundreds of ten-pound notes carefully folded into socks, underpants, and handkerchiefs.

"Who does she think took it? Not Rosie, surely?" he said.

"Well . . . it looks like it might have been. The bank says there was an electronic transfer of two thousand pounds to Rosie's account before she left. But Jenny Shaw told me Rosie was given the money to go on this trip by her father."

"Could the grandmother have got confused? How old is she?"

"Eighty-something but sharp as a tack."

Sparkes tried to concentrate on what he was being told.

"So two grand left the grandmother's account and ended up in Rosie's account? Could she have done it herself? And why didn't the bank raise the alarm earlier?"

"It didn't trigger an overdraft straightaway. Some direct debits went out yesterday and they put Granny Shaw's account in the red."

"The question is, could this be connected with Rosie's disappearance?"

Salmond shrugged. "Maybe she thought she was about to be found out. Maybe she decided to go into hiding."

"But what about Alex? Why would she run away?"

"Don't know. Perhaps she was an accomplice?"

Sparkes sat forward.

"Who are you talking to?"

"The bank's fraud department to nail down the dates, and I'm going to see Rosie's father, Michael Shaw, at home this afternoon."

Sparkes heard the edge to her voice.

"What? Come on. What are you thinking? What's your instinct on this?"

Zara Salmond smiled. "I thought you weren't doing gut reactions anymore, sir."

Sparkes made a face. He had sworn off listening to his gut after the Bella Elliott kidnapping case, when his obsession with the suspect, Glen Taylor, had caused the collapse of a trail and almost ended his career.

"I'm not. Well, not in the paperwork, Sergeant. But you always get a feeling." He looked at her meaningfully. They'd been through a lot together.

"I don't know. Something's not right," Salmond said.

"About?"

"About Rosie's father. I spoke to him yesterday, when his daughter was reported missing, and he was a bit closed, if you know what I mean. Didn't have much to say or ask. As if she was a stranger."

"Perhaps he was in shock?" suggested Sparkes.

"Yes, but he's making a big show of appearing devastated in the papers today."

"Do I detect a note of cynicism?"

"My gut didn't like him."

"Is that so? When are we talking to him?"

TWELVE

The Detective

SATURDAY, AUGUST 16, 2014

Mike Shaw adjusted his tie while he waited. Bob Sparkes watched him through the sitting room window as he waited outside for DS Salmond to lock the car door. It gave him a moment to read the middle-aged businessman standing on the other side of the double glazing.

It made slim pickings. Tallish, broadish, brownish hair, and an expensive shirt with one of those stupid, showy knots in his tie. *A Windsor knot.* Sparkes had refused to have one like that for Sam's wedding. He hadn't wanted to wear a deep pink tie in the first place, but had agreed if he could do his usual schoolboy knot. It had caused a bit of a fuss with Eileen, but he had stuck to his guns.

"I'm giving away the bride, not launching a new hedge fund," he'd said to Eileen. And there had been no more said. Sam hadn't minded. He didn't think she had, anyway.

DS Salmond nudged his elbow—she was ready. Sparkes stepped forward, clearing his throat as they knocked. Mike Shaw was expecting them, but he still looked up warily when they were ushered in by the latest Mrs. Shaw. Everyone did when they saw a police officer. Even the innocent.

"Thanks, Mrs. Shaw," Sparkes said warmly. "Is this your little one?"

Imogen Shaw, her hair unbrushed and exhaustion etched into her face, clutched the baby in her arms even closer. "Yes. Sorry—she needs another feed. I'll leave you to it."

Mike Shaw mouthed something to her and she closed the door behind her.

"I remember those first few weeks so well. Are you getting much sleep?" Sparkes said, attempting to settle his interviewee.

Shaw shook his head but his face remained expressionless as the detectives pulled out chairs at the dining table. He took one opposite them.

"What's this about? Has there been a development?" he asked, leaning on the table. "Surely you could have told me on the phone. I'd like to get back to work. Saturday's my busiest day and I'm up against it at the moment."

No hello, then, Sparkes thought.

"Yes and no. This is a bit delicate, Mr. Shaw, but I'll come straight to the point. Your mother, Mrs. Constance Shaw, rang us this morning to report that two thousand pounds has gone missing from her bank account. She only became aware when she was contacted by her bank, concerned that she had become overdrawn without discussing it with them."

Mike Shaw opened his mouth to say something, but nothing came out. His hand went up to his tie and he cleared his throat.

"Sorry, I thought you were here about Rosie."

"Well, we are, in a manner of speaking," Sparkes said gently. "Has your mother said anything to you about this?"

"Me? No, no. I don't understand why she didn't tell me."

"No? Perhaps she couldn't get hold of you at work."

"Yes, that must be it."

"Following her phone call, we have confirmed that two thousand pounds was transferred to your daughter Rosie's account on July the fifteenth, two weeks before she caught a plane to Bangkok."

"Rosie's account? Why are you looking at Rosie's account? What are you saying?"

"I'm saying that we are trying to account for the missing money."

Mr. Shaw half-rose from his chair in his agitation.

"I can't believe my mother would call the police like this."

Not disputing that Rosie may have stolen the money, though, Sparkes thought.

"Her granddaughter is missing and all she can worry about is money," Mike Shaw spat. "Typical. She is the most self-centered woman I've ever met."

"But if Rosie *has* taken the money, it may have some bearing on her disappearance. She may be afraid of being found out. You do see that?"

"This is ridiculous. I am sure we can clear things up. Perhaps my mother forgot . . ." Shaw blurted.

"Is your mother in the habit of forgetting things, Mr. Shaw?"

The man opposite nodded slowly as if processing the thought. "Well, she's eighty-two now. Her memory can be a bit dodgy."

"I see. She struck me as pretty on the ball when I spoke to her," Salmond said. She'd told her boss about the interrogation she'd undergone at the hands of Constance Shaw. There'd been two phone conversations and the older woman had wanted to know every step the police were going to take.

"So you think your mother may have given Rosie two thousand pounds for her trip? And forgotten?"

"Well, it's possible . . . I don't know."

"But I understood from your wife—sorry, ex-wife—that it was you who had loaned Rosie the money for Thailand. She was very adamant about it."

Shaw gave him a look. "I bet she was. Jenny is adamant about a lot of things, but we're not really on speaking terms so I wouldn't know what she was saying."

He paused.

Thinking time, Sparkes thought. *What has he got to think about?*

Shaw cleared his throat. "Look, I didn't lend Rosie any money. She asked, but I said no. I told her she was an adult now and to fund her own holidays. It was a bloody cheek of her to ask anyway. She's been so nasty to Imogen—my new wife. You should see the letter she wrote to her."

"I see," Sparkes said. *Moving on . . .*

"The thing is that your mother went into the bank and was shown her statements for the past twelve months," Salmond said.

Shaw tensed, then lowered his head to smooth his trousers, examining the crease intently.

"It appears that regular amounts have been paid into your personal account for the last year. Amounts that your mother claims she wasn't aware of. She says she stopped receiving paper statements when you put her accounts online."

"I thought it would be easier for her."

"She says she doesn't have a computer, Mr. Shaw, so easier how?"

"I could sort bills out for her, that kind of thing."

"What kind of thing exactly?" Sparkes said.

Shaw sat back and closed his eyes as if to remember.

He began talking before he opened them. "My mother is a very difficult, demanding woman, Inspector. I was doing a lot of work for her. I simply took what was owed."

"I understand you are a salesman for a carpet company, Mr. Shaw. What sort of work were you doing for your mother? Providing underlay?"

"No, of course not. I meant I was always paying for things she wanted out of my own pocket. I was always doing things for her."

"Managing her money?"

"Yes, she asked me to when my father died."

"She says you suggested it. 'Insisted on it' were her words. How are your own bank accounts, Mr. Shaw?"

"What do you mean?"

"It must be expensive having two families . . ."

"You cannot imagine," he said as he sank his head into his hands. "I've got one screaming for university fees and the other nagging about having the house redecorated."

"It sounds very stressful."

"You think? We went and bought paint at the weekend. Imogen chose Elephant's Breath. It was way over our budget, but she wouldn't listen. She said it was perfect for the baby's room and she had to have it. I've had to pay the mortgage on my credit card this month. And all this with Rosie . . ."

Shaw started to shake, his mouth twitching and his hands making the table tremble.

DS Salmond leaned forward into his eyeline. "This must be very upsetting for you, Mr. Shaw. Shall I ask your wife to get you a glass of water?"

He blinked. "No, I don't want Imogen to hear any of this. She's very emotional at the moment, with the baby and everything. Oh God, this is unbelievable. My daughter is missing and you are looking at my bank account. What sort of people are you? Can't you see that I am devastated?"

Sparkes made sure he didn't catch Salmond's eye.

"Of course. But, we have to act on information received, Mr. Shaw. You do understand?"

If he did, he didn't want to discuss it further.

"I'll speak to my mother and get this cleared up. I'm sure she's made a silly mistake."

"Right," Sparkes said. "We will also be contacting her."

"I need to get back to work now," Mike Shaw said as he rose.

Both officers nodded. "Well, thank you for your time. We'll be in touch," DS Salmond said.

The new Mrs. Shaw was hovering in the hall when they emerged.

"Is everything all right, Mikey?" she asked.

"I'll tell you in a minute," her husband said, ushering the police officers through the front door.

"Well?" Salmond said when they were in the car.

"My gut doesn't like him either," Sparkes said quietly. "And what the hell is Elephant's Breath?"

https://www.facebook.com/alexoconnor.333

Alex O'Connor

August 4 at 0718

. . . is eating duck feet and living the dream

She wasn't sure if it was duck's feet but it was something unidentifiable and it sounded more exotic than noodles. Certainly more exciting than Rosie's Maccie D's.

Alex had got into the habit of getting up as soon as it was light every day to walk round different parts of the city, while it was quiet and cooler. Mostly she went on her own, wandering by the river, catching boats to somewhere new, and taking photos she posted on Facebook and Instagram with emojis of champagne bottles and stars.

She should have been on a beach by now but Rosie wouldn't budge. She was having too good a time to want to leave. And Alex was too nervous to continue alone. So she carried on writing variations on *Alex O'Connor . . . is having the time of her life* on her timeline and counted the Likes, the Loves, the funny comments, from her friends and passing strangers. They helped bolster the fiction. She kept *Alex O'Connor wishes she'd never come* to herself.

The truth didn't have a suitable emoji. She was unhappy and homesick. This trip wasn't what she thought it would be. And she was beginning to admit to herself that she should never have come with Rosie.

Alex didn't talk about it to anyone but Mags. *Thank God for Mags . . .*

She couldn't tell her mum and dad the truth: *Rosie is legless and sleeping her way through the boys in the guesthouse. This isn't why I came to Thailand. She's ruining everything. I could kill her.*

They might insist on them coming home. And she was still hopeful in a tiny corner of her brain. She'd give it another week. And Mags could be her listening ear—she didn't know anyone well enough yet at the guesthouse.

The English lad from the first night had started appearing on the next stool at the bar more often. And sometimes, when she came down for her walk, he was downstairs and offered to go with her. He called himself JW, which made Alex hide a smile the first time. He didn't have much to say but was always pleased to see her. Maybe he was lonely, too?

She tried to encourage him to talk, just to be kind more than anything, and he started to open up, telling her about his trip, testing her reaction with a flick of his eyes. He was traveling alone. "Wow, you're brave," Alex had said longingly. And he'd smiled shyly. Pleased.

He'd sort of adopted her, telling her about his security measures—keeping his stuff safe and private. Alex had half-listened as he enumerated his precautions: watching the other people in the shared dorm, putting his money and passport in a special belt he'd bought, never taking it off. When she heard him say something about putting it in a plastic bag when he had a shower, she clicked back into the conversation.

"That's a bit extreme, isn't it?" She'd laughed. His eyes had flicked away.

"But you can never be too careful," she'd added quickly.

"No," he said. "Not in a shared room," he said and took a swig of his water.

"The Dutch schoolboys are using lockers out the back. Dummies. No one uses lockers. Everyone knows that's where your things are and it is the easiest thing in the world to open the lock."

"How do you know about lockers?"

"Stuff I've picked up along the way," he said.

She shouldn't have encouraged him, really. It wasn't kind. But she needed someone to talk to. And he was sweet. He listened, laughed at her jokes, hung on her every word. He'd taken over the role she'd expected Rosie to play.

She knew she wouldn't have done half the things she'd done so far without him. And he seemed to like her company, too. Perhaps a bit too much. She'd tried to keep things as friends, but it was becoming obvious he wanted more. He said she could call him Jamie but only when they were on their own.

They'd talked about lots of things in the way that lonely people do; revealing themselves too quickly in the rush for instant intimacy. He'd told her on the second day that he liked that no one knew who he was in Bangkok. No one was judging him. She'd thought she understood and she agreed, and as they'd walked on she had pointed out the weird and wonderful things on street stalls—scorpions, ducks so neon orange they looked as if they'd been painted. The heads were left on. Lolling there in front of her with eyes all covered with a white film.

"It's not like Tesco's," JW said. "You can see they are dead animals."

When they went out at night, the whole place changed. It got dark so early, even though it was summer all the time, and all the creeps and sex tourists came out of their hiding places.

She e-mailed Mags about them:

You can spot them a mile off. Old, white, fat, and tattooed. And desperate. They look like they're enjoying themselves, laughing and talking too

*loud, but they must know everyone hates them. Don't they? The tiny
women who look like children hanging on their arms hate them.*

Her real traveling companion didn't even stir when Alex got up
and clattered around the room. She'd usually been in bed for only a
couple of hours by then, anyway. They were seeing each other less each
day. And when she said something about a sunset or a pavement fish
stall, Rosie rolled her eyes.

It was just like the walk-to-school thing. Being away from home
had not made them BFs. If anything, it had magnified the yawning
differences between them. Alex found herself cast as the boring older
sister, always seeing the negatives, while Rosie was the fun girl having
a wonderful time.

Rosie liked telling people she was a free spirit. Alex thought she
sounded like an idiot and that being a free spirit seemed to mean getting drunk as often as possible. But if Alex tried to warn her about
anything, such as getting her drink spiked by strangers, she'd go all
sulky and say it was like being on holiday with her mum.

She wanted to tell Rosie that the thought of being free to do anything she wanted had kept her going when she was stacking beans at
Asda. But she couldn't. And she certainly couldn't tell her that she'd
been put in charge by the mothers, hers and Rosie's. They'd sat her
down and said, "You will look after Rosie, won't you?" As if she needed
protecting. And it was like they'd planted their radioactive seed of fear
deep under her skin.

THIRTEEN

The Reporter

"This is a waste of time. They'll turn up," had become Don's mantra. And they do, today.

The news came this morning. Don rang me as I was getting up.

"They've been found," he said. "But they're in body bags."

"Oh God," I said. "Where? What happened?"

"There was a fire in one of the crummy hostels off Khao San Road. It happened on Friday but the cops have only just found bodies. They say there was no register or anything and the building was unsafe to enter until today."

"How many dead?"

"Just two so far."

"And it's definitely Alex and Rosie?"

"There's no formal ID yet, but the word is it's them. I wonder if the parents have been told."

I'd had the exact same thought. I didn't want to ring them in case the police hadn't made the call. I'd done it once in my career and never forgotten the stomach-lurching realization that the person on the end of the line had no idea her husband was dead. And the frantic backpedaling as I tried to end the call without breaking the news.

. . .

ring Bob Sparkes to see what he knows. It's early—not even eight a.m. yet—but he won't mind. He's bound to be at work already.

But when he picks up, he sounds as if he's in an echo chamber.

"Bob, can you talk?"

"Not really. I'm at the hospital."

"Oh God, sorry. Have you had an accident?"

"No. It's Eileen. Look, I'll call you back."

"'Course."

And he's gone.

dial the O'Connors' number slowly, practicing the words I'll use depending on how they answer the phone.

If Lesley says, "Hello, Kate. You're an early bird," or similar, I'll pretend it's a routine check call before she leaves for work. Say I've heard there's some activity in Bangkok, get her to ring the Foreign Office. If she's in tears . . .

A stranger answers. An old woman. And I think for a moment I've misdialed.

"Sorry, I wanted to speak to Lesley but I think I might have the wrong number."

"It's me," Lesley says. *She knows.*

"The police are here, Kate. They say there was a fire in Bangkok and two bodies have been found. It's two girls. They're the right age, and they say they're ninety percent sure. So there's still a chance. They might need to use medical and dental records." Her voice sticks on the word "dental" and I try to speak, to comfort her.

"I am so sorry, Lesley. I really hoped . . ."

"We all did. We're going out there today. I've got to go, Kate. To be sure. And to bring her home if it is . . ."

. . .

Terry is quietly thrilled he's got a splash this early in the day.

"Fuck," he says. Hyperbole is not his thing.

"Do the families know? Have you spoken to them?"

"Yes."

"Great. File it asap, before the others are all over it. Ring me afterward."

When I finally run out of patience and phone Bob Sparkes back, he doesn't mention Eileen or the hospital.

"Kate, sorry about earlier. You've heard?"

"Yes, I got a call from our bloke in Bangkok."

"Right. We were alerted overnight and I sent DS Salmond round to tell the families. She's still with them, I think. They were completely unprepared for this. We all were, really."

"I know. I called Lesley just now and she sounds terrible. I've just filed the story."

"Have you? It's not confirmed yet, Kate. The bodies have to be formally identified."

"I know, I know. I've written it carefully. But it's them, isn't it?"

"I think the odds are it is," he says cautiously. "The descriptions match the missing persons reports."

"For goodness' sake, Bob. I'm not going to quote you. Anyway, the families aren't waiting," I add. "They're flying out there today."

And I'm going, too.

"Nina will sort out tickets for you," Terry says when he emerges from the Editor's office with the okay for us to go.

"Thanks, Terry," I say, wrestling my overnight bag out of my desk drawer.

"You get on your way. The picture desk is getting hold of Mick, and I'll get Joe working on it at this end."

Joe jumps up, then tries to disguise his excitement.

He's learning, I think. *Doesn't pay to look too eager.*

My young protégé sniffs like a pro and mutters, "I'll make some calls."

"Thanks, Joe," I say. "Everything I've got from Don and Lesley is filed and on the website. I've tried her again but she and Malcolm are packing and getting sorted, so you need to speak to their son, Dan. He's the one in charge of the Facebook site."

"On it like a car bonnet," Joe says, scribbling down Danny's phone numbers. "Wish I was coming with you."

The only Foreign he's been on was to the Jungle in Calais to interview refugees. "I went further on a school day trip," he'd complained to me.

"They're not sending anyone anywhere, Joe. It's not personal. It's a question of money," she'd explained patiently. "We used to be on planes everywhere but the accountants are asking, why pay for tickets when we can do the whole job online? I travel so rarely now I'm about to be busted down a tier on my airline loyalty cards."

"Next time," I tell him and head off as the adrenaline around the possibility of a real story in August mounts in the newsroom. I call Steve before I get in the lift.

"I'm going to Bangkok, love," I say. "It's ninety percent sure it's the two British girls who died in the fire. The families are going to carry out the formal identification."

"I knew this would happen," Steve complains. "It always bloody happens. As soon as I buy tickets to anything. We're supposed to be going to that David Tennant play tonight."

"Sorry, Steve. Take one of your mates at work instead. Take Henry.

Look, this is a good story—and the parents are flying out tonight. I've got to go."

"Well, ring me when you land."

"Of course. Oh, and, Steve, can you pay the credit card bill? And I was going to ring about getting rid of that old fridge. Number's on the top."

"Yes, yes. How long will you be away, then?"

"Not sure. A few days—a week at the outside."

I hear my husband sigh.

"I know it's a pain but I've asked to go on this story so I can try to get out to Phuket while I'm there. It's only an hour and a half from Bangkok by plane. I'm going to see if I can find Jake and talk him into coming home."

"Right. It's a lovely idea. But don't build your hopes up, Katie. He is an adult, not a little boy. Look, I've got to get back to work. Have a safe trip. And ring me."

In the taxi to the airport, I sit in silence, looking at a photo of Jake on my phone and imagining his surprise when I turn up at his project. *If I can find his project.* But I brush it aside. I focus on him laughing and me crying when we see each other. I hope it will be like that.

FOURTEEN

The Detective

MONDAY, AUGUST 18, 2014

DS Salmond had been the obvious choice to send to tell the families. Sparkes would have gone himself, but Eileen had a meeting with the consultant and he'd wanted to be there to hear the latest prognosis. He'd been sure it was going to be bad news.

Anyway, Salmond was better at that kind of thing than he was. She had the knack with the bereaved. Where some coppers were stiff and uncomfortable around grief, and others overinvolved, she managed to be warm and professional. He couldn't say where he fit on that sliding scale.

"They are still running on nervous energy, putting off the moment when it sinks in," she'd said when she returned to HQ.

"Did you see Mike Shaw?"

"Yes. I went to his house last. He was in shock, I think. Jenny had phoned him before I got there. He's going with her and was trying to get ready. His new wife wasn't happy, so I didn't stay long."

Salmond had gone to leave but had stopped. "Oh, and he said his mother had remembered lending Rosie the money."

"What? He said that while you were telling him his daughter's body had probably been found?"

"I know. Well, he did. And I'm certainly not ringing Constance Shaw about it today."

"No. But don't lose sight of it, Zara. It needs tidying away eventually."

He sat thinking about the girls. Not in a bar, causing their parents heartache, but in body bags. Every fiber of his detective brain was engaged. Where? How? Why did these girls die? Fire was a horrible killer. Nothing swift or unfelt. It looked as if they'd been unlucky, wrong place, wrong time. But . . . He searched for details but there was nothing to snag his attention. The problem was that he was doing it thirdhand, reliant on reports of reports via the parents at this stage, each fact filtered through different eyes and imperatives. He wanted to be there, seeing the scene, gathering the evidence, talking to witnesses, not in this stuffy office reading e-mails. He shrugged stiff shoulders and tried again. But as he read, his mind wandered back to Eileen. He'd been right. Time was shortening.

"You look wonderful today, love, better every time I see you," he'd told her as he entered her hospital room that lunchtime.

"I'll be home soon, Bob," she'd answered from her bed, a wind farm of fans ruffling the fibers of her wig.

Sparkes had sat in his usual chair, dark red leatherette, the front edge of its seat worn thin by the years of anxious spouses perched to catch every word and glance. He'd pulled the chair tight against the bed frame so that they could touch.

"How's the pain?"

"Okay. How's your day?" she'd asked, her eyes slightly unfocused but pointing in his direction. "Tell me your news."

"Oh, fine. Anyway, never mind that, love." Bob had leaned forward quickly to kiss her forehead. It'd felt damp and cold and he'd fancied he could taste the chemicals being piped through her.

His kiss had nudged her wig—she'd picked it from a hospital catalog the first time round and had gone for a new color.

"I felt like a change and I've always wanted to be a blonde," she'd said, chirpy, pale, bald, and holding up a helmet of ash-blond hair for inspection. He'd laughed—the first proper laugh since her diagnosis—and kissed her hard. A lover's kiss. The new Eileen had still stopped him in his tracks each time he'd come through the door, but when she took the wig off, stubble prickled her scalp and colored her back to brown.

"I might bleach it when I get home," she'd teased when she caught him looking. "What do you think? Sexy?" He'd smiled and held her hand. They'd been winning then.

He closed his eyes as Eileen flooded his head. He ought to be at home, getting ready for her discharge from hospital. Changing the sheets on the beds—one upstairs, one down in the sitting room, which she would choose between depending on how she was doing. She liked the duvet cover with rosebuds on it. He needed to iron it. And get that raspberry tea she loved. He'd do it later. He scribbled *R tea* and *ironing* on a yellow Post-it and went to stick it somewhere he'd find it later. But he ended up putting it back on the Post-it stack, where it curled with contempt at his inadequacy.

Sparkes breathed deeply to contain the panic beginning to constrict his chest. *Open your lungs,* the woman in Eileen's yoga DVD said. *Feel your breath open spaces inside you.* He had a go, but the dread about what "coming home" meant could not be exhaled. Eileen was coming home because there was nothing more they could do at the hospital. It was the endgame. Eileen's consultant had told them as they held hands, both clammy, he from fear, she from the drugs.

"It may be months but more likely weeks," she'd said kindly but firmly. There was to be no disputing the facts or appealing against the sentence. Afterward, they had sat in a sort of daze, not daring to look at each other, in case they had to talk about it.

"We'll talk at home," Eileen had said to break the silence. "Can you remember to get my raspberry tea?"

He would go and pick her up tomorrow morning, after the ward round. She'd be bright and cheerful for him. Eileen could still turn it on with the help of her morphine, but that would fade as the day wore on. He could picture her moving slowly round the house, touching things as if she were about to leave. The agony of cancer was changing her. There were times when she pushed away his attempts at loving attention. Times when she got angry, couldn't bear him to touch her. And it was at these darkest times that he realized how much he loved her. How much there was to lose. *Months, please make it months . . .*

He pushed himself away from his desk as if physical action could rid him of his thoughts, and he cast around for anything else, something to distract him from Eileen's illness for one last day.

FIFTEEN

The Reporter

MONDAY, AUGUST 18, 2014

The airport lounge is crammed with businessmen, ties loosened, spectacles pushed up onto their heads, glasses of pinot noir in their fists as they lounge in the leather armchairs. There's a football match playing on one of the vast TV screens and a ticker tape of news running under the smiling face of a presenter on another.

This is the part of the job I love most. Going on a Foreign. The last-minute arrangements, rushing to the airport while the news-desk secretary is still booking the tickets, pushing through queues, boarding as the plane doors are closing. The anticipation of the story waiting at the other end.

It's busy and I choose a table in a corner and sit down slowly, scanning the room. There'll be other reporters flying out to Bangkok to cover the story, but I don't see any familiar faces propping up the free bar. My colleagues must be going goat class.

I've used my gold loyalty card and a great deal of charm at the check-in desk to be upgraded to business class. *Maybe the last time I can pull that one,* I think, but I'm pleased with myself. I need to be alongside the families so we can talk. And they'll be bumped up to the front of the plane to protect them from the press. *From people like me.*

People in business lounges tend to fall into two categories: the Residents, feet up and on first-name terms with the staff, and the

Tourists, the first-timers, buzzing over the free sandwiches like excited wasps.

But the O'Connors and Shaws are doing neither.

I spot Lesley and Malcolm holding hands over a table near the windows. Both look exhausted, neither speaking. Lesley's staring at her phone as if willing it to ring. When she looks up, she sees me and raises a hand in recognition.

The mobile rings and she looks at the number, then hands it to Malcolm, gets up, and weaves between the tables to me.

"Can I sit down?" she says and collapses into a chair. "Sorry, you don't mind, do you? I feel a bit wobbly."

"Of course you do," I say. "Do you want a glass of water or something stronger?"

She shakes her head. "I don't want anything except for it not to be Alex," she says and bursts into tears.

"Oh, Lesley," I say, pulling my chair round to touch hers.

"I know I must sound wicked, wishing it to be someone else's child, but I can't bear it."

"You are not wicked," I say. "Just desperately upset. I understand that."

"I don't think anyone *can* understand."

I consider telling her about Jake. Share my bit of misery. *Me, too.* But she doesn't need to hear it. It doesn't matter what's happening to anyone else now. She cannot think about anything but Alex.

"And I'm frightened of flying." Lesley hiccups and almost laughs at the absurdity of her situation. "I can't believe this is happening. I should be at the pub quiz tonight. We're the Little Gray Cells. But instead I'm going to fly eleven hours to see if a body in a police morgue is my daughter."

"You are doing brilliantly, Lesley."

"No, I'm not. I'm falling apart, Kate. I don't want to get on the plane. What if there's news? We'll be up in the air for hours, out of contact. We won't know anything until we land. It's terrifying me."

I lean forward to be in her eyeline. To get her to focus.

"It's night there now. Nothing is going to happen until the morning. Things could be a bit clearer tomorrow. You need to try to get some sleep on the flight. Have you got anything you can take?"

Lesley twists a tissue in her restless hands into shreds. "I'll manage."

I nod, never taking my eyes off the woman disintegrating in front of me.

I fish my phone out of my bag and dial Joe's number.

"Hi, it's me. I'm at the airport. Look, can you ring or text me if there is any more news before we take off?" It's a given that Joe would, but I want Lesley to know that I am getting any new info.

Joe uses his telephone voice and I want to tease him, but not in front of Lesley.

"Yes, will do," he says. "Nothing on the wires at the moment, or on Twitter or the Facebook group. How are you doing?"

"Good, thanks. Speak when I get there."

I shake my head at Lesley. "Nothing new this end, but I'll ring the local reporter now to make sure we get any updates before we take off." I call Don's number.

"Hi, I'm on my way to you. What's happening at the moment? Anything I need to know before I board?"

"It's the middle of the night, Kate. So not much. The police've been trying to make the building safe to continue the search. I hope they're wearing hard hats—it looks like it was a hazard before the fire, never mind now. Smells terrible. Poor buggers flying out here to identify their kids."

I'm editing the information in my head to make it fit for public consumption.

"Have you seen any of the parents?" Don says.

Lesley's looking at me and I hope she can't hear Don.

"Yes," I say with what I hope is a telltale inflection.

"Ah, are you sitting with them?"

"Yeah, so . . . What are the police saying about the fire?"

"That *farang kee ngok*—sorry, Cheap Charlie backpackers—caused it. It looks like it wasn't full at the time, thank God, but a contact at the hospital says there's a possible survivor—a Western lad with burns who came in on the night of the fire. There are no other details about him yet, but I'm making inquiries."

"Which hospital?" I ask. "Have you told anyone else?"

"Not yet. I'm working on getting in to see him."

"I'll make sure we look after you if you keep anything you get for us. Just until I get there . . . Don?"

We both know that an interview with the survivor could be the next big story. Especially if he turns out to be the hero of the hour.

"As it's you, okay," Don says. "But I can't afford to fall out with the pack, so keep *shtum*. Okay?"

"Thanks. See you when I land. And, Don, can you text me if you hear anything new?"

"Yes, will do," Don says. "See you in the bar."

Lesley's leaning forward expectantly. "What did he say? Who's in hospital?"

"There's a boy who might have been injured in the fire, but it's all a bit vague at the moment."

Lesley's face droops with disappointment. "A boy," she repeats quietly. "Does he know what happened?"

I squeeze her hand. "I don't know. It's still very early in the investigation, Lesley, so nothing is certain."

Lesley nods but I can see she's not really listening. She looks like she's heard it all before. Because she has.

"My contact out there will call us if there's any news; he's talking to the police all the time."

She mouths her thanks and walks back to her husband to tell him what I've told her. Then she goes over to another table, where Jenny Shaw is sitting with her ex. She has her back to him.

Well, this hasn't brought them together, then, I think and lift my hand in silent greeting as Jenny looks across at me.

SIXTEEN

The Reporter

MONDAY, AUGUST 18, 2014

My phone rings and I see Lesley's head turn at the sound. It's Mick and I shake my head to show there is no news for her.

"Just checking in, Kate. How the fuck did you get upgraded? No chance when I tried. The airline girl looked like I'd asked her for a blow job when I suggested business class."

I turn away to smile so Lesley doesn't see.

"I've seen three other photographers in the queue for security," Mick says. "Going to be a pack job." I can hear the grin on his face. Mick loves a pack job—the drinking, the competition, the fun of being with a crowd of other journalists.

"How's it going on your end, then?"

"Okay. I've spoken to Lesley. They're all terrified, poor things. Anyway, I'm sitting with them on the plane. It'll make life so much easier to be with them when we land."

"Well, think of me when you're tucking into your gourmet meal and necking champagne."

"I'll bring you a doggie bag."

I wait until the families are dozing before walking back to economy. Mick is dead to the world, his head lolling.

"Mick," I hiss too loudly, and other heads rise in the seats around him.

"Hello, Kate," George Clarkson from the *Telegraph* says from the row behind. "I didn't know you were on board. How are you doing?"

"Yeah, are you up the front?" Louise Butler from the *Herald* calls across the aisle.

"Hi, okay, and yes," I say. "How about you, George? Haven't seen you since you moved from the *Mail*. What's it like in the deep end?"

"A lot less screechy and hatey." He smiles. "No one shouts. All very civilized."

I look around and count five papers and a TV reporter. I know them all. They're my people. I feel comfortable here, in the fug of airline food and flatulence of the cheap seats.

"Has either of the families spoken to you? Or are the flight attendants on security duty?" Louise says, and I realize they haven't seen my story, filed from the airport lounge just before I boarded. I hesitate. The reporters hear the pause and know the painful truth. They've been beaten to it.

"What are they saying? They must be in pieces," Louise says.

Feeding me the line. I simply nod.

"How did you get your desk to agree to pay for business class? My lot wouldn't. I had a go at getting up front to see the parents when they were serving the meal but I got caught."

Bloody Louise Butler. Little Miss Pushy, I catch myself thinking and get an unsettling glimpse of myself on a doorstep. I turn back to George.

"How are they, Kate?" he asks.

"Not bad. They're being picked up by the embassy."

"And you'll be in the car, all cozy with them, no doubt. But you'll give us a line, won't you?" Louise says, leaning over and touching my arm. "We're your mates."

George raises an eyebrow on behalf of the other reporters.

"I get that you want the story, Louise," I say, moving my arm away from her. "We all do. Look, I filed my talk with them just before we took off. Your lot can pick it up from the website."

"Listen to her," I hear Louise mutter, mimicking my voice, " 'Your lot can pick it up from the website.' Who does she think she is?"

"It's the middle of the night," I say, trying to get things back on track. "Everyone's tired and on edge. We should all get some sleep. Where are you all staying?"

Mick grabs my hand when I move off and I squeeze back. He gets up and follows me to the dividing curtain and we stop.

"When we land, try and get off as quickly as you can, Mick. I'll go ahead with the O'Connors and the Shaws and meet you at the scene. I'll get some photos and video on my phone in the meantime. Ring me when you're on the way—and try to lose Louise. She'll turn us over soon as look at us."

Mick grins. "She's toast."

"Right. And, Mick, don't say that in front of the families."

SEVENTEEN

The Reporter

TUESDAY, AUGUST 19, 2014

The embassy official gives me a long-suffering look when Lesley introduces me.

"Ah, Her Majesty's Press. I'm sure you can arrange your own transport, Miss Waters."

"She's coming with us," Lesley says. "We can squash up."

I don't say anything—I don't need to. Lesley's doing superbly on her own. Malcolm keeps quiet and the Shaws simply look away.

"Well, if you are sure," the official says, displeasure in every clipped syllable. "This way."

The mood of the group had dipped back to numb when Vice-Consul Clive Barnes met us at arrivals and told us there was still no confirmation of the identities.

"It was a multi-occupancy building and the police would like you to take part in the identification process so there are no mistakes," he said carefully.

I took the lead as the others stumbled along in my wake, pulling their suitcases behind them. I needed to make a friend of Clive.

"This must be the most difficult part of the job," I say, trying and failing to match his stride. "Coping with other people's tragedies."

"Indeed. But I expect you know all about that, Miss Waters. I cannot say I am happy about taking you to the scene, but it is what the families want, apparently."

This is going to be hard work.

I fall back in step with Lesley and gently take the handle of her case from her. "You look worn-out. Let me have it for a bit."

At the back of the group her husband trudges, weighed down with another case and carrier bags, his head lowered. Mike Shaw has his bag and Jenny's holdall. She'd let him haul it off the luggage carousel for her after pointing it out but made no attempt to take it from him. She walks just behind Lesley but the two women barely speak to each other.

Lesley holds her husband's hand as Clive Barnes loads suitcases into the boot of the waiting minivan. She looks frozen despite the heat, shivering, her teeth chattering when she tries to talk. *It's all too real now,* I think. *Not just on Facebook. They are here and their daughter is probably dead.*

Malcolm helps Lesley into the vehicle and I perch between her and Jenny, apologizing as I fight to fasten the difficult middle seat belt. The husbands sit in the row in front. Lesley and Jenny stare out of their windows at the traffic while the men try awkwardly to make conversation.

"I've booked you into a hotel close to the embassy," Clive Barnes says. "I'll take you there after you have identified . . ."

There is a beat of silence. He can't bring himself to say the word "bodies" and no one in the vehicle is about to help him.

Finally, Malcolm says, "Is it definitely Alex and Rosie they've found?" and I feel Lesley stiffen beside me.

"We cannot be sure at this juncture, but it has been confirmed it is two young Western women who match the descriptions of your daughters."

I stroke Lesley's arm and she leans into me and begins to sob.

Jenny turns her head farther away.

Malcolm is trying to carry on. "We want to talk to the police straightaway and go to the scene of the fire."

Clive Barnes sounds grateful. "Yes, of course. One of my colleagues spoke to the detective in charge earlier. The postmortem examination is later this morning and the police are still searching the fire site. It might be advisable to have an interpreter for when I'm not available. Shall I help arrange one?"

"What will that cost?" Mike Shaw mutters.

"Yes, please, Mr. Barnes," Malcolm says.

"Please call me Clive."

Lesley is still sobbing against me in the back.

"Oh, love," Malcolm says, twisting round and reaching through for her hand. "Try to hold on."

The vehicle stops at a barrier across a narrow alley. Beyond, I can see policemen in gray uniforms, with masks over their mouths, and workmen with heavy machinery. And Don Richards.

"It is probably best not to talk to the press," Clive Barnes says and checks himself. "Sorry, Miss Waters. It is our standard advice."

"I see. Of course, the press may well help put pressure on the authorities to find out what happened here." I try to keep my voice even.

"Yes, well. Shall we get out?"

The parents walk together and I see both Lesley and Jenny slip their hands into Malcolm's as they reach the police guard at the barrier. Mike is two paces behind, his isolation complete.

Don Richards steps forward immediately.

"Mr. and Mrs. O'Connor? Mr. and Mrs. Shaw?"

They look up expectantly.

"Hello, Don," I say.

"My dear girl. There you are."

I can hear the disappointment in his voice. I've beaten him to it.

"Oh God! Please let it not be her," Lesley whispers as she and the

others are ushered through. I go to follow, but my new best friend
Clive stops me with a look.

"Families only. Police instructions."

Shit.

I try to catch Lesley's eye, to appeal for her help, but the O'Connors
are oblivious to everything apart from the blackened skeleton of a
building. What remains of the guesthouse leans into the street like an
old drunk, vomiting the last of its debris. The floors look as if they
have all fallen through. A charred foam mattress is curled in the street
and ashes eddy round the feet of the investigators.

The stench of smoke and soot catch in my throat as I call after
them, "I'll wait here for you, Lesley." I don't know if she's heard but I
take out my phone to film them making their way toward the ruin.

I squat down on the curb in the dust and heat to type my story on
my smartphone. I need to get the copy sent straightaway and be ready
before the families come back. I use my thumbs to type quotes and a
description of the scene while Don Richards tries to read over my
shoulder.

"Bugger off, Don," I say when he pretends to snatch my phone.
"Do your own color."

"Doing it now, matey."

Standing beside me, he scribbles in his tatty notebook. "I'll send it
on my laptop in a minute. I'm on order for everyone," he says, thrust-
ing his book back in his pocket. "Here they come. That was quick."

I press Send and stagger to my feet to film the return. They look
like a funeral procession as they walk slowly back, heads down, Malcolm's arm round his wife's shoulders, holding her up.

"How are you doing, Lesley?" I say quietly as the group draws level.

"It's heartbreaking, Kate. Have you seen it?"

I step round the nearest police officer and look through a gap in
the barrier at the pile of stuff swept up. It's hard to see clearly but I

think I can spot the blackened frame of a backpack, or maybe it's the twisted frame of a bed.

"I can't see anything of Alex's," Lesley says. "That's a good sign, isn't it? Isn't it?"

I nod. "What are the police saying?"

Clive Barnes clears his throat loudly. "I think we should head for the police headquarters. And then the hotel. You must be exhausted."

"We're not sleeping until we've done everything we can," Malcolm says. "We need to talk to the police. Come on, Lesley."

Mike Shaw nods and tries to take his ex-wife's hand. She almost takes it—her defenses at zero—but something stops her and she bats him away.

"Jenny," I hear him hiss. "For Christ's sake. This is about Rosie, not us."

Her expression starts to crumble at the edges. "This wouldn't have happened if you hadn't given her the money to come."

I hear Lesley gasp and try not to catch her eye as Mike Shaw stalks off to the waiting vehicle.

"Let him go," Jenny says as Malcolm moves to go after him. "Walking away is what he does best."

"Be quiet, Jenny," Lesley says. "This is awful enough without you torturing Mike."

Jenny starts to cry and Malcolm leads her off.

Lesley catches hold of my arm as she passes. "Don't put any of that in the paper, will you? We are all so upset. It makes people say terrible things."

EIGHTEEN

The Reporter

TUESDAY, AUGUST 19, 2014

D on takes me to one of dozens of cafés nearby to wait for Mick, and we try to talk over the distorted din of the Eagles' greatest hits.

"Why haven't they got identities yet?" I stir my green tea leaves into submission. "Have they got the proper equipment? Can they do DNA here?"

"'Course they can. This is an international hub, not a third world country. But foreign travelers are not a priority. They get hundreds of tourist deaths a year—drownings and traffic accidents mainly—and the cops see them as a royal pain in the arse. They get them off their books as fast as they can. Death and mayhem are bad for the holiday business."

A sunburned boy in a T-shirt at the next table is obviously listening, practically falling off his chair to catch our words.

"Hello," I say, unable to ignore him any longer. "Are you staying in one of these death traps?"

He smiles an "I'm off my face" smile and waves his arms about a bit.

"Are you? Were you here when the fire started?"

He nods. "I was walking back to mine and saw the smoke and shit."

"Did you know anyone who was staying there?"

The boy laughs nervously. "No, I don't know who is in the next bed most nights, let alone in another hostel."

I turn back to Don and shrug. "Hopeless."

"He's right. Some of these places cram kids in everywhere. And the owner of this place has gone AWOL. No surprise, really. The place is a death trap—look at those wires." I gaze up at the ropes of tangled cables strung from building to building.

"They're always shorting out and there's rubbish and old gas bottles everywhere. The girls didn't stand a chance if they were in there."

"Where the hell is Mick?" I yell, startling the pothead next to us. "We're losing time." I ring his number and take a sip of the bitter liquid.

"Where are you?" I shout down the phone. "Don't know where that is . . . How long? Okay. We're in the café at the top of the alley. If you're not here in five, I'm going."

Don raises a questioning eyebrow.

"I need to talk to the possible survivor," I say. "It's the only exclusive line I've got."

Nervous energy is burning a hole in my stomach. These first hours on the ground make or break the story. I've got to be first everywhere, and I wonder where Louise is now, reporter paranoia kicking in.

She's probably sitting beside the survivor, holding his hand and getting the whole story. She's paid Don to keep me here.

"Bloody hell. I'm just going to go."

"We can't see him anyway," Don says. "Not yet. I went first thing this morning but it was a no-go. My bloke will tip me the wink when I can."

"This is them." I see a taxi pull up and Mick gets out, already apologizing. I stand, and the intensifying heat of the day makes me sway.

"Fucking airport security. Someone must have fingered me—both me and the bloke from the BBC got pulled in to be searched. Our money's on Louise."

"Where is she now? And the others?"

"The police headquarters. That's where the families are going.

There's talk of a press conference being sorted out later. George will ring me when he hears. I said we'd give him a line in return."

"Okay. We'll get it from the wires if they say anything there. Lesley said she'll talk to me at the hotel in a couple of hours, so we've got a bit of time. We need to get to the hospital before the pack hear about the possible survivor."

"Survivor?" Mick says.

"I'll tell you in the taxi." I throw my bag into the boot and jump into the front seat beside the bewildered driver.

"Get in, Don. We need you to translate. And ask him to crank up the air-conditioning—I'm dying here."

As we drive, I brief Mick and ring the news desk to make sure my copy has arrived. I want to talk to Terry but I've lost track of time. They're six hours behind in London, and the graveyard shift is still running the desk through the night. The Has-Beens and Old Beans. It'll be potluck who I get.

"Hello, Old Lags' Home," Gordon Willis, the paper's former Crime Man, growls. "Oh, it's you. Just been reading your stuff, Kate. All very moving if you like that kind of thing."

"Sod off, Gordon. It's an exclusive chat. Anyway, what are you doing on the desk? Can't believe they've let you back in the building. You're supposed to be retired and living on the *costas* with all the villains you've written about. What happened? Spent all your redundo on sangria?"

"I fancied a bit of a break from the hacienda. And they asked nicely. Have you seen Don yet?"

"He's sat in the back of our speeding vehicle, actually. I'll pass your best wishes on."

"Do. Where are you going next?"

"The hospital. To try to see a possible survivor—a lad with burns who turned up on the night of the fire. We've got it to ourselves at the moment. Tell Terry when he wakes up—and that I'm seeing the parents later, on my own, and that the girls' formal ID is expected today and the police are saying nothing."

"Okay. I'll get him to call you when I hear from him. Won't be for an hour or so unless you want me to wake him now."

"No, best not. Look, we're arriving. Speak later."

NINETEEN

The Mother

TUESDAY, AUGUST 19, 2014

Lesley focused on her surroundings: The room was lit by fluorescent tubes set into the ceiling; the floor was tiled with cream-and-black-speckled squares; the tall lockers were stainless steel. And the smell was indescribable. It took her several minutes before she could bring herself to look at the trolley. There was a white sheet covering the body except for a foot with lime green painted toenails exposed.

"Mrs. O'Connor," someone was saying beside her. Clive. "Are you ready?"

She wasn't, but how could anybody be ready for this? Malcolm took her hand. His felt so cold. Like stone.

"Yes," she said, because there was nothing else to say.

The sheet was peeled back by a mortuary assistant to reveal a waxen effigy of her daughter. Malcolm's hand convulsed in hers. She wanted to reach out and touch her child's face. To comfort her. But the assistant anticipated the movement and stopped her.

"Please don't touch the body," said a police officer, an austere man who stood to one side.

"Alex," Lesley corrected. "Please don't touch Alex."

"Can you confirm that this is your daughter, Alexandra O'Connor?" he continued, as if she hadn't spoken.

"Was," she said. "It's not her anymore, is it?"

The officer looked confused.

"This is our daughter," Malcolm said.

She'd wanted to stay, but Malcolm led her out to the waiting area, where Jenny and Mike Shaw sat in silence. Lesley didn't need to speak. Jenny's face crumpled at the sight of them and Malcolm took her hand. "It's Alex, Jenny. Do you want me to come in with you?"

Mike Shaw got up stiffly. "No, it's okay. We can manage."

His ex-wife stood at his side as the door was opened and they were ushered in.

W hile Lesley waited, listening to the echoes of misery in the adjoining room, she played with the idea that none of this had really happened. That she would wake up in a minute and be looking at the old alarm clock and hearing her youngest in the shower. Using all the hot water.

Mike and Jenny reappeared and she was back in the room. "I was just thinking, perhaps it was a dream," she said.

"No, love. I'm afraid it isn't," her husband murmured. "We need to try to think straight now."

Now. Now that we know for sure.

Lesley looked at Jenny's face, blank with shock. "I wanted to touch Alex," she said, "but they wouldn't let me."

"I thought it wasn't her for a second," Jenny said. "The girl on the table had a little rosebud tattoo on her shoulder. I went to say it wasn't Rosie, but it was. I didn't know she'd had it done. I tried to kiss her but they said I couldn't, that there will be time for that later. But there won't, will there? No more kisses. The last time was at the airport."

"How has this happened?" Lesley sobbed. "We need to find out why they died like this."

"We will, love," Malcolm said.

Clive stepped forward. "Let's go and talk to the police."

· · ·

The police colonel at the Crime Suppression Division was formal but courteous. He was accompanied by the interpreter hired for the families, a young man in a tight suit, Harry Potter glasses, and a ridiculous schoolboy quiff.

When they were seated, the officer immediately outlined the facts as he saw them.

"The victims were found together at the rear of the building," the interpreter said after listening and making notes, his words harsh after the musical lilt of the officer's account.

"But their room was on the top floor," Lesley said. "Alex said so in an e-mail. She joked about it being the penthouse."

"Not in a room. In a cupboard sort of place." The interpreter looked flustered.

"A cupboard?" Lesley said.

The interpreter asked the officer a question and nodded obsequiously before turning back to his audience.

"Bigger than a cupboard. A place for storing things. Cold things," the young man tried to explain, but the colonel had started to speak again and his tide of words was getting away from the interpreter, who lowered his gaze and started taking notes again.

"There was a party on the ground floor," he explained when the officer next paused for breath.

"He said more than that," Lesley challenged him. "It went on for ages. Why aren't you telling us everything?"

"I am, madam," the interpreter said, clearly stung that his professionalism was being questioned. "I was about to continue . . ."

"Good," Lesley said.

"There were drugs and alcohol taken at the party . . ."

"Our girls didn't take drugs," Jenny said loudly. "Why is he saying this?"

Her words were not translated back to the colonel.

"The police think maybe a candle was knocked over by drunk or drugged people at the party," he continued. "Or a cigarette not extinguished. High probability an accident."

"Did Rosie smoke?" Mike asked.

"No," Jenny muttered.

"The fire spread very quickly through the rooms. The front of the building was mainly wood. The two girls were hiding from the fire in the cold store. They died from . . ." The young man searched for the right words, putting his hands to his throat to indicate choking.

"I think he means smoke inhalation," Clive Barnes whispered quickly to end the pantomime before it became too graphic.

"And heart attack," the interpreter added. Lesley thought she saw Barnes roll his eyes.

"The owner of the hostel is being sought in connection with safety violations."

And with that, the colonel closed his file, raised his hands in *wai*, and made a slight head bow as he made to leave. Malcolm struggled to replicate the gesture. But Lesley jumped to her feet to stop the departure.

"Did no one hear them? They must have been screaming for help . . ."

The colonel remained standing and impassive.

"The officer says no one knew they were there until the bodies were found," the interpreter said.

"No one heard or saw anything? What about the others at the party?" Mike asked. "Where are they? What do they say about what happened? How did they escape and our girls didn't?"

The officer looked impatient at the question.

"They have not found any witnesses," the interpreter said.

"So you are saying that our daughters were the only ones in the guesthouse at the time of the fire? Where are all the other guests? You can't have a party with just two people, can you?"

The officer shrugged delicately.

"They have not found any witnesses," the interpreter repeated.

"We heard there was a young man with burns at the hospital," Lesley said, remembering her conversation with Kate.

"He is not relevant to the inquiry."

"What does he mean?" Lesley asked the interpreter.

The officer remained stony-faced as he rattled out a longer explanation.

"He says the young man at the hospital could not tell them anything," the interpreter said. "They are not even sure he was at the guesthouse."

The colonel spoke again, then shook hands limply with the families.

"He said they will release the bodies in the coming days," the interpreter said. "They will give you the documentation and you can take them home."

Afterward, Clive Barnes escorted them to the minivan again. "You didn't look very happy in there, Clive," Lesley said. "I don't think Harry Potter was telling us everything his boss said."

Barnes looked pained. "My Thai is not fluent, but he definitely skipped over some parts."

"What did he leave out?"

"That police had been to the guesthouse previously in connection with drugs. Let's say it was known to the authorities. There was a little more detail about how the girls were found. They did not suffer any burns or injuries—they must have died from smoke inhalation. The store they were in was metal, which would have kept out the flames, and they had wrapped themselves in some matting to protect themselves."

"Oh God." Lesley had an image of her frightened child, hiding from the flames.

"Why are they saying there was a party if there are no witnesses?" Jenny suddenly asked.

Barnes shook his head. "Perhaps the other guests have made themselves scarce because they don't want to be questioned about drugs by the Thai police?" he said carefully.

"Our girls didn't take drugs," Jenny repeated.

Barnes paused. "We don't always know what our children get up to when we're not there, do we?"

"Do you think that's why the boy in the hospital didn't say anything? He must know something if he was there," Lesley said. "The police should be questioning him again."

BANGKOK DAY 11
(WEDNESDAY, AUGUST 6, 2014)

FROM: Alexinnit96@gmail.com
TO: Magsishot@hotmail.co.uk
SUBJECT: ROSIE IS A COMPLETE NIGHTMARE

Hi, Mags,

It's been a mare of a day. First R decided she was definitely going to get a tattoo! She begged me to go and hold her hand. I told her it was a bad idea. That she wouldn't be able to go out in the sun, swim, or do anything that might cause an infection. But she wouldn't listen. I'm not sure how she can afford it—what with all the nights out. And her mum would kill her if she knew.

JW said it would hurt like hell and showed her his tattoo—a little dagger someone did for him one night with a needle and a bottle of ink when there wasn't anything on the telly, apparently. But she wouldn't listen. Course, she started crying as soon as the tattooist put his needle on her skin. She was shouting, "He's hurting me, Alex. Make him stop!" Sooooooo mortifying. She made so much fuss the woman who had taken her money came through and told her she was frightening the other customers. She was smiling like it was a joke—they smile all the time here, especially when it is completely the wrong moment—and said there'd be no refunds and told Rosie to basically sit still and shut up. She'd ordered a big gecko on her shoulder, like Lars has, but I persuaded her to go for something smaller. She chose a rosebud in the end. It looked horrible when it was finished, all oozy and bloody. Gross.

We came straight back to the guesthouse after so Rosie could have a lie-down, and I was helping her get her T-shirt over her shoulder so it didn't touch the wound and something really weird happened. You know when you get that feeling someone's watching you? And I thought I saw something move where our curtains don't quite meet in the middle. It made me jump and Rosie screamed because I touched her arm. It spooked us both. Rosie made me go and look. I was really scared. I pulled the door open slowly. I kept thinking about that horror film we saw, *Hostel*. I was really shaking. But there was no one there. There had been, though. I'm sure.

Rosie was more interested in taking some painkillers, but I got my emergency sewing kit out and sewed the curtains together. More soon, A x

Rosie was still playing her new tattoo to the hilt that night, wincing theatrically if anyone went near her and boring everyone to death with how much it hurt.

"It was like being stabbed," she told Mama, the only person in the guesthouse still willing to listen to her tale of woe. "They should have warned me."

Mama clucked and smiled as she inspected the wound. "Poor Rosie," she murmured. "I have something for this."

Wads of cotton wool were brought from the back room, the mysterious area where Mama appeared to live.

She hadn't been interested in Alex's report about a Peeping Tom. "Probably the fan blew the curtains," she'd said. "This is a good guesthouse. No problems here." End of subject.

I wonder if there's a Mr. Mama, Alex wondered, watching the landlady swishing around in a caftan and high heels as big as small boats.

Alex had made herself laugh out loud, and the nurse and patient wheeled round to glare.

"Shut up, Alex. I'm in pain here," Rosie said.

"Take this, dear," Mama said, putting a pill in her hand. "This will make it better."

TWENTY

The Reporter

TUESDAY, AUGUST 19, 2014

The doctor thought we were relatives. We hadn't said we were, but we'd screamed up to the hospital in our taxi and jumped out, looking desperate and Western, and the security people had ushered us through to an office immediately.

Don and a grave-looking young doctor had a conversation in Thai, strings of words playing up and down the register, ending with the doctor nodding and smiling sympathetically at Mick and me.

"What have you told him?" I'd asked, but Don had shushed me and walked me out.

"Doesn't matter."

"Tell me!"

"That you've flown out from England to see the fire survivor. He immediately assumed you were family."

"And you put him right? Don . . . ?"

Don had winked at me and said, "Shut up. You're in. Third floor, room six. Doctor says you've got five minutes."

I'd stood, undecided, as people milled around us, until Mick had nudged me. "Come on, Kate. We'll go and ask if he wants to see us. No harm in that."

I'd nodded and walked to the lift.

. . .

And here we are. Looking at an empty bed. Not just empty; the mattress has been stripped of sheets, ready for the next patient. Don goes outside to make sure we've got the right room and comes back in, shaking his head.

"This is definitely room six. I'll find a nurse."

When he comes back he looks grim. "He's gone. Discharged himself first thing. The nurse said there was nothing they could do to stop him."

While I was waiting for Mick, I fume silently.

"A name, an address?"

"No. She says it's confidential. She wanted to know who I was. I think she's going to find someone in charge. We might have to make a quick exit."

"I thought you said you had a contact here."

"I do. I've tried him but he's on a ward round."

I want to scream. *So close. If we'd been here a couple of hours earlier . . .*

I'm looking in the locker for anything with a name on it when the grave-looking doctor from the lobby and a female colleague come in.

"Hello," she says in English. "I was looking after this patient, Mr. Waters."

"It's Mrs. Waters, actually," I correct her.

She looks puzzled. "Sorry, not important," I say quickly.

"Do you know where your patient has gone?"

She shrugs. "No. The police might know. They came to talk to him. This morning he said he wanted to leave. He did not have money to stay."

"Was he English?"

"Yes, Mr. Waters, he is English."

"Mrs. Waters," I say again, trying not to show my irritation.

"You are Mrs. Waters?" the doctor says.

"Yes, yes. What else do you know about your patient? His name?"

"Mr. Waters," she says.

"Look." I am starting to feel as if I am in some bizarre comedy sketch.

Who's on first . . .

"Are you saying his name is Mr. Waters?" Don interrupts.

"Yes. The patient is Mr. Waters."

I feel like I am stepping off a precipice. "First name?" I croak, but I already know.

She pulls out a sheet of paper. "Jake."

TWENTY-ONE

The Reporter

"What's going on? Do you know him?" Mick asks, his voice suddenly loud. "Kate?"

"It's my son," I say and sit down on the chair beside Jake's empty bed.

"No! Stone me!" Mick says, pulling up another chair.

"I can't believe it's him," I say and hear Mick muttering, "Fucking right . . ."

The female doctor and Don are discussing something in hushed voices.

"Why did no one tell me?" I say. "Why was I not contacted after he came in?"

"He didn't want us to tell anyone," the doctor says. "It was his right, Mrs. Waters."

"Why? Why didn't he want us to know?" I shout into the empty air, and everyone starts moving toward me. Don helps me stand on trembling legs.

"Come on, love. We need to take you to the hotel. You've had a shock. Get her other arm, Mick."

"Was he badly hurt? Was he burned?" I ask, shaking them off.

"Not too badly," the doctor says. "His injuries were not so serious. He has burns to his hands and some scorching on his right cheek and nose."

She is talking about the thickness and surface area of the burns, the rate of recovery, and I try to take it all in but my mind keeps slipping back to an image of him trying to get out of the burning building. The panic he must have felt, roiling in my gut now. I want to hold him to know he is safe now, but I can't. I pat the mattress he once lay on instead.

"Does he know about the girls?" Don says to the doctor, and I suddenly remember why I'm here.

She nods. "The police asked him about them when they came. But we don't know if he understood. He was in shock when he was admitted. He couldn't speak for the first two days and he didn't mention them when he started to talk. But all of this is completely understandable in the circumstances."

I'm nodding as if I, too, understand, but the facts keep slipping away from me.

"And it was definitely Jake?" I say.

She holds up the sheet of paper to show me. It has his date of birth, his passport number. My boy.

Beside "Next of Kin" is written *Not known*.

"I have to call Steve," I say to Mick, and he signals to Don to leave.

"We'll get you some water," he says, and I hear them talking as they walk away.

"Bloody hell, you couldn't make it up," Don is saying.

I dial slowly, putting off the moment.

What am I going to tell him? What am I going to say? I don't know anything. Like why Jake was there in the guesthouse or what he's been doing. What has he been up to for the past two years?

Steve picks up immediately.

"Hello. You're early. Luckily I've just woken up. What time is it there? How was the flight? The play was wonderful—I'll try to get more tickets for when you're back."

"Steve, something's happened. It's Jake," I blurt.

"Jake? What? What's happened?" His voice is loud, spilling out of the phone into the room. "Are you in Phuket already? How is he? Can I speak to him?"

"Steve, I'm in a hospital in Bangkok. Jake was in the fire. The hostel fire I came out here to cover."

There is a beat of stunned silence as my husband wrestles with the news.

"What?" he shouts. "I don't understand. What has Jake got to do with the fire?"

"He was there, Steve. I don't know why. The police have talked to him. They came to the hospital and questioned him."

"Hospital? Police? Was he a witness?"

"I don't know."

"Oh Christ, is he hurt?"

"The doctors say he's not in danger. They say he's got burns on his face and hands."

"Haven't you seen him?"

"No. He's gone. Disappeared from the hospital."

"Disappeared?"

"Yes. Disappeared. I'm frightened for him, Steve."

"I don't understand, Katie."

"Neither do I. The doctor said he left after the police came. He didn't want us to know, Steve. He asked the hospital not to contact us."

I'm crying too hard to speak. "Take three deep breaths, my darling," says Steve. "I need to be able to understand everything you are saying. And I need to see your face, Katie. FaceTime me so I can see you."

I hang up and close my eyes, taking slow, juddering breaths, and letting the panic slide from my throat back into my stomach before FaceTiming Steve back. I can see the strain in his face when he appears on the screen.

"Now start again from the beginning," he says.

And I do. As if I am filing a story to a copytaker in the old days. *New par. He said, colon quote. Full stop.*

And Steve is talking in his calm consultant voice, telling me we will find him and how skin recovers, telling me we will bring him home as soon as possible, telling me everything is going to be all right. All the things I need to hear.

A nd when we reach the end of the story, I say, "I'm sorry, Steve."

"Why are you sorry?" he says. But he knows.

"I lost him. Just like you said I would."

He sighs. "This isn't your fault. Go to the hotel. We need to speak to the authorities. We need help to find him. But we will find him. Ring me when you get there. Okay?"

"Okay."

But nothing is okay. Everything has changed here in this room that smells of bandages and antiseptic. I'm not the reporter here. I'm the mother.

TWENTY-TWO

The Reporter

TUESDAY, AUGUST 19, 2014

Don is making calls to the Tourist Police and my ears prick every time I hear him say Jake's name. I wonder what he's telling them. Mick sits me down on a bench in reception and I try to think like a reporter. Where would an injured man with little money go? Would he check into the nearest hostel? Would he go to the embassy? Would he go to stay with friends? He'd need a pharmacy for painkillers. Did he have a prescription? I need to ask the doctor. She could alert the pharmacies. I write *pharmacies* on my notepad. My writing is shaky and my mind wanders back to the empty bed.

Where are you? I think. I've been asking this question since the first of May 2012 when he walked out of the house with his backpack and his hurt feelings. *I should never have let it go on this long.*

I need to do something. Anything. I call Clive Barnes at the number on his business card. He is not happy to hear from me.

"There is nothing for the media at the moment, Ms. Waters. You will have to wait. I'm a bit busy with the families of the girls, so if you will excuse me . . ."

I interrupt his formal leave-taking and throw myself on his mercy. I tell him about Jake. His voice changes instantly to victim-support mode, hiding any surprise—and any secret triumph he must be feeling at having Her Majesty's Press on the back foot.

"I see," he says simply. "You must be very worried. Please tell me his details—his date of birth, his passport number if you know it, description—and let me see what I can do. Try not to worry too much."

He is following a script, I think and try not to notice.

"Can I ask if you have told the O'Connors or Shaws?" he says. "I understand you are talking to them regularly."

"Er, not yet. I've only just found out myself."

"I'll tell them. We don't want them to hear it from the media, do we?"

A small moment of triumph, then.

"I would like to tell Lesley myself," I plead. "I can answer her questions. I will be talking to her as a mother . . ."

"As you wish. I'll be in touch, Kate. And please let me know if Jake turns up."

Mick is tugging my arm. "They're here," he hisses. Through the doors I see the pack clambering out of a convoy of taxis. They pour into the reception area and spot me immediately.

"Bloody hell, she's got here first," I hear Louise say.

Mick tries to head them off.

"Hi, have you been to the site of the fire yet? What about the press conference?" he says. "Are police saying anything about theories yet?"

"Not much coming out so far," George says. "We've heard the guesthouse was known as a good place to get drugs. Everyone's waiting on the IDs and the PM, so we're all filing color from the scene and interviewing the same stoned backpackers."

I try to laugh with the rest of them, but it feels fake.

"Never mind that—have you spoken to the boy who survived?" Louise calls across to me. She's not the sort to be distracted.

"No," I say and my voice trembles. Louise looks at me hard and the reporters come closer.

"You look upset," George says. "What's happened? Has there been a row? Are you being chucked out?"

"No," I say. "Nothing like that."

I take a deep breath and think about keeping quiet. But they're going to find out anyway. I would.

"The thing is, the survivor is my son Jake."

"You're joking! Your son?" George says, and there is a buzz of excitement among the reporters.

"Yes, I know. Unbelievable. I didn't realize until I spoke to the doctor."

"Wow," Louise says and I see her scribble something in her notebook.

"I knew he was in Thailand—I told you, George—but I thought he was in Phuket, saving turtles," I say, trying to explain but sounding hopeless.

"God, that must have been such a shock. How is he, Kate?" George asks.

"Not too bad, the doctor says. Some burns on his hands and face."

I feel like I'm talking to my friends—they are my friends, most of them—but more of them are taking down what I'm saying. Is this a press conference?

"How old is Jake?" someone asks.

"So, is he on holiday?"

"How did he get out of the fire?"

"Did he get his burns trying to save the girls?"

"Is he a hero, Kate?"

And while I'm struggling to find answers, Louise says:

"You'll get us in to see him, won't you?"

The reporters go quiet. I swallow hard.

"No, I can't. Jake isn't here anymore."

"Where is he, then? Have you squirreled him away in a hotel?" Louise snaps.

"No, I haven't. I haven't even seen him. He discharged himself this morning before I got here. I don't know where he is."

"What? He's disappeared?" she says, and everyone crowds closer round me so they don't miss a word.

"Do the police know?" a TV reporter asks from behind his video camera, and I nod. "They talked to him last night."

"So is he a hero or a suspect?" Louise says.

"Shut up, Louise," George says. "Ignore her, Kate."

I look at them, at the faces I know so well. They are people I have been scared with, laughed with, confided in, got drunk with, but suddenly I am the stranger in their midst. I am the story.

PART TWO

THE STORY

TWENTY-THREE

The Mother

TUESDAY, AUGUST 19, 2014

S he turned on Malcolm as soon as the hotel bedroom door closed.

"Why didn't you back me up? Sitting there, not saying a word."

"There was nothing I could say, Lesley. You and Jenny asked all the questions. And the police know what they're doing."

"Who says? I saw that embassy bloke roll his eyes when the policeman was talking. I want to know what happened to my daughter."

"*Our* daughter."

"Yes, yes, our daughter."

"That's what I want, too. You know that. We mustn't let this push us apart, love. It's what happens to couples when something terrible happens. They turn on each other. Blame each other. I've read about it in the papers."

"We're not like Jenny and Mike," Lesley snapped. Being reasonable was not what she wanted at that moment. She was so angry she felt she could burst. Her daughter. Her daughter was lying in a morgue and no one could tell her why. Why was Alex dead? Who was to blame?

Malcolm got into bed fully clothed, too exhausted even to take off his shoes, and closed his eyes.

"We can't sleep now," she shouted, startling him. "We've got to find out who is responsible for this. Get up!"

Malcolm turned onto his back and looked at the ceiling, tears rolling into his hair.

"Stop being so passive!" Lesley shrieked.

He reached out his arms to her and she collapsed onto the bed, folding herself into him.

"We will find out." He stroked her hair and stilled her clenching fists. "But we can't function without sleep, love. You are so tired, you can't see straight. Close your eyes, just for half an hour."

She waited for him to fall asleep, monitoring his breathing as it slowed to comatose, then rose and sat at the desk with the flimsy notepad she'd found on the bedside table.

She wrote *Things to Do*, just like she would if she'd been at home. But instead of writing *Phone bank, Buy cat food, DRY CLEANING!*, she put *Find out how the fire started. Who else was in the hostel? Was there a party? Where were Alex and Rosie? WHY DIDN'T THEY GET OUT?*

She was gripping the cheap hotel biro so hard it splintered.

When she looked up from the list, she saw her hollow-eyed reflection in the mirror.

"Why didn't you get out, Alex?" she said, but the bereaved mother looking back at her had no answers.

The phone rang and she picked it up quickly to stop it waking Malcolm.

"Mrs. O'Connor," a sweet voice sang to her from reception. "I have someone here to see you. Please hold."

"Lesley? It's Kate. I hope I haven't woken you. Can I come up?"

"Okay. But Malcolm's still asleep."

Kate looked terrible when Lesley opened the door. Her makeup was all smudged, as if she'd been crying. *What's she got to cry about?* flitted through Lesley's head, but she didn't ask. She couldn't summon up the energy.

"We'll have to talk in the bathroom," she whispered and led the way. She sat down on the toilet lid. Kate perched on the side of the bath.

"We've identified the girls. It is them," Lesley said in one breath. "I'd hoped they'd made a mistake, but it is Alex and Rosie."

"I am so sorry, Lesley."

"Yes, well. Now we have to find out what happened." She knew she sounded manic but she had to keep going or she would break down. *Keep strong,* she told herself, kneading her thigh with her fist to keep herself focused.

"Of course," Kate said. "What are the police saying?"

"That there was a party that night. That there were drugs and drink. That it was most probably an accident. That's what the interpreter told us. A candle or something like that."

"Right," Kate said. "Was there evidence of a candle causing the fire?"

"I don't know. They didn't say. The thing is, there are no witnesses, according to the police. It just doesn't make sense."

"Right," Kate repeated.

Why does she keep saying that, as if she doesn't believe me? "But Clive Barnes says he's heard about the boy you mentioned at the airport— the boy who got out alive. I want to talk to him and find out why my daughter didn't."

Silence filled the tiled bathroom. *Another tiled room,* Lesley thought and tore a sheet of toilet paper off the roll to wipe her eyes.

Kate looked as upset as she was and she passed her a piece of loo roll.

"Sorry, Lesley. I'm a bit all over the place. When did Clive tell you this? Did he have a name?"

"No. Why? Do you know who it is? Have you seen him?" Lesley asked.

"It's my son."

"What is? What are you talking about?" Lesley felt completely lost, as if she'd blacked out and come to at a different point in the conversation.

Kate leaned forward to tell her, nearly falling off the narrow lip of the bath. Lesley put her hand out to steady her.

"Careful," she said, but Kate brushed her away.

"I went to the hospital to try to speak to the survivor, and when I got to the room, I discovered it was my son Jake. The doctors told me. I didn't even know he was in Bangkok—we thought he was in Phuket. That's what he always told us. It was a complete shock."

"Your son?"

"Yes. Jake."

"Was in the fire?"

"Yes. I know it must be hard for you to take in. It was for me."

Lesley couldn't speak for a moment as she tried to make sense of it.

"What does he say about what happened?" she said.

"Apparently he couldn't tell the police anything when they spoke to him, Lesley."

"Yes, that's what the policeman said to us, too. But he'll be able to tell us what happened, won't he?"

"Not at the moment."

"Well, when can we go and see him?" Adrenaline surging through her, Lesley jumped up, threw open the bathroom door, and shouted Malcolm's name.

"What?" he groaned. "Alex?"

"Wake up, love. We're going to the hospital. We're going now," she said. Nothing was going to stop her.

Kate took hold of her arm to restrain her, but Lesley shook her off impatiently. "Come on, Kate. You can take us."

But there was something wrong. Hers was the only energy in the room. Kate looked flat and panicky.

"Hold on, Lesley. The thing is, I don't know where he is now. No one does. He left the hospital this morning."

"Why? Has he run away?"

Kate couldn't look her in the eye.

"Well, has he?"

"No," Kate said loudly. "He told the doctor he didn't have enough money to pay big medical bills."

"Didn't he call you to say he was in hospital?"

Silence again.

"No. He hasn't been in touch properly for a while. He came to Thailand to find himself. Sorry—you don't want to hear about my family problems. Look, there's no point going to the hospital. Honestly. He's gone."

"What are you talking about?" Malcolm said, his head still on the pillow, his voice deadened by exhaustion.

"Go back to sleep, love," Lesley said. She would deal with this.

"What are you doing to find him?" she asked.

"Everything I can, but I need your help. We are talking to different people, Lesley, but we can pool our information. Will you let me know as soon as you hear anything?"

Her turn for silence.

"And will you publish what I tell you, Kate?"

"No. Not now." The answer was too quick, but Kate decided to go with it. "I want to find my son."

"Okay. We're talking to Clive later and we're going to do a press conference in the morning. We want to talk to the media."

"There'll be lots of questions about drugs, Lesley. You do know that?"

"She didn't take drugs."

"No, but the police and local press may be telling a different story. Just be prepared."

"And what about you? You'll have to be prepared for questions about your son, won't you? We'll be in the same boat."

BANGKOK DAY 13
(FRIDAY, AUGUST 8, 2014)

FROM: Alexinnit96@gmail.com
TO: Magsishot@hotmail.co.uk
SUBJECT: Nightmare continues!

Hi Mags,

STILL waiting to set off for next stop—we've already
been here a week longer than we said—but R is being a
complete bitch and won't talk about it.

Went up to our room today and walked in on her and
Lars. Soooo embarrassing. Rosie shouted at me to get
out. I mean, it's my room, too. Lars came out still
putting on his shirt and said sorry. Rosie pretended
nothing had happened when I went in. She's weird like
that. She said Lars was taking her to another club
tonight. He's going to do some DJing. He calls himself
DJ Rappo. Crappo, more like!!! I think he has taken some
of my stuff. Well, someone must be. I keep losing
things—those earrings I bought for school prom have
gone. Rosie and I had a row about it. She says I leave
stuff all over the place. But I don't. I'm not imagining it.

I'm so desperate to leave I'm seriously thinking about
ditching Rosie and traveling solo. But it's too scary. I

wouldn't want to stay in a place like this on my own. There are weird people coming and going all the time—and the locks don't work properly. Maybe it's better to wait. The Dutch boys are going to Myanmar by bus on Monday, so she won't have anyone to play with after that. And I keep thinking maybe things will be different when we get on the road and it's just us. Maybe it'll be all right then.

I'm keeping busy, reading and people watching. There are so many visitors. Mama takes them through to the back. But they're not staying here. Sometimes they have a coffee or a beer at the bar. Sometimes they just drift off. Lots to look at, anyway. And there's a mystery English bloke here who I've seen a couple of times. He doesn't speak to us—sits smoking dope out of the window—under the sign that says "No Drugs Here." The boys he shares the dorm with call him The Stoner and I've only seen him a couple of times.

But there's something about him. He's older than us and interesting. I know that doesn't sound sexy but he is in a funny kind of way. Going to have breakfast . . . Back soon . . .

Part 2!

Turns out the mystery bloke isn't another traveler. He works here to pay for his keep—cleaning the showers and making the breakfasts. He's normally finished by the time I get back from my walk, but I didn't go this morning—too busy writing to you!

Anyway, he just spoke to me. Just the one word! It's a start . . .

I was sitting at the bar and the Dutch boys were at the other end, talking about a drinking game they'd been playing last night. They still managed to eat a huge omelet with chilies, some sort of meat, and what looked like clots of tomato sauce!!! Gross.

"Finished?" was all he said when he picked up the plates, and he put his thumb in the tomato sauce smears.

We got chatting about the terrible food—he said he knows how bad it is because he used to eat it, too! He's got a lovely smile. And he said he'd show me a better place up the road. He says there are fewer cockroaches—and it's cheaper. Win-win!

Wish me luck. A x

Afterward, she realized she hadn't even asked his name! One of the Dutch boys told her he was called Jake.

TWENTY-FOUR

The Reporter

TUESDAY, AUGUST 19, 2014

I ring Terry from my room, repeating the facts about Jake as I know them, numb now to the consternation my story causes.

"So he's a hero, then?" Terry asks uncertainly.

"Possibly," I say, willing it to be true.

"File what you've got, Kate, and I'll get Joe to pull it together in the office. There's some nice stuff from family members we can weave in. What are you going to do next?"

"Not sure, to be honest. Don is putting out feelers to contacts but it's a needle-in-a-haystack job. He could be anywhere."

For the first time in my career, I don't know where to begin. I normally love the hunt for the story, but this time it's personal. Everything matters desperately. And I'm afraid of what I'll find.

"You get on with it, then," Terry is saying. "And stay in touch."

I lie back on the bed—just for five minutes, I tell myself, before I have to act. I close my eyes to try to stop the chaos in my head. Ideas, thoughts, images, fears. I think about that time Jake jumped off the shed roof. He just sat there, holding his wrist like it didn't belong to him. Pale but composed. "It's probably broken," he said. It was Freddie who'd cried. "My brave boy," I'd told Jake over and over as we waited in Accident and Emergency for an X-ray. It came out later that he'd been trying to get his little brother to jump when he fell. But we let it go. He had a broken wrist, after all. I wonder what else we let go. My dad used to say we spoiled him. We argued about it. Horrible word, "spoil." Sounds so childish, but it means "harm or destroy." I lie there thinking, *Did we? Did we spoil our son?*

Everything is running at twice the normal speed.

"Slow down!" I tell myself out loud. "This is good news. He's alive. His injuries are not serious. He probably tried to save the girls."

But there is a voice in my head asking, *So why has he vanished?*

I sit up and start typing. *Write it and then hit the phone,* I tell myself.

The next time I ring in, Terry tells me the story is the splash, a spread on pages four and five, and there's a column by an MP who lost a child abroad.

"And Jake?" I ask.

"Three pars in the lead about him getting out alive and his injuries. Okay? One of the tabloids is ramping it up into full-blown hero stuff—they've got a photo of Jake from somewhere."

"A photo?"

"From your local paper, looks like. I didn't know he got a special prize for his A Level results. That you'd produced a genius."

"Yes." I remember the reporter and photographer turning up and Jake pretending not to be impressed. "I'm so proud of you," I'd told him, and kissed his cheek and wiped off the lipstick smudge. I'd watched as he posed for the camera, my confident, clever boy.

"Now go to bed and get some sleep," Terry says, hauling me back into the nightmare.

"Sure," I say. But I have no intention of doing so. I need to know everything that is going on. Need to get a grip.

"Is Joe in the office? Just want to touch base," I say.

"Yes. The golden child is sitting, watching a game show with the rest of the kindergarten. I'll get him to ring you now."

"Hi, Kate," Joe says when I pick up his call. "How's it going? Any word on Jake?"

"Not yet. Anything on your end?"

Joe rattles off the names of the people he's spoken to, but it's all background noise. "They were such lovely girls" seems to be the sum of his efforts, but it allows me to slip back into reporter mode. Just for a minute.

"Keep in touch with all of them," I say. "We want to hear anything they're hearing."

"Yes, Kate."

"By the way, did you win the face-off?"

"What?"

"Terry gave you up. And, Joe."

"Yes, Kate?"

"Daytime telly is for losers."

"Yes, Kate."

TWENTY-FIVE

The Reporter

TUESDAY, AUGUST 19, 2014

I go back to Khao San Road as soon as I hang up, telling myself I need to get some sense of what happened there. I'm scouring the crowd for my son. He's not here and the faces start to blur as I stare too hard, desperate for the familiar. People stare back and I start showing them the photo of Jake I have on my phone. It's a picture of him smiling at someone off to the side—maybe me. I can't remember now. It has been my screen saver for two years and I can't even recall the occasion. They all smile their sympathy and shake their heads, but I know they're not really looking—they're not taking him in. They need to remember his face. I go into a copy shop to get Jake's photo made into flyers. On the bottom, I have printed his name, my phone number, and "Please Help Me Find Jake." Like a woman in a story. Then I thread through the throng, handing them out. Kids take them, perhaps thinking it's a voucher for a free drink or entry to a club. I see them glance down and then stuff them in pockets or throw them down as they walk away. Why would they care?

I go and sit in the front row of tables at one of the bars, as far away from the loudspeakers as possible, but the disco music dings on my skull like hail.

I watch as herds of new arrivals parade past, girls in shorts, flashing white thighs and big earrings. They've clearly heard a good time is to be had here and their faces show their determination to have some of it. Their screams of laughter echo round the bar fronts, fighting with the music for my ears.

The boys are skinny kids by comparison, clutching bottles of beer, jostling one another, egging one another on with shoves and winks as the pretty restaurant fluffers pretend to tug down their tiny skirts but hitch them up farther instead.

Planet Good Time, I think, but a glance round the neighboring tables tells a different story. Blank, exhausted faces, busy anesthetizing themselves with plastic buckets of vodka and Red Bull or outsize bottles of Chang beer. Bored-looking couples are staring intently at their phones, not each other. A lone boy is warily eyeing the massage chairs in the shop opposite. The masseuses with young bodies and old faces are lounging on the wipeable upholstery like lizards waiting to pounce.

"Later," that boy is probably thinking. *"After a couple more beers. If I don't get lucky."*

It all feels a bit tired and cheap. *More like Blackpool with good weather,* I think.

"Gin and tonic," I shout to the hovering bar boy. His face doesn't register the request, but he returns with the drink and the bill. I show him Jake's flyer and he shrugs and points behind him. On the posts holding up the awning are taped a dozen photocopied pictures, each with its own heartfelt plea from a friend or parent. I take a big mouthful of my drink, welcoming the bitterness and buzz.

"On your own?" says a voice from behind.

When I look round, I see Louise is sitting two tables away.

"Yes," I say and turn back to my glass. I can't face her. The inevitable fake concern, the sly questions.

She comes over and sits down in the chair beside me. "I know this must be a very difficult time," she says and I laugh.

"Bloody hell, Louise, are you really going to try that on me?"

She shuts up. "Another gin and tonic," she calls across to the waiter. "Sorry. Old habits and all that . . . How are you doing?"

"Been better. Look, I really don't feel like talking, Louise. Why aren't you having dinner with the rest of the pack?"

"Don't fancy it—they're getting rat-arsed in the hotel bar. Have you eaten?"

I haven't, not since I arrived a lifetime ago, and the gin is beginning to make my head spin. But she doesn't wait for an answer.

"I'm going to get a bowl of something here," Louise says. "I'll order one for you, too. You need to eat. Keep your strength up."

She's doing a me, I think, and almost smile in recognition. *Mothering me, taking control.* I want to tell her where to shove her bowl of food, but it feels so nice to be looked after like this. Not to have to make decisions. So I let her carry on.

And I eat the sticky, sweet chicken and rice as if I haven't had food for days. As I finish, Louise puts down her bowl even though it's still half-full. *Can't ask questions if you've got your mouth full,* I think, marking her performance.

"Have you any idea where Jake might have gone?" she says. "He must be so traumatized by what happened."

I don't reply. I wait her out. But she is doing the same. We sit in silence as she fusses with her napkin, then wets her finger and tries to pick up stray rice grains from the table.

"What have you written?" I ask, the first to weaken.

"The girls, the mums, the holiday of a lifetime. The usual. And I've written Jake up as the reluctant hero, who risked all to try to save the girls and then slipped away to avoid the limelight."

"Right. I hear you got a photo of him . . ."

"Yeah, the local news agency found it. I think everyone has it. Nice pic but a bit old. I expect he looks a bit different now."

"Yes," I say. But I have no idea. I try to picture him with a beard, or shaven head.

"When did you last see him?" Louise asks casually, beckoning the waiter to order more drinks.

"Not for me, thanks," I say quickly. "I need to go back to the hotel."

I dig through my purse to pay but Louise waves it away. "I'll get this. It's all on expenses anyway."

And she picks up the flyer I've pulled out with my wallet. "This is a good idea," she says. "Mind if I keep it?"

Later, in the room, I scroll through the news websites and see my flyer, with the headline "Mother's Desperate Hunt for Hero Son." It's me. I start to dial Louise's mobile and stop. Everything I say now will be news. I need to say nothing.

TWENTY-SIX

The Reporter

WEDNESDAY, AUGUST 20, 2014

Terry is struggling to say the right thing. He can never get it right, and I've often wondered how he ever managed as a reporter on the road.

"Look, Kate, this is a big story, but I can't have you filing developments if you are part of it. You do see, don't you?"

I do, but I feel a door closing.

"Well, just for a couple of days, until I sort out Jake." I try to push back. I make it sound like it's nothing—like I'm dealing with a child having a tantrum.

"Yes, but what if things get difficult?" he says.

"Difficult?" I snap, but we both know what he means.

"You know how things can get," Terry says wearily. "I don't need to tell you." He doesn't. Perhaps it's started already.

"What's being said about Jake, then?"

"Not much and it's all pretty positive. He's being portrayed as the survivor who may hold the key to what happened."

"Well, that sounds okay," I say hopefully.

"I hope you've told Steve not to say anything."

I haven't, but I will now. And Freddie.

"Anyway, you need to concentrate on your family," he adds. The last nail in the coffin. When the news desk starts talking about your family, you know it's over.

"Has this come from the Editor?" I ask. Terry doesn't answer immediately, but of course it has. I'm being cut adrift in case my son and I damage his paper's precious reputation.

"Simon is very concerned about what you must be going through, Kate," Terry says finally. "He's got kids, too. He feels you need to focus on Jake. We all do."

"So who's going to cover the story here for us? Don?"

"I'm sending Joe out."

"Right, well, he'll be pleased to get his first big Foreign. When is he arriving?"

"He's on his way. He'll ring you when he gets in tomorrow. God, it must be tomorrow already there. Go to bed, Kate. Oh, and let me know if there is anything I can do to help. Okay?"

He's desperate to get off the phone and end his attempt to feel my pain.

"Okay," I say.

I look at the time on the television display. It's two a.m. I pick up my notebook and reread my list: hospitals, pharmacies, turtle sanctuaries.

When I ring home, I get my answerphone announcement and start speaking over myself, telling Steve to pick up.

"Kate? Sorry about that, love, but I've had to start screening calls. All your lot keep ringing to ask about Jake. Is there any news?"

"No, not yet. I've been handing out flyers in the area around the guesthouse."

"I should be there with you."

"I'm fine," I lie. "Let's see what happens in the next day or so, Steve. I think he'll turn up when he sees the coverage. And then I'll bring him home."

"God, I hope so. Freddie says he's getting friend requests from reporters on his Facebook page."

"How is he doing? I'll ring him now."

"He's okay, Katie. A bit confused—like we all are."

"I know. Look, I know I don't need to say it, but don't talk to the reporters. Even the ones you know. Especially not them."

"Why do you think I'm fielding calls? Never mind them; what are the police saying?"

"Nothing about Jake. Just that foreigners are to blame for the fire."

"You sound exhausted. It's the middle of the night there. You can't do anything else now. Get some sleep so you can think straight in the morning."

"Yes."

"Do it, Kate."

I leave a message for Freddie on his phone. "Darling, it's Mum. No news yet here, but I'm sure he'll turn up soon. I'm going to bed now. Don't talk to reporters . . . Love you."

TWENTY-SEVEN

The Reporter

WEDNESDAY, AUGUST 20, 2014

I'm woken by Joe, ringing from the lobby.

"Kate, it's me. I've just got here. The taxi driver overcharged me, the bastard. Can you give me a fill on what's happening?"

His nervous energy surges down the hotel phone, forcing me upright and making me want to kill him.

"I'll come down," I say as I drag myself out of bed. "Order a lot of coffee."

It takes me ten minutes to wash my face, dress, and pull a brush through my hair, and I can see from Joe's face when I walk in that I look terrible.

He turns away and I catch a glimpse of my reflection in the shiny chrome breakfast buffet. I look ninety.

"Are you all right, Kate?" Joe says, and I start to crumble.

"Don't be nice to me or I'll cry. And if you think I look bad now, wait until you see that."

Joe looks terrified.

"Don't worry—I'm fine. Not enough sleep, that's all."

"You've lost an earring," he says.

"Whatever. Let's leave my fashion crimes to one side and focus on the story. Have you seen any of the others yet?"

"Only Mick. He looks worse than you . . ."

"Thanks." I take a mouthful of hot coffee and burn my tongue.

"Where are the girls' parents?"

"Probably upstairs in their rooms if they've any sense. Avoiding us. Go and get some breakfast, Joe."

I sip my coffee and watch him prowling round the buffet, piling his plate with pancakes and flaccid bacon. He mimes, "Do you want anything?" and I shake my head. Can't think about food yet. I watch the second hand on the dining room clock tick away another minute and I try to make a plan for the day. Now that I'm not a reporter.

"What are you going to do this morning?" Joe asks as he comes back to the table, as if reading my mind, meaning, "What should I do?"

I reel off a list of people he needs to ring—Don, the police, Clive Barnes, and the parents—while he piles the food into his mouth, takes notes on his paper napkin, and nods.

"You need to get alongside Lesley and Jenny—I'll give them a call when you've finished stuffing your face."

"Ooooh, that looks good," Mick says, looming up behind Joe. "Unlike you, Ms. Waters."

"Have you looked in a mirror this morning, Mick? I think you win in the walking-dead stakes. How much did you drink last night?"

"A couple."

"Of gallons?"

"Fuck off. What's that on your plate, Joe? Looks like a skin graft."

"It's chicken bacon. Tastes like bacon, anyway."

"That'll do. Back in a mo'."

I wonder what Mick's been told by the news desk. More important, he'll know what the pack is doing. What they're thinking.

"Do you really need three fried eggs?" I ask as he returns.

"Shut up. It'll do me good. Something needs to."

"Where are the others?"

"Bed. Spoke to George from the *Telegraph* just now. We've got a presser at ten here."

Joe writes it in his notebook.

"Finished?" I say. "Come on—let's go and talk to the families."

"Wait for me," Mick says, folding the last egg into a slice of bread and picking up his camera bag.

Lesley is standing in the lobby when we emerge and she lifts her hand to greet me.

"Hello, how are you doing?" I say. "Did you manage to get any sleep?"

"No. How about you? Any news about your son?"

I hold her elbow and guide her to a group of armchairs in an alcove.

"Lesley, I'm being taken off the story while I sort everything out, but my colleague Joe Jackson is here to take over."

We both look over at Joe, who realizes I am talking about him and smiles and waves across the room at Lesley.

"He only looks about twelve." Lesley sighs.

"He's a good reporter. And a nice lad."

"If you say so. I had someone knocking on our door this morning at silly o'clock. I told her where to go."

Louise on dawn patrol, no doubt.

"Malcolm's upstairs phoning the airline. We want to take the girls home as soon as we can, but there's a lot of paperwork. I just can't face it."

"I can help you if you like, Lesley," I say. "Shall we meet after the press conference?"

Lesley nods, distracted by the arrival of her husband and the Shaws.

"How did you get on?" Jenny is asking Malcolm.

"I spoke to a very nice lady at the airport. I've got to call her back at eleven."

I signal to Joe to come over so I can introduce him to everyone. Mick throws the rest of his breakfast in a bin and shakes everyone's hand, holding on to Jenny's a shade longer than necessary. She flushes but doesn't draw back. "How are you bearing up, Jenny?" Mick asks and squeezes her elbow before letting go.

Poor woman—she needs a bit of TLC, I think. *I could do with some, too.*

Joe is chatting to Malcolm and Lesley about Bangkok and the crazy traffic, steering clear of the story and putting them at ease. *Good boy,* I think. *You'll be fine.*

The families have decided to go to the embassy early so they can use the phones there to ring home.

"My mobile bill is huge already," Jenny says. "I just can't afford it. I don't know how I'm going to pay for all this . . ."

Malcolm takes her arm as her face starts to collapse and says, "We'll sort it all out when we get back. Come on, Jenny. The car's here."

TWENTY-EIGHT

The Mother
WEDNESDAY, AUGUST 20, 2014

Clive had signed them in at the gatehouse and walked them into the embassy, past the smokers in the courtyard and through the waiting room for those who had lost passports or wanted visas. People looked up as they passed and Lesley felt their eyes on her. They couldn't know who she was.

Idle curiosity, my dad would've said, if he'd been here. She wished he were. Lesley clutched Malcolm's hand harder.

They were ushered first into what felt like the set of a costume drama. The wooden floor of the Ambassador's Residence glowed with polish and the sunlight poured through the high windows, filtered through voile curtains.

"It's like something out of a film," Lesley said and immediately felt ridiculous. They were there to talk about the death of their daughters, not to sight-see.

"Where should we sit?" she added quickly.

Tea was brought and they sat at a white-clothed table in the Garden Room, watched by a smiling portrait of the Queen and, through a window, a bronze statue of Queen Victoria. Nobody spoke for minutes at a time; the effort to find something to say seemed too great.

Clive was talking about repatriation plans and legal procedures and Malcolm was chipping in with "I sees" and "Of courses." The two women sat silently.

"We have got a bit of time before you have to be back at the hotel," Clive said. "Do you want to make any phone calls?"

"Yes," Jenny and Lesley gasped at the same time. "Please," Lesley added.

She had to sit and listen as Jenny wept down the phone to her sister; she held her fists against her stomach to keep her grief still while Mike sat beside her, hollow-eyed with shock.

Then it was her turn. Jenny curled up on the low settee with a box of tissues in the corner of the Visitors' Room and Mike went outside to have a cigarette. Lesley dialed home, then listened dully to the blare of noncomprehension from the receiver.

"It isn't working," she said, her voice made stupid by exhaustion.

"Did you put the international code in front of your number?" Clive said gently, taking the phone from her and dialing the number.

She could hear the ringing in her house and closed her eyes. For a moment she hoped no one would pick up. She was too tired to talk.

"Hello, this is the O'Connors. Please leave a message for Malcolm, Lesley, Dan, or Alex, and we will ring you back," the machine said.

Alex.

She couldn't speak. "It's, it's . . ." she finally stammered.

"Mum," Danny's voice broke in, "is that you?"

"Yes, darling."

"How are you and Dad doing?"

"Okay. We saw Alex yesterday. We're arranging to bring her home, Danny." She couldn't—wouldn't—use the word "body."

Her son was sobbing five thousand miles away and she couldn't do anything.

"Stay strong, my darling. We'll all be home as soon as we can. Is Auntie Sheila with you?"

"Yes, she and Uncle Rick came this morning. She's here now if you want to talk to her."

The phone was handed over like a relay baton.

"Les?" her sister-in-law said. "Are you all right? How's Malcolm?"

"We're in pieces, Sheila," Lesley said, her brave face no longer needed. "But we are bringing her home. Thanks so much for being with Dan. What have you told Mum? Does she understand?"

"Not really. Maybe it's a blessing. Don't worry about Dan. We've got him. Look after yourselves and ring us when you have time."

Back at the hotel, the arrangements for their press statement had been made. Clive Barnes pointed out the chairs for the reporters and the stubby black microphones placed on the table where the families would sit. A young woman was setting out printed name cards on the white cloth. They'd spelled her name wrong. Lesley O'Conner.

She went to say so but stopped. What did it matter? Alex was dead.

Standing in the anteroom ten minutes later, she could hear the growing buzz of voices in the conference room next door, the squawk of chairs being shifted, the chirp of greetings. Clive had said they would be brought in when everyone else was sitting. Like guest stars on a talk show, she wanted to say. She would have said a week ago. Only a week.

She looked at Malcolm, then at Mike, and Jenny, and they looked back.

"I wonder if they'll ask questions," Lesley said and realized she'd said that already.

"God knows," Jenny said.

"You don't have to answer any questions," Clive said firmly. "Probably best not to. It only encourages them."

He'd advised on the statement Malcolm was to read out. "Best to make it short and dignified," he'd said, and they'd written it together. Clive had read it through, nodded his approval, and added at the bottom: "We would like to be able to grieve for our daughters away from the public gaze and hope you will respect our privacy."

"Worth a try," he'd muttered.

When they were led in, a noise like a flock of birds taking off startled Lesley. The cameras of a dozen photographers were pointed at them and she stumbled under their gaze.

"Come on, love," Malcolm said.

The statement had gone well. Malcolm had managed to keep going until the end, when Lesley heard the choke as he said they were taking Alex and Rosie home. She'd put her crumpled tissue to her mouth to stop her lips trembling and then begun to lever herself out of her chair to leave. But a voice calling her name made her hesitate.

"Mrs. O'Connor," the voice said, "thank you very much for speaking to us today. We realize how hard this must be."

She'd tried to locate the person speaking, but she couldn't pick the person out from the sea of faces.

"Thank you for all your support," she said to the room.

A forest of hands shot up in response.

"When did you know it was Alex who had died in the fire, Mrs. O'Connor?" a man in the front row called.

"Yesterday," she answered.

"Do you know how the fire started, Mrs. Shaw?"

"No," Jenny answered, staring at the table.

"We've heard that there was a party that night. Were the girls at the party?"

"We think so," Lesley said.

"Do you know who else was there?" Joe called out from near the back.

"Was Jake Waters there?" a woman asked from the front row.

"Who?" Mike said.

"Kate the reporter's son," Lesley whispered to him.

"We don't know," she said to the woman. "He was taken to hospital with burns on the night of the fire. But that's all we know at the moment."

"Are you happy with the police investigation?" the same woman asked, leaning forward to hear their answer.

"Er . . ." Lesley started to speak.

"Are the police treating Jake Waters as a suspect?"

"A suspect for what?" Malcolm blurted, looking at the others for a clue. "What on earth do you mean? The fire was an accident. The police say so."

"It's just, we are hearing some disturbing things about the guesthouse. Did you know that Mama's Paradise is well-known to the police? It's known as the Sweet Shop locally. Apparently, it's where people go—sorry, went—to buy drugs," the woman explained as if they were children. Innocents abroad.

Lesley couldn't take her eyes off the reporter.

"And there has been a death there before. Late last year, a forty-two-year-old man died there in unexplained circumstances."

"No," Mike said hoarsely. "Of course we didn't know."

"I think that will have to be the last question," Clive Barnes said smoothly, practically lifting Lesley out of her chair by her elbow. "Thank you, ladies and gentlemen."

And it was over. But standing back in the anteroom, Lesley felt it was just beginning.

TWENTY-NINE

The Reporter

WEDNESDAY, AUGUST 20, 2014

Left on my own, I slump on a chair in the lobby, lost for a moment. I should be doing something. Shouldn't I?

Come on, Waters, get yourself moving.

I walk out to the taxis and ask to be taken back to Khao San Road.

The red-and-white tape that closed the alleyway to Mama's yesterday has been torn down and discarded in the dust. The police have gone as well. I walk up to the shell of the guesthouse, the smell of soot tickling my throat and making my eyes water as I arrive at what once must have been the entrance. The sign has survived somehow, hanging by its last screw, but its wording is gone, the wood charred and the paint blistered and flaking.

I peer in and then around. There's no one here to stop me.

"Hello," I call into the gloom, just in case, and then tiptoe in. I don't know what I think I'll find here, but when I hit a dead end in a story, my instinct is always to go back to the beginning and see what I missed. And this is the beginning.

I pick my way through carefully, and as my eyes grow used to the darkness I start to see the full horror of the blaze. A forensic investigator I interviewed once told me that a fire itself can tell you where it started, with a V-shaped smoke or burn pattern pointing like an arrow to the seat of the flames.

I start to look, and from what I can see, the worst of the damage seems to be at the back of the building, but I decide not to go farther in. The remains of the upper floors hang down above my head, with shards of wood and concrete balancing on one another like a circus act.

"Get out of there," a voice shouts. "Are you mad? You'll get killed."

I poke my head out of the darkness. The stoned boy from the café yesterday is standing in front of Mama's.

"What's it got to do with you?" I shout back. "I'm just having a look."

"It's dangerous. Bloody hell, you're old enough to be my mum—you should be telling me off."

His ridiculous indignation makes me laugh—for the first time in days.

"Oh, get over yourself," I say. "What are you? Fourteen?"

"Twenty, actually. Why are you poking around in there, anyway? The police have finished. It was an accident, they say. But then they always do."

"Do they?" I ask.

"If it's a *farang* like me. And the girls."

"Did you know them? The girls?"

The boy looks around quickly.

"What?" I ask.

"Just have to be careful," he says. "Lots of people are asking questions."

"Look, my son was in this fire, too."

"Your son?"

"Yes. And now he's disappeared. I'm desperate to find him." And I pull out one of the flyers from my bag.

He looks at it and then at me, his eyes wide. "Jake," he says. "You're Jake's mum?"

Ten minutes later, we're sitting in his room, him cross-legged on the floor, me on the end of his bed. Ross wouldn't talk in the street; he says he's afraid of the police and the reporters. I haven't told him I'm one, too. He doesn't need to know. He said he lived round the corner if I fancied a cup of tea, and I followed him. At the last minute, I texted Mick to say where I was going. As insurance.

Ross apologized for the mess when he opened the door and looked to see if I was going to tell him off. I'm someone's mum to him. But I just pushed the foil, straws, and dirty clothes off the mattress and sat down.

He starts to make tea for us on a camping stove and I tap my feet impatiently. He looks up and I stop fidgeting and smile encouragingly.

"How long have you lived here? You've made it very homey."

He laughs at my feeble attempt at conversation and turns back to the pan of boiling water. He hands me a filthy mug and I pretend to take a sip while he lights a spliff.

"Do you mind?" he says as if he cares.

Of course I bloody do.

"No, it's your place. You do as you please." *But can we talk before you get off your face?*

"So, you know Jake," I say, and he nods slowly, holding his breath. When he finally breathes out he says: "He works at Mama's—in the kitchen, doing the washing up and stuff. He says he doesn't earn much, but she lets him live there for free. He's been there for ages. He was there when I arrived and that was January 2013."

He's been here all this time, lying to us, pretending to be in Phuket, counting turtles. My brilliant son working in a shithole kitchen.

"I go there sometimes to see him," Ross says. "Or he comes here."

"You're friends, then?"

"Yeah, sort of." Ross takes another long drag. "We don't talk much. We smoke together sometimes. He knows where to get good shit. A little helper." And he giggles. I clasp my hands together to stop them slapping him.

"Little helper?" I ask, although I know.

"A bit of weed, that's all. He doesn't do yaba or smack. Nothing nasty," Ross says. "He's a good bloke, Jake."

A good bloke? I can't believe we are talking about my son taking drugs. He was terrible at chemistry, I find myself thinking. *Stop it.*

"Do you know where he is now?" I ask, desperate to get out of here.

"No idea. Goes his own way. I was surprised that he came back here after that bloke died."

"What bloke?"

"From Scotland. A bloke in his forties. He was found in his room at Mama's just before Christmas. The police said it was suicide, but . . ."

"But what?"

"Well, he didn't leave a note—let's put it that way. He looked like he'd been in a fight and his stuff was gone when they found him. His money and passport had been taken."

"Had he been murdered?"

"Don't know. He'd been partying the night before, really out of order. Jake had served him a lot of booze at the bar and he told me the bloke had been snorting Special K."

"Special K?"

"Ketamine. A lot of people take it here—makes you high really quick. It's ace."

I want to stop asking questions; I don't need to know any more. But I can't help myself.

"Did the police come? Were people questioned about the death? Was Jake questioned?"

Ross grins.

"No. Mama told him to disappear while she sorted it all out. She told him the cops always blame foreigners for crimes if they can. And his visa didn't allow him to be working there. Mama knows the score—she's got a thing going with the police. But it shook Jake up. He went off for a bit. A little holiday until things quietened down. It was the only sensible thing to do. And he stayed away while all the antigovernment riots were on. It was chaos here. Wild. But then he turned up back at Mama's. Said he didn't have anywhere else to go. Said he couldn't tell his mum and dad because it was what they said would happen. That he'd fail."

"I never said that," I say, but maybe I did. I try to remember.

"When did you last see him, Ross?"

"Last week. A couple of times. I saw him in the street and he said he was doing great. He'd met a lady, he said." Ross winked and smiled sleepily.

"That's nice," I say. "Did he say who she was?"

"Nah. But I think she must have given him the elbow because he came round a couple of days later in a bit of a state and wanted a smoke. It was very early—I was still in bed. But he banged on the door until I opened it. He looked awful. He'd got some sick or something on his trousers so I loaned him a pair of mine. His are still here, actually. I haven't had time to wash them, but you can take them if you like."

He fishes around in a heap of clothes and pulls out a pair of blue trousers and hands them over. "Sorry, they whiff a bit."

They stink and I push them to the bottom of my bag.

He smiles again. "Look, he's a good bloke. Don't worry—he'll turn up."

My head is buzzing with the unwanted information and I want this skinny kid to shut up now.

"Have you told anyone else what you know about Jake?" I ask. *Oh God, who else knows?*

Ross shakes his head.

"A reporter was asking last night, but I told her I didn't know anything. I didn't like her. She was pushy. In-your-face. You know? They must be trying to talk to you, too."

"They are, but I'm not saying anything either. Will you keep everything—the Scottish bloke, Jake smoking weed—to yourself, Ross? For his sake. The press will hound him if they find out. When they find him."

Ross nods sagely. He fumbles to show that his lips are sealed. I put my number into his mobile in case he hears anything and I leave him there in his sweet, numbing fug.

THIRTY

The Reporter

WEDNESDAY, AUGUST 20, 2014

George is outside the hotel, vaping and producing an industrial-size plume of fake smoke. It smells like cinnamon and apple when I get close.

"Hi, Kate," he says. "My new vice . . . Have you tried it? Disgusting but I can pretend it's healthy because it smells of fruit. One of my five a day."

George has been to our house with his wife and kids. A barbecue, I think. His son got stung by a wasp and I put vinegar on it, like my mum used to when I was a kid. It was a good afternoon with friends, lying back in old deck chairs, laughing about work, and drinking cold rosé.

He smiles his sympathy. "We missed you at the press conference, asking your killer questions. What have you been doing?"

"Yeah, it felt odd not being there. I'm grubbing around, talking to people but not getting far. Was there anything worth filing this morning?"

"Odds and sods. It was a statement and a few questions. I've just filed. The families looked like rabbits in the headlights, poor buggers. They've only just seen their kids in the morgue. And Louise asked them if they knew about the other death at the guesthouse."

My skin prickles. They are only one step behind me.

"Oh?" I say.

"Yeah, a plasterer on holiday who the police said committed suicide. His family say he definitely didn't kill himself—he'd just paid thousands to renew his Arsenal season ticket . . . But the Thai police wouldn't listen."

"Have you spoken to his family?"

"Yeah, they're nice people and it's a good line for the story. We're all filing it. That and the fact that Mama's was a known drug shop. Stoner central, we've been told."

"Christ," I say and hope I sound genuinely surprised.

"Didn't you know?" George says.

I shake my head. I need to get away from this. Need to close it down.

"Had Jake been at the guesthouse long?" he asks, burrowing into my silence.

"I just don't know, George. He's an adult. He stopped checking in with us when he left home."

"'Course," George says swiftly. "Can't wait for ours to fly the nest." And he stops. He knows he's said the wrong thing.

"Better get back to the phones," I say, as if I am letting him off the hook.

In my room I scroll through the stories about the earlier death. But what they don't know is that my boy was there. And ran away that time, too.

I go back to my list and ring another wildlife project in Phuket. *I'm just filling time, I know. He was never there. He was living another life while we told people his lie.*

There's a knock on my door and I open it to find Louise with that "I've got a story" look on her face. I've seen it too many times to mistake it.

"I'm a bit busy, Louise," I say, but she's ready for me.

"It's important you hear this, Kate. Before it's on the net."

"Hear what?" I say, falling for it. I should know better, but it's irresistible. I want to be in on the secret.

"We've found Jake's Facebook page."

"Oh, that!" I almost laugh. I'm on safe ground. "He hasn't used it since he went away. He hated all that. He told us . . ." *And I've looked, over and over.*

Louise half-smiles back. "Not that one—not the one in his real name. The other one. He's Jake Sherwood to his Facebook friends."

"Sherwood?" I gulp. It's my maiden name. "How do you know it's my Jake?"

"It's him."

"How did you find him?"

"My geek in the office tracked him down. Well, I spoke to a friend of Jake's here—a little wanker called Ross who tried to pretend he'd never heard of him. You can always tell when they're faking, can't you? I got him chatting about other stuff, got his name and where he's from, and he led us to online Jake."

"And is Jake posting?" I ask. "Do you know where he is?"

Louise shakes her head. "There's been nothing new since the fire. But there's other stuff on there."

My stomach tightens. "Other stuff? What stuff?"

"You'd better have a look. It's not pretty."

"Just tell me," I snap.

"He says he had to leave Phuket in a hurry. We've enquired at a bar he mentioned in a post and the owner says Jake worked there but left over a year ago. He told people he'd been robbed and the local mafia had threatened to kill him because he owed them money. Sounds like he may have got himself in trouble with the wrong people . . ."

Don't say anything. Don't give her anything she can quote.

I try to keep my face impassive. "Okay. I'll look at it myself."

"And there are photos . . ."

"I imagine there are." I edge the door shut. "Thanks for telling me, Louise."

Now sod off.

She turns and says urgently, "You need to look at them, Kate. They're going to be published."

I close the door as she's still talking and rush to my laptop.

When I find his page I start to cry. He's there. At a party on a beach, lit by a bonfire. His hair is waxed into stiff little horns. His eyes are black with eyeliner. And the caption reads, "I'm a twisted fire-starter."

THIRTY-ONE

The Reporter

THURSDAY, AUGUST 21, 2014

The picture is on the front of almost every paper. Of course it is. Even the *Post*. With Joe's byline and the headline "Is This the Missing Witness in Backpacker Fire?"

I ring and wake my office son.

"What the hell is this?" I shout into his ear.

"Everyone had the photo, Kate. An agency put it all round and I had to file copy to go with it. I tried to play it down, but Terry gave me an earful. Told me to harden up the story. I'm sorry, but it's such an incredible picture."

"Yes, but taken more than a year ago, according to Facebook. And he's dressed up as Keith, the lead singer of the rave band the Prodigy."

I knew as soon as I saw it. It was a family joke—after one of Jake's teachers called him a child prodigy at a parent evening, we started to tease him, calling him Keith, whenever he got a bit big for his boots. Jake loved it. He and Freddie used to dance round the kitchen, howling the words to "Firestarter." Bloody stupid song.

"Oh yeah," Joe says and starts singing the mindless chorus.

"Shut up, Joe. This isn't helping."

"Sorry. Look, I did say it was an old picture in the copy. I said it was taken a year ago in Phuket. Not sure if that was edited out . . ."

"Why didn't you warn me?"

"Because I knew you'd give me hell. I'm in an impossible position; you must see that. I'm working on this story, not living it with you. I have to do what the news editor tells me—he's my boss . . ."

"Whatever, Joe."

The hunt is on. Jake won't show his face now. Who would?

"Do you want to say anything? Give his side of the story?" I can hear the hope in Joe's voice.

"Sod off. I don't know what his side of the story is. And that's off the record. Everything is off the record. You do know that?"

"Yes, yes. I know, but do the others? What are you going to say to them? Some of them have been sent to Phuket. One of Don's boys is going for us. Terry wants me to stick with the parents."

"Oh God, has Lesley seen this?"

"I don't know."

I put the phone down on Joe and ring up to the O'Connors' room. Malcolm answers.

"Kate? We wondered if we'd hear from you today. Have you seen your son in the papers?"

"It's a fit-up, Malcolm. He was at a Halloween fancy-dress party over a year ago. He's dressed as a singer. Keith from the Prodigy. 'Fire-starter' is the title of their biggest song. This was a joke. Nothing to do with what happened here. You do understand that?"

But the phone has gone dead.

The others come knocking. *Tap-tap. Rap-rap-rappity-rap. Bang-bang.* They don't know for certain I'm in here, so I sit tight. But it gets harder. It is suffocating. I feel the room getting smaller and the walls thinner as they call through the door. "Kate! I know you're in there. Come to the door!" When that fails, there are the whispered entreaties: "Kate, it's me, George. Look, I can make things better. We need to talk."

I know if the tables had been turned, I would be there, ringing my hotel room throughout the night, doorstepping me at breakfast, slipping notes under my door.

I can hear myself on the other side of the door. I wonder how long they'll stay there. *How long would I stay?*

I listen to the conversations outside in the corridor.

"Do you think she's in there? I can't hear anything."

"She must be in pieces," someone else says.

"I bet she's filed it, though," Louise snaps. "She won't let a little thing like being his mother stop her."

I have my hand on the door handle, ready to wrench it open and give her a piece of my mind. But I stop.

She knows you can hear her, stupid. She's trying to goad you into saying something.

My phone rings. I've put it on silent so the reporters can't hear it.

It's Joe's number. I tiptoe into the bathroom and close the door in slow motion.

"Kate," he says when I finally answer, "are you okay?"

"What do you think?" I whisper.

"I'm going to come and say I've heard from you," he replies. "That you are going to the embassy. Hopefully that will shift them."

"Well, it could work, but then what?"

"Mick has booked you into a different hotel under his name. Get your stuff together, ready for when the pack leaves."

"Thank you, Joe." I can't say anything else. Emotion is choking me.

"You'll hear me outside in a minute. Mick will knock three times when they're gone."

Two minutes later I hear him arrive. George calls to him: "Joe, come and get Kate to talk to us. She needs to say something."

"I've just spoken to her. On the phone. She's not here. She's gone to the embassy to talk to Clive Barnes."

"Fuck," Louise says. "Are you sure? You wouldn't be screwing with us, would you, Joe?"

I hold my breath. I'm not sure he is up to screwing with someone like her.

"Shut up, Louise. You think everyone's like you."

Good boy. How could I doubt you?

"You can stand outside an empty room if you like. I'm going to the embassy." And I hear him walk away.

There is a moment's silence and I grip the edge of the bed harder.

"Wait for me—we can share a cab," George shouts down the corridor, and they all move off, grumbling and swearing.

The three knocks make me jump. I pull the door open a crack and there is Mick.

He gives me a quick hug. "Come on, let's go and play hide-and-seek with the wicked press," he says, picking up my bag. "I've got a cab waiting at the back entrance. Just in case they've decided to doorstep the front . . ."

He keeps up his banter in the taxi as we wind through the streets to a small, anonymous hotel.

He's already checked us in as a couple—Mr. and Mrs. Murray—and I lead the way up the stairs to the room.

"Right, got to get back to work or they'll be suspicious," he says. "But ring if you need me. I'm saving your number on my phone as Mum so no one sees it's you. I've told Joe to do the same. He did well, didn't he? Chip off the old block . . ."

"Not like Jake," I say.

"Don't be too hard on him, Kate. He was at a party. I expect everyone was dressed up. He's just been unlucky."

"I don't know. I don't know anything about him anymore. Go on. I'll be fine. And thank you, Mick. You are brilliant."

"The top banana, that's me. Keep your head down."

I can't ring Steve to let him know I've moved—he'll already have started ward rounds—so I lie on the bed and try to get my thoughts in order, but everything is dancing about in my head.

Why has Jake run away? Traumatized, the doctors say. That's it. He can't bear to remember that night. He must be so frightened. Or is he ashamed?

I try Lesley's mobile. She'll see it's my number and I keep my fingers crossed she'll pick up. It rings out too long and I am about to hang up when she finally answers, slightly out of breath.

"Kate? Sorry, I had to go in another room. Malcolm doesn't want to have anything to do with you."

"I understand that, Lesley. The story today must have been a horrible shock for all of you. Thank you for taking the call. You know that photo was taken ages ago? At a party?"

"Yes, yes. But it shook us up. Planted doubts in our minds. Malcolm keeps asking me if the fire could have been started deliberately. But the police would know, wouldn't they?"

"I suppose so, Lesley. Have you spoken to them today?"

"Malcolm did. They still say they think the fire was an accident. There is no new evidence."

Relief sweeps over me, making me trembly, and I fumble the phone. *This is ridiculous. Pull yourself together,* I tell myself. *Of course it was an accident.*

"It must have been terrible for you as well," Lesley says. "Seeing him like that."

We are still on the same side, then.

"I've moved hotels to get away from the reporters," I tell her, and she snorts in reply.

"Welcome to our world. We're getting on with the paperwork. The insurers are sorting out bringing the girls back and we are making funeral arrangements at home. I think keeping busy is all we can do."

"If I can help in any way . . ."

"Probably not at the moment. I'll have a word with Malcolm. He's so on edge. Normally he's the calm one, but the pressure is too much. We just want to go home."

"Of course you do. Have they said how long it will take to sort out?"

"A few days. Everyone is being so kind. We had a call from Hampshire Police. That nice DI Sparkes. Just to see how things are going and to pass on his condolences. But we need to see Dan. He's having to cope with it all without us and we never seem to be in the right time zone to speak to him."

"You'll be home soon," I say.

When she's finished, I start to dial Bob Sparkes. It's eight thirty a.m. where he is. I need to talk to a grown-up.

THIRTY-TWO

The Detective

THURSDAY, AUGUST 21, 2014

He'd wondered when she'd call.

The first stories about Jake's involvement in the fire had brought Zara running—*running*—up the corridor yesterday. He'd thought there must have been a terrorism alert at the very least and had met her at the door.

"What?" he'd shouted, blood pumping.

"Kate Waters's son. He was in the Bangkok fire with the girls. He tried to pull them out."

"What?"

"Your favorite reporter, sir. Her son Jake is in most of the papers today. He was there the night of the fire."

Salmond's eyes had been practically on stalks with excitement. Sparkes had groaned loudly.

"For God's sake, Zara. Calm down. I thought you were hammering down the corridor because of a lockdown situation. And she's not my favorite reporter."

"Sorry. I just couldn't believe it when I read it." Salmond had gone pink with exertion and embarrassment. "Sorry, I'll go and do something useful."

"Good."

After she'd gone, he'd found the stories and read them carefully, allowing himself a private "Bloody hell!" He'd almost rung Kate to tell her he was glad Jake was okay, but Salmond's "your favorite reporter" had galled him. Was he that transparent? Anyway, she wasn't. He'd speak to her when she got back from Thailand with her hero son.

B ut this morning, the sound of his sergeant haring down the corridor a second time was enough to tell him there was more to come.

"He's not a hero now," she said, pretending she'd just been passing despite the damning evidence of her flushed cheeks. "He's a Twisted Firestarter according to the press. It looks like he's gone on the run. Wait until you see the photo!"

"Thank you for that news flash, Zara. I'll have a look in a minute . . ."

He searched for it as soon as her head disappeared, and found it was dominating the websites of all the tabloids. It was grotesque. He didn't know what Jake Waters looked like, but he hoped this wasn't his normal look. Sparkes read the stories, noting the "No comment" from the Thai police, and looked back at the picture, trying to see Kate in the heavily made-up face. But there was nothing of her round the eyes or mouth.

Still, his son didn't look much like him—took after Eileen's side of the family. "God help him," he told himself. "He would have had better hair if he'd inherited my genes."

He wondered how the kids were today. Neither of them had asked if their mother was being sent home for the last time, and he hadn't had the heart to tell them. He thought they must know, but it was easier not to say it out loud. They would all take it one day at a time. He had the sensation of falling and he gripped the arms of his chair to save himself.

Jake Waters could be his displacement activity for the day. He was almost sure Kate would call now.

She did, forty minutes later.

"Hello," he said. "How are you doing?"

"Bloody awful, Bob. Have you seen the papers?"

"Yes. My DS just clocked up a personal best getting the latest news to me."

"It's a complete farce. This bloody photo was taken more than a year ago. It's nothing to do with the fire. Poor Jake is having his life trashed over a picture taken at a stupid beach party."

"I have to say I was surprised when I saw it. The reports I read yesterday said how brave he'd been."

Kate sighed heavily, making the phone line whistle. "That came from one of the doctors. They said they thought he must have been injured trying to get people out of the fire. And everyone went with it. For twenty-four hours. Until this photo was found. Classic hero-to-zero maneuver."

"Well, you know better than I do what the press gets up to when they get bored . . ."

She went silent.

"So, have you heard from Jake?" Sparkes continued. "Why do you think he left the hospital like that?"

"I have no idea. I'm so worried about him. But I could also wring his neck. Why the hell doesn't he come forward? They're saying he's on the run, but it's ridiculous. He's an adult and he has chosen to discharge himself from hospital. It's hardly a crime."

"Quite. But it's strange that he was allowed to leave—and hasn't turned up." Sparkes weighed his words carefully. If it'd been his investigation, he'd have made sure a potential witness didn't disappear.

"Was he badly injured?"

"No, thank God. Just some burns on his cheek and hands."

"So he could simply have gone off to recuperate. Or come home?"

"Home" reverberated in his head. It was where he should be. At home with Eileen.

"Home?" Kate said.

"Well, yes. If I was injured and traumatized, I might well head for home."

There was another telling silence.

"Does it make me a bad mother if I say I hadn't even considered that?" she whispered.

It might do, he thought. *Am I a bad husband, talking to you instead of caring for my wife?*

"Look," he said, shifting himself in his seat. "No one is perfect. And you're in the middle of a media storm, Kate." *On the wrong side for a change,* he thought, but he refrained from twisting the knife. "It's hard to think straight. Did Jake have a return plane ticket?"

"We bought him a flight home last Christmas. We e-mailed the ticket and he said he'd picked it up, but he didn't catch the plane. A friend of his said he was having a few problems at the time . . ."

"Right. But he might have banked it for later. Was it a flexible ticket? The embassy might be able to talk to the airline. Or the police may have already made the call, if they really are interested in finding him. Have you spoken to the investigating team?"

"No. Not yet. All the stuff about Jake is coming from the papers, not the police. I've been told by Lesley O'Connor that the cops are not interested in him. They said he was irrelevant to the inquiry. I don't know what he told them, but the police said they couldn't even say for sure if he'd been at the hostel. My sense is that the police are satisfied it was an accident and the girls died from smoke inhalation. Case closed."

"And what are the parents saying about that?"

"Well, they thought the same. But this coverage has unsettled them—of course it has. And there are new reports about a previous death at the hostel today. A suicide. Totally unrelated. But it ramps up suspicions, doesn't it? As far as I'm concerned, the press are looking for someone to blame and they've fixed on Jake because of that photo. It's classic. Trial by media if you look a bit odd."

"Yes, you have got form," Sparkes said, not letting her off the hook. "Do you remember that poor schoolmaster in Bristol who was practically accused of murder by the newspapers because he had a strange hairstyle?"

"Not my paper," Kate said quickly. "Anyway, I don't even know if Jake knew the girls. No one has come forward to say he did. And he's not here to defend himself. It is so unfair."

"I can put a call through to Interpol to see if there's any alert for Jake," he suggested. "If the Thais aren't looking for him, you could run it and spike the press guns a bit."

"Oh God, could you?"

"Let me make the call, Kate. Are you on your mobile number out there?"

"Yes. You will ring me as soon as you've spoken to them, won't you? And thanks, Bob. I am so grateful."

Afterward, Sparkes sat back and mulled it all over. He'd already put the call through to Interpol as soon as he'd seen the story.

And he hadn't told Kate about the chat he'd had with Hilary Young at the coroner's office the previous evening. It was police business, not for the media. He'd rung Hilary when he heard the girls' bodies were being repatriated. The local coroner would be opening an inquest as soon as they arrived in the UK and came under his jurisdiction, and Sparkes wanted to touch base about timings. He and Hilary had chatted about the case and wondered together whether the families had considered having the bodies cremated before coming home.

"It's cheaper and there would be no autopsy here if they did," Hilary had said. "They might prefer that. I hope the embassy is giving them all the options."

"I'll make sure they know," Sparkes had said. It had all been very run-of-the-mill stuff. But of course, Sparkes hadn't known then about Jake Waters going AWOL. That put a whole different complexion on things.

THIRTY-THREE

The Reporter
THURSDAY, AUGUST 21, 2014

I'm trying to make myself understood by the Thai police when my phone beeps and I see that Mick is trying to get through. I'll call him back when I've finished.

"My name is Kate Waters," I begin again. "Do you speak English?"

The voice at the other end, the third so far, says, "Sorry, sorry," and I'm put on hold while someone who can understand me is found.

"Hello, hello," I call into the phone politely when no one comes. I want to scream, "Pick up the phone," but it won't help. There's no one there. Just white noise. I hang up and try again. I know the number by heart now.

"Hello. My name is Kate Waters," I repeat, trying to keep the frustration out of my voice. "Do you speak English?"

There is the sound of mouth breathing and complete incomprehension.

"Don't put me on hold . . ." I shout when I realize what's happening, but too late—I am back in limbo.

The embassy, my first call, had been polite but firm. "We cannot get information about airline passengers, Mrs. Waters. I am sure you understand there is strict security around air travel. Perhaps the police can help you."

It takes another ten minutes and one final redial before I finally get through to someone who asks the magic question: "How can I help you?"

I fall over myself trying to tell my story in the simplest terms, editing my language as I go along. "My son is Jake Waters. He was injured—hurt—in the fire at Mama's Paradise Bar and Guesthouse. Where the two English girls died."

"Yes," the officer says.

"Can you understand me?" I ask.

"Yes," he says. I don't know if he can or not.

"Are you looking for my son Jake Waters?" I try.

"Yes," he says. *Why are you asking closed questions?* I shout in my head. *Ask him something he has to answer in words of more than one syllable.*

"Why?"

"We have some questions."

We're in business!

"What do you have questions about? I understand you have closed the case."

"That is a police matter. Do you know where your son is?"

"No, I am very sorry but I don't. I am desperate to find him, too."

"Yes. Well, please call me if you speak to him."

"I will," I say, but I cross my fingers behind my back like a child. I wonder if I will.

"Have you checked to see if my son has left Thailand?"

There is a pause. "Does he have a plane ticket?"

"He might do. I'm not sure . . ."

"I see. Which airline? We will check."

I give him the information I've found in my e-mail to Jake, carefully enunciating the reference number.

"Thank you, Mrs. Waters."

• • •

Bob rings to tell me Jake had been put on an Interpol alert list. "It's a Yellow Notice—saying he's a missing person. The girls were on the same list until their bodies were identified. So it's good news. A Red Notice—an international arrest warrant—would have marked him down as being hunted for a crime."

"Thanks, Bob, but I'm not sure the media will be interested in the nuances of color coding. They'll just write that Interpol is looking for him. I think I'll keep quiet on that one."

I finally call Mick back and he gives me his bad news. "There's more dirt," he says. "Joe has just had a chat with one of Jake's old girlfriends from school. It seems Jake was kicked out of university."

"Kicked out? He said he'd jacked it in because it wasn't the right course for him."

"Well, he didn't. He cheated and got caught."

I feel like I'm going mad. Everything I thought I knew is being pulled from under me.

"Put Joe on," I bark at Mick.

"Hi, Kate," Joe says nervously, and I can imagine the face Mick would have pulled as he handed over the phone.

"What is this crap you're writing about Jake being thrown out of university?"

"So you didn't know?"

"Of course I didn't know. What sort of question is that?"

"Well, it's a ring-in. A former girlfriend who saw the firestarter stuff in the papers and phoned to see if we were interested in her info. Terry passed her on to me."

"Who is she? Did she want money? I bet she did. Go on—tell me. I want every cough and spit."

Joe hesitated.

"What?"

"She said Jake was doing drugs. I'd better tell you that up front."

I close my eyes and wait for the horror to unfold.

"So, basically he was sent down for copying essays from the Internet. His ex says that he was clever enough to write them himself but he was too busy having a good time."

In my head, I can see Jake the morning we put him on the train to Durham Uni. He'd asked us not to drive him—"It's such a long way. The train is fine"—and he'd been embarrassed that we were there at the station, waving and making a fuss, but we didn't care. It was a rite of passage—our firstborn setting off for adulthood. He'd looked like a young Stephen Hawking with his geeky glasses—a bit of an affectation, we knew—and his beautiful smile.

What had happened to that boy? The one I thought I knew? Maybe the game had changed for Jake when he got to university. He'd never really had to try in order to succeed before. He'd always been top of the class at school. And if he thought he was going to fail—like the episode with the saxophone instruction, when despite having begged for lessons he gave up after just three months, as soon as it started getting hard—he just moved on to something else. *He'd got used to life being easy.* But there must have been lots of Jakes at uni. He'd said everything was fine when he rang home. But maybe there'd been hints if I'd cared to listen. I've always been so good at reading between the lines when I'm interviewing people, hearing the stutter of truth beneath polished lies. But not this time. I suppose I wanted to hear only good news. *Good news doesn't take as much emotional energy, does it? And I was busy with other people's bad news.*

I try to remember the phone calls, the clues I should have picked up. He'd said that everyone in his course had been top of their class and some of them were cleverer than him, but Steve and I had teased him about it. Poor Jake—it must have been a shock to find that he might have to work to keep up. He'd definitely tried at first. He'd told us about spending his evenings in the library—"You wouldn't recognize me, Mum. I'm almost a geek . . ."—how he'd read all the books on the course list and boasted when he got good marks for an essay.

But perhaps making an effort lost its shine after a while and he lost focus. If it was going to be that hard, maybe he thought it wasn't worth it.

Joe is still speaking, giving the gory details of my son's fall from grace, and I tune back in.

"The girlfriend said he started getting drunk every night and snorting a bit of coke. His friends were doing the same. He began gurning and sniffing in lectures and thought he was brilliant when he was actually speaking complete rubbish at tutorials."

"What an idiot," I mutter.

"Jake told her that his personal tutor gave him a friendly warning at the beginning of the second year. He told him he needed to spend more time on his essays. That drugs were not making him cleverer. That they were turning him into an almighty pain in the arse and he was in danger of failing. But Jake just denied it all and carried on. His friends were very worried about him, Kate."

"So worried, they're selling information about him. Nice." *Why didn't he tell us? He didn't phone as much, but why should he? He didn't need his mum checking up on him. Or perhaps he did. Did I ring him? No, I texted. Shorthand caring. Not the real thing. And then he stayed up in Durham for the summer. He said he was working.*

"Apparently he started nicking bits of other people's stuff from the Internet when he'd forgotten to do assignments," Joe went on.

"And then whole essays. They caught him. There was a formal disciplinary process and he was asked to leave."

"Christ" is all I can say.

"We're running it, Kate," Joe says quietly. "I'm so sorry."

"Really?" I say. "How is this a story? It's got nothing to do with the fire. I suppose Jake dumped this girl? That's why she rang. She's got an ax to grind." It is my last feeble attempt to kill the story. But I've trained Joe too well.

"No, she said she dumped him because of the drugs. They were changing him. And I've checked her story out. It adds up. The university has issued a statement confirming he was sent down."

"Well done, you." I hate myself for sounding so bitter. Two days ago, I'd have been cheering him on. But I can't now. You see, I've been where Joe Jackson is a thousand times, hoisting up the truth in triumph. We're taught that the truth is all that matters. My first news editor used to say: "It doesn't matter how beautifully you write a story. If it isn't accurate, it's worthless."

Everyone wants to know the truth. Except those who don't. Those who stand to lose by it. I know that now.

"I need to tell Steve," I say and put the phone down on Joe.

My poor husband goes very quiet when I spell it all out. "Oh, Katie," he says. "What happened to him?"

"I don't know, Steve. Maybe he got in with the wrong crowd?" And I wince at the tired excuse used by the parent of every child in trouble.

"Please come home, love. Freddie and I need you here. And we don't even know if Jake is still in Thailand . . ."

I feel desperate and angry that he is asking me to leave Thailand knowing Jake *may* be here, but I can't put up much of an argument to stay. "Okay," I say reluctantly. I make it sound as if I'm agreeing only for Steve's sake, but in truth, I'm too tired, too broken, to do anything else. I ring the travel agent and change my ticket for the next flight. In my other life, I'd have experienced the familiar ping of happiness to be going home at the end of a job. But it isn't the end, is it?

After I've packed, I turn on the television to shut out the silence, but the try-too-hard action movie fades to wallpaper and I sit there attempting to put myself in Jake's shoes. I try to imagine the shame, the devastation of the moment he was sent down from university. Maybe heading off to Thailand had seemed the obvious choice. He'd have a gap year and get back on track. He just needed a bit of R and R. Traveling, meeting new people to put things into perspective?

But it seemed Jake had slithered down the loser slope, looking for handholds and hiding from the truth. He'd cut himself off from his family, fending us off with the occasional e-mail and even rarer phone call. His friend here in Bangkok, Ross, had said Jake had felt he couldn't go home. Couldn't tell his mum and dad he was in trouble.

He couldn't let us know what he'd become. A failure.

THIRTY-FOUR

The Mother

FRIDAY, AUGUST 22, 2014

Malcolm had thrown himself into the complexity of the arrangements with something resembling enthusiasm. She knew it was because this meant he didn't have to think about the future without Alex, and she tried not to puncture his bubble of activity. She sat and watched him on the phone, talking about permits and documents. She'd have to ask him about them later. He was keeping a note of everything in his special book. Lesley noticed that his handwriting, which he had always been quietly proud of, was getting smaller and tighter.

He frowned as something was spelled out to him. It was almost as if he was at work in his office at the council. He looked businesslike and in charge. Not like a grieving father. Until he caught her eye and his face sagged.

"Sorry," he mouthed and held up five fingers to show how long he'd be.

"I'll get us a coffee," she mouthed back.

Lesley listened at the door before opening it. She knew the drill now. Smile and say nothing. The reporters had worked out a rota to camp outside their room in pairs when the hotel had threatened to throw them all out if they kept blocking the corridors.

"So sorry, Mrs. O'Connor," the charming manager had said,

smiling. It had taken a bit of time to get used to the permanent smiles. At first Lesley thought they were mocking her when she complained about the door knocks late at night.

"Why are you laughing about this?" she'd said to the girl on reception. "It's very upsetting." The girl had smiled even more and Lesley had marched off. Clive had told her later it was a cultural tic that tripped up many Westerners.

"She was smiling her apology and then her embarrassment when she saw you were upset," he explained.

"How was I supposed to know that?" she'd said to Malcolm. "Bloody silly carry-on. Do you think I should go and say sorry?"

"Just leave it, love."

She'd got used to hearing the next shift of reporters arrive, settling down on the chairs they'd placed outside her door. They looked as if they were in a dentist's waiting room.

She wondered who it would be now. Joe from the *Post*? She hoped so. He always jumped up when she appeared. Lovely manners. He reminded her a bit of Dan. Or George from the *Telegraph*. He was serious and respectful. Not like some of the others. Louise Butler, for one. She always stood too close, pretending to care. But she didn't fool Lesley, not with that hard mouth.

It was quiet outside and when she opened the door there was no one there. She almost felt disappointed. *Get a grip, Lesley,* she told herself. *You're supposed to be avoiding the press.*

But she still looked up and down the corridor, hoping to see them. The truth was that the reporters and photographers had become their neighbors, the familiar faces in a country of strangers. They asked how she was, how she was coping, and talked about Alex. And Lesley knew things about them. All Kate's troubles, obviously, but also that Mick was getting married—"The price of a bit of salmon and some salad for the reception is a fucking scandal," she'd overheard him say outside her door—that Joe was saving up to buy a flat, and that George had developed a jippy stomach. She almost took some Imodium out to him but Malcolm said it was a step too far.

She'd still asked him if he felt better the next time she saw him.

And she waved to two of the photographers who were having breakfast when she got to the dining room.

Malcolm was writing on the hotel notepaper when she came back to their room, carrying two cups with coffee slopped into the saucers.

"Mind you don't drip on your notes," she called from the en suite as she unrolled toilet paper to soak up the spills.

"The undertakers are sorting out the civil registry death certificate, the certificate of embalming, and the document for the transfer of remains to the UK," Malcolm said. "Clive says we can book flights home."

She sat down hard on the loo seat. "Transfer of remains" was like a punch in the stomach.

They'd decided to bring the girls back intact because they couldn't bear the thought of them being cremated without a funeral.

"Are you all right in there?"

"Yes, just catching my breath. Do Jenny and Mike know?"

"No, I'm just about to go and knock. Who's outside this morning?"

"No one. Bit strange. Wonder what they're doing. I'll go."

Jenny Shaw wasn't dressed. She couldn't face the physical effort of taking her pajamas off, choosing clothes, and pulling them over her head, she told Lesley when she let her into her darkened room. She wanted to go back to sleep and never wake up.

Lesley wanted to shake her but opted for brisk action, instead.

"I'll open the curtains, Jenny. Things always look better in day-light."

"Rosie is still dead, even in daylight, Lesley," Jenny said. And Lesley wheeled round to face her.

"I know. Of course I know that, but we need to keep going. We can't just collapse in a heap. There are things we need to do, Jenny." She cast about for tasks that Malcolm hadn't already got in hand.

"We need to buy clothes for the girls. To give to the undertakers."

"Clothes?" Jenny said as if she didn't understand the word.

Lesley sat down next to her on the unmade bed. Jenny's grief dripped down the walls of the room. It was there in the tortured sheets, the discarded empty miniatures from the minibar, and the untouched dinner congealing on the bedside table.

The world had stopped here in this room. She turned to Jenny and took her by the shoulders.

"Don't you think we are all dying inside, too? You are not alone in this, Jenny. Mike is in bits, too."

Jenny hugged herself. "Mike's going home. That's how in bits he is. Imogen needs him, so he's leaving me here to sort everything out. Selfish bastard."

Lesley tried not to react—it would just wind Jenny up further—but she was furious with him. *Couldn't he have waited a couple more days?* she thought. She'd get Malcolm to go and see him and try to persuade him to stay.

"Look, Jenny," she said quietly, "we can't change what has happened. But what we can do is make sure everything is done properly so the girls can come home with us. Malcolm's doing his bit and we need to do ours. Come on. Get dressed, and we'll go to the mall near the embassy."

I t was while the two women were flicking mindlessly through the racks of unsuitable clothes that Jenny asked the question that changed everything.

"What were they wearing when they were found?" Jenny said.

And they both stopped, letting the hangers clatter back into place.

"I don't know, Jenny. The police colonel said they had wrapped themselves in matting for protection from the fire, didn't he?"

"But nobody mentioned their clothes. Nobody has offered to give me Rosie's clothes. I want to know what they were wearing. There must be photos from the scene. Ring Clive."

Lesley fumbled with her phone and stood as rigidly as one of the mannequins. "Clive, it's Lesley. We want to know what the girls were wearing when they were found. Well, ask someone. Someone must know."

The two women clung together for a moment before pushing past the assistants to get to the exit.

Lesley's phone was ringing as they walked down the hotel corridor.

"Clive? Let me get into the room. We're almost there. Okay. What have you found out?"

The silence in the lavishly decorated bedroom stretched into minutes as she listened, pressing the phone to her ear so hard it was leaving a mark on her cheek.

Jenny was looking at her, trying to read her eyes.

Malcolm sat on the bed, uncomprehending, but Lesley knew he would wait for her to finish. He liked a complete story—couldn't bear soap operas with their cliff-hangers and dramatic drum solos. Their son Dan teasingly called him a box-set sort of man.

When she hung up, she sat heavily on the bed beside him.

"Tell me," Jenny said, jumping out of a chair. "What did he say?"

"They were naked, Jenny."

THIRTY-FIVE

The Detective
FRIDAY, AUGUST 22, 2014

Sparkes was toying with a flabby lasagna in the staff canteen when Salmond found him.

"That looks revolting," she said, plonking herself down.

"Thanks for that," he said, pushing the plate away and then covering the remains with his napkin so he didn't have to look at it again.

"I'm having my lunch—twenty minutes of carbs and quiet. Whatever it is, can't it wait?"

"Not really," the DS said seriously. "Our two girls were naked when they were found in the cold store."

Sparkes got up and led the way back to his office.

Salmond recounted the hysterical phone call she'd had from Lesley O'Connor and her follow-up call to the Bangkok embassy.

"She's right. The vice-consul has confirmed it with the police. Their report states that the bodies were naked and no clothing was found at the scene."

"And they've known this from the start? And not mentioned it? Bloody hell. We need to see their report and find out what else hasn't been mentioned. Is this just shoddy police work? Or is it a deliberate obfuscation of the facts?"

"The second one," Salmond said, "whatever the word is. It doesn't fit their theory that the girls died trying to escape from the fire, does it? This evidence opens up all sorts of scenarios, none of them good."

"No. What the hell was going on in that guesthouse?"

"That's what Lesley said."

"How did you leave it with her?"

"I said I'd find you and you'd ring her back."

The conversation didn't start well. He got Jenny Shaw first and she wouldn't let him get a word in as she ranted about the appalling investigation, the lies, the missed evidence. He let her wear herself out and made notes to himself until she stopped.

"Jenny?" he said into the silence.

"Yes, I'm still here," she muttered. "We all are. I'll put you on loudspeaker."

"Okay. Why did you ask the police the question? Is there anything else you need to tell me?"

"No, I don't think so. Lesley and I were buying clothes for the girls to wear for the journey home. And I was thinking about a dress she'd bought just before she left. And I wondered if she'd been wearing it when she died. I don't know why. I have such strange thoughts."

"It was an excellent thought, Jenny. It may be a step toward finding out the truth about what really happened."

"Except the police here don't want to know. They've closed the case."

Lesley's voice came on the line. "They won't listen, Inspector. We've been down there to try to talk to the colonel, but he's unavailable. A junior officer came down and smiled at us. He insisted the death certificate was the final word on the subject. We asked for a copy of the police report, but he said no. I suppose it might contain other things they don't want us to know," Lesley said. "When we pressed him about them being naked, he said, 'Perhaps they took their clothes off because it got too hot?'"

Sparkes groaned. "Really?"

"I think he would've said anything to get rid of us."

"I will take this up with the Thai police," Sparkes said. "What you need to know is that I will be investigating the deaths—I have discussed the new developments with the coroner for West Hampshire and he has asked me to look into them."

"Thank God," Lesley said.

"Obviously, it is very important that the girls are not cremated in Bangkok. We need to be able to carry out an autopsy. If the bodies are embalmed prior to repatriation, this may help preserve evidence of how they died."

Malcolm spoke up. "I'm organizing all of that now, Inspector. I'll be in touch as soon as we have a date."

"Thank you," Lesley called from across the room. A distant voice.

"Do you have any further questions?" he asked, more from habit than from a desire to prolong the agony.

"No. None until we get home," she said.

THIRTY-SIX

The Mother

MONDAY, SEPTEMBER 1, 2014

She'd made herself focus on getting Alex home, shutting her mind to all the questions and horrors of the last days in Bangkok. She had closed down to a narrow strip of activity, ignoring the increasingly lurid headlines about the girls' naked bodies and Jake Waters—"The Murky Truth about 'Fire Hero'"; "Drugs Turned 'Hero' into Monster"—and the casual questions of the last couple of reporters left in the hotel.

For days she hadn't been able to look any further than landing at Heathrow. But when they'd finally unlocked their front door, she'd felt something break inside her. She'd come back to the real world— her little life of work every morning, weekly pub quizzes and super- market shops, singing along with the radio while she ironed Malcolm's shirts. But it had no longer meant anything to her. She'd felt like an actor in a play. Going through the motions as she opened the pile of post at the kitchen counter, pretending to read letters from the bank and insurance companies.

The need to know the truth about what had happened to Alex filled her head like the ocean roar of tinnitus.

She needed to know whether someone had deliberately hurt her child; she needed the physical evidence the Thais were ignoring.

Had someone drugged her? Raped her? Left her to die in a fire?

She caught herself, hauled herself back from the edge of madness.

She had to be strong now. *I can't save you, my darling girl,* she told Alex. *But your dad and I have made a pact that we won't rest until we know the truth. We will get you justice.*

Lesley didn't really know what justice would look like. But it was a goal that others seemed to understand, especially the press. They'd written that an inquest had been ordered in Hampshire, and the pictures of the coffins had made the front page, but the story was slipping gradually out of sight now. The political party conferences were on the horizon and the news agenda was moving on. The Silly Season that Kate had told her about had been folded and put away like beach towels.

"We've got Thai death certificates," Malcolm had told the coroner's officer, an unexpectedly cheerful woman in a busy dress, when they'd sat in her office in Winchester, the morning after arriving home. "I've had all the paperwork translated."

"Call me Hilary, Mr. O'Connor. That's very good. I've already got copies from the funeral directors," she'd said, rustling around the room with all the documents.

"We need to find out what happened," Lesley had heard herself say, as if in another room.

"Of course you do."

And Lesley had found herself trying to identify the birds flying across Hilary's dress. *Cranes? Herons?*

"And the funeral . . ." she'd heard Malcolm say.

"I'm sorry, Mr. O'Connor. We cannot release Alex's body until all investigations are complete."

The coroner's officer had leaned forward and patted his hand. "We will get things done as quickly as we can. The postmortem is scheduled for the end of the week."

When they got home, Lesley had gone to bed and cried for the rest of the morning, burying her face in the damp pillow, until Dan came in with a cup of consoling tea and broke down at the sight of her. She made herself stop.

I won't cry again until Alex's funeral, she promised herself later, picking up a tea towel to dry the dishes on the draining board.

Jenny and Mike had been told the same thing in an apparently identical meeting. Lesley had volunteered Malcolm to go with them—to referee if needed—but Jenny's sister, Fran, had come from somewhere up north to help.

"That's good," Lesley had said. "You need family around you."

"Fran never stops talking," Jenny had complained. "I won't get a moment to myself while she's here."

Lesley had given her a hard stare and Jenny had added lamely, "I know she means well."

When Fran and Jenny got back, Fran had recounted to the O'Connors the whole conversation the Shaws had had with the coroner's official. Lesley had tried to interrupt, muttering, "Yes, well, she said the same to us," a couple of times, but Fran wanted her moment.

"How was Mike? How is he coping?" Lesley had asked. He'd disappeared back to his other life as soon as the meeting had ended, according to Fran.

Jenny, who had not said a word since sitting down, had suddenly come back to life.

"Who knows? He looked like he wished he wasn't there."

"He's lost his daughter as well, Jenny," Fran had said, marching straight onto the thin ice.

"He lost her a long time ago, when he walked out on her. I don't want to talk about him. This is all his fault."

Malcolm had picked up his cup and said, "Anyone for another coffee? There's more in the *cafetière*."

Fran had looked at him gratefully. "I'll have one. I'll come with you, Malcolm." She had still been talking as they left the room.

Left alone, Lesley had tried to talk to Jenny, but the other woman wouldn't meet her eye.

"It isn't Mike's fault, Jenny," she'd said. "You know that. But I understand how hurt and angry you are. Because I am, too."

Jenny had sagged in her chair. "She wouldn't have died if she hadn't gone. And she wouldn't have gone if he hadn't given her the money."

"Jenny . . ."

"I know, I know," Jenny had snapped. "I'm being unreasonable."

Lesley had looked down at her hands. Not the moment.

"The thing is, Fran keeps going on about him," she'd carried on. "Picking at the scab. What Mike must be feeling, how sad Mike must be. He should be here with me, Lesley. I need him."

She'd looked as shocked as Lesley when the truth tumbled out.

"Have you talked to him about how you are feeling?" Lesley had said quickly.

"No. I can't. I can't bear the thought of Imogen answering if I ring."

"Then ask Fran to ring and get his mobile number."

Jenny had nodded.

THIRTY-SEVEN

The Reporter

MONDAY, SEPTEMBER 1, 2014

The white, handwritten envelope was still damp when I picked it up off the doormat, presumably having sat in a postman's bag during the morning rain, and the ink had smudged. I opened it without thinking, my thumb finding the weakness in the flap and ripping it apart as my eyes flipped through the rest of the post.

"Great," I said when I glanced at the first line and sat down at the kitchen table. "A bloody speeding ticket." And I threw it aside. The last mean kick of a bastard day.

It's Steve who reads it properly when he gets home an hour later. "Hello," he shouts above the radio news, playing at full volume to reach me wherever I am in the house.

"Katie, turn it down, for God's sake! The whole street must be able to hear it."

I poke my head round the kitchen door and stick my tongue out at him. "I see Mr. Sunshine is home. Bad day?"

He grunts. It has clearly been a very bad day. I know his noises by heart now. Twenty-five years of marriage have fine-tuned my ear to the nuances of his verbal tics.

"Me, too. Let's have a glass of wine and toast self-pity," I say, kissing him lightly. We're drinking more lately. Taking the edge off the panic that is simmering just below the surface.

He sits down wearily, exhaustion dragging his eyes into the pouches beneath them. "I've been on my feet for twelve hours. Horrible surgery list today," he says.

I keep quiet about my woes. They are pathetic in comparison. I'm on light duties at work, kept away from anything meaningful by Terry. I'd had to insist on coming back, pointing out that I wouldn't be working on the fire—and that they needed me. "It's not as if you are mob-handed, Terry," I'd said. "I'll do rewrites if you like. I need to keep busy."

The Editor had me into his office on my first day back—just for a two-minute chat, to reassure me of the *Post*'s commitment to me—but he's avoided me in the days since. And my name is not going in the paper.

"Best to keep a low profile for a bit, Kate," Terry advised. So I've spent the past ten days bashing out fluff and battling with celebrity agents who want to tell me what I can and can't write.

"You win. You had the worst day," I say.

Steve is staring into his glass.

"Cheers." I clink his glass of sauvignon blanc with mine and we each take a mouthful.

"Anyway, what do you want for dinner? There's the rest of the fish pie to finish. Or we could order a takeaway."

"Don't mind," Steve says. "Anything will do. You look tired, love."

"I am," I mutter. "I'll stick the pie in the microwave."

"Okay. Any messages on the answerphone when you got in? Anything in the post?" he asks, as he always does.

"Your mum left a message about Sunday. Looking forward to seeing us, et cetera. A reminder about the home insurance and one from the dentist about my next checkup. And there's a speeding ticket."

"Kate! Not another one," he says. "Why do you have to drive like Jenson Button all the time? It is costing us a fortune in fines."

"Shut up and drink your wine," I say. "Anyway, it might have been yours. I didn't read on."

"Where is it?"

I find the limp envelope on the counter, hand it to him, and turn back to the fridge, searching for vegetables I've forgotten to buy.

"Well?" I say. "Who is the guilty party?"

"It's Jake," Steve says.

I stare at him.

Steve holds up the sheets of paper as proof.

"This speeding ticket is for him. Our son was apparently driving at eighty-two miles per hour on the A3 on August the twenty-sixth. That's last week. In a hire car. The car company has passed the ticket on."

"Jake?" I say. It's the only word I really heard.

"Jake," Steve repeats and takes my hand.

"He came home . . ."

THIRTY-EIGHT

The Detective

TUESDAY, SEPTEMBER 2, 2014

He and Salmond had been to see the families the day after they'd returned and the two mothers had welcomed them eagerly.

"It is so good to finally be able to talk to a detective who knows what he's doing," Lesley had said as her opening gambit.

Sparkes had smiled encouragingly, but he hoped this was not just going to be foreign-police bashing.

"We'll listen to what they say before making any kind of judgment," he'd told Salmond on their way there. "But the families weren't there when it happened, so let's not lose sight of the fact that this is all thirdhand information."

Malcolm O'Connor had sat nodding his agreement as his wife and neighbor set out what they knew. Or what they thought they knew. *Hard to be objective about the evidence when your emotions are fully engaged,* Sparkes thought.

"As we told you on the phone, they were not clothed when they were found, Inspector," Lesley O'Connor had said, marking off "the facts" on her fingers. "But the police over there refuse to investigate whether there was a sexual assault."

Sparkes noticed that Malcolm O'Connor had automatically looked up at the ceiling at the mention of sexual assault.

Always hard for fathers, flitted through Sparkes's head. He saw that

Lesley hadn't noticed. She was focusing on itemizing the catalog of mistakes by the Thai police.

"They only taped the scene off for twenty-four hours and then anyone was allowed to walk all over any evidence. It was completely unprofessional. They made no effort to find witnesses. No one else who was at this supposed party has come forward. There must have been others staying at that guesthouse, but the only person we know about, Jake Waters"—she spat the name—"has gone on the run."

"I'm not sure 'gone on the run' accurately describes it, Mrs. O'Connor," Sparkes had said, putting his hand up to stop her. "Jake Waters discharged himself from hospital. And hasn't been in touch with his family or the police. He may not know we want to talk to him."

"Well, he must be living on a desert island, then."

"That is possible in that part of the world, as I understand it," Sparkes said carefully.

"Inspector, it's been all over the Internet. The press think he has questions to answer," Jenny had added.

Luckily, the press are not the final arbiters, he thought. *God help us if they donned horsehair wigs officially.*

"And the girls have been slandered by the Thai police. They've made them out to be bad girls so they can blame them and cover up the truth. Can't you see?"

Lesley's voice had risen as the accusations tumbled out, and she'd half-stood as she made her final plea. Malcolm O'Connor had reached for her arm and gently pulled her back into her seat.

"I understand how upset you are," Sparkes had said. "You want answers. We all do. And we will try our best to find those answers. The results from the postmortems will help establish how your daughters died."

The word "postmortem" had silenced everyone, and Lesley started to cry.

"I can't bear it," she'd sobbed. "I know you have to do it, but I don't want anyone to touch Alex again. She's been handled by police officers, mortuary assistants, embalmers, the undertakers. And someone at that guesthouse. Somebody stripped Alex and Rosie and wrapped them in coconut matting. But what else did they do? I keep thinking about hands on her skin. And I can do nothing to stop them."

"But this needs to be done, love," Malcolm had said firmly. "I wish it didn't, but we need physical evidence. Alex has the key to what happened."

"And Rosie," Jenny had added. "They would want us to know, wouldn't they?"

"Yes, Jenny," Malcolm had answered. "They would."

Sparkes had listened to them rationalizing everything so they could bear it.

"Where is Jake Waters?" Sparkes said now. "What did he see?"

"He's probably still in Southeast Asia," Salmond replied unnecessarily.

"We don't know that. We need to talk to his mother, to make sure she hasn't heard from him."

"I thought you had," Salmond said slyly.

"Not officially. Not as part of our investigation. We need an update on the Bangkok situation. They might have heard something and not bothered to tell anyone. You set up the liaison with the Thais and I'll talk to my mate at Interpol.

"And we need sight of the girls' e-mails, texts, WhatsApps, Facebook, tweets. We've got passwords from the parents, haven't we?"

"We've got Alex's—she always used the same one for everything. Jenny Shaw said she doesn't know Rosie's."

"Well, make a start with Alex."

"On it," she said and scurried out of the office.

. . .

She returned looking harassed. "DC Collins is mining the online stuff—he's brilliant at it."

"Thank God someone is." Sparkes laughed. "And the Thais?"

"Police Colonel Prasongsanti of the Crime Suppression Division has no information on the whereabouts of one Jake Stephen Waters, DOB March 15, 1992," Salmond recited.

"Okay, I'll phone Kate Waters. I'm not going to jump in the car—it's a bloody long way to go to find out she has heard nothing from him."

"Maybe I should do it, sir. It would make it more . . . more formal."

"Go on, then." Sparkes read the number from his contact list and the sergeant dialed and put the call on loudspeaker.

"Hello. Kate Waters." Her voice was brisk.

"Hello, Mrs. Waters. It's DS Zara Salmond from Hampshire Police."

"Hampshire Police?" Sparkes could hear Kate orienting herself. "DI Sparkes's colleague? We've met, haven't we? Must be a couple of years ago now. Was it in court?"

"Yes, that's right. The Building Site Baby case, if I remember. Look, I'm ringing because Hampshire Police have started their own investigation into the circumstances of the deaths of Alex O'Connor and Rosie Shaw."

Silence.

"Hello?"

"Sorry, yes. I just wanted to move away from my desk. I thought the investigation was closed."

"It is in Bangkok, but the bodies of the two girls have been repatriated and the coroner has asked us to open an inquiry."

"Of course. Sorry—I'd forgotten how that worked. So, how can I help you?"

"We would like to locate your son Jake Waters," Salmond said smoothly.

"You and me both," Kate muttered.

"To ask him about the night of the fire in Bangkok."

"We don't even know if he was there, DS Salmond." Kate's voice fizzed.

"Which is why we need to speak to him, to check where he was. He could be an important witness."

"Okay."

"Have you had any contact with your son, Mrs. Waters? Have you any idea where he is?"

"Does Bob Sparkes know you are calling? We've already been in touch on this matter."

"Yes, DI Sparkes is aware of the request."

"I would rather talk to him, if you don't mind."

Sparkes shook his head.

"He's not available at the moment, I'm afraid." Salmond was crisp and to the point. "So, have you heard from your son?"

There was the slightest of pauses.

"No, I haven't."

Sparkes scribbled *Has anyone else?* on a piece of paper and waved it under Salmond's nose.

"Has anyone else heard from him?"

The hesitation again.

"I'm not sure," Kate said.

"Not sure? What do you mean?"

"Well, I'm not sure if it means anything, but I've heard he may be back in the UK."

Sparkes's eyebrows disappeared into his hair.

"What makes you think that?" Salmond asked.

"He's had a speeding ticket."

THIRTY-NINE

The Reporter
WEDNESDAY, SEPTEMBER 3, 2014

D S Salmond had wanted me to come in immediately when she phoned yesterday, but I asked if we could postpone it till this morning. I pointed out I was a good couple of hours away and I had to finish a story. I didn't tell her I was writing some nonsense about the hottest Augusts in history. I wanted to keep the upper hand.

We made an appointment for eleven today. I told Terry I had a doctor's appointment and he waved it through. He doesn't want me in the newsroom.

My return has been much more difficult than I'd imagined. Steve had warned me but I suppose I'd been looking forward to coming home to the mother ship, to being surrounded by friends and colleagues. But my experience with the pack has left its mark. I've become wary of those innocent-sounding openings.

"You must be devastated, Kate," Gail, one of the feature writers, a woman I've known since we learned shorthand together, had said as she hugged me. "And poor Jake. Having those terrible things said about him."

I could feel myself tense as I waited for the dewy-eyed sympathy to turn to a grilling.

The thing is, we just can't help ourselves. We want to know everything, and I know I would have asked some of the same questions:

"Didn't you know about the university issue?" "What do you think he's been doing out there?" "Do you think he had anything to do with the deaths?"

When I didn't come up with the goods, people backed off and started talking about me instead. I got worn down by the bone-aching awkwardness of it all. I'd walk into a room and the conversation would stop.

I became paranoid when people looked away, pretending to be busy. I couldn't decide if it was because they think Jake's bad or I am.

I'm still asking myself the same questions. Searching for answers, writing e-mails to him every day, begging him to get in touch. I'd hoped Freddie might have heard something, but he says not. We've packed him back off to university—he said he'd stay with us but I could hear the reluctance in his voice. He needs to be back in his normal life. He couldn't do anything but sit around the house here, trying to make us feel better. He's a lovely boy but patience isn't his strong suit. I think the agony of the wait for news was wearing him out. We ended up following each other from room to room, making endless cups of tea, watching *Antiques Roadshow* so we didn't have to talk. Because there are only so many ways to say "This can't be happening."

Platitudes were the safe option. But the atmosphere grew thick with what was going unsaid. I found myself wondering if Freddie had secret moments of glee—at seeing the golden boy of the family knocked off his pedestal—but I beat myself up for even thinking it. He loves his brother.

Ironically, I feel most comfortable with the one reporter I can hold responsible for Jake's notoriety. Joe quietly brings me coffee and gobbets of the office goss.

I've decided to keep a low profile until this whole thing is over.

Until we get the inquest verdicts of accidental death and the girls can be buried. Then I'll make them all suffer for having suspected him. When it's finished.

Steve was relieved when I told him about the call from Hampshire Police. He'd wanted to ring them as soon as we got the speeding ticket but I'd said no.

"It's probably a mistake. I'll ring the car hire people. And if it really is him, there's a chance he'll get in touch. Or come home. He won't if I tell the police and it gets leaked to the press. It will all blow up again. Please, let's wait."

I'd rung the car hire company right away and waited while Vivaldi's greatest hits played on a loop. Not the Nigel Kennedy version. My head was full of Jake and, as I smoothed the creases out of the official letter on my desk, I stroked his name with my finger. I'd told myself it must be an administrative error. Insisted. And Steve had gone along with it because the pain involved in admitting our son had returned home without telling us or making any contact was too much for either of us to bear. So, admin cock-up it was.

The person at the other end finally announced herself and I explained.

"I've received this letter," I said. "It says my son was speeding in one of your cars. But he's in Thailand. So it must be a mistake."

"Do you have a reference number?"

Ten long minutes later, the woman at the car hire company had moved from professionally caring to "computer says no" mode. She had begun using my name in every sentence—never a good sign—and wouldn't budge from the official line that the speeding fine was a police matter.

"I'm afraid, Mrs. Waters, that I cannot discuss this any further with you—only your son."

"But he's in Thailand."

"He'll have to take it up with the police, Mrs. Waters. They issued the speeding ticket, not us. We are just passing on the correspondence to the person who hired the car," she repeated.

"I see."

"Is there anything else I can help you with at this time?"

"Is that a joke?"

The phone went dead.

I was still trying to decide my next step when DS Salmond had phoned to ask a direct question and I knew I couldn't lie.

've got the letter in my bag. And the envelope. But I imagine DS Salmond has already been in touch with the car hire people. She sounds like the efficient sort.

She comes out to the reception area of the police station to meet me and guide me through to an interview room. Bob Sparkes is already there. He looks up from his folder and smiles.

"Hello, how was the drive?"

"Good, thanks." I'm about to call him Bob but it suddenly doesn't feel right. I settle for not calling him anything.

DS Salmond is asking the questions, anyway.

"When did you receive the notice from the car hire firm?"

She must know already if she's any kind of detective, but I play the game.

"It arrived in the post on Monday morning but I didn't see it until I got home after work. I thought it was for me. I get a few . . ."

"When did you realize it related to your son?"

"A bit later that evening. My husband spotted his name on it."

"But you didn't contact the police?"

I glance across at Bob Sparkes, but his face is giving nothing away and he looks down at a piece of paper.

"Well, I couldn't believe it was right. I wanted to get in touch with the hire people to check if there was an error. Of course, they wouldn't discuss it with me. They said they could only talk to Jake. And that it was a police matter."

"Quite. Has your son been in touch with you directly?"

"No. No," I repeat when she gives me a long look. "I would tell you."

"Like you did about the speeding ticket?"

"Okay. That was a mistake. I'm sorry."

"It's important, Kate," Bob says, and I nod.

"Has the hire company given you any details to confirm it was Jake?" I ask.

"He used his driving license and a credit card to hire the car."

"Has he still got the car?"

"No, that one was returned," Salmond says.

"So he's hired another one?"

Sparkes smiles. "So quick, Kate. Yes. Jake has hired another car. We're looking for it—and him."

"What will happen when you find him?"

"We'll ask him some questions about what he heard and saw on the night of the fire."

"If he was there."

"Quite. Remember to pay the speeding fine." Salmond snapped her notebook shut.

t was the Dutch boys who'd started it. Them and their stupid drinking games. They'd been necking beer all day by the look of them, those great big bottles of Chang, but they wanted some fun, they said, when they finally rolled up at the guesthouse with a bottle with no label.

"We're leaving tonight. We want a going-away party!"

Alex had been worried. They'd been all red-faced and sweaty in that dangerous "it's about to kick off" way. Eyes flitting over the girls and then at each other, as if they had a plan. She'd given Rosie a warning look, but she'd just laughed and Lars had thrown his arms round her and given her a big kiss on the cheek.

"My beautiful English girl," he'd sung right into her face. He'd kept his arms round her, and Alex could see Rosie was beginning to struggle to get free.

"Come on, Lars," Alex had said. *The Head Girl.* "What have you got in the bottle?"

"The man said tequila." Diederik had belched and then put his hand over his mouth.

"Look out. He's going to be sick," Alex had said as she pushed him toward the toilets. Lars had let go of Rosie and helped Alex steady his friend.

"He's okay. He's okay."

"He will be in a minute." She'd steered Diederik into a stall and closed the door on him. *Don't need to hold his hair like a girl. He can get on with it himself,* she'd told herself. The noises told their own story, and when he'd come out, he'd been grinning happily and wiping his mouth on his bare arm.

"Let's start again," he'd shouted and rushed back into the dorm to begin a new game.

R osie was down to her underwear when Jake came in an hour later. "Who the hell has puked in the bogs?" he asked in an icy sort of voice that shut everyone up.

"And what is going on here?" He was looking at Rosie. She tried to cover herself with her hands and Alex almost felt sorry for her.

She wanted to tell Jake that she'd tried to stop the game but her friend wouldn't listen, just kept downing the stuff in the shot glasses and losing the dares, but she kept quiet. She'd had enough of making excuses for Rosie.

And though she wasn't nearly as wasted as her friend, she was a bit tipsy. She'd started off matching her shot for shot, fed up with always being the sensible one, but after a while, when her head started spinning, she'd begun tipping her drinks into a bin behind her when the Dutch boys weren't looking. Anyway, the boys were all about Rosie. Alex had watched as they circled her friend, her stomach clenching but secretly relieved it wasn't her.

Jake was really angry but Lars had jumped up and started dancing round the room. He was a six-foot-four-inch schoolboy in a pair of Superman underpants and suddenly they'd all laughed. Alex couldn't help it. He'd looked like a stick insect on crack. Rosie had put her T-shirt back on and Jake calmed down. He'd picked up a shot glass and sat on the floor with them.

"I know a game," he'd said.

He wrote their names down on bits of paper napkin and they each had to pick one out and then pretend to be that person. The others had to guess who it was. If they got it wrong, they had to down a shot of tequila or whatever was in the bottle.

Alex got Jake, so she sat and waited. She didn't need to scrutinize him for telling details—she'd memorized him already: the way he straightened his glasses when he was being serious, his crooked smile, his way of chewing the thumbnail of his left hand when he was listening. The others carried on, getting rowdier, clowning about and insulting one another. Diederik got Rosie's name and started ripping off his clothes and flirting with Lars, kissing his cheek and ruffling his hair. They all knew who he was supposed to be, but it was so funny they let him carry on. Rosie laughed the loudest of all and Alex knew she would disappear with Lars as soon as possible.

When it was Jake's turn, he put his head down and looked at each of them from under his lashes. Not in a sexy way. Secretly. Like a Peeping Tom. Alex realized instantly who he was impersonating and looked across at Jamie to see if he'd recognized himself. He looked like he had no idea. He mouthed, "Who is it?" and Alex pointed at him and mouthed back, "It's you." The word "Me?" formed on his lips but didn't get any further. Jamie looked horrified. She could see him thinking, *Is that what they see? Am I this weirdo?*

The others were getting bored now, so Jake messed with his hair, making it stand on end like Jamie's in the mornings, and Lars shouted, "JW!" and the ordeal was over.

But Alex knew Jake had been watching them. He knew who they were.

Hours later, when Jake went to finish the washing up and Rosie was walking Lars and Diederik to the bus station, she sat with Jamie on the floor of the dorm. He'd carried on drinking after the game.

She tried to get him onto his feet, but his legs wouldn't cooperate and they ended up in a heap, laughing hysterically.

When they stopped, he looked at her with his unfocused eyes. "I love you, Alex," he said. She tried to start laughing again but found she couldn't. "I've loved you since I saw you on the plane."

"What are you talking about?"

"You smiled at me on the plane over here. Don't you remember?" She didn't, but she thought it must be the drink talking.

"I followed you onto the bus, but you didn't notice me. Anyway, we ended up together, didn't we?"

"Hush, Jamie," she said. He took hold of her hand.

"I know you're too lovely for me. Most girls are." He took a deep breath, and it was as if something had been released in him, words spilling out: "Spud, one of the blokes on the last building site where I worked, called me 'a bottom-feeder'—he told the others I only went after ugly girls because they were easy. I wanted to tell him they were nice girls. Kind. But I could hear the game starting. The 'make Jamie angry' game. So I breathed slowly, like they taught me, laughed with him, and then got on with mixing plaster. But I didn't stop thinking about it. Flicking through the girls I'd gone out with. There weren't many, really. And I chose them because they didn't give me that 'Who the hell do you think you are?' look. The one mean, pretty girls always give me, making me feel I'm nothing. So I stopped. I started looking for girls who smiled nervously when I walked up to them in a pub or a club. Who giggled, as scared of rejection as I was, when I spoke to them. They made me feel good, and that can't be a bad thing, can it?"

Alex felt battered by this flood of confidences but shook her head. "No, that can't be a bad thing."

"Do you like me, Alex?"

She nodded, unable to do anything else. She wanted to say, "I like you very much as a friend, Jamie," but his sudden vulnerability frightened her. She couldn't hurt him.

He smiled happily and slid slowly sideways on the floor. She picked a sheet off his bunk and put it over him.

FORTY

The Detective

THURSDAY, SEPTEMBER 4, 2014

A notification had pinged up on Sparkes's screen twenty-four hours earlier: *Alex O'Connor PM.*

He didn't remember putting it on his Outlook calendar—he'd scrawled it in his desk diary. *He's very analog,* he could hear Zara Salmond saying somewhere. She must've put it online for him.

He was in the office early to prepare. He didn't mind them. Postmortems. They were part of the job. But, to his quiet delight, Salmond always made sure she was standing in a corner of the forensic mortuary—"Away from the head end"—if she had to be there. Wonder Woman, as she was known in the department, had a chink in her body armor.

The police had been asked to attend by the West Hampshire coroner, an impatient, silver-haired solicitor who pushed proceedings along at a clip but still managed to charm the bereaved.

Sparkes didn't know what the examinations would show. Evidence of a sexual assault could be very difficult to detect in an embalmed body. And of course, there might be nothing there. Nothing to find. Maybe there'd been a misunderstanding about the clothes. A mistranslation. And the absence of clothes was all they had at the moment. It was all completely circumstantial.

But that wasn't what the families wanted to hear, and he wondered if they would be able to get on with mourning their children if the coroner agreed with the Thais that the girls had died accidentally in the fire. He doubted it. But at least they could hold their funerals.

Eileen had talked about her funeral the night before. She wanted her name in flowers, people singing "The Old Rugged Cross" and wringing their hands, she'd said and laughed at his horrified face. "Bob, I'm joking. If you sing 'The Old Rugged Cross' I'll sit up in my coffin. How about 'Ding-Dong! The Witch Is Dead'?"

He'd tried to play along, but inside he was dying.

"So," she'd said finally, reading the list on her lap. "Lilies on the coffin. Donations to Cancer Research. The poem from *Four Weddings and a Funeral*, all the verses of 'Amazing Grace,' and David Bowie's 'Starman' to finish."

She tore the page out of her notebook and handed it to him. "All sorted."

Apart from the dying part, he thought, and his stomach tightened into its default knot of fear. *This is ridiculous,* he told himself as he fought the nausea down. *You've seen death so many times.*

But usually after the event. And not people he loved. He'd seen lots of bodies, but this time he'd be there when death took place. And he was terrified. He couldn't really say what of. The way the palliative nurse had described it, all would be serenity. Eileen would simply slip away. But she would be gone. And his future without her would begin.

DS Salmond tapped on his half-open door and roused him from his thoughts. He put his hands to his eyes in case he'd cried without knowing. It happened sometimes.

"Did you remember the O'Connor PM is today?" she asked.

"Come in, for goodness' sake. I'm always talking to your disembodied head. Yes, of course I did. Remind me who's doing it."

"Aoife Mortimer. Hilary at the coroner's office told me."

"Oh good. We should go. She likes a prompt start."

"Right. Well. Are you sure you need me to come, too?"

"Yes. You can drive."

In the car, Salmond sucked a strong mint in a preemptive strike against the smells that always turned her stomach.

"Why do you think the Thais didn't do a PM? Very sloppy," she said, conversationally.

"Not a decision I'd be comfortable with. But let's see what Aoife finds, shall we?"

They didn't have to wait long.

The CSI photographer was taking her first pictures of the body of Alex O'Connor when Sparkes and Salmond entered the mortuary viewing gallery.

"Morning, Bob," Dr. Mortimer called up to him. "Hello, Zara. How are you feeling today? I've put a stool in the corner for you. Just in case."

Sparkes tried not to grin and moved forward to look down at the body on the slab.

"Christ, the embalmers have really gone to town with the formalin," he said. The concentration of the embalming fluid was so strong that his eyes were burning.

Aoife Mortimer nodded. "I'll come up. Shall we get on with the briefing, while we can still breathe?"

Sparkes ran through the story so far, carefully prefacing each fact with the words "according to the Thai police." The pathologist made notes and then walked down to the mortuary floor to begin.

She put on an extraction airflow hood to protect herself from the formalin, put her notebook down on the sheeted table behind her, and looked up at Sparkes—her eyes level with his feet. "Right," she said. "Shall we?"

There was silence in the room as she walked round the body to do the initial, visual scan of the mottled, waxy body on the table.

"Let's get this postmortem makeup off," she said quietly to the technician at her side.

"I suppose they were trying to cover the marks of the embalming needles in the neck, but they have put this on with a trowel," Dr. Mortimer said.

The orange pancake foundation gave the dead girl the macabre air of an end-of-pier show dancer.

Sparkes tried not to breathe through his nose as the pathologist began washing the makeup off Alex O'Connor's face and neck to expose the skin.

"That looks like bruising on the neck." Aoife Mortimer reached forward to move the young woman's hair back. "Can you see that, Bob? Where the foundation makeup was."

He peered down from his perch. Decomposition had muddied the skin, but he could see a deeper-colored pattern of bruises and scratches.

"Christ, it looks like she's been strangled."

Salmond shot off her stool and came to look, her hand over her mouth.

Her eyes said, "Told you," when she turned to her boss.

"Let's not get ahead of ourselves," Dr. Mortimer said coolly, spotting the look. "I'll need to complete the examination before I can come to any firm conclusions."

She continued her meticulous external inventory of the body and Salmond returned to her place of safety to scribble notes on the back of a folder.

Dr. Mortimer worked her way down the girl's body. She spent time examining the pubic area, moving backward and then in close, observing carefully from different angles. Sparkes knew she was looking for the glint or reflection of dried fluids.

Alex is telling us her story. Sparkes nodded to himself.

It had been a difficult day and was about to get worse. That morning, she and Rosie had had the big showdown about moving on that had been brewing for days. But when Alex had walked into the bar that evening, she'd found Rosie busy flirting with Jake, batting her eyelashes slowly in time with his jokes. Her infatuation with Lars apparently forgotten.

Alex had felt as if she'd been slapped. Rosie must have known how she felt about Jake—she'd talked about him a couple of times, when they were alone in their room. Testing out how she felt, how others saw him. Rosie hadn't sounded that interested then, but she was all over him now. Alex's prior claim certainly wasn't holding her back. And Jake had looked as if he was enjoying it.

"Rosie, I'm talking to you," Alex had shouted.

"What now? I'm busy . . ."

"I can see that." Alex had moved closer, screeching chairs out of the way. "I don't know why I'm wasting my breath, but we need to get those tickets today. The cheap ones might sell out if we don't."

Rosie shrugged.

"We're supposed to be leaving on Friday, after we get our exam results. We agreed."

"You agreed, not me. I want to stay here. I'm having a good time. Jake wants to show me a new karaoke club. Don't you, Jake?"

"Well, I was just telling you where it is. I've got no plans to go there," Jake had said quickly and moved off to safety behind the bar.

"Jake!" Rosie had tried to call him back, then turned on her friend. "You drive everyone away, Alex. Everyone thinks you are such a miserable cow. Why can't you just relax and enjoy yourself?"

"I am. I just want to see more of Thailand. I came to travel, not sit in a guesthouse for weeks on end, taking drugs and throwing myself at anything with a pulse."

"Shut up! I'm having a good time and you can't bear it. What's your problem?"

"You! You're my problem. And how long can you go on 'having a good time' if you carry on spending money on club booze and tattoos? Do you even know how much you've got left?"

Rosie had pulled a face, back to a sulky child. "Mind your own business, Alex. You're not in charge of me."

"Fine. But I'm leaving on Friday night whether you come or not. In fact, I'm going to buy my bus ticket tonight. You can do what you like."

Jake was pretending to dry the glasses and Jamie was studying his phone in the corner, but of course they'd heard it all. Alex hated public rows. Her mum said they were common and Alex knew she got all red in the face and tearful. But it couldn't be avoided this time. She'd been dancing around the subject in her head for days. According to the original itinerary, they'd been due to be toasting their A Level results in Ko Phi Phi, "gazing out at monolithic rocks in an azure blue sea," Alex had read from her guidebook. But it looked as though they would be in Oxxi's Place yet again, gazing out at a sea of drunks.

When Rosie stormed off, Jamie came and sat by Alex and stuck at her side for the rest of the morning, sympathizing, saying everyone was tired of Rosie. Of her strops and her whining.

She finally gave him the slip after lunch, when he went to the toilet. She just needed some time on her own. She knew he'd be hurt, but he was in her face all the time now. Egging her on to fall out with Rosie, pressing her to go traveling with him instead. She couldn't face telling him there was no way she'd do that. She could see the vulnerability in his eyes. She couldn't tell him the truth—she just didn't fancy him.

Alex went for a walk down to the river, to watch the boats and clumps of watercress gliding on the current. She'd said to Rosie that she'd go off alone, but she knew in her head she wouldn't. She was too nervous. What was she going to do? Her mind kept returning to Jake. He was lovely. She wasn't sure her mum would approve—he definitely needed a shower and to cut his toenails—but her mum wasn't here to cast her beady eye on him . . .

He was a bit of a lost soul—and Alex couldn't resist a lost soul. The idea of having someone to rescue, like Lizzy with Mr. Darcy or Belle with the Beast, was so romantic. It could occupy her for hours.

She knew that Jake had been to university but it hadn't worked out. He'd told her on their first date—she was calling it a date even if it had been him showing her where to eat safely. He said he hadn't got on with his tutor so he'd decided to leave. Alex thought it was a bit extreme but she hadn't liked to say so.

"What did your mum and dad say?" she'd asked instead. It was the first thing she'd thought of when he told her. She'd imagined telling her mum and the hurt it would cause.

"Oh, they didn't care," he'd said. "I'm an adult. I didn't need their approval." But he couldn't look her in the eye.

"When are you planning to go home?" She'd tried to change the subject.

"Not sure. No plans."

He hadn't spoken again as they walked back to the guesthouse, and she'd been sure he wouldn't ask her out again. But when they got to the end of their alleyway, he'd cleared his throat and she'd stopped.

"The truth is that I fucked it all up. My family doesn't know, but I couldn't hack it at uni. I failed and I couldn't tell them. They had so much invested in me being a success. It's all they ever talked about. They were so proud of me doing law."

"Mine are a bit like that. I feel like they're planning my future for me sometimes. They want me to succeed so hard it hurts. It's a huge pressure."

Jake nodded. "I nearly went home last Christmas. I had a ticket but I knew it meant telling them everything and whenever I thought about telling them the truth, I could see them standing on the station platform, waving me off to university. And I chickened out. And ended up here."

"Do they know what you're doing now?"

"No. It's been another fuckup. I can't get into it now. I rang recently when I was a bit pissed. I'd missed my mum's birthday and I just wanted to hear their voices but I didn't know what to say when my mum answered."

Alex had reached out to touch his hand.

"I'll get in touch with them properly when I've sorted myself out," he'd said, his voice shaky.

"You should, Jake," she'd said. "Ring them!"

He'd sort of nodded. "I'll see. Thanks for listening. But please don't tell anyone about what I've said."

"'Course not."

She'd wondered as she walked up the stairs why he'd chosen her to tell his secrets to, but she didn't really care. He had; that was all that mattered. She found herself singing in the shower as she imagined falling into his arms and what those lips would feel like. Not that he'd given her any sign of taking the next step. He hadn't even held her hand yet. Still, there was time. She'd work on it. She'd started putting on a bit of makeup to make him notice her in that way.

She hugged herself when she thought about him noticing her. Then stopped. She needed to get a move on. Rosie was already hurling herself at him. She was shameless. So Alex would have to be, too. She tried to imagine Rosie's face when she announced Jake was coming to Phi Phi Island with her. That would stop her blond ponytail bobbing for a bit. Alex texted Jake before she lost her nerve and asked if he wanted to go for a drink later. He replied straightaway: *Great. Take you to my favorite place . . .*

She didn't get back until nearly six o'clock and Jamie was still sitting there, waiting for her.

"Good grief, Jamie, have you been there all day?"

"Where have you been?" he said. "I was worried."

"I'm fine. I just needed to clear my head," she said. She caught a glimpse of herself in the mirror behind the bar. She looked all lit up. Jamie looked so miserable, she gave his arm a squeeze and told him she was sorry.

"That's okay. Where shall we go to get something to eat tonight?"

"Ah . . . Actually, I'm going with Jake to one of his favorite bars."

Jamie's face fell and she felt irritated. She had every right to go out with Jake, but she didn't say anything. She didn't say that she was more excited than she'd been about a boy for ages. That Jake had such nice eyes. And lovely hands. And that she was going to wear that top her mum didn't approve of. She'd tell Mags later.

Jamie just looked at her with his mouth open.

"Alex," he croaked. But she didn't want to hear. She was sailing away from him on her way up to her room to shower and get ready for Jake.

"Be careful," he called after her as she climbed the stairs.

FORTY-ONE

The Detective

THURSDAY, SEPTEMBER 4, 2014

Five hours later, Sparkes was trying to drink a cup of coffee in the staff canteen. But it curdled in his mouth as it met the all-pervading residue of embalming fluid. The aftertaste of death.

"Right, then," he said when Salmond joined him with a copy of the pathologist's preliminary findings. "Where are we on this? Anything we didn't hear in the mortuary?"

"No, don't think so. She's sending oral, vaginal, and anal swabs to the lab with the other tissue samples. It's a twenty-eight-day turn-around at the moment, so we're looking at the beginning of the month for the results unless we call in favors and push them up the schedule. But she's listed the bruises, defensive scratches, a fractured hyoid, torn fingernails, all indicating manual strangulation. It's a bloody scandal this wasn't picked up by the police in Bangkok. You wouldn't have needed a postmortem to see the external marks. Just a pair of eyes and a brain."

"Yes, let's stick to the facts as we know them, shall we, Zara? I'm assuming no cause of death is mentioned in the prelim?"

He had a copy of the Thai death certificate for Alex O'Connor in front of him, which stated, "Inhalation of smoke and toxic gases."

"No, but she's put, 'No soot detected in the airways beyond the vocal chords.'"

"It appears she was not alive when the fire started," Dr. Mortimer had said to Sparkes in the mortuary without lifting her head from the exposed trachea.

"**W**hat time is Rosie Shaw's PM starting?" Sparkes looked at his watch.

"We've got about twenty minutes. Do you want a sandwich?"

"What do you think?"

"I'm having one. Can't do this on an empty stomach."

"On you go."

He waited until his DS was out of earshot and rang Eileen at home.

"Hello, you," she said. "I've got my guardian angel, Helen, here, telling me I need to eat more." Helen, the palliative nurse, was no doubt sitting in the old Lloyd Loom chair by Eileen's downstairs bed. *I should be there.* The thought flitted through Sparkes's head, trailing guilt behind it.

Eileen was disappearing in front of him, her color changing to gray as if she were fading away. He'd kissed her three times that morning as he left. He couldn't stop kissing her.

"Sorry, just need to this morning," he'd told her.

"Don't apologize, Bob. Give me another one," she'd said.

"**H**elen's right," he said now. "How are you doing? What time is Sam coming this afternoon?" Their daughter came every day, swapping roles to become the mother.

Their son came and went, often hovering in the doorway as if he feared he might catch something or get too involved.

Eileen made a supreme effort with him, forcing brightness into her voice, laughing at his stories. It was heartbreaking to see. It made the dread uncurl its black tendrils to choke Sparkes.

"Don't be hard on him, Bob. He's so afraid of it," Eileen had said after one particularly difficult visit. "Nothing bad has happened in his life until now. He's never had to deal with failure."

"Failure? You've got cancer, Eileen. It's not a life choice."

"Mmmm. Well, I suspect our son secretly sees it as such. He can't help it. It's the way he's made."

"We'll need to go and see the parents when the Shaw PM is over," Sparkes said as soon as Salmond returned with a disgusting-looking egg mayo sandwich. He almost preferred the smell of formalin. "I'd rather tell them tonight. It's not fair to keep them waiting. Are you all right to work late?"

"No problem, boss. Neil's got a parent evening at school, anyway."

"Good. Who's the Family Liaison Officer?"

"Wendy Turner. I'll ring her in a minute and brief her."

Aoife Mortimer came through the canteen swing doors and waved.

"Just getting an energy bar. Are you ready?"

She eyed DS Salmond's bulging sandwich and raised an eyebrow. "Is that wise?"

Sparkes couldn't help a small rush of anticipation when he entered the mortuary for the second time. He wondered if Aoife Mortimer felt the same. He glanced at her profile. The hood covered her whole face, but he knew, beneath it, she was giving nothing away.

He eagerly scanned Rosie Shaw's face and neck for telltale bruises and hesitated. He leaned forward in his chair to get a better look but there was nothing to see.

"No visible signs of bruises or other external injuries to upper body," Dr. Mortimer dictated into her tape recorder. "Gray-blue discoloration of skin pronounced, indicating decomposition of tissue pre-embalming."

"She didn't die the same way as Alex O'Connor, did she?" he said and heard the note of disappointment in his voice.

"It doesn't look like it."

Dr. Mortimer was swabbing the teeth and palate for samples. "What appear to be soot particles present in mouth," she told her machine.

"But not in the trachea," she added hours later. "This girl wasn't breathing when the fire started either."

"So what killed her?" Bob Sparkes said, more to himself than to the pathologist. "Was she attacked?"

"It's far too early to say. I can see no external wounds or defensive injuries. I've taken swabs and samples for toxicology and we'll have to wait for the lab results. Sorry I can't say more."

"When can we have the full report?"

"The usual length of time, Bob. We're looking at mid-October for the full monty. They're stacking up in the labs."

"We can't wait that long. I'll put through a request to prioritize the DNA swabs from both girls. We need to know who's done this."

"Well, good luck with that."

She was so deep in her head, she didn't realize what she was seeing at first when she pushed open the door. She knew she needed to check in with the mums—it was her day for a text—and was planning what to tell them.

Rosie was sitting cross-legged on the bed with Alex's handbag emptied onto the sheet in front of her.

"Oh," she said, startled, and started stuffing brochures and timetables back in. "Sorry, I was looking for a paracetamol."

Alex nodded uncertainly. That's what she was doing, wasn't it?

"They're in the side pocket of my backpack. Where they always are."

"Oh yeah. Sorry. I forgot."

Alex picked up her bag. The air in the room felt charged, as if something was about to happen. Something bad.

"My arm is feeling better," Rosie said, pointing to the site of her tattoo, as if everything was normal, but her voice was high and tight.

"Good."

"Are you going out?"

"Yes. I came up to get changed. I'm going out with Jake."

"Oh!" Rosie pulled a face.

"Yes."

They were talking but not looking at each other. Alex pulled her emergency wallet out of her bag.

"I'll come, too. I'll pay tonight," Rosie said quickly. Too quickly.

"No, thanks," Alex muttered, opening her wallet. "We want to be on our own. Anyway, I need to get the money out for my bus ticket. I'm losing track of how much I'm spending. I never seem to have as much money as I thought. Maybe I should keep a record . . ."

"Stop fussing," Rosie snapped.

Alex put her wallet on her lap.

"I'm definitely leaving," she said.

"I want to stay."

"Then stay."

Alex went to pull out the notes she'd carefully counted the day they'd arrived. They weren't there.

"What's the matter?" Rosie said loudly, her concern sounding fake and overdone.

Alex looked up at her. "It's gone. My money's gone."

"No! Someone must have taken it."

She isn't going to win any Oscars, Alex thought.

"Where is it, Rosie?"

"What the hell do you mean? I don't know!"

"That's what you were doing when I came in. First you try and take Jake; now you're taking my money."

Rosie's face was a dull red. "I . . . I . . . I can't believe . . ." She tried to voice her outrage, but Alex could see her mask slipping. There'd be tears next.

Rosie didn't disappoint. She cried like a baby and Alex sat with the lump in her stomach hardening with every sob. She couldn't bring herself to touch Rosie. To comfort her. She wanted to punch her.

"Where is the money?" she asked, hardly recognizing her own voice. It startled Rosie, too.

She pulled two twenty-pound notes from under her thigh. "This is all I've got. The rest is gone." She hiccupped.

"All of it? There was two hundred pounds in there when I last checked."

"I'm so sorry, Alex. I was going to put it back. I will—I'll pay it back. What are you going to do? Don't tell anyone, please."

"I don't know what to do," Alex said, more to herself than to Rosie. She didn't. She felt totally alone and vulnerable. She wished more than anything that she could go home and her mum could sort it out. She needed time to think.

"I'm going to move into another room," she said finally. "I don't want to be in here with you. I can't trust you."

Rosie's weeping intensified.

"Don't hate me," she wailed.

"Shut up, Rosie. It's always about you, isn't it? How do you think I feel?"

"Upset. I know you're upset. I can explain . . ."

"Can you? I doubt it."

"Alex, listen to me. Please. I've got myself into trouble."

FORTY-TWO

The Detective
THURSDAY, SEPTEMBER 4, 2014

"Knew it," DS Salmond said as she buckled herself in.

"Don't get smug. No one likes a smart-arse," Sparkes muttered. "Is the Family Liaison Officer in place?"

"Yep, Wendy is all sorted. She's there. The meeting is at the O'Connors' house."

"Well, come on, then. I need to get home tonight at some point."

"'Course, boss. Sorry."

DC Wendy Turner opened the door and pulled a worried frown. "They're all very agitated, sir."

"Thanks for the heads-up. Hardly surprising, really."

Sparkes put on his professional face as he walked through the sitting room door and went to shake hands with everyone.

"What did the postmortems show, Inspector? What news have you got?" Lesley said, halting the attempt at formalities.

"Give him a moment, love. We're here to listen, Inspector," Malcolm said.

Sparkes hated these moments. Some coppers loved them. The Poirot complex, he called it. That moment when, in their heads, they call everyone into the library and give them all the answers. He knew the huge effect his words were going to have on these four people and hesitated. Nothing could be unsaid after this. He wanted to choose his words carefully, but the overthinking made him stumble.

"Thank you. Er . . . I know you've been waiting so I'll come straight to the point. Right, well, we have the preliminary findings from the postmortems. It's not the full report, obviously, but what the pathologist has found is, er, evidence that suggests neither girl was alive at the time of the fire."

The faces staring up at him looked lost in his fog of words. Why hadn't he kept it simple?

"Sorry, what I'm saying is that it appears both girls were already dead when the fire started," he clarified, and the faces lit up with understanding for a split second, then collapsed.

"They were murdered, weren't they?" Jenny Shaw blurted. "Somebody killed them and set the place on fire to hide what they'd done."

"How did they die?" Malcolm murmured.

"We are not sure about Rosie yet, but there are signs that Alex may have been strangled," Sparkes said, keeping steady eye contact with Malcolm O'Connor. The father's jaw pulsed and his lips pursed to contain his grief.

"Strangled. Who strangled our darling girl?" Lesley screeched. "Where is Jake Waters? He must know something. Only the guilty hide, don't they?"

"Or the frightened," Sparkes added.

"What would he be frightened of? The truth?"

"We need to take a step back here, Lesley. I know how devastating this news must be, but we need evidence, not guesswork and accusations, at this point. Let's wait for the report from the lab to see if there's anything to prove who was involved."

"But how long will that take?" Lesley wailed.

"The full report will take another four to six weeks, as you've probably been told by Wendy. But we've asked the lab to prioritize some of the tests. We may have results next week, but I can't promise."

"But what about Rosie?" Mike Shaw asked from behind Sparkes. He was standing near the door as if about to make his escape. "Was she strangled, too?"

Sparkes turned to him. "We don't know yet, Mike. There are no visible signs of injury on her body," he said carefully. "But the labs may help us understand how she died."

They all fell silent, struggling to absorb the tsunami of information. It was Malcolm O'Connor who spoke first.

"Why didn't the Thai police find this out?"

"I don't know," Sparkes said. "We will be sharing these findings with them and talking to them."

"You might as well not bother," Lesley said. "They don't care what happened to the girls. But you do, don't you?"

I t was seven thirty when they emerged, but Sparkes was not ready to go home. One more thing. He liked a tidy desk.

"Right, quick trip to southeast London," he said and pretended not to hear Salmond's muttered "You're kidding."

"I thought you needed to get home, sir," she said.

"I do, but Sam is with her mum. And I want to get things finished."

He rang to tell Kate they were on their way.

"Is your husband home?"

"My husband? Have you found Jake? Can't you tell me what's going on?" Kate had pleaded.

"No, it's best to talk face-to-face."

K ate Waters's house was not what he expected. He thought journalists and hospital consultants earned a fortune, but this was a modest terrace, probably ex-council, within a shout of the market traders in Roman Road. Still, London prices meant it was probably worth three times as much as his place.

There were red geraniums wilting in a terra-cotta planter on the windowsill.

"She wants to water those," DS Salmond said, pushing the bell.

Steve Waters greeted them at the door. He was shorter than Bob Sparkes and the detective felt unaccountably pleased.

"You must be DI Sparkes," he said pleasantly. "And DS Salmond. Please come in, both of you."

Kate was sitting quietly in the living room. The television was on and her laptop was open on her knees. She closed it, muted the telly, and stood when the officers entered.

"Hello," she said. "You made good time." She sounded very calm, but Sparkes noticed the hint of a tremor around her mouth.

"Come and sit down and tell us what this is all about." Steve Waters guided them to a sofa.

"This shouldn't take long—thank you, Dr. Waters."

"It's Mr. Waters—sorry, not important. It's just, surgeons are misters for some reason . . ."

Of course they are. Sparkes cursed his stupidity.

"Yes, sorry. Well, anyway. The postmortems of Alex O'Connor and Rosie Shaw were carried out today."

"Ah!" Kate breathed.

"It appears neither girl was alive when the fire started."

Kate held his gaze.

"How did they die, then?"

"There are still tests to complete, but we have strong indications that one of the girls was strangled."

Steve Waters gasped.

"And you have come all the way from Southampton to tell us this?" Kate said. "Why?"

She knew why. Sparkes knew that she knew.

"Is this about Jake?" Steve asked quietly.

"Yes, Mr. Waters, it is. We are launching a murder investigation and this development has made it even more urgent that we speak to your son. To see what he may have seen or heard in the days and hours before the fire."

"Of course," Steve said.

"We also need a sample of Jake's DNA—from a hairbrush or toothbrush, that kind of personal item."

"You want his DNA? Absolutely not," Kate said loudly. "You just said you wanted to talk to him as a possible witness. What are you not telling us? The Thai police have not accused him of anything. It is only the papers who've pursued him. And there is nothing to connect him—"

"We are gathering evidence all the time, Kate. The picture is getting clearer about what happened to Alex and Rosie. A DNA sample could rule him out of our inquiries."

There was a pause.

"We haven't got anything, anyway," she said, but she sounded less sure now. "He didn't leave a toothbrush here—he'd left home. And we've cleared out his room."

"You'd be surprised what we can get DNA samples from. Can I send someone from forensics?"

"Oh, all right, then. If it will help rule him out." He could hear the fear in her voice, feeding her aggression.

"What else have you found out?"

"We'd prefer not to disclose that at the moment," Sparkes said firmly, giving his sergeant a warning look. He didn't want to say anything about the sex swabs.

"I see," Kate said.

"When are you putting this out to the media? Are you holding a press conference?" She was back in charge of the conversation, and

Sparkes found himself sitting up a bit straighter. He wondered if this was how her interviewees felt.

"Oh God!" her husband whispered to himself.

"They'll have to have one, Steve. It's the next step," Kate said.

"Yes," Sparkes said. "We're planning one for the morning. We'll be asking for the public's help in tracing Jake—and any other possible witnesses."

"Who else are you looking for?" Kate asked.

Ever the reporter.

FORTY-THREE

The Reporter

THURSDAY, SEPTEMBER 4, 2014

When they've gone, I go into the downstairs loo and lock the door. I can't bear to see Steve. He's sitting on the sofa with his head in his hands and I think he may break down. I've seen him cry only a handful of times since I met him—when the boys were born we'd cried together, then when his dad died last year. And when I left him that time. The boys had been small and he'd never been there—always at work or thinking about work. I'd just wanted to make him realize, but I'd gone too far and it had taken months to get us back on an even keel.

I felt detached when Bob was telling us about the postmortems. I sort of clicked into reporter mode, weighing the information, writing the intro in my head. But this is us. Not some story to be picked over for the best quote.

They've found someone's DNA on the girls rings in my head like an alarm. *They will know who did this.*

Get a grip, Kate, I tell myself in the mirror. *Jake had nothing to do with this. And Steve needs you.*

He looks up when I come back.

"What are we going to do, Katie?" he says. I knew he'd ask that. He wants me to take charge of this, to make it all right.

"What are we going to tell people?"

"Well, they know the police want to talk to Jake. It's been all over the press."

"But they don't know the girls were murdered, do they?"

"One of them," I say. "One of them was murdered. We don't know about the other one."

"For fuck's sake, Kate. Stop nitpicking. One girl or both girls—it doesn't change anything, does it?"

It doesn't. "I'm sorry. You're right," I agree. "We need to tell the family quickly. Now. You ring your mum and I'll ring Freddie."

We pick up our phones and I go into the hall. I can hear him apologizing to Dorothy for ringing so late. *She's probably in bed. We should have rung tomorrow morning. She won't sleep now.*

"Sorry, Ma," Steve says. "Just wanted to let you know that there's been some news about the fire in Bangkok. Well, I suppose it's about Jake in a way . . ."

Freddie picks up and I'm immediately thrust into the surround sound of a rowdy pub.

"Mum! Has something happened?"

I want to shout "No"—he's too young to bear the full load of my fears—but he is part of this. "Sort of. Can you go somewhere quieter for a moment, love?"

"Have you heard from Jake? Has he turned up?"

"No, not yet. There's some stuff that's going to be in the papers. One of the girls was murdered."

"Not Jake . . ." he whispers.

"They don't know who killed her, Freddie. But they are going to announce a murder investigation in the morning and say they urgently need to speak to your brother. I wanted to warn you."

"Oh, Mum!"

"I know, love. I know. They want a DNA sample. To rule Jake out," I say and hear how hollow this sounds. "But we haven't got anything left of his at home."

"I have," Freddie says. "I've kept some of his T-shirts and that baseball cap he wore to annoy you."

"Have you? I didn't know."

"Yeah," he says, and I hear the tremble in his voice. "They're in my cupboard. Stupid, I know, but they smelled of him. I missed him, Mum."

And I hadn't noticed. I'd been too busy putting on my own brave face.

"I'm sorry, Freddie. We'll find him."

Later, Steve and I sit hugging our cups of coffee in silence.

"He had nothing to do with this, Steve," I say again.

"No."

"I'm going to find out who did do it." And I suddenly feel lighter. "That's what I'm going to do. I'm going to find the people who were at the guesthouse. Find the others. That's what I'm good at."

Not being a mother, plainly. But I can do this.

"Katie," Steve says, "you can't make this right by banging on doors and hounding policemen. Jake is our son. We are responsible for him. And if he has done something wrong, we have to stand by him and help him take his punishment."

I stare at him. He doubts Jake. He can't be part of my plan, and I draw the fences around me closer.

I ring Joe Jackson from the kitchen and give him the heads-up about the postmortems.

I can hear the excitement in his voice building as I drip feed him the details I've decided to share.

"Dead before the fire started?" he says. "Strangled? Bloody hell. And I can file this now?"

"Yes, Joe. It's going to be put out there by the police in the morning. You'd better ring the O'Connors and Shaws straightaway. You can include a quote from me, that this must be a heartbreaking development for the families but there is nothing to connect my son with these deaths."

"Got it."

"And, Joe, you owe me big-time now. I'm going to call in favors. Understood?"

"Absolutely. Happy to help."

We'll see.

Mama had given her a hard look when Alex asked for her own room.
"You are not sharing with Rosie?"

Alex had given her a hard stare back.

"No. I need another room. Just for me."

She was not in the mood to explain or discuss. She needed her own space. End of.

Rosie's confession had left her shell-shocked. She'd realized she didn't really know this girl sharing her room, but nothing could have prepared her for what Rosie had revealed.

Her friend had stopped crying abruptly, perhaps realizing Alex wasn't buying the little-girl act, and wiped her eyes on her T-shirt.

She'd lain back on the pillows, speaking to the ceiling, maybe so she didn't have to see Alex's reaction, and announced that she'd had to get away from home because she was going to fail her A Levels.

"I don't care, but my mum is going to go mad."

"How do you know you're going to fail? Maybe you're just being paranoid," Alex had said.

"I wish. I missed an exam. A whole paper. I went to a party that turned into an all-nighter. I hooked up with someone and didn't wake up in time. Mum thought I was on a study weekend with my biology group. But I needed to have some fun. I was sick of studying. I don't want to go to uni anyway. That's what my mum wants, not me."

Now that she'd started, Rosie almost looked like she was enjoying herself. She was the center of attention again, where she belonged. And everything was someone else's fault. She was always the innocent victim.

"Never mind that. What about my money? Why were you stealing from me?"

"I wasn't stealing it. I told you I was borrowing it. I'll pay you back, Alex."

"When?" But Rosie was telling the bare lightbulb hanging over her the next installment of her sob story.

"I had to, Alex. Everything cost much more than I thought. The tattoo was four thousand baht, remember? Even though I didn't get the big one."

"You didn't have to have it done," Alex exploded, but the excuses continued to flow as Rosie examined her glittery fingernails, which she'd spent the afternoon painting.

"And everyone is ripping me off."

"Who?"

"Well, the tattoo place. And . . . and the scooter bloke."

"What scooter bloke?"

For the first time, Rosie sat up and looked at her.

"It wasn't my fault, Alex. Honest. I hired a scooter from him. Lars wanted to ride round Bangkok on one, but he didn't have enough money for the deposit, so I paid it. It was a proper rental shop and we were having a great time, but we left it outside a bar while we had a drink. It was all locked up, I swear. But when we came out, it was gone. The bloke went mad when we told him. He turned round and said I owed him thousands of baht to replace it."

"Seriously? What were you thinking? It's one of the best-known scams in Thailand. It's on every travelers' forum. These con men have duplicate keys to the bikes and steal them themselves, then charge you."

"I didn't know."

"Whatever. Why didn't you tell me?"

"Because I knew you'd go mad. I thought I could sort it out myself and you wouldn't need to know."

Alex almost laughed. Almost.

"Did you tell the police?"

"I wanted to, but the scooter-shop man has my passport. I had to leave it as a guarantee when we hired the bike. I asked Mama if she'd come to the police with me, but she said I'd be arrested if I didn't have a passport. And that the police would probably plant drugs on me. But she said if I gave her money, she'd pay them off. She'd sort it out. She said she'd make sure I didn't get into trouble. She says she's done it for foreigners before."

Rosie stole a look at Alex before collapsing back and burying her face in the pillow.

There was a stunned silence. All Alex could think was, *You've ruined everything.*

"I should have told you," Rosie said quietly.

"You think? Have you told your mum?"

"Of course not."

"What about your dad? Maybe he could lend you the money to get your passport back."

Rosie sat up and tried to laugh. "He won't. I had to threaten to tell Imogen about his latest girlfriend to get the money to come here in the first place. I saw him snogging one of the shop assistants in a car outside his work. It was a bit of luck. He'd never have paid up otherwise. But he gave me the money to shut me up and get me out of the way. I don't know where he found it. He said he was completely broke, living on credit cards. But he did."

Alex stared at her, *Who are you?* running through her head.

. . .

"Here." Mama thrust a key into her hand. "Ground floor. Through there." As she pointed, Alex noticed that her silver-painted fingernails matched Rosie's. *Thick as thieves,* she thought. *Thieves anyway.*

"Thanks." Alex shouldered her hastily packed bags and tramped off into the gloom at the back of the guesthouse.

Rosie came clattering down the stairs, calling her name, but Alex ignored her. She was too furious to say anything sensible. She'd tell Mags all about it.

"Mama, she knows," she heard Rosie say as she marched off.

FORTY-FOUR

The Detective

FRIDAY, SEPTEMBER 5, 2014

Mags Harding rang that morning.

"I need to talk to someone about Alex O'Connor and Rosie Shaw," she told the switchboard operator, her voice shaking. "I've just seen the news on the television."

"All right, let's slow down a bit. How do you know Alex and Rosie?" the operator asked gently. "Let's start there."

Minutes later the teenager's call was put through to DS Salmond, who listened carefully, then pitched up at Sparkes's office door.

"We've had a call in about the girls, sir," she said.

"That was quick. What are they saying? Anything about Jake Waters?"

"Yes, in a way, sir. It's about what was going on before the girls died. What was really going on. The caller says that Alex was her best friend and wrote her e-mails about how things had gone wrong pretty much from the beginning. There were all sorts of problems and fights."

"Really? What about?"

"Sex and drugs and rock and roll, it seems. According to the e-mails, Rosie and Alex were arguing over Jake Waters."

"Were they? So they definitely knew him. He was there."

"Oh yes. And there's much more. Rosie had got herself into trouble with a con man. And in her last e-mail Alex said she had caught her stealing her money. Oh, and that Rosie had blackmailed her father into giving her the money to go to Thailand."

"Bloody hell! But why didn't our tech genius DC Collins see these e-mails on his trawl?"

"She used a different e-mail account. One we didn't know about. She used it for private stuff, according to her best friend."

"So, who is the best friend? I thought that was Rosie."

"Apparently not. Call in was from Margaret Harding—known as Mags. She was the girl who was due to go to Thailand with Alex and dropped out."

"Oh yes, Rosie was a late substitute."

"Alex was e-mailing her friend Mags the whole time, apparently. The last message was on August the twelfth—more than forty-eight hours after the parents got their final one. These e-mails paint a very different picture from the one we've seen on social media. The 'bezzies on tour' was a bit of fiction, it appears. Alex told Mags that she hated Rosie."

"Why didn't she get in touch sooner, when the girls were first reported missing?"

"She'd been sworn to secrecy by Alex and she didn't want to get anyone into trouble. The e-mails Mags Harding has forwarded to me are pretty explicit—not parent reading material. And, like everyone else, she thought the girls would turn up. And then when they did, she thought their deaths were an accident and no one needed to know about the e-mails. But they might now. Now it's a murder inquiry."

"Right. Let's have a look, then—and get Collins onto it."

The e-mails—sometimes three a day—cataloged the growing tension between the two girls in Bangkok, the fights, the silences, the anger, and the theft.

Sparkes started reading them out at random. "*Rosie is completely out of it tonight. Can't get any sense out of her.*'"

"*Rosie is legless and sleeping her way through the boys in the guesthouse. This isn't why I came to Thailand. She's ruining everything.*'"

"*'Another row with Rosie. Had enough.'*"

"*'Rosie is hitting on Jake. UNBELIEVABLE!'*"

"Why didn't we know any of this before?" he said. "We were told they were having a great time."

Salmond got up Alex's Facebook page. "Because that's what Alex wanted us to think. Look, for example, on August the second. When she told Mags that Rosie was sleeping her way through the blokes, she posted a photo here on Facebook of the two of them clinking glasses. *'Living the dream with my roomie,'* it says here."

"Why would she pretend to be having a good time?"

Salmond looked at him. "Because that's what she wants her 'friends' to think. This is her public profile. It has nothing to do with what's really going on in her life."

"Public profile?" Sparkes said. "She was a schoolgirl from Winchester, not on *I'm a Celebrity . . . Get Me Out of Here.*"

"Ah, but we are all stars of our own reality shows now, sir. Didn't you know?"

"Shut up, Zara. What a load of bollocks. Whereas, these"—he waved at the screen—"raise some bloody serious questions about what was really going on on this trip."

The drugs, the casual sex, the stealing. The high-risk behavior. Was this why they died?

"We need a statement from Mags Harding asap and full access to her e-mails from Alex."

"She's on her way in and bringing her phone so we can check it."

"Right. Call me when she gets here—I want to be there for the interview. I suppose I ought to call Bangkok with this, for appearance's sake . . ."

"I'll talk to the Thais," Salmond said. "The big question is, do we share this with the families?"

Sparkes scrolled back through the e-mails, giving himself time to think. "I think we have to. If we are passing them on to the Thai police, they may leak. I don't know how secure they'll be and it will be a hundred times worse if they see them in the press first."

"Do you want me to do it?"

"No, I will. Tell the Family Liaison Officer I need to see them at midday, after we've interviewed Mags Harding. I'll go to them. I'm going to tell Mike Shaw first as he's the star turn in these. He might clam up in front of the others. Then his ex-wife and the O'Connors. Don't imagine that's going to be pretty."

He tried to imagine Jenny Shaw's reaction when he told her. *Disbelief, probably. No one wants to hear that their child has a dark side. Especially when she's dead.*

And the last line Alex had written to Mags was ricocheting round his skull. It said simply:

"I hate Rosie. I could kill her."

FORTY-FIVE

The Reporter

FRIDAY, SEPTEMBER 5, 2014

I've watched the press conference three times already, the highlights playing on a loop and on the ticker tape running underneath the perky Sky News presenter. Each time they use the photo of Jake I gave them, I close my eyes as if it is too bright to look at directly. I know it's coming—it's in exactly the same slot in the report—but it shakes me each time. Closes me down.

I'd decided to go into work this morning, but Steve was horrified at the idea.

"Why would you?" he'd said.

"Why wouldn't I? You are," I'd snarled.

"That's different, isn't it?"

He'd wanted to say his was a proper job that mattered. That people's lives depended on him. But he held himself back. Probably telling himself that now wasn't the time.

But I didn't let him get away with it. Why should I?

"What? What were you going to say? That my job isn't as important as yours?"

"Stop it, Katie. I wasn't going to say anything about your job. Look, neither of us has slept. We are both horribly stressed and you've been told to stay at home. I'm going to be late for my first patient. I've got to go. Go back to bed."

I'd let him kiss me good-bye and continued our row in my head while the kettle boiled. I won. I think I did. I wasn't going back to bed. I'd get on with something—keep busy.

But here I am instead, sitting and watching the rolling news and closing my eyes every fifteen minutes.

It is Joe who breaks the gogglebox spell. I've put my phone on silent and left it on the hall table to avoid talking to reporters. I hear it buzzing on the polished wood and turn up the telly. But Joe comes to my door and knocks. *Rap-rap-rappity-rap.* I've taught him well. I pull aside the net curtains and see him, in shirt and tie, looking at my flowers.

"I know, they need watering," I say when I open the door. "Come in quick. Is anyone else out there?"

"No, I did a recce before I knocked. Golden rule number hundred and twenty, isn't it?"

"Shut up. Coffee?"

"Go on, then. It'll be my third this morning. I'll be flying when I leave here."

"Why are you here, anyway? Why aren't you with the parents? Does Terry know?"

"Not exactly. I've filed the presser and they've sent Gail from features down to do the big interview."

Should have been me, I think, like the abandoned girlfriend at the back of the church. But Gail will do a lovely job.

"I told Terry I'm meeting a contact. Well, I am, really. You're my best contact."

"That, Joe, is tragic. Contacts are people who can tell you things—people who know stuff. Like coppers and politicians."

"Like you," he says. And he's right. I know the stuff he wants.

"So, big brownie points from Terry for the scoop last night, I imagine." I veer away from me.

He grins. A look of pure happiness. "He said, 'Fuck!' Terry's never said that before about any of my stories."

"I'm happy for you. Now sit down and I'll tell you what we're going to do."

We've made a list. I like a list. A tiny piece of order in a chaotic world. We're going to find the other witnesses, but we need more info to stand any chance of tracking anyone down.

"What have we got?" Joe says.

"I've rung Ross in Bangkok. Jake's friend. He says there were a couple of Dutch boys at the guesthouse. He thinks one might be called Lars."

"Well, we're halfway there, then . . ."

"Sarcasm is banned from this desk," I say, banging the kitchen table. "Okay, where is the information we need?"

"Internet. Traveler forums. Facebook. Instagram. Twitter," Joe says, his fingers twitching to get started.

"Yes, yes, but what about the actual people who know?"

"Well, Jake, obviously."

I shoot him a look. We've already had the "He had nothing to do with the death of those two girls" conversation.

"And Rosie and Alex," I say.

Joe looks confused.

"They were writing home, weren't they? Well, Alex was. Rosie seems to have left it to her to pass on their news. Alex can't have been texting and e-mailing just the parents. She was all over social media, so there might be other e-mails. We need to see them. She'll have dropped in all sorts of little bits and pieces of gossip about the others in that godforsaken hostel."

Joe lifts his head and looks at me. He raises his eyebrows and I nod.

"Yes, there may be stuff about Jake, too. But it could be information that could help him."

"I'll call DS Salmond. I'm ringing her every day, anyway. She's too busy to talk usually, but she might help."

"You need to work at it, Joe, to get her onside. Chat to her about the case, about the hours she's working, about police pay. About other stuff. You need to build a connection. Show her you're a reporter she can trust."

"Sounds a bit touchy-feely to me."

"Being a reporter is touchy-feely, you idiot. We're not here to observe the news happening through a telescope—or Google. You've got to plunge yourself into this job so you can feel things, see things up close, understand them. You've got to get your hands dirty. Right up to the elbows."

"All right. I've got it. Do I need to write it down?"

I go to swipe him with my notebook and laugh. I could hug him for making me laugh today.

"Right. Lecture over. So don't barge in today with a request to see the e-mails. She'll say no and put everyone on their guard. Who else has got the e-mails?"

"Mum and Dad?"

"I saw the ones they got when I did the first interview. They were pretty tame stuff about temples and tuk-tuks. We need to find the friends the girls confided in."

"I'm all over it," Joe says, bending over his screen, not speaking, scribbling notes before he burrows his way into the ether.

FORTY-SIX

The Mother

FRIDAY, SEPTEMBER 5, 2014

She'd watched the press conference too many times. So many times that she caught herself mouthing the words of DI Sparkes along with him while she waited for the photo of Alex and Rosie to pop onto the screen just after the headline.

And the photo of Jake Waters. She'd taped the whole segment and frozen the frame with his face staring out of the screen. Not the horrible photo on the beach, where he looked like the devil, but a new one where he looked like someone's son. He had glasses on and had wavy hair and a lopsided smile.

"Did you do this?" she asked the face. "Could you have done it?" She tried to imagine her own son hurting someone, but the image wouldn't come. Not her boy, then. But could someone else's? Could Kate's?

She looked up, startled, when Malcolm appeared at the door.

"Stop torturing yourself." He sighed.

"I keep looking for some sign in his face, Mal. What do people who strangle girls look like? Do they look like that? Normal?"

"I don't know, love. The police know about this sort of stuff, not me. I can't bear to keep going over and over what happened. I feel so terrible that I couldn't stop it." He sat down and cried silently, his shoulders heaving with the effort. Lesley looked at him and then back at the screen. She hit the rewind button and play, focusing on Bob Sparkes's face.

She'd boiled two eggs for breakfast and then lost heart, leaving them to harden and turn gray in the cooling water. Malcolm had still been sitting, white-faced, in the front room. She'd draped a throw from Alex's bed round his shoulders without saying a word, leaving him to his grief. She couldn't take his on as well. Not today.

Wendy Turner rang at ten. "Wendy? Is there any news? Has someone phoned in? Have they found Jake Waters?"

"Hello, Lesley. I see you were bothered by a reporter last night. You could have called me—that's what I'm here for."

"It was very late. I didn't want to bother you, and Joe Jackson already had the information anyway. We couldn't stop him writing it, could we?"

"No, I suppose not. Anyway, I'm calling to arrange a meeting with DI Sparkes. He wants to see you all to talk through some things. Can he come at midday?"

"Yes, of course. He can come earlier if he wants. What is this about?"

"No, midday is what he said. Let's wait until he gets there, okay?"

It wasn't, but nothing was within her control anymore. She'd have to bear the wait.

"How are you doing, Lesley?" Wendy asked her.

"Terrible. Malcolm has shut down completely and I'm just going through the motions."

"It might be worth talking to the doctor about getting something to help you cope."

"We don't need pills. We just need to find out who killed Alex."

"I know. But pills might help you get through this period of uncertainty."

Period of uncertainty. A new euphemism to add to the lexicon, Lesley thought. *This difficult time, your sadness, your grieving. No one has said, "While we find your daughter's murderer," yet. I wonder how long it will be before they do.*

"Thanks, Wendy. I'll talk to Mal about it."

She sat holding the phone in her hand, staring into space. This stasis was killing her. She dialed Kate Waters.

"Where is he?" she screeched. "Where is your murderer son?"

"Who is this?" Kate whispered, shock muting her voice.

"Lesley. It's Lesley. Did you know what he'd done? When you were pretending to be so concerned about us?"

"Of course I didn't. What is the matter with you? You are talking about my child. My son hasn't murdered anyone. The press and the police have got it completely wrong."

"That isn't what they're telling us."

"What are they telling you? Look, I understand how distraught you are. But my son had nothing to do with your daughter's death. Please believe me."

"You can't possibly be sure. You weren't there. And he was a druggie when he was at school—before he got chucked out. You said you didn't know about that either. So really, you don't much about him, do you?"

Kate put the phone down. Lesley tried to feel a moment of triumph, but she felt as dead as the line.

FORTY-SEVEN

The Detective

FRIDAY, SEPTEMBER 5, 2014

Sparkes cleared his throat. "I'm very sorry you were bothered by the media last night," he said, his nervous energy making his coffee cup ring like a bell as he stirred it.

"Bloody reporters," Jenny snapped. "Who told Joe Jackson about the postmortem results? We certainly didn't."

The others shook their heads firmly. They were crammed into Jenny's tiny kitchen this time: him, Wendy Turner, and the O'Connors. He looked at their tense faces and was quietly glad Mike Shaw wasn't there.

Sparkes had gone to see him first, at the carpet showroom. Shaw had looked sweaty and ill sitting in his office-cum-stockroom. He'd moved some flooring samples from a chair for the detective and they'd sat, knees almost touching.

"How are you bearing up?" Sparkes had said. They were so close, he could smell the saccharine notes of chewing gum on Shaw's breath and the stale cigarette smoke beneath. He'd sat back an inch, trying to find some personal space.

"Shit," Shaw had said. "I'm feeling shit. Sorry, but this is a fucking nightmare."

Sparkes had nodded sympathetically. "It must feel like that. It's a terrible time for you all." *And about to get worse.*

"Mike, now that we know more about how the girls died, we need to piece together what was going on in that guesthouse. I need your help."

Shaw had looked at him properly for the first time. "My help?" he'd said. "What can I tell you? I was thousands of miles away when this all happened. I hadn't heard from Rosie since before she left. I don't know anything." He'd spread his hands out in front of him.

Sparkes had reached for a folder he'd put on the floor beside him. "I want to show you some e-mails that Alex sent to a friend about Rosie," he'd said. "They may be important."

Shaw's eyes had widened and he'd reached for the sheaf of paper.

"I should warn you that you are mentioned," Sparkes had added.

Mike Shaw's hand had faltered, but he'd taken the printouts. Sparkes had watched as his eyes darted over the lines and knew he'd found the incendiary quote when his face suddenly sagged.

"Oh God, has Jenny seen these?"

This is all about you, then. Not your dead daughter, Sparkes had noted as he'd shaken his head.

"Not yet. I'm meeting the others in half an hour. I thought it would be fairer for you to see them first."

"As I'm the one having his character assassinated." Shaw had loosened his tie.

"Will you be coming to the meeting?"

"What do you think?" he'd muttered. "I wasn't going to go anyway. To be honest I thought it best to keep out of the way with the way things are between me and Jenny. We had another row after you left last night. She accused me of abandoning her and Rosie all over again. I just can't deal with it anymore, Inspector. Malcolm said he'd call me afterward."

Shaw had opened a drawer in his desk and taken out a packet of cigarettes. "I'll open a window," he'd said after lighting one and inhaling deeply.

"That would be good," Sparkes had said. "Isn't it illegal in the workplace?"

"Oh, bloody hell, go on—arrest me." Shaw had smiled grimly.

Sparkes had waved the smoke toward the window and carried on.

"I realize how difficult this is," he'd said, "but I need to ask you if what Rosie told Alex is true. About Rosie forcing you to give her money."

Shaw had sat up straight and stubbed the cigarette out in what Sparkes hoped was an ashtray hidden in the drawer. "I can't see that it has anything to do with what happened," he'd said.

"We need to test the truth of what Alex says. She also says Rosie was taking drugs. That there was jealousy over men they'd met and rows. That may have something to do with what happened. You do see that, Mike?"

Shaw had opened and closed his mouth as if about to deny everything but ended up nodding wearily. "I don't know if Rosie took drugs before she went—she might have done. I didn't really know what she was doing. I should have, but Jenny made it as difficult as possible. Changing arrangements, canceling visits at the last minute. I saw her less and less. She used Rosie to punish me for leaving. For being happy with Imogen . . ."

"But your daughter came to see you about the trip?" Sparkes had prompted.

"Yes. Rosie came." He'd put his head in his hands. "I hadn't seen her for ages. I thought when she got older she'd be free to choose to see me, but I guess Jenny had done a good job of turning her against me. Anyway, there was a horrible scene. She saw me having a quick fumble with one of the girls here—it was nothing, really, the sort of thing that happens in offices every day," he'd said.

Well, maybe in your office, Sparkes had thought, glad Zara Salmond wasn't there to bristle at the "boys will be boys" remark.

"But Rosie overreacted, said she'd tell Imogen. My new wife wouldn't have understood." Shaw had looked away. "You can imagine."

Sparkes had nodded and Shaw had plowed on. "I had to stop her, and she said she wouldn't say a word if I gave her the money for the bloody holiday."

"And where did you get the money? You told me you were paying the mortgage by credit card."

Shaw had laughed, a bark of fake amusement. "Don't play games with me, Inspector. You know where Rosie got it. From my mother."

"Did you arrange the transfer from her account?"

"I can't remember."

"And did your mother know?"

Shaw had stood to end the conversation. "This is old ground, Inspector. And we have covered it. My mother has withdrawn the allegation that money is missing. I'm sure you've got more important things to be getting on with. Like finding out how my daughter died."

"Yes." Sparkes had stood, too, and taken back the printout. "I'm going to show the e-mails to your ex-wife now."

"I'll make sure to switch my phone off," Shaw had said. "What a fucking nightmare."

There were tiny stacking stools to sit on in Jenny Shaw's kitchen, and everyone looked as if they were balancing on one cheek.

"I don't know who told Joe Jackson," Sparkes said. Well, he didn't for sure. He could take a good guess, but he didn't want the discussion to disappear down that rabbit hole for the next hour. He cleared his throat again, indicating a change of subject. But Lesley was deaf to his nonverbal signals.

The e-mails were going to remain the elephant in the room, swinging its trunk, biding its time.

"Never mind that—have you had any sightings of Jake Waters since the press conference?" she said. "Where is he?"

"No, Lesley, but we are getting helpful calls from the public." They weren't. There were the usual no-hopers. "He looks like the bloke in the chip shop. Except the chip shop bloke is black . . ." was his favorite so far.

He squeaked his chair closer to the table and leaned forward to try to gain their full attention.

"I've come to tell you about some information we've received this morning."

"What information? What are you talking about?" they chorused.

"We've been made aware of some e-mails that Alex sent to a friend, talking about difficulties she and Rosie were having."

"Difficulties? Alex didn't tell us about any difficulties. She said they were having a great time," Lesley said. "And why are we only hearing about them now?"

He sighed. "Because we've only just heard about them."

Jenny was speaking over them both, demanding to be heard.

"Tell us what is in these e-mails."

"Well, there are a number of them. They were written to Margaret Harding."

"Mags? She didn't say a word about them to me," Lesley said, alarm making her voice loud and high-pitched. The walls of the kitchen bounced the sounds, distorting everything into an angry buzz. "I called her right at the beginning to ask if she'd heard from Alex, and she said she'd heard nothing—just like us. Then she rang us to say how sorry she was when we got back from Thailand. Why didn't she say anything to us about this?"

Sparkes held up his hand to halt the flow.

"She'd promised Alex she wouldn't say anything at the time. The e-mails contained some tricky stuff that Alex didn't want you to know about. Mags is a teenager. Sometimes they don't make the best decisions. No doubt you'll have a lot of questions, but maybe it would be better if you read the e-mails before we discuss them—"

"Do they mention drugs?" Lesley said, cutting him off.

"Yes."

"Show them to us," Jenny barked.

"Please," Malcolm added.

Sparkes pulled out copies of the printout and DC Wendy Turner handed them round as he left them to read. He went out into the hallway. "I'll just check in with the office while you are looking at them," he'd said, desperate to escape for a moment. He looked at the photos of Rosie near the front door. Birthdays through the years. Variations on a girl in a party dress, blowing out candles on a cake and smiling for the camera.

The growing tension in the kitchen seeped out into the narrow hall, eddying round his feet as he texted Salmond. It was unbearable. The parents exclaimed quietly when they hit the first signs of trouble, the first accusation. But just "Oh!" Nothing more. Then they'd edged forward in an eerie silence, perhaps unsure of what they would find next.

Ten minutes later he was called back in by DC Turner. He could see the distress in their faces.

"Has anyone else seen these?" Malcolm took the lead.

"Only DS Salmond and myself. And Mike."

"Mike's seen them?" Jenny shrieked. "When? Why did he see them first? Why isn't he here now to answer your questions?"

"I saw him on his own this morning, Jenny."

"He couldn't face us, could he? Cowardly bastard. And up to his old tricks again. Still messing around with the office girls. The saintly Imogen won't forgive him, will she?"

"Stop it, Jenny!" Lesley slapped her hand down on the table. "This is not about you and your marriage breakdown. We need to focus on the girls."

Jenny reddened. "I'm sorry. I can't help it; it just brings everything back."

"That's natural, Jenny," DC Turner said quietly, closing the subject.

"Who else is going to see these e-mails?" Malcolm doggedly pursued his question.

"We won't be sharing them with anyone else apart from the Thai police at this stage," Sparkes said carefully.

"Thank God," Jenny said. "Isn't it enough that she's dead? Does she have to have her character dragged through the mud?"

Sparkes left that hanging.

None of them looked at one another while he talked about the possible ramifications of the information.

"Alex talks about other people at the guesthouse. Rosie's friend, possibly boyfriend, Lars, and the other Dutch boy, Diederik. And a boy she names as Jake and JW who she likes."

"Jake Waters," Lesley said quietly. "The Stoner, she called him. He's in loads of these e-mails. And she doesn't always like him. She says she wishes he would get out of her face in one of them."

"And anyway, most of this isn't true," Jenny added suddenly.

The O'Connors wheeled round to look at her.

"Oh, Jenny," Lesley said. "Of course it is."

Her daughter's litany of blame was dancing in Sparkes's head.

"My daughter wouldn't steal money. And she didn't take drugs," Jenny insisted. But her voice trembled.

"We don't know what they were doing," Lesley said.

No, Sparkes thought.

"Why didn't Alex tell us how unhappy she was?" Lesley whispered to her husband. "Why did she pretend?"

"I don't know, love," Malcolm said. "They were young and on their own. We all did foolish things when we were that age."

"I just don't believe it. I'm sorry," Jenny stated, as if for the record.

"We can't have this conversation," Lesley said. "You're too upset to think straight."

"Shut up, Lesley. I'm not," Jenny screeched. "I know exactly what I'm saying. This is all lies."

FORTY-EIGHT

The Reporter

FRIDAY, SEPTEMBER 5, 2014

After I put the phone down on Lesley, I can't speak. It isn't just rage at the hideous injustice of it. I feel shocked and bloodied, as if I've been physically attacked. *Where is your murderer son?* bangs against my heart.

In the silence, I slide down the wall to the hall carpet, trying to catch my breath and thoughts. Trying to hoist my "Jake Is Innocent" banner out of the dirt.

I don't know if Joe has heard any of it, but when he puts his head round the kitchen door, I have my answer. He looks as ashen as I feel.

"Are you okay? Was that Lesley O'Connor?" he says.

I nod.

"She's upset," he says, trying to comfort me. "She doesn't know what she's saying."

But she does.

"I don't want to talk about it. Come on, let's get on with something useful," I say and try to lever myself up. "How far have you got?"

"I've found someone," he says, pulling me to standing.

It had taken Joe less than thirty minutes to locate Mags Harding—the original travel companion—who featured heavily on Alex's

Instagram account back in the day. He rings the news desk to say he's going down to Hampshire on a tip and we head out to his car.

"What did they say?" I ask, plugging my phone into his charger.

"Sounds interesting . . . It's what they always say when they're not listening."

"It's good to be off radar sometimes, Joe. Come on, let's get a wiggle on."

He drives like Postman Pat, sticking to the speed limit all the way even when I shout, "For God's sake, why are you driving at one mile an hour? You're not ninety. Put your foot down!"

"And how many speeding tickets have you had this year?" he says. "You could probably pay for a new car with the fines."

That shuts me up. But I'm still screaming in my head when he slows for every traffic light.

Mags Harding is waiting for us at a burger bar. Her suggestion, obviously. She'd been excited when Joe had rung her from the house. We were her first reporters, she'd told him.

"Bingo," I'd crowed when he told me. "First in."

I let Joe order the double cheeseburgers for him and Mags—"I'll have a coffee, thanks"—while I warm her up. I introduce myself as Kate, Joe's colleague. No surnames to trigger any alarms.

"How are you doing? You must be so upset about Alex," I say, opening the door to our chat.

"Yes. We've . . . we'd been best friends since primary school. I still can't believe it's happened. First the fire and now they're saying she was murdered."

Tears fill her eyes and she chews at a nail.

"You were supposed to go with Alex to Thailand, weren't you?"

The finger comes out of her mouth and I notice a tiny sliver of nail drop onto the table. Mags flicks from sorrow to wide-eyed teen drama and back again. I can see her thinking about her escape from the clutches of death. Starring in her own survivor's special.

"It could've been me, couldn't it? I said that to my mum. If I'd gone. If I hadn't dropped out. It could've been me. It's so horrible."

"Absolutely. Why didn't you go, Mags?"

"It was the money. I really wanted to go and I kept thinking I'd start saving the next week, but it didn't happen. I just couldn't afford it. I kept putting off telling Alex. I thought she'd go mad. It was all she talked about. Thailand."

"And did she go mad?"

"No. I think she was too shocked to say much. I still feel guilty. I kept saying sorry, but I let her down, didn't I?"

She wants me to say she didn't. I pause while Joe puts the burgers on the table and disappears to fetch my drink.

"You mustn't beat yourself up. Her mum said she was having a brilliant time over there before . . . before all this," I say, watching her hand hovering over the stack of animal snouts and eyelids.

"Well . . ." Mags says. She takes a bite and limp lettuce falls out onto the table. She doesn't bother to pick it up. Salad's clearly not her thing.

Joe sits down and joins her.

I wait them out. It will take only a couple of minutes for them to devour their meals.

Mags wipes her mouth with a napkin and smiles at me with shiny lips.

"Better?" I ask and she nods.

"Sorry. I was starving."

"So, I was saying that Alex's mum said she was having a great time in Thailand . . ."

Mags pulls a face. "Not really. Actually, she was having a terrible time with Rosie."

"Why? I thought they were best mates."

"No, I was Alex's best friend," Mags corrects me. "Rosie was the last-minute substitute. I couldn't believe she was going with her. I said to her, 'Are you sure, Alex? Do you even know anything about her?' But she said it'd be okay. I knew it wouldn't. They didn't go out to-gether at the weekends like we did. Rosie hung around with the Dan-gerous Sisters at school—the girls who slept around and got drunk all the time. She wasn't one—a dangerous sister—her mum kept her on a tight lead after her dad left. But she wanted to be."

"And that wasn't Alex's idea of fun?"

"No way. People probably think we're a bit geeky. We like Harry Potter . . ." she adds.

"So how did they get on in Thailand?"

"Not good. Rosie was a complete nightmare, Alex said."

"Did you speak to Alex, then?" Joe says. "FaceTime her?"

"Once, right at the beginning, but the time difference kept catch-ing us out. We e-mailed most days instead."

"She must have been so glad to have you to talk to," Joe says, and I sip my coffee and sit back.

"We've always been able to talk. Peas in a pod, our mums said. We told each other everything. She knew I wouldn't tell anyone else. And I didn't. Her mum rang me when Alex stopped e-mailing, but I kept my promise. I said I hadn't heard from her that week—I wish I'd said something then, but I couldn't show Lesley some of the stuff Alex wrote. It was about drugs and sleeping with boys. Parents never want to hear that, do they? I only went to the police when they said Alex was murdered."

"The police? When did you do that?" I ask.

"Just this morning, actually. I thought that was why you got in touch."

"Right," I say. *Moving swiftly on* . . . "Anyway, it was a very good thing to do, Mags," I say, and she looks grateful.

"I'm not sure Jenny, Rosie's mum, will think so."

"Why? Because the e-mails said Rosie was having a wild time?"

"Well, yeah. But more because she'd stolen money from Alex and blackmailed her dad into paying for the trip."

Mags picks up the last of her onion rings and dips them in tomato sauce while I try to keep my face straight.

"That would be upsetting," I admit. "When did all this happen?" I say.

"It was in the last e-mail I got from Alex. A couple of days before the fire. She wrote to say she'd just caught Rosie trying to get off with the bloke Alex liked and then going through her handbag. She'd stolen nearly two hundred pounds. Spent it on a tattoo and God knows what. And then Rosie had turned round and said she'd caught her dad kissing another woman and she said she'd tell his new wife if he didn't give her money. Alex was so shocked. She told me she was going to leave Rosie there. She was considering coming home. Then nothing . . ."

"Wow," Joe says. "That's insane."

"I know. I'd never have believed it if Alex hadn't told me herself. Look, here—you can read the e-mail."

Good boy, Joe.

Mags hands him her phone and he scrolls down, tutting and raising his eyebrows like a pro.

"You don't mind if I take a copy of this?" he says, and Mags shrugs.

"Sure."

"I'll forward it to my e-mail and I'll put my number in your phone so you can contact me again."

She smiles and twirls a lock of hair between greasy fingers.

"Can I take a photo of you?" he asks, picking up his own phone.

Alex's new room was next door to the dorm and she could hear the murmur of the boys' voices as she vented her anger in an e-mail to Mags, listing Rosie's crimes in capital letters and ending I HATE ROSIE. I COULD KILL HER.

She wondered if she should tell someone else about the missing money. About Rosie. About Mama.

Maybe Jake can help. But what can he do? The money's gone. I'm never going to see it again. But people should know what's going on. Shouldn't they? Mama could do it to them, too.

Alex went to stand in the shower, wanting to block out her thoughts and sluice off the sour stickiness of her spent fury. It was a horror show in there, the smell of slimy tiles and testosterone marking it out as the boys' bathroom. She automatically blocked holes in the plasterboard walls with new twists of toilet roll before taking her clothes off—she was careful since the shadow at the window of their room. She closed her eyes and tried not to breathe until she was under the cold water.

She didn't want to get dressed in the swamp, so she wrapped a towel around herself, grabbed her clothes, and crept back to her room. But as she turned the key, Jake suddenly appeared from the dorm.

"Alex? What are you doing down here? Don't tell me you've used our shower? That must have been traumatic . . ."

She clutched her towel and clothes tighter, her exposed skin prickling under his intense gaze. "Er, I've moved into my own room. Look, I need to get dressed."

"Are you okay? You look upset. Are we still going for that drink tonight? When I've finished my shift? Come and find me in the bar when you're dressed."

She nodded and got through the door as quickly as possible. He was so nice. Maybe he'd know what to do.

The beer was poured and ready for her on the counter when she emerged. The bar was busy and Jake was serving, so she perched on a stool and waited. Across the room, she could see Rosie deep in conversation with Mama. They looked up as if they could feel her eyes on them, but Alex turned back to the bar. She didn't want to talk to either of them.

Keep calm, she told herself. *It's not you who has done anything wrong.* So why did she feel like she had?

"All right?" Jake asked when the crowd thinned. "Is your beer still cold? Jamie bought it for you."

"Yes, thanks." She turned to seek out Jamie. He was sitting alone and stony-faced at a table at the back of the room. She raised the glass in thanks to him and took a sip.

"So, what's going on? Why have you moved out?" Jake said. "Although I can probably guess . . ."

"Can you? I doubt it . . ."

He raised his eyebrows. "Well, I've heard you arguing . . ."

"It's a long story," Alex said, suddenly unsure of what she wanted to tell.

"We've got all evening—I finish in a couple of hours," Jake said and smiled.

It was the smile that did it. It made Alex melt inside.

"Rosie has stolen my money," she said.

"Rosie? Really? Are you sure?" He looked over at the accused, and Alex saw her former roommate raise her head. *She must have heard her name.* Rosie pulled a face and turned back to the ever-attentive Mama.

"Yes. I caught her going through my bag. And she admitted it. But that's not the worst thing. She's been scammed out of a load of money by some bloke who rented her a scooter that got stolen."

Jake's lovely eyes narrowed.

"And Mama has scared her to death saying the police will get involved and plant drugs on her." She didn't get to tell him about Rosie paying Mama to help her. A customer took him off down to the other end of the bar to make a complicated cocktail before she could continue, and she sipped at her beer again. It was flat. She took a handful of peanuts from a bowl on the counter.

When Jake returned, he picked up the conversation as if there'd been no break. "Well, the scooter thing is in the Ladybird book of scams, but getting arrested? Perhaps Rosie is ramping it up to distract you from the fact that she's nicked your cash. Make you feel sorry for her. She pulls the little-girl-lost thing quite a lot, I've noticed. She's a bit of a nightmare, really, isn't she?"

"I thought I was the only one who knew," Alex said gratefully. "She said you all thought I was a misery, bringing everyone down."

"I wouldn't believe everything she says. No one thinks that. We all think you're a hero, coping with Princess Rosie."

Alex tried to smile.

"What about the money, though? Have you got enough to carry on? What are you going to do?"

"I don't know."

"You could talk to Mama about it," he said carefully.

"Mama? I think she might be part of the problem."

"What do you mean? She knows a lot of people; that's all I'm saying. She knows how things work. She's helped me in the past."

"How?"

"Well, things got a bit sticky last year. The police were being difficult about my visa and she sorted it out. I owe her."

"Well, she's made it clear she doesn't like me. I'll think about it."

"Got customers. Let's talk about it later," he said as a crowd of noisy travelers flooded in.

Later, she couldn't pinpoint exactly when she'd started to feel ill. The evening had seemed to disappear. It had blurred at the edges at some point. She remembered Mama's face, looming up at her, but Alex's mouth had felt as if it had stopped working, so words fell out half-formed, and she was swaying dangerously on her stool. She needed to get to a toilet, but she didn't know where she was. Was she still in the bar?

"What's happening to me?" she'd wanted to say, but all she'd heard was a series of slurred sounds. She'd felt hands lift her. Then nothing.

When she woke the first time, her head was hammering, and when she tried to push herself up, she vomited on the floor by the bed. She felt too weak to care and closed her eyes against the daylight. When she woke the second time—was it the second time?—it felt like it was getting dark again and the vomit had gone. A plastic bowl was beside the bed.

She tried to get up, but her legs shook too much and she crashed back down. The sound brought Jamie to her door.

"How are you feeling?" he said. "You look terrible. I'll get you some water."

Alex didn't speak. She opened her mouth and immediately retched. Her ribs and stomach muscles felt bruised and she ached as if she'd been punched repeatedly.

"Lie still," Jamie said. "I won't be a minute."

"What happened to me?" she croaked when he returned with a glass.

"I don't know. Maybe you ate something bad. You collapsed near the loos. You poor thing. You've been so sick."

She tried to remember what she'd eaten. The peanuts? She'd had only a couple of handfuls. But her head hurt too much to think.

"I put you to bed. I've been popping in and out to make sure you're okay."

Tears leaked out of Alex's eyes onto the pillow. "I feel so ill," she said. "I wish my mum was here."

Jamie sat on the bed and stroked her hair. "Don't worry. I'll look after you."

"Does Rosie know I'm ill?"

When Jamie didn't answer, she gripped his arm. "Tell her to text our mums to let them know we're okay. I didn't do it yesterday. They'll worry. And Rosie never remembers. And don't say I'm ill. My mum will fret."

"Will do. Now, sleep."

Alex lay as still as she could to avoid triggering the retching. She reached a hand under her pillow for her phone, but it wasn't there. She'd find it later, she told herself.

FORTY-NINE

The Reporter

FRIDAY, SEPTEMBER 5, 2014

Joe is going to drop me back home, but as we drive up the street, I see reporters sitting on my garden wall. "Reverse ferret," I say, ducking down into the footwell, and Joe drives past and turns into the next side street.

"How many were there?" I say as I scrabble back into my seat.

"Three. And a photographer. It's probably the agencies. They looked very young."

I almost laugh. "Like you?" And he grins at me.

"Ah, but I drive like an old man . . . Where are we going?"

"Just to the corner. Leave me here," I say when we get to the end of the alleyway at the back of my terrace. "I'll ring you when I've combed through the e-mails."

He's forwarded the whole e-mail thread to me, thousands of words in scores of messages that began on July 27 and unspool to August 12. We've agreed he won't file anything from them yet.

"There's a lot of work to do, Joe. None of this info has been checked—especially stealing the money. Alex O'Connor could have made the whole thing up. We need to work it first."

He'd nodded, but I could see the disappointment.

. . .

I creep along the back of the houses, waving to next-door Bet in her garden. She's putting washing out and waves at me. I put my finger to my lips and point to the front of the house, and she smiles conspiratorially and beckons me into her kitchen.

"Come in," she says, pushing her moggy, Albert, off a Formica stool. "Take the weight off your feet."

"Have they bothered you, Bet?"

"They've tried. I told them to eff off. Bloody vultures. One kid called me 'love.' Cheeky bugger."

I smile at the thought of someone trying to butter up Bet. God knows, I tried at first, when we moved in a million years ago. But she can spot insincerity a mile off and is impressed by nothing. She's what my dad would have called "her own person."

She's looking at me for my response, but I can hardly join in slagging off the press.

"They're just doing their job, Bet. They'll push off eventually. Ignore them."

"Hard when they are saying those things about Jake. I told them. He's a lovely boy. Known him all his life and he wouldn't hurt a fly."

Her words are unexpectedly kind and I don't manage to steel myself in time. As I sit and cry, she rummages for tissues, then brings pink loo roll instead.

"Better out than in," she says as consolation. "You mustn't hold things in. Bad for you."

I sniffle pathetically and try to pull myself together. "I'd better go, Bet. I've got to make calls to the family."

"Take this packet of biscuits. I bet you're not eating properly."

I tuck the digestives into my handbag.

"Will you be talking to Freddie? Give him my love, won't you? How is he doing? What does he think about it all?"

"He's being very supportive," I say. But I don't really know what Freddie thinks anymore. I wonder if he blames me for Jake staying away, getting into this mess. We'll have to be very careful about what we say to each other. I'll try to protect him, but perhaps he'll do the same for me. He might be more open with Steve. They can talk about me. I'll ring him again tonight.

I hurry round to my back gate and lock it behind me. We don't usually lock it—never had to before. The boys used to ride their bikes home from school and stick them in the shed before bursting through the back door. It's been so long, the key has got rusty in the keyhole and I struggle with it. Then I stand in the sunshine for a moment, hidden from everyone by the tall brick walls that separate the gardens and watched by Albert, now lounging on our shed roof. I need time to think. Except thinking takes me back to the boy Jake was. *Where is he now? What did we do wrong?*

I shut my eyes and take a deep breath.

The list, Kate. Back to the list.

I fetch my laptop from the sitting room. This morning before Joe and I left, I'd drawn the curtains to keep out prying eyes and lenses, but coming in from the bright sun, I am blinded by the sudden darkness. I feel my way to the sofa and open the lid of the computer. I go to sit down but I can hear them talking outside. I think I even recognize voices. It is so surreal to be cowering in here with my friends outside, but I straighten my shoulders and walk away from them.

I've got a job to do, too.

It is a fishing operation, casting my net across every word contained in this stream of teenage consciousness.

I copy the e-mails into one document and search for different keywords. I start with "Jake." I have to. I need to know what the police know. His name comes up repeatedly but I notice she also she calls him JW. Mostly in the later e-mails. JW this, Jake that. Alex seems of two minds. Sometimes she is all about my son, talking about how kind he is, his lovely eyes, his beautiful hands, how she hopes he will ask her out. How she tries to catch his attention. What he said, how he looked at her. My son the heartthrob. But at other times she is impatient with him, complaining that he is in her face. *Girls,* I think. Not that I know. Never having had one.

It is only later that I realize Jake is also referred to in the first e-mails when Alex talks about someone called the Stoner, who sits smoking joints in the dorm when he isn't clearing tables. It's him. I put this other Jake away and move on.

A search for "Lars" leads me to his friend Diederik. They were moving on to Myanmar. And there's a reference to Amsterdam— *"Suppose he smokes dope all the time at home—he says everyone does it in Amsterdam"*—and Lars's plan to study sound engineering when he gets back. Alex doesn't sound impressed by him. She says she's frightened for Rosie, that she's so out of control, doing drugs with Lars. She must have expected drinking and clubs—what teenager wouldn't? But she'd been put in charge of a girl she didn't really know. Alex's fears are spelled out in full and I feel for her. She was so out of her depth. At eighteen to be dealing with this must have been terrible.

Bloody Rosie, I catch myself thinking. *Stop it, Kate, you're getting too involved already . . .*

On and on the e-mails go, with Rosie spinning further and further out of control in Alex's innocent eyes. "It'll be all right" became her mantra, and I can picture her crossing her fingers when she was thinking it, like in a child's game. But the growing sense of impending doom shouts out at me.

Why didn't you do something, Alex? If only you'd rung home. Your mum could have told you what to do. That's what mums are for . . .

I find another bit about Lars—Rosie was sleeping with him by then, according to Alex.

> Went up to our room today and walked in on her and
> Lars. Soooo embarrassing. Rosie shouted at me to get
> out. I mean, it's my room, too. Lars came out still
> putting on his shirt and said sorry. Rosie pretended
> nothing had happened when I went in. She's weird like
> that. She said Lars was taking her to another club
> tonight. He's going to do some DJing. He calls himself
> DJ Rappo. Crappo, more like!!!

I google "DJ Rappo, Lars, and Amsterdam." He's there, smiling sleepily at me from his profile picture. Lars De Vries. He's got his own website. "Thank you, social media," I hear myself say out loud.

I've got there ahead of Joe. He's annoyed to be a step behind—"I had to drive back to the office, Kate. Cut me some slack"—but as excited as I am when I give him the name. "Okay, I'll ring whoever we use in Holland. Who do we use?"

I tell him. I can't ring. I'm persona non grata since the postmortem results and the launch of a murder inquiry. Off the rota. In the long grass. Out. Terry rings me to see if I'm all right, to tell me to take some time off. It's nice of him. It's not his fault I'm in this mess, but he's still a mate. Mick rings, too, of course. But it's so awkward. We're all watching our every word.

I stay in the world of online anonymity, hunting down my quarry. *I could make a living doing this*, I think. *If it all goes wrong.*

The website is all about Lars's music—hip-hop and grime, apparently. *Is that where they shout at one another while they run round the stage? God, I'm so old.* But I see he's posted an upcoming date at a club. In two days. I ring Joe back. He's gloomy when he answers. "De Vries is one of the most common surnames in the country," he says. "I've just looked and there are hundreds of them."

"Never mind that. Pack your grime gear—whatever that is—we're going clubbing."

Joe persuades Terry it's a goer—"I told him Lars could tell us what was going on at the guesthouse and he might have photos of the girls." I suspect he said "with Jake" during the conversation, but I don't say anything. I just want to go.

Steve isn't keen. "You're not working and you need to be here in case Jake turns up," he says.

"I am still employed. I'm on compassionate leave. And I'm only going for one night. I'll be in touch all the time. It's only across the Channel."

"North Sea, actually. Well, if you think it will do any good . . ."

He's too exhausted to argue with me further, and I'm grateful.

Rosie was gone. Alex looked again through the window of the room they had shared. Her Girl Guide badge handiwork on the curtains had been unpicked by someone. The bed had a different-colored sheet and Rosie's rucksack had gone. She tried the handle of the door again, rattling it weakly in its flimsy frame. Mama appeared at the top of the stairs.

"Stop that!" she screeched. "You break it. Rosie not there."

"Where is she?" Alex's head was swimming. It had taken a huge effort to make it up the stairs on her wobbly legs.

"She's gone to meet her friends."

"What friends?"

"Dutch boys. She's gone to find them."

Alex stood with her hand still on the handle, trying to process what she was being told. Mama had vanished back down the stairs, her high heels click-clacking on the concrete.

"But she didn't have any money . . ." Alex called after her. "You took it."

She walked slowly down to her room. She stopped at the door to the dorm and knocked.

Jake opened it. It was the first time she'd seen him since the night she'd been taken ill. He looked surprised to see her. "I didn't know you were up." There was no warmth in his voice today.

"Rosie's gone," she said.

"Yes, I heard."

"Did you know she was leaving? Did she tell you?"

"No, no. Why would she tell me? Mama said she'd gone." And his eyes strayed away from her as if he was anxious to end the conversation.

"Jake, did she leave any message for me?"

"I don't know anything about it. I've just said so. Look, I'm sorry I can't help . . ." And he started to move off.

"I hate her," Alex hissed, stopping him in his tracks. "I really hate her. She's done everything she can to wreck our trip because she is completely selfish. Anyway, she'll just have to get on with it. It's her funeral. If she wants to swan off without a word, she can. See how far she gets. Mama said something about her joining Lars, but how can she? She hasn't got any money."

Jake turned to face her. He looked tired and stressed. His lovely eyes were red-rimmed as if he hadn't slept.

"Look, don't worry about Rosie. She was bad news for everyone. You are better off without her," he said. "Maybe you should think hard about going home. This is such a mess."

"What do you mean? Do you know why she's gone?"

He shook his head. "You look like you need to go back to bed, Alex," he added.

She felt nausea stirring in her gut again and gripped the door. She didn't want Jake to see her throwing up. Had he seen her being sick before? She tried not to think about it.

"What happened that night?" she said.

"What do you mean?" he snapped at her, and she felt unnerved by his change of tone.

"When I got ill . . ."

"Oh, okay. I have no idea. It got really busy and Mama sent me to get some more stock from a friend's bar. You said you'd wait, but when I got back you'd gone. I was a bit pissed off, actually. We were supposed to be going out, remember? I went to look for you. Anyway, Rosie told me that the faithful Jamie had taken you back to your new room."

"I don't remember any of that. I'm really sorry, Jake. I was looking forward to going out with you. Jamie thinks I must have eaten something bad."

"Good old Jamie," Jake said bitterly. And Alex tingled with pleasure despite herself. He sounded jealous.

"Jamie is just a friend, Jake. I don't fancy him. We can go out another night—properly this time."

"Maybe. Let's see when you are feeling better . . ."

"Perhaps I'll lie down for a bit," she said and staggered back to bed.

As she lay down, she put her hand under the pillow, automatically feeling for her phone. It still wasn't there; it hadn't materialized magically overnight, and she sat up again slowly. She had to find it. She emptied her backpack on the bed, then her handbag, sifting through everything over and over.

"Oh God!" she wailed. Jamie's head appeared round the door as if he'd been standing outside.

"Are you okay?"

"My phone. Someone's taken it. And Rosie's gone. And I feel so ill . . ."

Jamie came in and put his arms round her. "Don't worry, Alex. I'll look after you."

She was too weak to do anything but relax into his hold, and she felt him rest his chin on the top of her head.

She tried to reconnect with her anger about Rosie, but it had

gone—like she had—replaced by a sick dread about what she was going to tell their parents.

"I've got to find her, Jamie," she said. "What am I going to tell her
mum? She'll hate me. She told me to look after her, that she was depending on me, and now Rosie's gone off to Myanmar without any
money. She doesn't even know where it is. Oh God! Can I use your
phone to look at my e-mails, to see if she's been in touch?"

Jamie hesitated.

"Please?"

"Look, don't waste your time. You are well rid of her," he said. "She
was a complete bitch. You don't know the half of it . . ."

"What do you mean?" Alex felt herself going hot. "The half of
what?"

"Nothing, nothing. Sorry, my phone's being a bit temperamental.
Let me get online first." He fiddled with it for thirty seconds and then
threw his head back in frustration. "The bloody Wi-Fi's down. I'll go
and tell Mama to reboot it," he said as he disappeared out into the
corridor.

When he returned, he looked excited. "Mama says she's had a text
message from Rosie. She says she's sorry and has gone away to
think things through."

Alex stared at him. "Why didn't she leave me a message?"

"I don't know, but it's good news she's gone," Jamie went on. "I'll
come with you to Phi Phi. You're going to need a friend to travel
with now."

She shut that idea down with one look.

"Good news? How can this be good news? It's a complete disaster.
And stop talking about bloody Phi Phi."

Jamie looked as if she'd slapped him. She opened her mouth to soothe his hurt feelings but stopped herself. She didn't have time to look after anyone else. She had to focus on herself for once.

"I'll have to tell our parents," she said, more to herself than to the sulking boy in front of her. "And they'll want to know what's been going on. All of it. Oh God, they'll go mad. They'll blame me."

"What for?" Jamie said. "This is all Rosie's fault."

FIFTY

The Reporter

SUNDAY, SEPTEMBER 7, 2014

We arrive in heavy traffic and Joe wants to get a cab into town, but I persuade him that the train will be quicker. And cheaper. I'm funding myself now.

Nina has booked him into a four-star hotel. "Sounds nice," he says. "It's got a swimming pool and gym."

"We're not going to be swimming, Joe. Don't tell me you packed your Speedo?"

I grit my teeth and go on Booking.com to get a cheaper rate at his spa retreat.

The plan had been to doorstep the club for DJ Rappo's arrival, but the gig doesn't start until the middle of the night—eleven thirty, it says on the poster outside the club, and I groan.

"That's a twelve-hour wait. And I can't stay up that late," I say. "I'll turn into a pumpkin. Someone here must know where he lives."

I can see the looks I'm getting as soon as I step through the door. No one my age normally enters its portals.

"Hi," I say to a bored-looking girl wiping down the bar.

"Er, hi," she says.

"Is Lars in yet? DJ Rappo?"

She laughs. "No, he'll still be asleep. Doesn't get up until after midday."

"Where is he living these days?" Joe asks. "Since he got back from Myanmar? I heard he had a great trip."

"Yeah, he loved it. He's back in the Gibraltarstraat flat, staying with one of his friends."

"Oh, Diederik?"

"Yeah. Do you know him?"

"A bit. It'll be good to see them. Remind me—what number is the apartment?"

"Forty-two. Second floor. Tell Lars not to be late tonight."

"Good work, Joe." I mean it. We walk fast, following his phone's directions, and press the button on the panel for flat number 42.

There is a pause and a sleepy voice says, "Hello," and someone buzzes us in without waiting for a reply. On the stairs, we speed whisper our plan. "I'll start," Joe says. "Go in with the reason we're here, the fire, et cetera. And you chip in when we get going. Okay?"

It's his show today. And that's fine. His training wheels are long gone.

"Fine. Don't tell him my surname, though. I'll just be Kate. And Sherwood if necessary. It's my maiden name."

We're still talking when we reach the apartment door. It's ajar and Joe calls, "Hello?" as he pushes it open. A figure in boxer shorts and a T-shirt appears. He smells musty and his hair needs washing. Badly.

"Hey, who are you?" he says.

"Lars? I'm Joe from London."

"Do you want Diederik? He's out but back soon."

"Well, I'd like to talk to both of you. I'm a reporter from a British paper."

"A reporter? Really? What's going on? What are you doing here?"

He sounds aggressive and has taken a step forward, crowding us back toward the front door. We're about to find ourselves out on the stairs again.

"Lars, I'm really sorry to turn up unannounced," I say quickly. "We'd have phoned to make an appointment but we didn't have a number to call."

He falters. He clearly wasn't expecting politeness. He looks a bit unnerved.

"We've flown all the way from England to see you. We've come straight from the airport."

"Really?"

"Yes. Actually, I don't suppose I could use your loo? I'm desperate." I fix an apologetic wince on my face. "Please?"

He falls back and waves us through.

I take my time so Joe gets a chance to get going. But when I come out of the bathroom, wiping my hands discreetly on my trousers rather than the grubby hand towel, Lars is talking about clubs in Southeast Asia and opening a beer for Joe.

He doesn't know, rattles in my head. *He doesn't know about the girls.*

"Thanks so much," I say. "It was a lifesaver."

"So . . ." Joe says nervously. "I was just telling Lars we are writing about backpackers in Thailand."

He's bottled it.

"Yes. That's right. More specifically, the dangers young people face when they travel," I say, pushing us back on track. "It's obviously prompted by what happened to your friends."

Lars looks at me and lifts an eyebrow.

"Your friends Rosie and Alex in Bangkok."

Lars puts down his bottle. "Rosie and Alex? Right. Yeah. So what about them?"

"When did you get back from Asia?" I ask gently.

"A week ago. What's happened?"

"It's a complicated story, Lars. Come and sit down."

He lowers himself onto the floor and sits cross-legged like a child at story time.

"There was a fire at Mama's Guesthouse while they were staying there."

"No! When?"

"In the early hours of August the fifteenth."

"Oh my God, we had just left. Me and Diederik. We caught the night bus to Yangon on the eleventh, I think. Rosie came to the bus station to say good-bye. Is she hurt?"

"I'm afraid so. Rosie and Alex died, Lars."

His head jerks and he stares up at me. There is a moment's silence in the flat while he takes it in.

"Died? Both of them?"

"Yes. Their bodies were found after the fire. The thing is, the police believe they were dead before the fire started."

"Oh my God, someone killed them?"

"I'm so very sorry to bring you this news," I say. "To be the one to tell you. I honestly thought you would have heard about it."

He shakes his head. "We've been on the road and the Wi-Fi in Myanmar is terrible. I'm still catching up with friends now. Oh God, those poor girls."

"Did you spend much time with them?" Joe says.

"Well, we were together a couple of weeks. Rosie and I got quite close. But not Alex. She didn't like me, I think. She was with another boy all the time."

"Jake?" Joe asks, and I shoot him a warning look.

"No. Well, she liked Jake very much, I remember. He worked there and he was someone for her to turn to when things got a bit out of hand. Like when she fell out with Rosie. But she was always with Jamie. He was her friend. Following her around like a puppy dog."

Jamie?

"Was Jamie staying there, too? Was he another Brit?" I say. "It's the first time I've heard his name."

"Yes. Well, I think so. I can't tell you much about him—he didn't talk about himself, really. He preferred to watch people. Maybe he was shy—I don't know. He was funny, though. He slept on all his stuff in the dorm. Like we were going to rob him! And he had a big thing for Alex. But she didn't like him that way." He suddenly snaps his fingers. "Jamie Way. That was his name. I remember now. Rosie used to call him 'Jamie Always in the Way' as a joke."

Is he the JW in the e-mails? I wonder, trying to reread them in my head. *When did she write about JW?*

"Who else was there? The police said there were parties there every night," Joe says.

"That's bullshit. We used to go out most nights. And there were just us six staying while we were there. Four boys in the dorm and the girls upstairs. And the owner, of course. Mama. She was a big character . . ."

"Big how?"

"In every way . . . and she knew everyone. She could get you anything you wanted. Mama's Sweet Shop, she called it."

"Drugs?" Joe says.

"If you wanted them," Lars replies, suddenly wary.

"Did Rosie get drugs from Mama?" I ask. *She was getting them from somewhere.*

"Sometimes," he says. "Look, Rosie was fun. We both liked having a good time and she didn't have a problem with trying new things."

"Was anyone else selling drugs there?" And I hold my breath. *Don't say Jake!* I shout in my head.

"You are kidding," Lars says. "Mama wouldn't have liked that. She was strict about it. It was her place."

"Have you got any photos from the guesthouse?" I ask. He nods and fetches his laptop. "I've downloaded them all. I was going to make a collage for the wall . . ."

But you probably won't now, I think.

He pulls up a picture of the six of them. "I put the camera on a timer for a group photo. It was the last evening before we left. It was a great night."

They're in a room with metal bunk beds behind them. And there's Jake. My heart lurches at the sight of him, thinner than when he left, scruffier, but smiling. Everyone looks like they are having a good time at first glance. But when I reach past Lars and zoom in on the faces, one by one, I see not everyone is laughing. Alex isn't. And there is a boy standing behind her. His face is blank.

"That's Jamie," Lars says.

FIFTY-ONE

The Reporter

The *Post* has used the photo of the friends at the guesthouse big.

"The Last Photo Taken of Murdered Gap-Year Girls," the headline shouts above an exclusive interview with Lars. Joe has written it well. He's got all the best quotes in and named everyone who was at the guesthouse. Jamie Way is in there. Then I spot a quote from one of Alex's e-mails to Mags. Just a line, not mentioning drugs or theft but clearly identifiable as one of her messages.

You idiot, Joe. You've tipped off the police that we've seen the e-mails and you've not even used the best stuff. What a waste. I wonder what Bob Sparkes will say.

I ring Joe and he's had a call from Sparkes already—and Jenny Shaw. "Not a happy conversation with Jenny," he admits. "She said it was an invasion of Rosie's privacy."

"But you didn't use the stuff about her stealing and her dad shagging around, did you? Still, she knows you know now. Must be galling for her, never mind Mike Shaw. What about Bob Sparkes?"

"DI Sparkes didn't want the e-mails released either, but he didn't spend too long on that. He was more interested in asking a lot of questions about Lars and Jamie Way."

"That's good. Have you put him in touch with Lars?"

"Yeah, he was pleased with that, I think. Looked good, though, didn't it?"

"Fab. Now, where is Jamie Way? Meet you in the café round the corner from the office in an hour. Let's find his birth certificate. I'm sure Bob Sparkes's team is doing the same thing."

Joe has done the heavy lifting by the time I get there, trawling through the births registers from 1985 to 1995, by the time I get there. I told him to spread the net wide. Jamie Way looks the same age as the girls in the photo, but you can never tell.

"He might be older and hiding it," I say. I interviewed a bloke once who was in his thirties but pretended to be seventeen to re-sit his A Levels. People do the strangest things. And I've always suspected that people reinvent themselves a bit when they travel abroad. It's so easy to embellish or redact our lives when no one knows the truth.

There are five births that could fit our Jamie Way.

"We don't know where he was living in the UK, so we'll just have to contact all of them," Joe says, poking at the foil round a pat of butter with his knife. "I'll order the birth certificates."

"Okay. But we can look for the parents of each of them online in the meantime—trace their marriages and birth details. Give me the first one and I'll make a start on my laptop while you eat your toasted tea cake."

Joe takes a big bite and chews. "It'll take a day or so to get the certificates."

"Yes, but we may not have to wait. The paper's only just published the photo. You've put a come-on at the bottom, haven't you?"

"Yes, the usual 'If you know any of these people, please call . . . '"

"Well, let's see what we get from the readers. Someone may recognize him."

And of course they do. A building-site manager from Portsmouth gets in touch with the news desk and they pass the details on to Joe. He dials and puts the phone on loudspeaker.

"Hi, is that Mr. Watson? Thanks so much for ringing in. I hear you have some possible information about the photo we used today."

"Oh right! Yes," Mr. Watson says loudly, and the couple at the next table tut. "Well, I think it's a bloke who used to work with me. But he had a different name."

"Did he? What was he called, your workmate?"

"Jamie, but Jamie Lawrence. Funny kid but a hard worker. He had the makings of a good plasterer."

"How do you spell Lawrence? With a W? Funny how?" Joe says.

"Quiet, but when he got wound up he used to go a bit mental. Do you know what I mean? Bit handy with his fists if someone pushed him too far."

"And did he get pushed too far a lot?"

"He was the youngest on the gang so . . ."

"Right," Joe says wearily. "And where was he living when you worked together?"

"Dunno. Bedsit, shared flat, that sort of place. He didn't talk about it. Don't think he had any family."

"When?" I'm mouthing.

"So, when did you last see him, Mr. Watson?"

"Er, am I being paid for this?" the caller asks, and I sigh.

"Well," Joe says, switching to a script, "we don't normally pay for information."

"Oh, maybe I'll ring the *Herald* instead then . . ."

I make alarmed eyes.

"But, as I was about to say, I might be able to put a fee through for your help. A hundred pounds?"

"Lovely," Mr. Watson says. "Right, well, he left the site in July. He'd been saving to go off and travel the world for a while. It was all he talked about. Thailand this, Thailand that. He was all excited about it, said he was getting his first passport. But he wasn't himself in the last few weeks before he went. Miserable—you know, moody. We were going to have a few beers to send him off but he didn't show up at the pub."

"And has he been in touch since he went?"

"We got a postcard at the site office. The secretary did. She used to talk to him when he looked a bit down. Used to mother him. Anyway, it just said he was in Bangkok and having a great time."

I mime taking a photo and Joe waves me away, impatiently.

"I don't suppose you have any photos of Jamie?"

"No, we don't go in for selfies on the building site. But I could ask down at the pub. He used to hang round there."

"Which pub is that?"

"The Black Swan. Bit of a dive, but it's home."

The barmaid at the Black Swan says she'd been about to ring us, when Joe calls her. "I saw the piece but I had to wait for my shift to finish. Jamie's a nice bloke. Always bought me a drink," she says. "Am I going to get paid for this?"

"I'll ask," Joe says. "But I can't promise anything. Anyway, where did Jamie live? Was he a local?"

"Oh yeah. He lived down past the docks. He had a room in a shared house. With students, I think. He didn't know them before—it was just somewhere to put his head down, he said."

"No girlfriend?"

"Not now, I don't think. He was going out with someone last year, but it fizzled out. I think he was a bit full-on for her. He would be for me. He's lovely but a bit needy. Do you know what I mean?"

"Yeah, I think so. Has he got family in Portsmouth?"

"I don't know. He didn't like talking about his family. He was adopted, he said. But I think he spent part of his life in a care home. Just from things he said."

I love barmaids. They are the ear to every door, hoovering up information with a practiced smile. Like me.

"That's so helpful. Thanks. I don't suppose you've got a number or e-mail for Jamie?"

"No, sorry. I don't really swap numbers with customers. Leads to misunderstandings."

"Right, well, can I give you my number in case you see or hear from him?"

"No probs. And you'll check about the payment? I earn peanuts here."

"I'll be in touch," Joe promises.

"Well, that's interesting," I say as soon as the phone goes down. "He was Jamie Lawrence before he got to Bangkok. I wonder why he changed his name. And if Way is the name he was born with. Before his adoption."

Joe looks for a Jamie Lawrence listed on the electoral register in Portsmouth and finds one living in what looks like a shared house.

Bingo! And all while sitting in a café.

Bob Sparkes tries to sound pleased to hear from me, but I'm not fooled.

"Don't worry—I'm not ringing to whine, Bob. I've got some info that could be important about Jamie Way—the boy Lars said was at the guesthouse."

"Okay, I'm listening."

"We've had a ring in from someone who used to work with him.

They say he was Jamie Lawrence when he lived in Portsmouth. He was working on building sites just before he set off for Bangkok."

"Was he?"

"And the story is backed up by a barmaid at his local."

"I wonder why he changed names."

"Something to hide, maybe? The barmaid said he mentioned being adopted. We've found what could be him in a multiple-occupancy house."

"I don't know why we bother, Kate. You are all over this," he says, and I can hear he's smiling.

"Sorry, Bob. I'm not trying to best you. You've got a million things to do. I've got one."

"We've already got Interpol and immigration looking for Jamie Way—I'll give them this new name straightaway as an alias. Thanks for passing it on so quickly."

I can hear he's about to end the call and I interrupt his good-byes.

"Bob, this is just a thought, but do you think this boy, Jamie, could be the JW in Alex's e-mails? Lars says he spent all his time following Alex around. And reading the e-mails, I've noticed that she uses a different tone when she's talking about Jake, as if she is the pursuer."

He hesitates. Perhaps I've pushed too far.

"I'll look at that, Kate," he says, adding as I knew he would: "Don't suppose you've heard from Jake?"

Putting me back in my box.

FIFTY-TWO

The Mother

MONDAY, SEPTEMBER 8, 2014

"Bloody Mags Harding," Lesley shouted across the kitchen table, sweeping the paper off onto the floor.

"Les! Look what you've done." Her husband started picking up the pages and folding them back together.

"It must be her who's given the *Post* Alex's e-mails. Bob Sparkes said the police were the only ones who had seen them apart from her. And it definitely wasn't anyone from his team. He's as fed up as we are."

"I bet he's not flinging newspapers around the room," Malcolm muttered.

"Jenny's doing her nut. She rang to say she's given the reporter a real earful and she's coming round to discuss it with us."

"Oh God," Malcolm said and stopped his origami exercise. "I'm not sure I'm up to this, love. I can't face another scene with her."

"Then go and have a bath. I'll deal with it. Go on. Don't just sit there."

He lumbered to his feet, all energy gone, and padded out. She listened to the sound of his feet on each stair, counting them like the tick of the clock. She registered the whine of the extractor fan that needed a squirt of WD-40 and the gush of water as he turned on the taps. She was so deep in her thoughts that she sprang to her feet as if to run when the doorbell rang. She wished she could run away most days. *Just leave all this behind.*

She opened the door and Jenny started immediately, her eyes bright with anger. Lesley stood back to let her pass. "Malcolm's in the bath," she said. "He's not coping today."

It gave Jenny pause but not for long. She sat herself down at the table where the remains of the *Post* held center stage and she banged her hand on it.

"This rag . . ."

"There's no need to shout, Jenny. I'm right here."

"This bloody rag has got its hands on the e-mails. Can they do that? Can they just publish private things like that?"

"I don't know. I wouldn't have thought so—have you spoken to the paper?" She knew Jenny had, but it seemed the kind thing to do, to allow her to tell the whole story.

"Oh yes. I rang first thing this morning. Spoke to that child, Joe Jackson. Hopeless. Then I tried to speak to the Editor but he was in a meeting. Hiding from me, more like."

Lesley rose and assumed her role as tea maker and comforter. "On the plus side," she ventured cautiously. Jenny's face darkened.

"There is no plus side."

"Hang on; hear me out. On the plus side, they only used a couple of sentences—and nothing about Rosie and the drugs or Mike and the money."

Jenny banged the table again, sending ripples across the tea in the cups. "But they can. They could print any of those lies, couldn't they?"

There was a strange stillness in the room, and as Lesley turned to look at Jenny she felt as if she were moving in slow motion.

"Lies?" she said, the word elongating unnaturally, to fill the air between them. "What on earth do you mean?"

"I mean, why would Alex write those things? Those awful things," Jenny gabbled. "Rosie wasn't like that. Not before your daughter dragged her off to Thailand and put her in danger, anyway. I should never have let her go. Anyway, I think Alex was jealous of her, jealous that all the boys liked her, and she just wrote this stuff out of spite."

Lesley could feel the heat rising through her core. She spoke slowly, hardly trusting her voice to work.

"Shut up! What a wicked thing to say. You should be ashamed of yourself. But I understand why you would say it. After all, no one wants to admit their daughter took drugs, slept with anyone with a pulse, and stole from her friend. You must be devastated."

Jenny's face was scarlet and there was a tiny pearl of perspiration on her top lip. She gulped for air, then hissed, "She didn't do those things. Aren't you listening to me?"

"I think you need to go home, Jenny," another voice broke in. Malcolm, in his old striped dressing gown and with bare feet, stood in the doorway. She whirled round to face him. But he stopped her dead.

"Perhaps you should speak to Mike about the money he gave Rosie," he said. "You are right—we only have Alex's word for what happened in Bangkok. But your ex-husband is here. You can ask him face-to-face."

Jenny fled in tears, slamming the front door behind her.

"Do you think she will?" Lesley said.

"I don't know. I don't think she's interested in the truth, Les. Only her own version. But I can't have her talking about Alex like that."

"No. Mal, it was awful . . ."

He led her into the front room to talk it all through. It had become their panic room, the place where they could say the unsayable and leave it there.

When she'd railed and cried herself to a standstill, Lesley looked up at her husband. "I'm going to ring Mags and ask her to come and see us. I need her to tell me everything she knows. It's not her fault this happened, and we haven't talked to her properly since we got back. She was Alex's best friend."

Malcolm nodded.

"Perhaps we can give her something of Alex's as a keepsake."

"That's a lovely idea. I'll go and pick something for her."

There was another message via Mama. Jamie said Rosie had texted to say she needed time on her own. That she was with Lars. He had loaned her money.

"How strange," Alex said. "It's as though Rosie can hear what I'm saying. I think Mama is making it up."

Jamie had gone quiet. "Why would she?" he said in the end. And Alex couldn't think of a reason.

She'd asked to see the messages, but the landlady had snorted in reply. "You are not Rosie's friend. She messaged me," she'd said.

Alex felt completely isolated. She wasn't e-mailing Mags—she didn't have a phone and she wouldn't have done so even if she'd had one. She couldn't trust her friend to keep Rosie's disappearance a secret. It was too serious to keep quiet. She thought she'd probably sound the alarm if it were the other way round. So radio silence until she had sorted it out, got Rosie back.

Alex wasn't receiving any help closer to home. She was getting increasingly fed up with Jamie's constant badgering about Phi Phi. She lost it with him when he tried to bring it up again in the bar. There was no one else around—she wondered if Mama had stopped taking guests.

"For God's sake, Jamie! I am not thinking about that. I have to get Rosie to come back. Don't you understand?"

He clearly didn't. "I thought you'd be happy that Rosie had gone. You complained about her all the time. You said you wished you'd never come with her. That you were going to ditch her."

"Jamie! I haven't got time for this. I need to talk to someone who can help me. I need to talk to Jake. Don't give me that look! He knows how things work here. He'll know what to do."

"Maybe Jake could go to Myanmar and find Rosie. He obviously fancies her . . ." Jamie said quietly.

"Don't be stupid," she shouted. "He doesn't fancy her. She was throwing herself at him. He was embarrassed by it."

"Well, if that's what you want to believe. It didn't look like that when I saw them."

"When did you see them?"

"The other night when you were supposed to go out with him. They were getting drunk together. Rosie was all over him, sitting on his knee, and Jake wasn't trying to get away. In fact, they went off together. Upstairs."

Alex closed her eyes against the images. "Shut up!" she shouted, as if she could blot out his voice. "You're making this up, trying to upset me."

"No, I'm not. Ask Mama. She saw it, too. I'm not saying this just to upset you. I'd want to know if my friend was doing that behind my back. It was a revenge shag. How low could she get?"

"Leave me alone, Jamie," Alex sobbed and ran from the room.

She hated him, too, now. *A revenge shag. Was Rosie really capable of that? And was Jake so weak he'd go along with it? She didn't know what to believe.*

. . .

Alex suspected Jamie was standing outside her room again. She pressed herself against the door to listen. She could hear a rustle and tried to ignore it. She needed to get dressed and buy another phone. *Come on, Alex. You can't put this off any longer.*

As she was pulling on a pair of shorts, she thought she heard whispering outside. She crouched by the door and listened. She heard Jake mutter: "Everything okay?"

"No."

"Is she still asking about Rosie?"

"Yes."

"I'll talk to her," Jake said and tapped on the door just above Alex's ear. She lurched backward and sat down hard on the concrete floor.

"Come in," she called, struggling to her feet.

"How are you feeling, Alex? Oh, sorry—you're getting dressed," he said when he caught sight of her. "Is that a good idea?"

Her face burned at the sight of him, but her anger made her feel stronger.

"What do you care what I do?" she snapped.

"Er . . . Look, I can see you're upset, not thinking straight."

"Wrong. I know exactly what I'm doing. I'm going to buy a phone and ring home. I have to tell my parents what's happened."

"Look, Rosie is an adult. You can't dictate what she does," he offered.

"No, so I hear."

Jake looked at her carefully. "What do you mean? What have you heard?"

"Forget it." Now that he was there in front of her, she couldn't bring herself to ask him if he had slept with Rosie. She couldn't face the humiliation.

Jake took a deep breath. "Alex, you should make your own decisions about your trip. You could carry on on your own. Let Rosie do what she likes. That's not your responsibility."

"Of course it is," Alex shouted. "I can't just abandon her. What am I going to do?"

"You could go home," he said.

"You didn't when things went wrong for you."

"No, and I wish I had. I've made bad decisions, Alex. Don't make the same mistakes I did."

Jake put his arm round her to comfort her and she tried to pull back, but she felt safe for the first time in days. She rested there, breathing him in, listening to his heartbeat, telling herself Jamie was lying. She could have stayed there forever, but Jake let go suddenly when Jamie barged in, uninvited, pretending he hadn't been eavesdropping outside.

"Sorry, didn't realize I was interrupting," he said sullenly.

"You are," Alex snapped. "Would you mind closing the door behind you?"

He slammed it instead.

FIFTY-THREE

The Detective

MONDAY, SEPTEMBER 8, 2014

Jamie Lawrence rang all sorts of bells. Social Services, police records, Youth Courts, the Probation Service—all spewed him out. They all used different terms and weasel words—"challenging" was his personal favorite—but the consensus was clear: a troubled boy. He'd been put into care by his mother at the age of four. *Poor kid. He must have known all about it at that age. All about his mum not being able to cope,* Sparkes told himself.

Foster carers followed—Sparkes counted three moves in less than a year—then adoption by the Lawrences, a couple in their forties who'd never had children. Jamie's records went quiet then for about ten years before he exploded back onto the scene as a teenage thug. He was eventually put back into care by the Lawrences "for his own protection." They, too, were unable to cope with the troubled boy.

Local authority homes; petty crime; fights; court appearances; second, third, and final chances peppered the documents in front of Sparkes. On his seventeenth birthday, Jamie left the state system with his Pathway Plan for getting a job, according to the social worker's last word.

But the odd thing was that he seemed to stop getting into trouble. He just disappeared off the radar and stayed there.

Until now, Sparkes reminded himself. He had a bad feeling about

Jamie. The building-site boss had said he lost his temper—"went a bit mental"—when things went wrong. If people said the wrong things. And there was an awful lot going wrong in that guesthouse, according to Alex's e-mails. *And you wanted to replace Rosie as Alex's traveling companion. Did you make sure you could? Did you do something to make it happen? Did Alex find out?*

All this was whirling round his head as he looked at the party photo, trying to read the expressions on their faces and map the dynamics of the group.

He stopped only when answers to his inquiries started to trickle into his inbox at mid-morning. More red flags unfurling.

It turned out that Jamie Lawrence had traveled from London to Bangkok on the same flight as the girls, on a newly issued passport.

Did he see them on the plane? Or follow them from the airport? he thought. *I wonder if there's CCTV of him at Suvarnabhumi arrivals. Or Heathrow departures.* He called Salmond in.

"Get on this, Zara. Let's see if airport security can find the girls on CCTV and see who is milling around them, shall we? I think we're on the right track at last. What else is on your list?"

"I've interviewed the building-site boss, the barmaid, the other tenants in his rented flat."

"What did they have to say?"

"Kept himself to himself. As per . . . Liked power ballads, apparently."

"Really?"

"Whitney Houston on repeat. The others complained."

"So a romantic, then . . ."

"Hmmm. His ex-girlfriend said he was moody. Got jealous about nothing and then went quiet. She got fed up and ended it last year. She said . . ." Salmond pulled out her notebook. "She said he had a problem with trust. She's been reading too many advice columns, if you ask me."

"A troubled boy. Maybe Alex gave him reason to be jealous. Her pursuit of Jake was pretty full-on according to her e-mails. Maybe she didn't hide it."

The detectives sat and nodded at their own thoughts.

"Let's get on with it," said Sparkes. "It looks like a case is finally building. I can feel it in my gut."

It was all going so well. Until he got a message to call his Interpol contact.

"Bob, sorry it's taken a while. Mad busy here. Anyway, your Jamie Lawrence has turned up on our system. He's on remand in Bangkok as part of a drugs investigation."

"Christ, you've got him. That's brilliant. When was he arrested?"

"Last month. The Thai police lifted him on August the fourteenth."

"But that's the day before the fire. Can you check the date?"

Sparkes drummed his fingers on the desk while he waited, his brain racing. *The Thais have got everything else wrong; they must have cocked this up as well.*

"Hi. No, that's right. Probably not what you want to hear. Sorry, but I've seen the arrest report online. Arrested on Thursday, August fourteenth, at fourteen oh five. With a two-gram bag of cannabis."

"Shit! Can you send it over? What a pisser.

"Salmond, get in here!" he shouted into the empty room and drew a line through the name at the top of his pad.

FIFTY-FOUR

The Detective
TUESDAY, SEPTEMBER 9, 2014

He'd been waiting all morning for a call from the techies. Sometimes he thought they were winding him up when he phoned to see if there was any news, pretending they didn't know who he was, calling him DI Sparkle behind his back. They liked a joke down in the labs.

"Inspector, I'm pushing the button on your sex-swab reports now," a voice said down the phone. "Come back to us if there's anything you don't understand."

Bloody cheek.

"Thanks. Will do."

"Exhibit RMS3 (low vaginal swab) tested positive for semen. Full DNA profile was obtained."

The minute traces of bodily fluid taken from Rosie Mary Shaw's body showed traces of semen.

The lab had run the DNA extracted from the traces through the database and come up with nothing. But with Jamie Lawrence out of the picture, Sparkes was laying bets that there would be a match with Jake Waters.

Christ, poor Kate, he caught himself thinking. *Never mind Kate. Poor Alex and her parents. They're the victims here.*

He read through the results again, ticking them off against his inbuilt checklist.

Salmond knocked.

"I heard the labs had sent some results, sir."

"Did they tell you they found semen on Rosie Shaw?"

"No. Christ. I bet it's Jake Waters. We've got him."

"Except we haven't. Unless he's turned up overnight and no one's told me. Where the hell is he? Why are we not getting any sightings or credit card use apart from hiring the two cars? He must be using cash and sleeping rough. It's been two—no, three—weeks since immigration confirms he flew in. How has he been invisible for that long? His photo has been everywhere."

Kate Waters had complained loudly about the picture—Jake's driving license photo—claiming it made him look like a criminal.

"Everyone looks like an ax murderer in those photo-booth pictures, Bob. Please use another one. I'll send you one of ours."

But the new picture hadn't shaken loose any witnesses. There'd been no calls into the police station beyond those from the usual loons and attention-seekers.

"Anyway, Zara, what we might have is that he had sex with Rosie. Not that he killed her. Let's confine ourselves to the facts for a moment, shall we? We don't even know if it's his DNA. This afternoon we should get the results from the hair we found in his baseball cap. Can you chase it up? I want to talk to the grown-ups about next steps. I think someone has to go to Bangkok. Speak to Jamie Lawrence, see the crime scene, and try to get at least some of the original reports. We are getting nowhere doing it on the phone."

Salmond's face lit up. "Who? Am I going?"

"Stop grinning like a monkey. It's not a jolly," he said.

"'Course not. But I've never been to Bangkok."

"Well, don't pack your bags yet. They may say no."

D CI Chloe Wellington nodded her way through the points in his special pleading. She had a meeting at eleven—"It's mandatory, so make it brief and to the point, Bob"—and it focused him on what they had so far.

Two dead girls.

Both died before a fire, perhaps set to destroy evidence of murder.

One strangled and the other possibly raped.

British suspect/witness now in hiding in the UK.

British witness, Jamie Lawrence, in custody in Bangkok.

Dodgy investigation in Bangkok that missed almost all of the above.

"A nd what will it cost?" DCI Wellington demanded.

"We're pricing it out now, but we'll need a team of four including a scenes-of-crime officer and a photographer."

"And an interpreter," she added, glancing at the clock above the door. "Get me the ballpark figure asap so I can put it in front of the commander. But in principle, yes. You should go."

"Not sure I can," Sparkes said quietly.

"Well, that would be your call, Bob. But I can't see it working without you."

S almond practically burst into song when he told her.

"Team meeting in thirty minutes. Can you get someone to look at airfares and hotel prices? We need to do a budget this afternoon."

"On it."

. . .

The afternoon post brought evidence of pulmonary aspiration of food in Rosie Shaw's lungs. Microscopy had identified "multiple areas of vegetable matter in the small airways and air sacs."

"Looks like she choked on her own vomit," he told Salmond. "Poor girl."

"Had she passed out drunk, do you think?"

"Probably, but she may have taken drugs, too."

Sparkes scrolled back through Alex O'Connor's e-mails for the message where she'd said her friend was messing about with drugs. He was pretty sure she hadn't specified which, but he wanted to check.

Rosie's completely out of it tonight. Can't get any sense out of her. She's just sitting there, panting, and her eyes are all glazed and scary. God knows what she's taken. I asked Lars—one of the boys—but he just laughed. Said she was fine, he'd taken something, too. I'm putting her to bed and I'll try to talk to her about it in the morning.

It sounded like ketamine—the dissociation and the labored breathing. He wondered if it was the first time Rosie had taken it. It was a club drug—small amounts snorted or shoved up your jacksie to make you high quickly. But it didn't always last long. Maybe she'd kept taking bumps to keep the high going? You could take too much—especially if you were out of it already—but people didn't usually die from an overdose unless they'd taken something else as well. Or had too much to drink and choked. To be sure he'd have to wait for the tox results from the fluid Aoife had managed to get out of a vein in Rosie's groin, but he'd put money on the drug being there.

"I'll go and tell the Shaws," he said.

. . .

Sparkes drove to Winchester slowly. He needed thinking time, to weave in the different scenarios. Alex strangled. Rosie choking. What was the time frame? How were the deaths linked? Was one death the consequence of the other? But which?

He was still deep in his head when he pulled up. Mike Shaw was waiting outside in his car.

"I thought we'd go in together, Inspector," he said nervously as Jenny watched from the window.

They were sitting in chairs at opposite ends of the sitting room, so Sparkes had to keep turning his head, as if he were at a tennis match.

Jenny started crying immediately and Mike had got up and sat on the arm of her chair, patting her back awkwardly as Sparkes described their child's last moments.

"She wouldn't have known anything about it," he said. It was what everyone wanted to hear. That no one had suffered.

He'd left them to their grief and gone back to the office.

Salmond rang him just as he was closing down his computer. And his work brain. He needed to get home to Eileen.

"I'm out the door, Zara. Is it important? Is it the DNA result?"

"No—tomorrow, they say. But it looks like Jake Waters has surfaced."

He flicked the computer back on. "Where is he?"

"Kingston upon Thames. Buying fuel and withdrawing cash at an ATM in a garage forecourt just off the A3. There's a watch on his accounts and the bank alerted us immediately."

"And?"

"He drove off before we could get there but we've got him on the garage CCTV. He's still driving the second hire car, the Skoda. We're looking for him on the ANPR cameras on the A3 to see where he's gone. His number plate will ping up in one of the control rooms if he stays on the main roads. He won't get far."

"Well, what have we got at the moment? Any security camera material to identify him?"

"The usual crappy blurred images. He's got a baseball cap pulled down over his eyes and what looks like a scarf over the lower part of his face. The bloke who served him said he made him nervous. Said he looked like he was wearing a bank robbery kit when he came in, all wrapped up on a sunny day."

Has it been sunny today? I can't have looked out of the window all day.

"Who've we got at the scene?"

"Me and a two-man team to mop up the staff and witnesses before everyone disappears. And I'm coordinating the vehicle alert to other forces."

"Is he going home? Have you spoken to Kate Waters yet?"

"No. Next on the list."

"I'll do it."

He dialed, working out what he wanted to say as he pressed the buttons. She was so sharp, she'd probably guess right away, and he didn't want to risk Kate tipping off her son and sending him deeper underground.

He fleetingly wondered what he'd do if it were his boy. Would he turn him in? Of course he would. But what if he were being tried by the media? What if the case seemed circumstantial? Could he put his hand on his heart and say he'd do it?

"Hello," Kate said, picking up immediately and stopping him midthought. "Have you got some news?"

"There's been a possible sighting of Jake at a petrol station in Kingston."

"Kingston? Southwest London? Why would he be there?"

"I was hoping you'd know. Is there any reason you can think of for him to be in that neck of the woods? Any friends there?"

"No, not as far as I know. It's somewhere you drive past, isn't it? How do you know it's him?"

"Well, money was withdrawn using his credit card and he was driving the second car he's hired."

"Okay. More importantly, have you found Jamie Way, or Lawrence, or whatever he's calling himself now?"

It was his turn to hesitate.

"What? Have you got him?"

"No, the Thai police have. He wasn't there, Kate. He was in prison in Bangkok on the night of the fire. He's not our man."

He could hear the crushing disappointment in her voice as she muttered, "No . . ."

"Right, better get on."

He rang Helen the palliative nurse next to tell her he'd be late.

"Don't worry, Bob. She's sleeping. She won't know."

"How's she been today?"

"Same. See you in a bit."

Jake had left her room soon after Jamie, saying he had to go and see Mama. "I'll be back soon," he'd said and stroked her hair. "Try to rest."

Alex had thought about resting for a moment, had even lain down on her bed, but she couldn't. *Make a plan and then carry it out,* her mum would say if she were here. But nothing seemed real about the situation and she felt as if she were in a play. She got out her notebook and wrote *Plan to Find Rosie* at the top of the page, putting off the moment when she would actually have to act.

Okay, she told herself. *What is the priority?* She wrote: *1. Go to Wi-Fi café to use the Internet,* then crossed it out. She needed her own phone so her parents could ring her back. She had to speak to them, not just send an e-mail or text.

She put on her sun hat and walked slowly in the draining heat, sticking close to the stalls to catch the shade of their awnings. First to the ATM to queue, then withdraw enough money to buy a phone and some credit. Then to the nearest fake-electronics shop to find a cheap smartphone.

It seemed to take hours, but she finally made it back to her room and fumbled the SIM card into place with sweaty fingers.

When the phone came alive, she tried to sign into her e-mail account, but there was something wrong with her password. It was so long since she'd had to remember it. Gmail kept telling her to retry. She punched it in again more deliberately this time, as if Google were a slow child. No match. When she clicked "I Don't Know My Password" she was told a link had been sent to her phone. Except she'd lost her phone. She wanted to scream. It was like one of those cheap puzzles where you had to slide tiles around endlessly to find the sequence. She'd just phone home. She knew that number.

But still she hung back, torn between the comfort of hearing her mother's warm voice and the panic her call would unleash. She'd always been the reliable daughter, but not anymore. She screwed up her eyes, forcing herself to start dialing, and then stopped. It was still the middle of the night in Winchester. She felt relief wash over her at being able to postpone the evil moment.

"I'll try Rosie!" she shouted. She could ring Rosie now. *I can make her come back and stop all this,* she told herself. And Mum need never know.

But she couldn't remember the number. It had been saved on her phone under Rosie's name and she hadn't seen it for years. She tried to force the digits to magically appear in her head—there was a double eight in it, she was sure—but she came up empty. If only she could find her old phone. The thought made her dial her own number— *maybe it's fallen down the back of something.*

She waited, telling herself the battery must be dead by now and it would click straight to voice mail. But it began to ring in her ear. She held the phone away from her head and listened for its ringtone— "Happy" by Pharrell Williams. She and Rosie had both put the same one on their phones when they flew to Bangkok. *God, that was only just over a fortnight ago.* Alex clutched the phone, remembering when she had still felt happy.

She could hear Pharrell. But it wasn't in her room. She must've left it in the bar. She walked as fast as she could down the corridor, but the sound was getting fainter, not louder. She stopped and stood, turning round like a radar dish to pick up the tinny sound. It was coming from the dorm.

Alex pushed open the door as the sound stopped.

"Crap," she blurted and started to redial the number.

"Have you got a new phone?" Jamie said as he came in behind her.

"Er, yes. I think my old one is in here."

"In here? Why would it be in here?"

"Don't know. I heard it ringing."

"Oh! I've got the same ringtone as you," Jamie said and sort of laughed. "I was just coming to answer it." His voice sounded flat.

"No, you haven't," she said. "You've got 'I Will Always Love You.'"

"Used to. Got fed up with it and changed it. I downloaded 'Happy.'" And he picked up his phone to play it to her.

She retreated, unsure and feeling like a fool, and sat on her bed to think what she was going to say to her mum and dad when she finally took the plunge. She'd wait until they got up—or until they got back from work. She could give herself another few hours.

FIFTY-FIVE

The Detective
WEDNESDAY, SEPTEMBER 10, 2014

They'd found the car late the night before, burning on a piece of waste ground in South London.

Salmond had rung to tell him. "He must have realized there were cameras at the service station," she'd said. "Our little firestarter is on foot now."

"Anything left for our boys to work with?" He kept his voice low to avoid disturbing Eileen downstairs.

"Not much. It'd really taken hold before someone rang it in. Not an unusual event round there, apparently."

"Bob." Eileen's voice had floated up the stairs.

"Sort out Jake Waters's DNA sample, Zara. Got to go," he'd said and ended the call, feeling as guilty as if he'd been speaking to a mistress.

"Coming, love," he'd called back softly. How was he going to tell her he wanted to go to Bangkok? He wouldn't. He couldn't go. How could he? She might . . . He wouldn't go.

"Was it work?" she said when he bent down to kiss her head.

"'Course. Nothing to worry you."

"Go on, tell me."

He sat on the edge of her bed and took her cold hand.

"The car Jake Waters was driving has been found burned out. He's disappeared again."

"Never mind. Clever copper like you will find him."

"Not feeling very clever at the moment."

"Sorry, love."

"Don't be daft, Eileen. I just mean that there are more important things to think about at the moment. You."

"Shut up. I'm fine. Me and my mate morphine are doing a great job. Now do yours."

"I'm trying. The thing is . . . The thing is, we need to go to Bangkok for a couple of days to interview a witness and talk to the police there."

That gave her pause for thought. She struggled to sit up and he helped rearrange the pillows behind her.

"When are you going?"

"I'm not, Eileen. How can I?"

"Oh, do stop it, feeling sorry for yourself. Get on with it, Bob. Go to Bangkok. I'll be fine with Sam and Helen Angel. It's only two days."

"But you might . . . I need to be here," he blurted.

"Stop being so melodramatic. I'll be fine. The doctor and Helen are happy with me. They've got the pain under control and that is the main thing."

"But . . ."

"Look, if I promise I won't die while you're away, will you go?"

His eyes filled and he fought to control the tremble in his lips. Eileen clocked it all and patted his hand. "Just go, then come back and tell me all about it. I'm getting quite a taste for police procedurals."

He had to smile. She'd never been interested in his job before. She'd complained about the hours, the pay, and the toll it took on him. But now that she was dying, she wanted to hear every detail of every case. She'd even started reading detective novels. The darker the better.

"Let's talk about it in the morning."

"What is there to talk about? I thought we'd agreed."

He kissed her again and slid into the narrow bed with her, curling himself around her.

The results were back when he got to his desk that morning. It was a match. Jake Waters had had sex with Rosie Shaw. *But what else had he done?*

"You've seen?" he asked when Salmond knocked.

"Yes. Could it have been rape?"

"There's no physical evidence of that. And Alex said in her e-mails that Rosie was throwing herself at Jake."

"It could have got very ugly if Alex found out . . ."

Sparkes nodded. "We say nothing about this to anyone else. This is becoming a very complex inquiry and we don't want anyone jumping to conclusions and leaking it to the press before we find Jake Waters."

"All right, boss. But the families are getting impatient for answers."

"Say there's a delay in getting some of the results. Toxicology takes time. Lab problems. Be creative. The Shaws are still coming to terms with Rosie's cause of death, so let's just get out to Thailand and see what we can find there."

FIFTY-SIX

The Detective

FRIDAY, SEPTEMBER 12, 2014

The flight had left him completely drained and fogged. He'd tried to sleep but it wouldn't come. And Salmond had snored and fidgeted beside him. They'd looked at each other when the lights came on and breakfast service began.

"Bloody hell, we look like the living dead," she'd said. "Hopefully, we will scare the Thai police into helping us."

He'd nodded and spooned the yogurt and orange segments into his zombie mouth.

A hot shower and clean shirt had made him feel more human for his meeting with Colonel Prasongsanti at the Crime Suppression Division. Twenty minutes later, he wondered why he'd bothered.

The meeting was an exercise in excruciating diplomacy. It was certainly nothing to do with the investigation, as far as Sparkes was concerned. The senior Thai officer was courteous to the point of parody, bowing, making a speech about the importance of cooperation with the British police, inquiring about policing in their country. But nothing about the girls.

Bob had made gentle approaches to the subject, thanking the police officer and telling him how much they were looking forward to working with his team. He'd had to wait for the translator to do his linguistic to-and-fro, before being equally gently rebuffed.

In the end, he made a direct request for the police reports. Colonel Prasongsanti's smile became fixed as he listened to the translation.

That's a no, then.

"Colonel Prasongsanti regrets that that is not possible at the moment. The reports are still in progress. But you can visit the scene."

Well, that's something.

"That is very helpful. Thank you. And when is he hoping to have the reports?"

"Soon."

"Please could we meet the investigating officers?"

"So sorry, they are busy on other cases at present."

Sparkes smiled grimly at his counterpart.

"Perhaps they could spare us an hour. We would be so grateful. We simply want to learn from them . . ."

He'd pressed the right button. The colonel nodded gravely.

"He will arrange a meeting. Later today. Someone will call you on the number you have kindly provided."

"Thank you so much," Sparkes said, bowing in unison with his host.

"Well, that was like drawing teeth," he hissed at Salmond as they walked back to the main entrance.

"What a bloody pantomime," she hissed back. "I wonder who they'll let us talk to. No one who knows anything, obviously."

"Let's see. We'll just have to get on with our own stuff. Come on, let's get down to the scene. Where are Jason and Nicole now? Do we need to pick them up?"

They'd left the scenes-of-crime officers at the hotel, fighting jet lag with strong coffee. The pair had clearly not stopped at two cups. They both looked a bit wired when they got in the taxi, and Jason Fellowes started outlining his plan at a slightly faster speed than normal as soon as his bottom hit the backseat. Sparkes listened without speaking in the front, mentally running through his own checklist.

When they pulled up at Mama's Guesthouse, they all stood outside and spent five minutes taking a long, hard look at the building, its neighbors, access, the people around them. "Sniffing the air," Sparkes called it.

For him, it was a key moment, seeing the scene with fresh eyes. As fresh as twelve hours on a plane would allow, anyway. He rubbed the grit from his eyes and tried to relate what he was seeing to the descriptions in Alex's e-mails and Lars's photos. The building looked like an old hand-tinted photograph. The soot and ash had turned it black and sepia, but there was the odd flash of color. Shreds of a scarlet banner advertising whisky at the back of the bar, a melted yellow plastic crate.

He oriented himself: the terrace where Alex and Rosie drank beers when it rained; Mama's desk beyond the bar; the concrete stairs to the girls' room; the grilles on the windows of what must have been the dorm—the "boy nest," Rosie had called it, according to Alex.

"Right," Sparkes muttered. The others had been waiting for his signal and moved forward.

"I love a bit of flophouse chic," Salmond said, suiting up alongside Nicole. "I've got one for you, boss."

Sparkes took the white overall and stepped into it before pulling on latex gloves. They were maintaining standards even though the entire population of Bangkok had probably already stomped through their scene of crime. But the dressing up was attracting a bit of a crowd. Mostly bored tourists but some of the stallholders were moving round to get a better view, too.

"Come on, let's get on with this," Sparkes muttered, anxious to get away from the audience. He was already sweating in his suit and re-gretted not removing his tie before zipping himself in.

Nicole Ratner was taking her first videos and led the way. Sparkes moved through the ruins behind her, getting the measure of it all in his head. He didn't speak until he'd walked right round the site. It was his way. He picked a route through the debris of the ground floor, locating himself and fighting the urge to scream with frustration. He was amazed—no, horrified—at how much potential evidence had been left lying around for weeks, for scavenging dogs and passing opportunists to pick at. Bottles from "the party" were still rolling around beneath the heat-twisted frames of beds in the dorm. Charred belongings—a melted phone, a bracelet, unidentifiable bits of plastic and metal—floated on the sea of ash, probably just lying where they had last been flung.

The Thai police had originally said a candle knocked over at a party was responsible for the fire, but it looked to Sparkes as if the fire had started at the back of the building, at the end of a corridor.

Funny place to have a party, he thought. *And if a candle fell over on this concrete floor, it would just go out. You'd need something else to keep it going.*

He traced the scorch marks along the walls with his eyes to what must have been a door. There was nothing left of it now, just a gaping hole. He'd lay odds that the fire was started here, against the door. Was it started deliberately? To stop people going out? Or coming in? Or to stop people seeing what had happened beyond it?

The doorway led into a small courtyard, hemmed in on all sides by blank neighboring walls, and littered with blackened gas bottles and puddles of red plastic. The cold store, where the bodies had been found four weeks earlier, filled one corner. It looked homemade. It was basically a big metal box, dented, patched, and rusting where the edges met. The seal on the door was perished and ash blanketed an external air-conditioning unit. He wondered how the hell someone had managed to get it into the courtyard in the first place. Must have been built on the spot.

Inside the metal box, the drinks crates were still in one piece, stacked against a wall, the bottles clinking when he stepped onto the uneven floor. It stank of rotting food and rat shit and Sparkes put his hand over his mask to double bag his breath. It was only when he turned to come out that he saw the coconut matting heaped in the deep shadow by the door, the same spot, he guessed, where it had been thrown to one side by the officers who had uncovered the bodies.

"We need that," he said to Jason, who'd joined him in the claustrophobic space.

"Okay, boss," Jason said. "Nicole is photographing everything before I start sifting."

Sparkes found a patch of shade at the front of the building and drew a rough floor plan in his notebook. He made his notes meticulously. It was important—more so these days when he could become distracted so easily.

When Salmond found him, he was thinking about the distance from the dorm to the spot where the girls were discovered. "All right, sir?" she said, pulling off her gloves and hood.

"Yes. Well, apart from the fact that this crime scene is a bloody disgrace. Has Jason got the bottles from the dorm?"

"Yes. All bagged up and labeled. There are fingerprints everywhere, of course, but he's concentrating on the cold store. He says there's a lovely handprint inside, near the door."

"Probably the police or souvenir hunters. But we need everything."

"I don't think they were killed in the cold store—do you, boss? It's very confined—I can only just stand up straight in there—and he'd have had to kill one girl while the other one did nothing."

Sparkes nodded. "There were no marks on the bodies to suggest restraints. But they may not have been killed at the same time, of course. I think they must have died in the building, though. The only access to that courtyard is through the guesthouse, and the street outside is never empty—look around! This must go on twenty-four hours a day with the number of all-night clubs and bars in the area. Carting about two dead bodies might have been noticed. Even here."

"My bet is the dorm," Salmond said, taking the cap off a bottle of water. "Could have been a sex game that went wrong. Autoerotic asphyxiation? Like that MP—with the satsuma."

"Satsuma?"

"Might have been a clementine."

"Right, well, let's not worry about which small citrus fruit it was. Blimey, Zara, is this jet lag kicking in?"

Salmond grinned. "A bit."

"Who was the last person to see them alive?"

"The people at the party, according to the Thai police. Except there don't seem to have been any. The only other people staying at the guesthouse were the two Dutch lads, Jake Waters, and Jamie Lawrence. Lars and Diederik left on the eleventh and Lawrence was in prison on the night of the fire, according to the cops."

"We need to go and see him as soon as possible to see what he knows—and to get his prints. Trying to get forensic material out of the Bangkok lot is a waste of time."

Sparkes looked at his notes again. "We only have the police's word that the girls were alive that night. They could have been murdered and hidden days before. Aoife couldn't give more than a loose guide to when they died because of the uncertainty about the temperature in the cold store. When was Mags's last e-mail from Alex?"

Salmond pulled out her phone and scrolled silently. "August the twelfth," she announced. "The night Alex caught Rosie stealing from her bag."

"So they could have died at any time during the seventy-two hours before the fire."

"Yup."

Sparkes's phone rang. A local number. "Hello, Detective Inspector Bob Sparkes," he announced.

Two Thai officers—the more senior with faltering English—arrived half an hour later. They smiled broadly during the greetings and led the way into the guesthouse to point out areas they had examined. They had obviously been told they were there to instruct the British officers in how to conduct an investigation.

"I understand you believe a candle may have started the fire," Sparkes said with a smile. He was catching on.

"Why do you think it was a candle that started it? Did a witness say there was one?"

"The owner," the officer said. "She said many parties here. People drunk. They light candles. Candle knocked over." He made to leave, his work done.

"When did you speak to the owner? I thought she had disappeared," Sparkes said.

"Soon after the fire. She was very helpful."

"But I understand you have not found any other witnesses."

"Just owner. She lost everything in the fire. It was the fault of the foreigners who died."

"Except the autopsy in England showed one girl had been murdered. Strangled," Sparkes insisted, casually blocking the doorway to keep the officers there. "We sent you the report."

The two Thais talked between themselves for a moment.

"The case is closed. We have duties. We must go," the senior man said.

"Thank you very much for showing us how you work," Sparkes said, trying to keep sarcasm at bay. "Could we have a copy of your report? It would be so helpful."

"Not possible, sorry." And they were gone.

. . .

The team reassembled in the café at the end of the alley.

"We need to speak to the owner urgently," Sparkes said. "She was there. Ask the neighbors. They must know where she is. And I'll ask the embassy to get us in to see Jamie Lawrence."

Then we'll go home.

FIFTY-SEVEN

The Reporter

FRIDAY, SEPTEMBER 12, 2014

The decision to come had not been hard, really. I was chasing down every line in this story to find out the truth of what happened, the truth of my son's part in it, and Jamie Lawrence seemed to be the only person alive who might know. *Apart from you, Jake,* I tell myself. *But you're not here. And I've got to know what I'm protecting you from.*

I explained all this to Steve as soon as I'd heard that Jamie was in prison in Bangkok. He'd taken it all in as he helped himself to chicken dhansak from the foil container that was sitting in a pool of red oil on the table.

"So why have you got to go? Why can't you wait for your friend DI Sparkes to see him and report back?" he mumbled.

"Because I have questions I want to ask him. He may not want to talk to the police."

"But he'll want to talk to you?" Steve arched an eyebrow and drank his beer.

"I'll get him onside, Steve. I'll persuade him."

"I'm sure you will, Katie. No one is resistant to your charms, are they?"

I pushed my plate away. "Don't get nasty with me. You are exhausted; I get that. So am I, but I have to find out what he knows. You must understand that."

Steve didn't respond. He took another mouthful of curry.

"Don't you?" I said, louder. "This boy could be the key to every-thing."

"Actually, Jake is the key to everything. Shouldn't you be pouring your energies into finding him? This other boy has already been ruled out of the investigation by the police. He wasn't there. This is just displacement therapy, Katie. An expensive distraction—it'll cost a fortune for you to go. And you might end up not even getting in to see him."

"That's not fair. I've tried everything I can think of to find Jake." I had. I'd tracked down his friends from school, from university, even the treacherous girlfriend, and spoken calmly while corrosive desperation built in my stomach. I'd rung boys he used to play football with on a Saturday; visited pubs he used to drink in, libraries he'd studied in, cafés, shops he'd used. But nothing. No one had seen or heard from him.

"Anyway, I'll get in. I've got into harder places than that."

A wildlife park after hours to find a chained-up elephant and a *Midnight Express*–style prison in Bulgaria sprang to mind.

"And I've got some money tucked away."

"Our holiday money, you mean."

"Whatever. This is important. I'm going."

He speared another piece of chicken and chewed on.

And here I am. Groundhog Day in Bangkok, watching the same high-rises blur together from the speeding taxi. Don is already on the job for me. I'm having to pay him out of my own pocket, but he is worth his weight in gold. If anyone can help me get into the remand prison, it's him.

We meet at the same café at the end of the alley and I automati-cally look for Ross at the surrounding tables. He's not there so I turn back to Don and try to concentrate on what he's telling me.

"I can get you into Klong Prem prison this afternoon. It didn't cost much, but you can only have thirty minutes with the prisoner."

"Genius, Don. Will you come with me, in case I need an interpreter?"

"Sure."

"It's bloody Kate Waters!" A woman's voice rises above the hubbub of the café. I swing round in my chair. DS Zara Salmond is sitting two rows back. And not sitting anymore. She's striding between the tables, a woman on a mission, as the two people with her watch in astonishment.

"What on earth are you doing here?" DS Salmond calls over customers' heads, unable to wait until she arrives tableside.

"Er, hello," I say. "Just following up a story."

"Really? Wait until the boss hears you're here."

I twist round but can't see Bob Sparkes.

"Is he here?"

"You bet. He's making a call round the corner."

I get up quickly. I want to talk to him on my own, not with an audience of nosy tourists and shouty police officers.

We almost bump into each other as I round the corner into the alley. He's got his phone in his hand and is in another world.

"Bob," I say, making him jump. I keep walking, steering him back the way he's come so we are standing in shadows.

"Kate? What the hell are you doing here?"

"Your sergeant just shouted the same question at me. I'm here for the story, of course."

"What story? I thought you'd handed over to Joe Jackson. You're supposed to be on compassionate leave."

"Well, I like to keep busy. And Joe is doing something else at the moment. How are you doing? How have you got on with the Thai police?"

"Let's just say we are doing our own thing. Our team is working the crime scene and trying to track down the owner. The police are now saying she's a witness."

"Really? I might be able to help with that. I'm meeting one of Jake's friends later. He might know where we can find her."

"Right," he says, looking pained.

"We could go together, have a quiet chat with him," I say, slipping back into our normal working relationship.

"Not really, Kate," he says, bringing me back to reality. "I appreciate the offer, but we're looking for your son in connection with a murder inquiry . . ."

"Sorry, stupid of me."

"Anyway, what are you hoping to find here? Jake is in the UK. Shouldn't you be there for when he turns up?"

"Christ, you sound like my husband."

Sparkes smiles. "He has my every sympathy . . ."

I burble on; I don't want him to know about the prison visit. He might try to stop me.

"This is where whatever happened, happened. I need to find out the truth, Bob, for Jake's sake. And I can't sit around, waiting. It's like an itch that I have to scratch."

"I know," he says. He does. We are cut from the same cloth.

"I've got to get on," I say. "Time's cracking on."

"Where are you going next?"

"Going to see a man about a dog," I say. "How about you?"

"Same," he says and winks.

FIFTY-EIGHT

The Reporter

FRIDAY, SEPTEMBER 12, 2014

The queues at Klong Prem prison were long and I chewed at my nails, wondering if we would get in before visiting ended.

Don's contact had given him Jamie Lawrence's full ID and building number and he'd assured me we could just turn up. There were dozens of rules for visitors: no books or magazines with pictures of women (clothed or otherwise), no money, no food items. We could, however, pay for toiletries and food, including, bizarrely, KFC meals, and get them delivered by the prison service.

"Is that extra punishment?" I tried to joke.

"The daily menu inside is rice and fish heads," Don said. "He'll be grateful for whatever we send in."

"I hope he's not a vegetarian," I said to Don as I handed over the money for a bucket of fried chicken, toothpaste, and soap.

"Don't worry—he can use any of this as prison currency if he doesn't want it."

We moved through the system slowly, showing passports, being searched, filling in forms in echoing halls, and following signs to the Visitors' Room. Eventually, we sat on a bench and waited to be called.

. . .

A sudden flood of people into the room signals the end of the previous visit and I ready myself. I know what I want to ask, what I hope he'll tell me. *What I hope he won't.*

Names are being called and visitors are jumping up and running to the cubicle they've been allocated.

Don suddenly stands. "That's us," he says. I haven't heard my name or anything approximating it, but he grabs my arm and says, "We can't hang about. We haven't got long. It's the booth right at the end."

We walk fast, past the others, already perched on our side of the security grille and leaning hard toward their loved ones. The noise is deafening as dozens of voices compete with one another and bounce round the walls.

There are two high stools and a plastic telephone receiver in our half of the booth. I sit down and peer through two metal grilles—one inches from my face, the other a meter away, across a no-man's-land, where a figure sits with his phone to his ear. I screw my eyes up to get a better look. "He's Thai," I say to Don, and he puts his face against the grille to check.

I pick up the phone and say, "Jamie?"

The man says something I don't understand.

"It's not him," I shout at Don. "Have we got the right booth? Oh God, we're losing time."

He marches over to a guard at the desk behind us and returns. "Right place, wrong prisoner. He was here for the last visit. Our bloke is being brought now."

I clean the telephone receiver with a wet wipe, then the grille, as the Thai prisoner is escorted away and our man comes in.

I sit looking, unable to speak.

"Pick up the phone," Don says.

I do. The figure opposite does the same.

"Hello, Mum," he says.

FIFTY-NINE

The Reporter

FRIDAY, SEPTEMBER 12, 2014

Jake can't speak either now. We stare at each other.

Here we are. Sitting across from each other. He is so still it looks like he's been carved on the top of a tomb. But it's him.

"Jake," I whisper above the angry buzz of voices around me. And his head moves, a tiny flicker.

He puts one hand up to his face, covering it so that he looks as if he is peering through a crack in a wall. Not quite in the room.

"I can't believe you've come," he says.

Don reaches across to poke me. All he can hear is my end of the non-conversation. "You've got his name wrong, you bloody amateur," he explodes. "It's Jamie. Now ask a question, for fuck's sake. We haven't come here just to look at him."

I try to say something but my throat is so constricted I can only squeak.

Don grabs the phone from me and starts in. "Hello, Jamie. Sorry about that. My friend is a bit jet-lagged. How are you doing? We're reporters and we've come to see you to talk about Mama's Guesthouse."

I make a grab for the phone, startling poor Don into letting go.

"Jake," I say. "What are you doing in here?"

Don's face is a picture.

"It's my son," I tell him. "It's Jake."

. . .

My boy and I talk slowly, feeling our way through the minefield of questions that need answering. I clutch the phone, as I have done before, thousands of miles away, to hear every word. Don sits with his head next to mine so he can hear as well, making notes and occasionally interrupting with a follow-up question.

Jake tells us that his passport was stolen by Jamie and replaced with his own. He doesn't know why. He realized only when he was arrested in a bar near the guesthouse. The police searched his backpack and found Jamie's passport and a small bag of cannabis.

"It was a setup, Mum. Someone had told the police where to find me. They came straight to my table. They planted the drugs on me. I didn't understand what they were saying; they were shouting things and they looked at my documents and just assumed I was Jamie Lawrence. I didn't tell them my real name because I thought I could sort it out and no one would ever need to know I'd been arrested."

Us, he means. He didn't want us to know. His judgmental family.

"Has there been a hearing?" Don asks.

"No, I'm on remand."

"Why didn't you get a message to us, Jake?" I say.

He sighs into the phone. "I'm sorry, Mum. I was going to. But . . ."

"You see, you told us you were in Phuket, saving wildlife or something. We haven't really known where you were for two years . . ."

"Mum," he says. And I stop.

"Sorry. I didn't mean to interrogate you." *That is for later,* I think. "It's just been such a shock, finding you here."

We are back at the beginning.

"So, why did you come, then, Mum? What did you want to ask Jamie about?"

"The fire at the guesthouse," I say. He jerks his head up.

"What fire? When?"

"The night after you were arrested. Didn't you know?"

He shakes his head. "None of the guards speak English. I don't hear any news in here."

"Two girls staying there were killed."

"Two?" he shouts, his hand going back up to his face. "Oh God! Alex?"

Why isn't he mentioning Rosie?

Don looks at me. He knows there's something off about Jake's reaction, too. I shake my head and mouth "shock" at him.

"I know it must be distressing, love," I say, ramming the explanation home—for my own sake as much as Don's. "The police are investigating—here and at home. They are saying Alex was murdered, Jake. She was strangled before the place was set on fire."

His face has collapsed and he is crying. I put my hand to the grille—it's as close as I can get to touching him.

"Don't cry, angel," I say. It's the first time I've said those words since he was a toddler, and I start to cry, too.

"Who do you think killed her, Jake?" Don asks. "Was anyone being weird around her? Paying her too much attention?"

My son tries to steady his breathing. "We joked that Jamie was Alex's stalker," he says, his voice raspy and flat as if all the life has been knocked out of him. "He was trying to get her to go to Ko Phi Phi with him after Rosie . . ."

He stops.

"After Rosie what?" I say.

"I'm trying to remember," he says, his voice unsteady. "Rosie took off the day before I was picked up. She told Mama she was going to Myanmar with some Dutch boys. Jamie was so happy. He thought he would have Alex to himself."

"Dutch boys?" I say. "Do you mean Lars and Diederik?"

"Yes. How do you know their names?" He raises his head and looks at me hard.

"I've talked to Lars, Jake. I've been covering the story," I say. And I try to see his eyes, to see if he's lying. When he was little, I could always tell. He'd look away first or down at his shoes if he was fibbing. "Freddie did it . . ." As he got older, and the lies became subtler, it got harder. "I tried to ring but my phone ran out of credit . . ." But I could still spot the fake sincerity in his voice. "Honest, Mum . . ."

If I were fronting him up—if he were a story—I'd come straight in with "Rosie didn't go to Myanmar with the Dutch boys. We know that, don't we?" But I don't know what he'll say. I don't want him to lie to me. I'm not ready for that.

Don says, "She never left the guesthouse. She was the other body."

"It's been a huge story," I interrupt. "Your face has been on the front of every newspaper in the UK since the fire. The police are looking for you in connection with the deaths, Jake. You are in a world of trouble."

"Oh God! But why aren't they looking for Jamie?"

"Because as far as they're concerned, he's in prison in Bangkok."

His head goes down again.

"I—we will get you out of here," I say. I have no idea how, but I have to give him hope.

"Okay," he says.

"Hang on in there," Don says. "We need to sort out a lawyer immediately. I know one who might be able to help. Then we'll talk to the police about your real identity. Okay?"

Jake nods. He doesn't look at me. The bell rings and we start our good-byes.

"I'll come tomorrow," I say. "I've sent some food. KFC," I add, hopelessly. He's being hustled out of his seat to make way for the next prisoner.

"I love you, Jake!" I shout through the grille, but he makes no sign that he's heard me.

SIXTY

The Reporter

Don and I wait until we are outside before we speak.

"Can we get him out?" I say. It's all that matters now. I can deal with everything else later. Whatever that is.

"Let's see," Don says. "I'll ring my bloke. And we need to get the British embassy involved. It's a case of mistaken identity and we can prove who he is. It's a start, and if we were on home soil I'd be optimistic. But we're not in Kansas anymore . . ."

While he rings his man, I ring mine.

"Steve, I've found Jake," I blurt.

"Have you?" His voice is suddenly loud, spilling out of the phone. "Has he rung you? Where is he? How is he? Can I speak to him?"

"Steve, he's here. In Bangkok."

There is a beat of stunned silence as my husband wrestles with the news.

"What?" he shouts. "What is happening?"

And I explain slowly, unpicking the knots in the story for myself as well as my traumatized husband.

. . .

I t's Don who spots Bob Sparkes and Zara Salmond in the visitors'
queue.

"They must be going in to see Jamie Lawrence," he says when I try
to duck behind a pillar. "We need to tell them what's happened. They
may be able to help spring Jake."

I'm still not sure, but I cross my fingers.

"Inspector," Don calls across, and I try to smile.

Bob looks supremely fed up when he sees us. He doesn't smile
back, just rakes his hair with his fingers, leaving sweaty cornrows.

"Have you been in?" he snaps. "I should've guessed that's where
you were going."

I try to look apologetic. I need him onside. "We have, Bob," I say,
but I'm suddenly fighting back tears. I clench my fists against them.
Try to straighten my face.

"Kate? What's the matter? What's happened?" he asks.

"It's Jake," I gulp.

"What about him? Has Jamie told you something?"

I shake my head and Don carries on for me, filing the story in
three sentences. "It's Jake Waters they've got in there, not Jamie Lawrence. Jake says he was stitched up by him. His passport was swapped
and drugs planted on him so he was arrested."

"Bloody hell," DS Salmond says. "So who's been driving round
Surrey in the hire car?"

DI Sparkes looks up at the sky and then at me. "Are you sure
it's him?"

"He's my son. Of course I'm sure."

"I'm assuming you weren't sitting face-to-face and you haven't seen
him for a while. I'm just saying that people can make mistakes."

"It's him!" I shout.

"And what did he say? What did he tell you?"

I blow my nose on a tissue DS Salmond has handed me as the queue turns and watches us with naked curiosity before shuffling forward a few steps.

"He said when they first started calling him Jamie, he thought it was a good thing. That he could sort it out and no one would need to know he'd been in trouble. He's an idiot, Bob. But he was not involved in that fire. He didn't even know about it until I told him. He was inside Klong Prem, sleeping on the floor of a cell with seventy other prisoners."

Sparkes doesn't want to hear Jake's sob story and waves the *Midnight Express* details away with his hand. "What about the girls? Does he know anything about what happened to them?"

"He said Rosie left before the fire. To go to Myanmar."

"With the Dutch boys . . ." Don adds quietly.

Bob Sparkes raises an eyebrow. "Except, of course, she didn't . . ."

"He was told that by the woman who owned the guesthouse—Mama. Have you talked to her yet?" And I hurry on to Jamie past the questions about Jake.

"Jake says Jamie was a strange lad who followed Alex around and was trying to pressure her into traveling with him instead of Rosie."

"Does he think Jamie killed them?"

"He doesn't know. But he said Jamie was very happy when Rosie disappeared."

Salmond got her notebook out.

"So she disappeared on August the thirteenth?" she asks, pen poised.

"I think that's right. It was difficult to talk through two grilles with everyone else shouting around us."

"I imagine it was," Sparkes says. "I need to talk to Jake myself. He's a person of interest in our investigation until we rule him out, and I need to be absolutely clear about his identity myself. Before I contact the Thai police and my lot."

"I'm not sure prisoners can have more than one visit a day," I say. I'm not sure I want my son interrogated by DI Bob Sparkes. "They've got a million rules."

"Leave that with us. Zara's made a friend in the prison service and they've smoothed our way. Now tell me some family secrets I can test Jake with."

I run through pets' names, Jake's school, teachers' names, his A Level results, his first girlfriend. But all the time I keep running our conversation in the prison through my head.

"Two?" he'd shouted. As if he was expecting only one body. He hadn't known about Alex. But Rosie? What will he tell Bob Sparkes?

"**W**hat are you going to do with this, Kate?" Bob is asking. "Are you telling your newspaper about this?"

For a moment, I feel as if I don't know. But I do. If I don't do it, Don will.

"Yes. Of course I am. I need to get him released. Don's getting him a lawyer and I'm going straight to the embassy to tell them. They've got the wrong person in prison. That must count for something with the Thai authorities."

"Right, well, good luck with that," Sparkes says. "I'd better give our press office the heads-up—what time is it there?"

"Early yet, sir," Salmond says.

"But I'm not confirming your story, Kate. Not until I've seen him and am sure."

"Be gentle with him, Bob," I say. "He's been through hell."

SIXTY-ONE

The Detective

FRIDAY, SEPTEMBER 12, 2014

When he came out, Sparkes was reenergized. It was Jake Waters. They were doing a blood test in the prison infirmary to set the seal on it, but it was definitely him.

"Come on, Zara—keep up," he said, striding back to the taxi rank and turning his phone on again. "We need to tell HQ immediately and put Jamie Lawrence's photo out officially."

"I'm pretty sure that Kate Waters has released the story, sir. I've got loads of missed calls on my phone."

"Yeah, me, too." There was one from Eileen, but Sparkes was dialing DCI Wellington as he got into the taxi. He would ring Eileen as soon as he'd got rid of the business end. He couldn't wait to tell her the latest twist in the tale. She'd love it.

He talked to his boss in short bursts as they careered through the traffic. She knew everything already. The *Post* had been onto them before publishing Kate's account while he was inside the prison, but she'd fended off inquiries until she could speak to him.

"Say that blood tests are being done to confirm the identity of the man in Bangkok," Sparkes said. "Why haven't we got Jake Waters's DNA results from Rosie's body? We need to put a rocket under the lab boys. And, most importantly, put out the message that we want to talk to Jamie Lawrence urgently. The *Post* has got his photo from the Dutch boy, Lars. Let's get it blown up and out there."

U p in his room, he took off his sweat-sodden shirt and stood under the air-conditioning unit to dry off. He felt as if his brain were boiling inside his skull.

He sat on the bed with a towel round his shoulders and rang Eileen back.

Sam answered the home phone.

"Hello, love," he said, still buzzing. "I've missed a call from Mum. Put her on. She won't believe what's happened here."

"I can't, Dad. She's not well."

The towel slipped off as he braced himself against what was coming.

"What's happened?"

"She lost consciousness in the night. I'm so sorry, Dad. Can you come home?"

He was fighting one arm into the sleeve of his damp shirt already, adrenaline coursing through his body.

"I'm coming. What is the doctor saying, Sam?"

His daughter's voice faltered. She was being so brave it broke his heart.

"That it could be a matter of hours, Dad."

He wouldn't be there. He knew that.

"Were you with her, love?"

"No, Helen was. She just slipped into a coma during the night and Helen rang me as soon as she realized. Why did you go to Bangkok, Dad? Why aren't you here?"

He couldn't speak for a moment. The guilt and grief flooded his head, washing out every other thought.

"Dad? Are you there?" Sam's voice was his life belt, dragging him back to shore.

"I'll find out about a flight now, love. Kiss your mum for me. Tell her to hold on until I'm there. Tell her I love her."

"Oh Christ," he told his knees when it was over. He found himself on the carpet. Had he fainted? He didn't want to get up. He wanted to lie there. But someone was knocking on the door. He struggled to his feet and opened it a crack.

"Bob! Are you okay?" Kate said. "You look terrible."

He let her in. He didn't have the strength to do anything else.

She led him to a chair and helped him put his arm in the other sleeve of his shirt.

"It's freezing in here, Bob. You're shivering. I'll turn the AC down."

"I need to get home," he said. "I need to get a flight."

"Why? Oh God, is it Eileen? I'll call the airline for you now. Where's your ticket and passport?"

He fished them out of his jacket pocket without a word. The ticket was limp with the morning's perspiration, but Kate took it and sat on the bed with her phone.

He watched her as she tried to persuade the airline to change the flight. *This is what she looks like when she is working me.*

"Bob," Kate said, her hand over the phone, "they want to know what sort of emergency it is. We need to say or you'll have to buy another ticket. It will cost a fortune. You're on a cheapo fare."

"Eileen's dying," he said. And Kate's eyes widened.

"My friend's wife is dying from cancer. He has to get home tonight," he heard her say. "Is that the earliest flight? Nothing else? What about other airlines?"

She was all business as she finally got off the phone. "Okay. The next direct flight to London leaves at midnight. There are connecting flights that leave a bit earlier but they take much longer and there is the risk of missing your connection. So I've changed your ticket to the midnight flight. With the time difference, you'll be in London at six thirty tomorrow morning."

He nodded. It was hopeless. He wouldn't get there in time. His head dropped and Kate took his hand.

"We'll leave for the airport in four hours, Bob. Do you want me to tell DS Salmond?"

"No, I'll do it."

"I'll get you a brandy," she said and rummaged in the minibar. "I think I'll have one, too."

S almond came immediately. "Oh God, sir, I'm so sorry. What can I do?"

"Nothing, Zara," he said. "Kate's sorted out the flight, but I want you to stay and finish off here."

"Of course. It'll be all right. You'll get there."

Kate passed her a miniature and ripped the plastic bag off the tooth mug in the bathroom.

They all sat in silence, sipping their drinks, each in their own bubble.

Reality punctured the silence when Salmond's phone went off.

"It's DCI Wellington," she said and passed the phone to Sparkes.

The two women retreated into the bathroom, to give him some privacy, while he told his boss his news.

"Zara," he called after he finished. "You need to speak to the DCI and update her on what's going on re Jamie Lawrence."

"Are you going to be all right, sir?" she said, and he nodded.

"I'll stay," Kate said. "And I'll take him to the airport. You get on with the investigation."

She hadn't seen Jake for hours. He'd told her he'd be back soon. He'd been all distracted, but he'd stroked her hair as he left. She held on to that.

She didn't understand what was going on. She hated it when boys did that. Messed with your head. One minute really into you, the next, so not interested.

Anyway, she had other things to think about . . . But her mind kept straying back to Jake and the lovely dip above his top lip. And Rosie.

She took a deep breath and read through her new to-do list again, stumbling at every line. *Find Rosie; Phone Mum; Go home?*

She'd got her ticket out and laid it out on the bed beside "A & R's Final Itinerary." She and Rosie hadn't moved past page one, but she leafed through the rest of the trip, picking out highlights she'd never see now. Tears fell onto the pages, blotting the damp paper, smudging the details of their adventure. The reality was so grubby and sleazy. She went to screw the pages up and throw them across the room but stopped herself. She needed the airline phone number—she was sure she'd copied and pasted it into the itinerary—and found it in a list of "Useful Contacts." Just above Rosie's mobile phone number. Alex grabbed her phone and dialed. The phone went straight to voice mail.

Rosie's chirpy voice filled her head. "Hi, too busy having a great time to take your call. Send me a text if you need me . . ."

She begged Rosie to get in touch. "Please! We can sort things out. I haven't said anything to our parents yet. But I'll have to soon. Ring me, Rosie!"

She sat for a while with her phone in her hand. Was Rosie screening her calls? She'd text her as well, to ram the message home. Then she'd go and see Mama.

Mama glared at Alex as she approached.

"I need to know why Rosie left, Mama," Alex said. "It's very important."

The landlady's mouth clamped shut, her purple lipstick almost disappearing.

"I'll have to go to the police and report her missing if you don't tell me." Alex tried to keep her voice strong.

The purple lips reappeared in a ghastly smile.

"That would be a mistake," Mama said. "That is why Rosie went." And she told Alex about Rosie crying because she was so ashamed of herself, about begging Mama to lend her money and get her passport back from the scooter man.

"She wanted to run away from all this—and from you." Mama pointed at Alex.

"Why me?"

"You hated her. We all heard you." Then she shook her head. "You and Rosie are big trouble."

Alex stood her ground in front of Mama's desk.

"Please show me the text messages she sent. I need to see them."

Mama slid her phone off the desk into her pocket. "Private," she said.

Alex stood silently, grim faced.

"What? What else?" Mama said. "I am too busy for this."

She reached up to scratch her scalp and Alex noticed she was wearing her missing earrings.

"Where did you get those?" she snapped, pointing at the girlish flower-head studs, and Mama put a hand to an earlobe.

"Rosie," she said and half-smiled. "They were a good-bye present. Now go away." Mama waved her off.

"Was Rosie sleeping with Jake?" Alex blurted. The question had been burning a hole in her stomach.

Mama's eyes narrowed. "Who told you that?"

"Jamie. He told me to ask you."

"You are a bad girl. Making trouble for Mama's Guesthouse."

"Where is Jake?" Alex's voice was suddenly louder. "Did he have anything to do with Rosie leaving?"

"Not your business," Mama snapped. "I want you to leave now. I need your room."

Alex couldn't settle anywhere. She paced the corridor from her room to the dorm, then back again. She wouldn't talk to Jamie beyond asking where Jake was.

"When is he getting back?"

Jamie repeated that he had no idea, irritation making his voice more clipped, his breath shorter.

Alex watched him. When he thought she'd gone, she could see he was counting slowly with his eyes closed, like a child playing hide-and-seek. When he opened them, he looked startled to see her so close.

"What?" he said. She carried on staring.

"Nothing. Do you think Jake is avoiding me? I really want to talk to him before I go home."

"Stop talking about going home. We can sort this out. I can have a word with Mama if you like."

"No, I'll ask Jake to do it when I see him. He's worked here for ages. He knows Mama best."

"I can't believe you want anything to do with him after what he did."

"You don't know what he did, Jamie. You're just making it up."

"Well, I know what I saw. And heard."

"What? What did you hear?"

"Rosie shouting at Jake. Saying she would tell you about sleeping with him."

"Shut up!" Alex shrieked.

"If you don't want to believe me, that's your problem."

Alex turned away. "I'm going to see if I can find him."

"I'll come, too," Jamie said. "You shouldn't be on your own."

She wouldn't walk with him, so he trailed behind her. They went to all the usual places, but Alex noticed that he didn't really bother looking.

When they got back, Alex checked her phone again for a message from Rosie. Nothing. She phoned the airline to find out about changing her ticket. There were seats, but it was going to be expensive. She'd have to ask her parents to do it—and to pay the extra cost. When she rang them.

"I'm hoping I can take a flight home tomorrow," she told Jamie when she ventured back into the empty bar.

He looked stunned. "But we were going to talk to Mama about you staying."

"No, we weren't, Jamie. You were. I don't want you to. Even if Rosie comes back. How can I trust her again? I'm going to ring home and tell them and then get on the plane . . . I'm sorry, but I've got to leave. You'll be fine." She went to put her arm around him, but she didn't want him to get the wrong idea.

"I won't," he said, his voice muffled by emotion. "I want you to stay, Alex. Please stay with me . . ."

She pulled back and straightened her crumpled shirt.

"No, that's not going to happen."

He looked like he might cry. "Look, I'm going to start packing. Maybe we can have a drink together later."

"A bit of a party?" Jamie said.

"Well, maybe," she said doubtfully.

SIXTY-TWO

The Reporter
FRIDAY, SEPTEMBER 12, 2014

"Do you want me to leave you alone?" I ask, not wanting to go. He looks smaller somehow, curled in against the pain.

"No, I could do with some company," he says. "Even a hack . . ." He tries to smile.

"Ever the charmer." I smile back, trying to keep the gentle joshing going. It's what we do when things are blacker than black. We make a joke. A bad one. It's bravura, I suppose. Showing we can laugh in the face of anything.

"Shall I pack your bag?"

"Thanks, Kate. Is there another brandy in the minibar?"

I fish all the bottles out and lay them on the carpet in front of him. "No brandy, but there's whisky or gin. Or a beer?"

I leave him choosing and start emptying his drawers into his suitcase. I'm surprised he's had time to unpack—most blokes don't bother—but his underwear and socks are neatly sorted and his shirts are hanging in the wardrobe.

"Looks like you were planning to stay for a month, Bob," I say. "Not a light packer, then?"

"I couldn't concentrate when I was getting ready, so I put everything in. I shouldn't have come, should I?"

I go and sit opposite him on the bed and automatically stroke his arm. I can't help it. It's muscle memory for this sort of situation, but it makes me prickle with embarrassment and I go to pull my hand back. But he doesn't recoil. He takes my hand and squeezes it. "Thanks for being here, Kate. I appreciate it."

"Why don't you FaceTime Sam?" I say. "Then you can see Eileen for yourself. Speak to her . . ."

He puts on a clean shirt, turning away from me as he takes off the old one. The skin on his back is still damp and the fabric clings immediately.

I find my phone tripod in my bag and set it up on the desk. Using it will be easier than trying to hold the phone in shaking hands. "I'll go in the bathroom, shall I?"

"No, stay. I might balls the FaceTime thing up and need you."

He rings his daughter and I catch a glimpse of her on the screen, puffy eyes and Bob's mouth.

"Can I see Mum?" he says. I can see the strain in his face in the mirror above the desk as he searches for her.

"Hello, love," he says when Sam arrives at the bedside. The figure in the bed stirs at the sound.

"I'm here, love," he breathes. "I know you can hear me, Eileen. I want you to know how much I love you and that I'll be there in person in the morning. You promised you'd be all right until I got back. Will you wait for me? Please, love."

He's crying and I try not to look, but I catch myself glancing at the tragedy in the mirror.

"Move the phone, Sam, so I can see all of her."

Sam runs the phone over her mother, starting at her sleeping face, as white as the pillowcase, and moving over her curled hands on a rosebud duvet cover.

"We're all here," Sam says, panning round to show the others, looking shyly into the camera. "And we'll all be here when you get back, Dad."

"All right, darling. See you in the morning," he says.

I make him get into bed and rest afterward. He's exhausted and he closes his eyes against it all, lying on his side with his hands held together under the pillow. I turn the main lights off and sit quietly until I think he may be asleep.

Then I tiptoe into the bathroom and make my own call home.

SIXTY-THREE

The Mother
FRIDAY, SEPTEMBER 12, 2014

She switched on the kitchen television as she made the second tea of the day, standing in her nightie and old cardigan, turning up the sound a bit so she could hear above the kettle's rumble. Their Family Liaison Officer, DC Wendy Turner, had rung at the crack of dawn with the news there'd been a major breakthrough.

"Lesley, Jake Waters has been found in Bangkok. He's in prison."

"What? As well as Jamie Lawrence?" Lesley had said, trying to make sense of the words.

"No. The police thought it was Jamie Lawrence, but it was really Jake Waters."

"I don't understand, Wendy. What do you mean?"

She'd thought she'd got it straight when she put the phone down and turned to Malcolm.

"They're not looking for Jake Waters anymore," she'd said. "He's in prison in Bangkok. It is Jamie Lawrence they want to talk to now. It's him they think killed Alex."

Hours later, the Scottish referendum buildup was playing in the background as she stirred Mal's sugar in. As she lifted both cups to take them upstairs, Alex's face appeared on the screen. She slopped both back onto the counter in her haste to get to the remote control.

It was suddenly blaring into the room, the "astonishing development" in the backpacker murder.

"Mal," she screamed. "Come down here. It's Alex."

Malcolm ran down the stairs in his T-shirt and boxers, his face creased with sleep.

"Look!" she said pointing at the screen. "The press have heard they've got Jake Waters."

Malcolm sat down on a chair and rubbed his eyes.

"Can we turn the telly down?" he said. "I've got a terrible headache."

Lesley muted it and rang Wendy Turner's mobile phone. Engaged. But as soon as she put the phone down, Jenny called.

"It's doing my head in, Lesley," she said. "It's awful. Just when I think I know what happened, everything gets thrown up in the air again. I just want to know who killed our girls. That's all."

"I've tried Wendy again just now, but her phone's engaged. There's no one else I can ring for information. DI Sparkes and DS Salmond are in Thailand. I don't know how to get hold of them."

"Ring Kate Waters. She'll know."

Kate's mobile number rang out and Lesley tried to sit still.

"Hello, Lesley," Kate answered. "Have you heard?" There was no call for pleasantries now. Mother shorthand was all that was needed.

"Yes. It's unbelievable. Do you know what happened?"

"I went to see Jamie Lawrence earlier and found Jake in the prison."

"But how was this mistake made? Do they look the same?"

"A bit—same sort of height and hair color. But Jamie's passport was in Jake's bag. And Jake went along with it, told the police he was Jamie. He didn't want us to know he'd been arrested. And the police didn't question it. He was a skinny foreigner with a small bag of cannabis in his backpack. I don't think they were too interested in checking his ID. They just locked him up."

"And it was Jamie in the hospital?"

"Yes, with Jake's passport. And Jamie at the hostel when the fire started. Jake had nothing to do with that, Lesley."

There was silence as both women reran the last shouted phone call in their heads.

"I'm sorry I said those things, Kate. I was so desperately upset . . ."

"I know. It was a terrible time for all of us. But the police will catch Jamie now. Now they're looking for the right man."

"What are they doing? Are you with DI Sparkes and DS Salmond?"

Kate went quiet again. Then she whispered down the phone: "Look, Bob Sparkes has got a family emergency—he's flying back tonight. Zara Salmond is finishing things up here. Give her a ring in an hour or so."

"Oh goodness, what has happened?"

"It's personal, Lesley. I'm not sure Bob would like people to know. Is that okay?"

"Of course. What did Jake say about the girls, Kate?"

"He was very upset when I told him about Alex. I think he liked her a lot."

Lesley started to cry. She felt as if she was standing on a precipice in the dark, the stress of not knowing what would happen next crowding her head with what-ifs. She couldn't see an end to it. She couldn't bear to even try to step forward anymore.

"Try and stay strong, Lesley," Kate was saying. "I'm going back with a lawyer to see him again, to try to get him out. He'll be able to tell us more then."

"Will you call me afterward?" Lesley asked. "Please . . ."

SIXTY-FOUR

The Reporter

MONDAY, SEPTEMBER 15, 2014

I still haven't heard from Don, and I drum my fingers on the hotel desk. He's been busy all weekend with me snapping at his heels, urging him on. He's got the lawyer on board and we've talked endlessly to the embassy, the police, and the press.

Give him another five minutes, I tell myself. *He's probably on the phone to the lawyer again.* We're taking him in to see Jake later this morning. I look at my phone, like a junkie, automatically checking every thirty seconds for messages or e-mails.

Bob sent a simple text yesterday to tell me Eileen had died. He didn't say if he'd got there in time.

I hope he did. I'd waited for a long time after he headed off to catch his flight on Friday. I'd just stood there, weighed down by his quiet grief. He hadn't cried again. He'd stitched it under his damp skin, holding it in until he reached home.

"Thanks, Kate," he'd said as he shouldered his bag and put his passport in his breast pocket. "Better go through. Security can take an age . . ."

I'd wanted to hug him, but he looked too brittle to touch. "Have a safe trip, Bob. Try and sleep. You'll be there sooner if you do."

He'd tried to smile.

"Go on. There's a car booked to pick you up at the airport."

"Okay, good-bye."

He'd reached out a hand and stroked my arm, then turned and disappeared into the throng.

I'd taken the train back into the city. After so much intensity, I couldn't bear the isolation of a taxicab—I needed people around me, even strangers. Especially strangers. I watched their faces, writing their stories in my head.

It was very late when I got to my room and switched on my laptop. Jake's face was everywhere again. But this time he was the victim, not the perpetrator.

"The Wrong Man . . ."

The press had had a field day, beating up the Thai police over the mistakes they'd identified: "Ten Reasons They Got It Wrong," "The Devastating Mistakes in Full," et cetera. It's a complicated story but the editors had pulled out all the stops—*adding value*, the watchword on back benches—so there were sidebars, bullet points, and graphics to hammer home every line.

It looked amazing. But I'd wondered if it would do any good. Would it shame the Thais into releasing Jake?

I should have gone straight to bed when I got back to the hotel, but I poured myself a glass of château minibar and kept replaying Jake in my head. The moment we recognized each other. His reaction to the news about Alex. Rosie.

I'd ask him more questions when I got him out.

He doesn't look any more rested when I see him again. But then neither do I.

All the plates are spinning now. The embassy is attempting to work its diplomatic magic behind the scenes, and the lawyer is doing all the talking at the prison. I have to wait my turn. When the lawyer and Don go off to talk to the prison authorities, I lean forward.

"Did you sleep last night?" I say. He shakes his head. His eyes are pouchy and the bristles on his face make him look old.

"Did you get the food I sent?" He nods.

"We need to talk, Jake."

"When I get out, Mum. My head is all over the place. I'm trying to make sense of it all."

"We all are," I say. "Especially about Rosie. Do you know what happened to her?"

He shakes his head slowly.

"The police are going to ask you the same questions. You do know that?"

"The inspector already has and I told him the same thing. I don't know. She disappeared the night Alex got drunk and had to be put to bed. I was supposed to be taking Alex out but I ended up doing an extra shift. I was told Rosie'd gone to Myanmar on the bus to meet the Dutch boys."

He rattles it off, this neat little tale. And I shiver.

"Did you believe that?" I say gently.

Jake looks across no-man's-land at me. "Why are you asking that? What was I supposed to think? It was possible."

"Who told you?"

"Mama, the woman who ran the guesthouse. She's the person the police should be talking to."

"And Alex?"

"She was alive when I left the guesthouse for the last time. Honest, Mum. She was talking about going home. It was a horrible mess."

The bell clangs and he looks up. I can see on his face the relief that he can leave.

"Stay strong, love," I call and put my hand up to the grille.

He nods and stumbles away.

Ross is nervous when we finally meet. Jittery. Slopping his coffee onto the table as he jumps up to greet me. He'd blown me off the last time and I wondered if he'd turn up today.

"Hi." He pulls out a chair for me and I catch it before it tumbles to the ground.

"Watch out," I say. "Are you okay?"

"Yeah, yeah. Sorry, I'm all over the place. I'm trying to get clean. It's only been a few days."

"That's great, Ross," I say and smile encouragingly.

"I had some bad stuff the other day and ended up in hospital. Anyway, I'm trying . . ." He signals to a waiter for another coffee. "So, do you think you'll be able to get Jake out of prison? Is he okay?"

"I've just seen him—it's unbelievably grim. But we're working on getting the Thais to release him."

Ross nods and holds up crossed fingers. Like he's five and we're playing a game. *When do boys grow up? Probably only when they have children of their own,* I think, stirring my coffee. *When they finally get the whole being-an-adult thing.*

Ross has finished his drink and is looking edgy. "I'd better get off to the pharmacy," he says. "Pick up some stuff."

"Absolutely. Look, just one thing. Jake said I should speak to Mama, the woman who owned the guesthouse, but I don't know where to find her. Have you seen her lately?"

Ross looks at me sideways. "Well, not seen her, but I heard from someone that she'd turned up at a cousin's place. She's staying there for a while."

"I'd love to talk to her about Jake. Can you give me the address?"

"She might not want to talk to you."

"I promise not to say you gave it to me."

He writes it down on a paper napkin with my pen.

The woman sitting outside the house on an orange plastic chair is in what looks like full stage makeup and a wig, wafting her face with a bamboo fan.

"Hello," I say, "you must be Mama."

She curls a lip but stays seated. "Who are you? What do you want?"

"I'm Kate. I've been to your guesthouse." *It's not a lie. I have. I've stood in the ruins.*

She shrugs and rolls her eyes at another woman, sitting beside her. A small, drab peahen beside her own flamboyant display.

"I don't remember you, but so many people stayed."

"I just wanted to say how sorry I was to hear about the fire. It must be terrible for you to lose everything like that."

Mama looks interested for the first time and waves her companion out of her seat for me. "Yes, it is terrible. I lost my home, my business, my money."

I tut sympathetically and the cousin is sent off in search of cool drinks. She returns with water in plastic cups.

"Were you at home when it started?"

She nods. "Sleeping in my bed. I woke up and smelled the smoke." She mimes the moment she realized.

"Wow! How did you get out?"

"I climbed out of a window. I broke my arm when I fell." And she lifts the sleeve of her dress to show me a grubby cast. "I went back to my home village to recover. But I had to come back to Bangkok to sort out things."

"You were so lucky to get out alive," I say, laying the sympathy on with a trowel. *She was there. At last, I'm talking to someone who was actually there.*

"Very lucky."

"How on earth did it start?" I ask. "I heard it was a candle knocked over at a party."

The eyes narrow. "That's what the police say, but there was no party. One of the English boys did it," she says and fans herself for dramatic effect.

I am the perfect audience. I sit forward and gasp with disbelief. "How do you know?"

"I saw him. Running away. I smelled the lighter fluid he used." She spits on the pavement in disgust."

Jamie. Jamie Always in the Way.

"Those poor girls," I say, and Mama's face hardens behind the makeup.

"I heard one of them, Rosie Shaw, had left to go traveling in Myanmar . . ."

"That is what she told me."

"Did she?"

"The last time I see her. The night before the fire."

"Oh," I say carefully. "I thought she was supposed to have left two days before."

Mama fans herself rapidly. "Yes, yes, that is correct. Two days before. I can't remember everything."

"You must have been a good friend to her. I heard she sent you text messages?"

"Well, the English boy, Jamie, said to tell people that. People were getting upset about her disappearing. He said it would make them happier."

"Jamie?"

"Yes, he was always whispering in my ear, telling tales. He said he saw everything," Mama says almost to herself.

"Did he? What did he see?"

"He was always watching Alex. He wanted her more than anything. He even drugged her once to stop her going out with Jake."

"Really?" I can't believe what I'm hearing.

"Yes, he put something in her beer and then put her to bed. Safe away from everyone else."

Mama's cousin suddenly interrupts us, coming out of the door with a phone. She waves it at Mama, who excuses herself. "Sorry, this is important."

I sit with the cup of water warming in my hands and wait. *Rosie never left. Jamie made up the text messages. Did Alex find out? Was that why she was killed?*

When she returns, Mama is furious.

"Who are you?" she hisses from the doorway.

"I told you, Kate . . ."

"You are British police—my contact told me."

"No, of course I'm not. You're right—the British police are in Bangkok, looking into the death of the two girls. But I'm not with them. I'm the mother of Jake Waters."

She actually laughs. A deep, dirty rumble. "I am glad I'm not," she says and closes the door on me.

It takes the rest of the day for the results of Jake's blood test to come back, confirming the mistaken identity, and for the Thais to release him. I spend much of it in taxis, running round the city collecting and delivering pieces of paper, phoning home to get Steve to scan documents or Joe to find a number. I'll thank him properly when I get back. With Jake.

In the end, his release is done very quietly, without fuss or any admission of blame. The Thai way.

I stand and wait while Jake is brought through, the heavy clunk of slamming doors marking his passage toward me. I've got the emergency passport, plane tickets, and my luggage with me—Don and the lawyer thought it best to leave immediately, before anything else could happen. I hold Jake's hand in the taxi and he presses back.

"Nearly home," I whisper. "Dad and Freddie will be at the airport to meet us."

SIXTY-FIVE

The Reporter

TUESDAY, SEPTEMBER 16, 2014

They are not the only ones. The arrivals hall is rammed with film crews and reporters. I should have expected it, but I'm not firing on all cylinders. I spot Steve at the back of the throng, waving frantically, and push our trolley as fast as I can toward him, with Jake hanging on to the handle like a toddler in Sainsbury's. But it's like swimming against the tide. The reporters crowd in, ducking under the photographers' lenses, blocking our way and firing their questions at us.

"How does it feel to be home, Jake?"

"Are you suing the Thai authorities?"

"What's the first thing you're going to do?"

"Have a pint of beer, then sleep for a week," my son says and smiles his beautiful smile. The cameras beep and whir to capture the moment of release.

Then we move forward like a rugby scrum, the reporters still keeping their heads below the lenses and walking backward as we edge forward. Steve is wading through the crowd to meet us. He finally breaks through and folds Jake into his grasp and holds him long and hard.

"You're a wonderful sight," he says, and then hugs me, too.

"Still ugly," Freddie says and man-bumps his brother.

"Come on, let's get you home." Steve takes his eldest son by the arm.

"Do you want to say anything to the parents of Alex and Rosie?" a familiar voice shouts over the hubbub.

Jake stops smiling. I grip his arm to stop him, but he is searching for the source of the question.

"That I am so sorry . . ."

"Sorry about what?" Louise Butler calls back.

"Sorry that they died."

"Do you know how Rosie died, Jake?"

He looks stunned by the sudden change of tone, and Steve and I hustle him forward, away from the questions.

Joe Jackson appears at my side. "Can we get a few words on our own, Kate? An exclusive interview? I can come to the house."

SIXTY-SIX

The Detective

THURSDAY, SEPTEMBER 18, 2014

Bob was putting on his socks, sitting on the unused side of the bed. The others were waiting downstairs and he knew he should hurry, but he needed five minutes with Eileen. All the talking had been done, the endless cups of tea and the poring over photo albums and the remembering. The ritual of loss had been observed in every detail. But he ached to be alone with his wife. To hear what she had to say about it all.

He closed his eyes and summoned her. As she'd been last Christmas, before it came back. She'd presided over the kitchen like a battle general, cursing the roast potatoes that wouldn't crisp up and whisking the lumps out of her legendary, terrible gravy. And she'd smiled in the middle of the chaos.

"Well, this was worth getting better for, wasn't it?"

It had been. Every minute had been worth it.

She'd still been alive when he'd touched down at Heathrow—"She's still here, Dad," Sam had said when he phoned home. But when he was somewhere on the M3 she'd slipped away from him.

"She didn't regain consciousness, Bob," Helen Angel said at the door. "I am so sorry, but it was peaceful. A good death."

He'd sat on the Lloyd Loom chair and held her cold hand, starting to rub it warm from habit, then stopping.

"Hello, love. I'm home."

. . .

He'd put Eileen's instructions in his inside pocket, against his heart, when he and Sam had gone to the funeral directors to talk about arrangements for the service. "I might try to sneak in 'The Old Rugged Cross,'" he'd said, and Sam had laughed.

"She'd haunt you forever if you do."

"That would be nice." He'd smiled back.

The funeral went well, with everyone laughing and crying over "Starman" at the end, then tea and more tears in Eileen's chosen garden-center restaurant, surrounded by the heady scent of late blooms.

"She'd have loved this, Bob," his sister-in-law whispered. "You've done her proud."

He hoped he had. *Have I, Eileen?* he wondered.

Everything is perfect. Now, go and help Sam with the oldies, his wife murmured back.

"When are you going back to work?" one of the aged uncles asked, dropping crumbs down his black tie.

"Tomorrow," he heard himself answer. "I've got a case on that I need to finish. It'll keep me busy for a bit. Then I'll take some time off."

He couldn't leave it unfinished. There would be time for grieving later.

There'd been sightings of Jamie Lawrence overnight. The boy he'd been looking for had been hiding in plain sight, it seemed. But his photograph had ended that. Every man and his dog had seen him. Salmond had sent a text to let him know, and he'd responded immediately, unable to sleep and grateful for the distraction.

"When did you get back?" he'd asked when she picked up the phone.

"A couple of days ago, or maybe yesterday. Sorry, still not sure what time zone I'm in. Were you awake?"

"Yes. Not sleeping."

"I'm so sorry, sir."

"Thank you, Zara. We all are, but we are coping. We've had time to prepare."

"Do you want me to keep you in the loop re Jamie Lawrence?"

"Definitely. Eileen's funeral is this afternoon, and I'll be in to-morrow."

"Sure?"

"Sure."

It hadn't been much of a party. Just a case of drinking enough to dull the misery she felt. Jamie had drunk recklessly, disappearing to Mama's cold store for more booze and sending bottles skittering across the floor as he emptied them.

It was late, way past midnight, time to make the call.

"I'm ringing home," she said, more to herself than to the boy slumped on the floor. "Mum and Dad will be back from work now. I've got to. But what am I going to say? What would you say to your mum, Jamie?"

He'd looked at her blankly for a moment. "My mum? Which one?"

"What? You've got a stepmum? Like Rosie?"

"Actually I've had four, if you include the two foster mums."

"Oh!"

He took a deep breath as if he were about to dive into a wave, and there was nothing she could do to stop him.

"I was in care and then adopted. Then, when I got too much for my adoptive mum, I lived in a home until I was seventeen."

"Oh, Jamie," she said, pushing a bottle out of the way and squeezing in beside him.

"It's all a long time ago. I don't tell people usually. Because it makes them think I'm different from them. My social worker said I was too sensitive—that not everyone is judging me. But they are."

And it all tumbled out. About his childhood. His mum couldn't cope. He had vague memories of her—her smell. A burning smell. Cheap cigarettes constantly burning down in the ashtray or between her nicotine-stained fingers. Matches being struck, that smell of stale ashtrays.

"She sometimes smiled at me," Jamie said, off somewhere in his head. "And I'd hug her legs. Then she'd cry. I remember being hungry."

Then there were the foster mums. Alex tried to keep up with the moves, but Jamie was talking faster and faster. "The first was old and smelled funny. Lots of children. I was in a crowd but on my own. I was only four. I kept a matchbox that belonged to my real mum in my pocket. To put things in."

Alex reached for his hand in sympathy and held on tightly.

"That must've been awful. You were so little," she said.

"Yeah. The second foster mum was younger, but I was wetting the bed and she cracked one day and slapped me. The social worker saw the mark and then there was mum number three. My adoptive mum— and dad. I'd had to change school to live there. I was wearing the wrong uniform and the children stared. And one asked, 'Why are you wearing a blue jumper?' I didn't know. I had to talk to the nice lady in the staff room. With biscuits and squash. I was punching and biting the other children. That was the worst time. And when I got into more trouble later I ended up at the home. I was glad in a way. I'd had enough of families by then."

"Did you ever try to find your real mum?" Alex said, fascinated and horrified in equal measure.

"I thought she was dead—one of the foster mums told me that. But I got my full adoption certificate and my original birth certificate when I needed a passport to come here. It was the first time I really knew who

I was, I suppose. When I saw my mum's name, Anita Way, I thought I'd go and look at the house where she'd been living when I was born. The address was on the certificate. It wasn't that far—up near Kingston. I caught a train from Portsmouth and changed at Clapham. When I found the address, I stood on the pavement trying to remember living there. A woman walked past me up to the door and I asked her if she knew Anita who used to live there. But it was her."

"No," Alex breathed.

"I thought I must be hallucinating, but it was Mum. She didn't know it was me until I told her. And she went all panicky. She pulled me in so no one else would see me. It was funny; she didn't smell the same. She was smartly dressed. There was a big telly in the living room. Other children's things. She had another family. She didn't care when I said I'd been told she was dead. 'I was,' she said. 'Dead inside.' When I tried to ask her why she put me in care, she got angry.

" 'You were a mistake, Jamie.' " He imitated a woman's voice, high and harsh, and Alex shivered. "She said it wasn't her fault. She didn't find out until it was too late to get rid of me. My dad wasn't around. She'd been young and she couldn't have me in her life now. She hadn't told her husband about me. Or her kids. I said I was one of her kids but she said I was her dirty secret."

There was a silence. And Alex wondered if there was more or if he'd told anyone else. She hoped he had. She didn't want to be the keeper of his secrets. She had too much to deal with already.

"I shouldn't have gone to look, should I?" Jamie whispered to himself.

"This is not your fault," she said, taking charge. "It was a wicked thing to say. You didn't deserve that."

"But now you're leaving me, too."

"Oh, Jamie, please let's not start that again. You are going to be fine," she said. "Come on, you need to go to bed. You're going to feel awful in the morning."

She left him climbing onto his bunk and went to her room. She was thirsty after the beer. She needed a bottle of water. Mama kept them in the cold store—she wondered if it was open. *Must be. Jamie went out there earlier to get beers.* She'd go and help herself. She was leaving in the morning anyway. She didn't care what Mama would say.

The guesthouse was quiet. She wondered if she was the only person still awake as she crept through the door into the courtyard. She'd been out there a couple of times to find Jake, chatting to him while he did his chores. The door to the cold store was stiff, and she put all her weight into pulling it open, hoping it didn't make a noise. It was pitch-black inside. She got her new phone out and pressed a button to light up the screen. She was shivering at the sudden drop in temperature and quickly reached into one of the crates for the water, then turned to leave. She stumbled, stubbing her toe on something solid but soft. She steadied herself against the crates, making the bottles chime, and flicked her phone down at her feet. There was something sparkly. She reached down to pick it up and recoiled violently, wetting her pants in fear.

Rosie's glittery fingernail.

S he didn't remember shouting, but she must have done because Jamie was suddenly there, pulling her out of the cold store.

"Rosie!" she said.

He went to look and came out too quickly.

"She's dead," he said. His voice sounded dead as well. Why wasn't he shouting or something?

Alex was too shocked to cry. She was cold and she shook until her teeth chattered. She wanted to speak but her jaw spasmed every time she tried.

Jamie tried to lead her inside, but she pulled back.

"No," she said between her clenched teeth. "Can't leave her."

"She doesn't need you now, Alex. Rosie is dead."

"Who did this?"

"I don't know," he hissed. He didn't seem drunk anymore.

"We need to get an ambulance and tell the police. Tell someone."

"I'll do that. You go to bed."

She snorted in disbelief and her anger released her jaw. "Bed? My friend is dead! What are you talking about?"

"I'm your friend, Alex," he said quietly.

"Of course you're not. We've only known each other five minutes. I'm going to get the police—there's a police station at the corner of Khao San Road." She was shouting into his face, but his expression didn't change.

"You came out here earlier to get beers. You must've seen her," she suddenly screeched.

"No. I didn't."

"Oh God, you did, didn't you? And you didn't say anything. Did you do this? Did you kill her?"

Jamie turned his head slowly to look at her. His eyes were blanks in his face.

"Stop shouting," he said.

SIXTY-SEVEN

The Detective

FRIDAY, SEPTEMBER 19, 2014

Jamie Lawrence looked up at him through his lashes. He was dirty, his nose was running, and the healing burns on his face were a dull red.

"Hello, Jamie," Sparkes said, reaching down to pull him up to standing. "We've been looking for you."

The younger man blinked. He'd been asleep in the bin store of a children's home, curled up like a stray cat.

The Neighborhood Watch volunteer who lived opposite had noted him wandering around the day before and rung it in to the local police.

"Possible intruder at Meadow View. Young male, baseball cap, scarf over face."

The duty sergeant had noted the details with a small sigh. *Probably an inmate returning after curfew. Who breaks into a children's home?*

But the next shift noted the cap and scarf and rang the Southampton incident room. "We may have a sighting of your suspect," the Kingston DI said. "What do you want us to do?"

"Scope out the grounds but don't go in," Sparkes said. "I'm on my way."

. . .

The intruder was still asleep when Sparkes had creaked open the bin store door and ended the hunt. There was no chase, no wrestling to the ground, no cursing or punching. Just a blink.

"I am DI Sparkes and this is DS Salmond. We want you to come with us."

Salmond put the handcuffs on as Sparkes read him his rights.

"Jamie Lawrence, I am arresting you on suspicion of the murder of Alexandra O'Connor on or about August the fourteenth, 2014. You do not have to say anything. But it may harm your defense if you do not mention when questioned something which you later rely on in court. Anything you do say may be given in evidence," he said and felt a small flicker of triumph. *Got you.*

The boy had blinked again.

His solicitor, a dusty duty man, sat next to him in the interview room. "Can you give us your name, please, for the tape?" Salmond said, shifting to get comfortable on her plastic chair.

"Jamie Lawrence." The voice was boyish, as if it had only just broken.

"Why did you go to the children's home? Was it one you'd stayed in?" Sparkes asked. He was fairly sure it wasn't, but he wanted to ease in gradually.

"No, but it was near where my mum lives."

"Your mum? I thought she moved to Norfolk when you were taken into care."

Salmond had spoken to Sylvia Lawrence and she'd said she wanted nothing to do with her adopted son. "He broke my husband," she'd said in a tight little voice. "I wish we'd never set eyes on him."

"Not her," Jamie said, frowning and fiddling with the grubby bandages on his hands. "My real mum. Anyway, she wasn't in, so I started driving around and saw the sign for this council place for kids. It looked like home. Funny, isn't it?"

Sparkes shook his head. "No, we look for the familiar in everything, don't we? We look to anchor ourselves in safe waters."

It was a line from a book on coping with loss he'd bought and read secretly. Like porn. Grief porn. He cleared his throat. *Shut up. You'll be singing him a bloody lullaby in a minute.*

It was getting late and Sparkes wondered if Sam would still be there when he got home. He'd left her folding Eileen's clothes into an old suitcase. "She wanted me to send them to the charity shop," she'd said. "It's on her to-do list. Do you remember when she bought this dress?" She'd held up a sparkly number her mother had bought on a whim last Christmas. "You said she looked like the fairy on the top of the tree. I don't think she ever wore it again."

He'd picked up Eileen's favorite jumper and buried his face in it. It smelled of her still. "I'm keeping this," he'd muttered and put it under his pillow.

"Tell us about you and Alex," he said. "We've been told you spent a lot of time together in Bangkok."

Jamie nodded. "We were best friends."

"But you'd only just met."

"It didn't matter. We felt like we'd always known each other."

"Is that how Alex felt, too?"

"Yeah." Jamie didn't meet his eyes. "We were going to go traveling together."

"That isn't what she told her friend Margaret Harding. She said you wouldn't leave her alone. That you were in her face."

Jamie's head jerked up and he pushed his chair away from the table. "No. We were in love."

"But Alex wasn't, was she? That must have been very hard for you. You were desperate to keep her, weren't you?"

Jamie was nodding along, lulled by the gentle sympathy.

"You even drugged her," Sparkes added quietly.

Jamie's face flushed and the fists were back.

His solicitor came to life and interrupted. "What evidence is there for this, Inspector?"

"We have a witness," Sparkes said.

"The owner of the guesthouse, Mama," DS Salmond said. "She says you put Rohypnol in Alex's drink to stop her going out with Jake Waters. It made her ill for days." In truth, her conversation with Mama had been informal—the landlady had vanished again before her request for an official statement could be sanctioned—but she'd confirmed the details from her talk with Kate Waters.

"I couldn't let her go off with him," Jamie said, moving onto the edge of his chair. "I didn't know it would make her so sick. I used too much. Anyway, I was protecting her, making her safe."

"Safe from Jake? Why was he a threat?"

"He was trying to take Alex away!" Jamie shouted, and his solicitor put his hand on Jamie's arm.

They were almost there. Sparkes leaned forward and said gently, "Why don't you tell us what really happened on the night Alex died?"

"I don't know. I expect it was an accident," the young man opposite said, his voice squeaking as he spoke the words.

"What was an accident?"

"Alex dying," he whispered.

The solicitor was about to speak but Jamie kept going.

"I didn't mean for it to happen. I loved her. I didn't want to hurt her ever. But she pushed me away. I tried to hold on to her. It all went wrong."

Salmond pushed a box of tissues across the table. Jamie took one and wiped his eyes and nose, wincing when he brushed his burned skin.

"I need to understand how it all went wrong, Jamie," Sparkes said, leaning back, giving the suspect room to tell his story.

"She agreed to have a farewell drink with me. I was a bit drunk already—I'd helped myself to some beers from the guesthouse—and I was upset that she was leaving me. I must have held her too tightly. She stopped breathing . . ."

"Why was Alex leaving you?"

"Because of Rosie. Rosie had disappeared and Alex wanted to go home. I couldn't bear it when she said that."

"Was it just the two of you at the farewell party?"

Jamie nodded. "There was no one else left. Jake had been arrested."

"Did Alex know?"

"No, she thought he'd just gone off. I let her think that."

Sparkes saw Jamie's bandaged fists clench on his lap.

"She was supposed to hate him." His voice was getting louder. "I told her Jake had slept with Rosie, but she didn't believe me. I was so jealous when I'd walked in on them. I wanted her so badly my hands went all tingly when I saw her. It was how I felt when I thought about Mum. My real mum, I mean. I hate it when I think about her. Brings up all these feelings that the social worker said I need to let go. But they won't be let go. They feel as though they are rooted in my stomach." The young man reached for his abdomen as if to locate the feelings. "They are always here, smothering all my other feelings, strangling them when good things happen to me."

The words electrified the atmosphere and Jamie looked down at his hands.

"I'd stolen Jake's passport and wallet from his bag the day before, after I saw him with Alex. I broke into his locker and took his things from his backpack. I put my own passport in there so he wouldn't notice straightaway."

"Why did you do that, Jamie?"

"I'd decided I'd be Jake if that was who Alex wanted," he told his fists. "Sounds mad, doesn't it? Do you think I'm mad?" His eyes flicked back up to Sparkes.

The detective shook his head gently. "Go on."

"I probably would have swapped them back again the next day when I'd calmed down, but he never came back. Jake was arrested before I could. Mama must have fingered him to the police. They'd fallen out big-time—I heard them arguing. Jake was saying Alex wouldn't stop talking about Rosie. That it was all going wrong. Like the last time, with some Scottish bloke. That the police would come and he didn't have any money to give Mama to pay them off. Mama told him to shut up before anyone heard him."

"But you already had . . ." Sparkes said, and the younger man gave a small smile.

"I heard everything that was going on. No one ever noticed me in that place," he said. "Anyway, Jake picked up the little backpack he took everywhere and marched out without even looking at me. Mama must have made a call. Jake always said she was well in with the police. He was gone. Rosie was gone. I was sure Alex would come with me to Ko Phi Phi. She'd have to or she'd be all on her own."

"But she didn't want to?"

"No." Jamie's voice dropped so Sparkes had to lean forward to hear. "She didn't even want to talk about it. All that stuff I'd done to make her take me. For nothing."

"What stuff, Jamie?" Sparkes said, matching his tone.

The younger man closed his eyes for a moment. "The stuff I've told you about. Taking Jake's passport, telling Alex about him and Rosie. That."

There's more, Sparkes knew, but Jamie had rushed on with his blame game.

"All she could talk about was Rosie. Where was Rosie? And she was going to go home. She said there was nothing to stay for. I was gutted."

"Where were you?"

"In the dorm."

"Was she drinking?"

"Yeah, a bit. I'd got her the beer she liked from the cold store. We were sitting on the floor and I was going to tell her I loved her but I ended up telling her about being put into care. I thought maybe it would make her feel sorry for me, make her change her mind, but she didn't really want to know. She said she was going to ring home and tell them everything. I didn't know what to do. I thought she'd gone to her room but then I heard her shout from outside. I ran out and she was crying, saying she'd found Rosie."

The tension in the interview room was palpable. Sparkes was in the dorm with Jamie, clambering to his feet, walking down the corridor to the back door and out into the hot night.

"Did you see Rosie's body?"

"I saw a bit of her face. She had a mat over her but I could see her hair."

"Where was Alex?"

"In the yard. She was shaking and crying and I tried to make her feel better. I told her I would sort it out. But she got angry with me. I tried to help her up. But she struggled. She started to shove me away as though she wanted me out of her sight. I should have let her go but I hung on. I kept thinking, 'No one's going to push me out again.' And she was screaming. I think I'd frightened her. I didn't want to, didn't mean to. I just wanted her to stop. I pushed against her neck to stop the noise and held my hands there while she struggled, banging her hands against me and the wall. 'Stop it, Alex,' I said. I think I said. Then she did."

Jamie picked up his tissue from the table and dabbed his eyes.

Sparkes was replaying the hideous dance of death in the dirty court-yard. *It probably only took a couple of minutes,* he thought, watching the younger man slump back in his chair.

"Was Alex conscious?"

Jamie shook his head slowly. "She didn't speak after that," he said. "Her face was all gray and she fell to the ground. She'd wet herself—her legs had streaks of piss down them and her shoes were covered in splashes. I couldn't stop looking at her legs. I didn't want to see her face again. I felt as if I'd been standing there for hours. The air was all thick around me like it was setting, like a jelly, and when I turned my head, it felt like slow motion. Have you ever felt that?"

Sparkes nodded. "What did you do, Jamie?"

"I remember I told myself I had to undo this. Had to rewind. But I couldn't. I'd have to hide what I'd done so no one else would know. I took all her dirty clothes off to make her nice and clean again and put her with Rosie. I tucked the matting round them both and then I took out my matches and looked for something to make a fire with."

SIXTY-EIGHT

The Detective

FRIDAY, SEPTEMBER 19, 2014

They took a break when Jamie asked for painkillers for his burns. The fire had exploded into his face when he squirted more lighter fuel on Alex's smoldering clothes, he'd said. It was taking too long to catch. He'd been frightened that people would put it out before it could destroy everything. He'd got the inflammable liquid on his hands, and the flames had jumped on them when he'd tried to protect his eyes. He said he couldn't be sure who had put him in a taxi to the hospital, but he thought it might have been Mama.

Outside the interview room door, Sparkes and Salmond crushed plastic water cups in their restless hands and reviewed the situation.

"He's saying it was an accident."

"Well, he would, wouldn't he?" Salmond said. "But where is his remorse? It feels like it is all about him, not Alex. As if he sees himself as the victim."

Sparkes had felt the same, manipulated by the narrative and those flirting eyes.

"Did you see the eye thing he keeps doing? Looking up through your lashes is classic passive-aggressive technique. Submissive but controlling."

"If you say so, sir."

"I do. I was reading about it the other day."

"I prefer Jack Reacher." Salmond swallowed the last drops of water.

"On we go. We have another dead girl to sort out," Sparkes said and dropped his cup into the bin.

"Tell us about Rosie." Sparkes plunged back in. And Jamie blinked. "What about her? She was dead. I told you. Alex found her in the cold store."

"And when did you see Rosie in there?"

"I told you, after Alex found her."

"But you've told us that you went and got beer from the cold store earlier that evening."

"I . . ." Jamie closed his eyes.

"I'll ask you again. When did you see Rosie in there? The first time."

"The day after she was supposed to have gone off to join the Dutch boys," he said finally. The submissive glances had stopped, Sparkes noted. Jamie Lawrence was on the defensive.

"So you knew she was dead and that her body was outside the back door for two days?"

Jamie nodded. "I was too scared to tell anyone," he said. "I thought people might think I had something to do with it."

"But not too scared to push her to one side to get a beer?" Sparkes snapped. "Did you have anything to do with the death of Rosie Shaw?"

"No. I thought maybe she'd got off her face. Maybe she'd choked on her own vomit."

He'd paused for a beat before offering this theory and Sparkes knew he was almost there. The word "maybe" was a fig leaf. A hedge against the truth.

"How do you know that she choked?"

"I don't. I'm just guessing. That's the sort of girl she was. But I wasn't there so I don't know."

"I wasn't there." In a minute he's going to say the big boys made him do it.

"Do you know who was there?"

Jamie picked at the bandage, fraying the threads, and shook his head.

"All right, when was the last time you saw Rosie alive?"

"I can't remember now. I probably saw her in the bar or something. She was always around."

"Until she wasn't," Sparkes said. "You must have all been talking about it. Rosie vanishing like that. It must have been the only topic of conversation at the guesthouse."

"Yeah, I suppose so. I was sick of hearing about her, if I'm honest."

"You didn't like Rosie?"

"No. I hated her. We both did. Me and Alex." Jamie had unraveled a long thread and was wrapping it tightly around a finger, making the tip turn white. "She was a little bitch. Always making trouble. Alex tried to look out for her at first but she wouldn't listen. Taking drugs, having sex with people she'd only just met. She was sleeping her way through the blokes in the guesthouse, you know?" Jamie shook his head in disgust.

"Did you sleep with her, Jamie?"

He looked genuinely shocked. "Me? Of course not. I was faithful to Alex, but pretty much everyone else was in her bed."

"Jake?"

"Yeah. Like I said before. I told Alex."

"Did that cause trouble between the men who slept with her? Arguments or fights?"

"Not really. No one liked her enough to fight for her."

Poor Rosie, Sparkes thought. *Poor lost little Rosie.*

"What drugs was Rosie taking?"

"K mainly. Lars got it for her before he left."

"Where was he getting it?"

"From Mama. Everyone knew she sold K, weed, and yaba. And a bit of heroin sometimes."

"And roofies," Sparkes said, leaning forward, and Jamie looked away.

He was tiring. Sparkes was turning to Salmond to signal the end of the interview when Jamie spoke again.

"Can I ask a question now?"

Sparkes looked back at the boy. Jamie was looking up through his lashes again as if he wanted to please Sparkes, unsettling the detective.

"Er, yes. What do you want to ask?"

"Have you talked to Jake?" he said. "You should ask Jake about what happened to Rosie."

SIXTY-NINE

The Reporter
FRIDAY, SEPTEMBER 19, 2014

Bob Sparkes sounded very serious on the phone. And he cut me off when I tried to ask about Eileen and how the funeral had gone.

"I can't get into that now. I'm ringing on official business. DS Salmond and I are driving up to London now. We need to speak to Jake. Is he home?"

"Yes, he hasn't left the house since we got back. He's with Joe Jackson at the moment being interviewed about the whole nightmare. He wouldn't let me do it—suppose it would have been a bit weird. Anyway, Joe is on the case. A miscarriage of justice finally righted."

I'd made Joe wait a couple of days. I said Jake needed to rest, but the truth was that I needed to hear the story first. To make sure it was safe to tell.

"Is this to tidy up loose ends or something? I thought you and DS Salmond had finished talking to him. He made his statement in Bangkok." I kept my tone light, but my head was buzzing with unwanted thoughts.

"We'll be with you in another hour."

I put the phone down and stick my head round the door of the living room where Jake and Joe are talking. "Can I have you for a minute?" I say to my son.

He lopes out, shoeless and in a pair of Freddie's slightly too-short jeans.

"I've just had DI Sparkes on the phone. He's coming to see you. Needs to tie things up. Loose ends. You know."

Jake's face falls.

"It'll only be a quick chat, I'm sure," I say, but we look at each other for a beat too long. "You've made your statement. Anyway, how's it going in there? Is he asking the right questions? Are you sure you don't want me to sit in?" I keep my voice bright, but Sparkes's call has made my stomach tense, as if preparing for a blow.

"No, we agreed. Anyway, what did the police say? Exactly?" Jake asks.

"Just what I told you."

"Do we need to ring your lawyer friend?"

I look at my son and try to see what he's thinking. "I don't know. It could look like you have something to hide if we have a lawyer present . . ."

"I'm just saying it might be best. I don't want any trouble."

"No, of course not. I'll ring him to see what he thinks. Leave it with me."

He nods and is about to say something else, but I cut him off. "We need to go shopping for clothes before Mick does the photographs," I say, trying to get us back on track. "You came home with nothing."

And then I remember the pair of trousers he left at Ross's.

Joe appears in the doorway. "Okay to get going again, Jake?" he says. "I'm on deadline."

"Okay. Will you make us a cuppa, Mum?"

D I Sparkes knocks quietly and I swing the door wide open in welcome. *Nothing to hide here.*

"How are you doing?" I say. But the intimacy of the hotel room in

Bangkok has gone. He doesn't look me in the eye as he comes in, wiping nonexistent dirt from his feet on the mat.

"Is Jake here?" he says.

"Yes, I said so on the phone. He's through there. With Joe Jackson."

"Perhaps it's best if you remove the reporter from the room," he says to DS Salmond. I go to protest, but he silences me with a look.

Salmond goes into the living room and there's a short exchange before Joe comes out, pushing his laptop into his bag. He's not happy.

"What's going on, Kate?" he says. "I'm being chucked out."

"Go and have a coffee down the road," I say. "The police just need to have a word with Jake. I'll give you a call in a bit . . ."

I have no idea if I will, but I just want him to go. For him not to witness what is unraveling in my own house.

I close the front door on Joe and go through to the living room. Jake is sitting on the sofa, pale and coughing nervously.

"What is this about?" I say. My voice sounds angry. But I feel more frightened than outraged.

Sparkes looks away. He is arresting Jake in connection with the death of Rosie Shaw on or about August 13, 2014.

Jake stumbles to his feet.

"We will be taking you to Southampton for questioning."

"You need shoes, Jakey," I say and try to catch his eye. He turns away from me and I can't speak.

SEVENTY

The Reporter
FRIDAY, SEPTEMBER 19, 2014

We'd agreed I wouldn't say anything if the police ever came back. We'd been sitting together, my son and I, the night before last, while the others slept. Both of us still on Thai time.

I'd tried not to interrogate him on the plane home, gently teasing out the details of his time in Bangkok while we ate our food, but he'd tired quickly and fallen asleep beside me.

Steve had asked all his questions in the car from the airport, never pressing our son, letting him meander off into the minutiae of life in the guesthouse and prison. Safe ground. Freddie had listened in silence. We'd all let him off lightly.

We'd fed him and run a bath for him. And let him sleep. "We've got him home," Steve had said when we finally fell into bed that first night. "I can't quite believe it."

"It's wonderful, isn't it?" I so wanted it to be wonderful, but *What isn't he saying?* was drowning out the cheers of joy. "We need to talk to him properly, Steve," I'd said, turning to face my husband.

"We will," he'd murmured, already half asleep. "Plenty of time."

I lay beside him, rerunning every word Jake had said, testing the statements at the core of his story, pushing at the details that propped them up, probing them like a bad tooth, looking for the weak point.

But I caught myself holding back when I got too near. When something jarred.

"Why would he lie?" became my mantra.

I think I know what happened to Rosie," he'd said quietly.

"You've told us what you know, Jake," I'd said, desperately shoring up the family conspiracy to stick our fingers in our ears.

He'd looked at me and I'd held my breath.

When he didn't speak, I'd whispered, "Okay. Tell me the truth, Jake." Like I did when he was small and I'd found a broken ornament or a missing packet of biscuits.

"She was drinking from a bottle of fake tequila when I last saw her. She was lying on her bed, shouting at me. I thought she'd be fine—she'd just have a hangover in the morning. But she wasn't fine. She died, Mum."

"When did she die?" I'd whispered.

"I don't know. Sometime between me leaving her and Mama trying to wake her the next morning."

I'd felt my hands tightening around my mug of hot milk.

"Okay," I'd said carefully, hardly trusting my own voice. *What did you do?* I was screaming in my head. *Oh God, did you kill this girl?*

"Why was Rosie shouting at you?"

Jake's head sank onto his chest. "We were both a bit drunk and upset." His voice had petered out.

"What about?"

"I shouldn't have slept with her." He'd looked up, eyes wide with distress. "But she kept on and on about wanting me, touching me, kissing me. And we did it. We had sex. But I knew she was just doing it to get back at Alex. She had this smile on her face. Like she'd won. It was horrible and we had a row. I told her not to tell Alex and she laughed.

I told her to shut up, that Alex might walk in on us, and she yelled in my face that Alex couldn't. That Jamie had put something in her drink. To stop her going on a date with me. Mama had seen him do it. She was yelling that she was going to tell Alex. Tell her everything. The whole guesthouse could hear. I was scared, Mum. Everything was so out of control. I just wanted it all to stop and I left her there."

"God, what a nightmare," I'd heard myself say. I could see it. I could hear the anger in their voices. I could smell the sharp stench of loathing. I'd kept looking at my son, afraid that if I looked away, there would be a stranger there when I looked back.

"I was sure she'd tell Alex when she woke up. But she never got the chance," he'd gone on. "Mama found her dead the next morning when she went to talk to her about money. She came and woke me up and told me."

Jake had taken a deep breath. "Mama said Rosie must have choked in her sleep. She said she had sick all over her hair, Mum."

"Oh God," I'd said, horrified at what I was hearing. "But you didn't tell anyone. Why didn't you call an ambulance? Or the police? Why didn't you tell anyone?"

He'd closed his eyes and put his hands to his mouth as if to shut himself off completely. But I wouldn't let him stop now.

"Jake, tell me!" I'd said, pulling his hands away. "Did you hurt her?" I couldn't bring myself to use the word "kill." It's too finite. It cannot be unsaid.

He'd thrown his head back in shock. "No! Why aren't you listening to me? I didn't do anything to her. I knew you wouldn't understand—you weren't there. You don't know what it's been like, my fucked-up life. All I can tell you is that I had to keep quiet . . . there was going to be terrible trouble. Mama said it would be like the last time."

"The plasterer who died," I'd whispered.

Jake had nodded. "The police came that time, questioning all the foreigners in the guesthouse. Mama said I'd be arrested and locked up because I didn't have the right visa. They can throw away the key, Mum. I gave her all my money to sort it out for me. She sent me to her home village for a while, and when I came back, it had all been dealt with. The police said John had killed himself."

"But he hadn't?"

Jake shook his head wearily.

"He'd been attacked in his room and robbed."

"Christ! Who attacked him?"

"I don't know," he'd said. "He was doing all sorts of risky stuff and hanging around with dodgy people. But this time it was going to start all over again with the police. I'd slept with Rosie the night she died. I thought I'd definitely be arrested. And this time I didn't have any money to pay Mama to deal with it."

"*It?* You are talking about an eighteen-year-old-girl, Jake," I'd said.

"I'm so sorry, Mum."

And I'd listened, increasingly numb to his pleading, the excuses curdling in my stomach.

Perhaps he'd sensed my heart hardening, but he'd chosen that moment to deliver his coup de grâce. "And no one knew where I was. You and Dad didn't know. I'd made sure you didn't. I'm sorry—but my life was a complete mess. I didn't want you to know. I kept thinking about how you and Dad used to joke-boast to people about me becoming a barrister. You put such pressure on me, Mum. I know you didn't mean to, but you did. And I was cleaning toilets in Bangkok. I needed to turn things round, get a real job or something so I could come home a success. But time just kept passing."

I'd reached over and taken his hand. "I didn't know you felt like that."

"I've been an idiot, but I had no one to turn to. You'd have known what to do, Mum, but I couldn't bear for you to know. Please help me now. They might put me in prison. They won't believe I have nothing to hide. Please . . ."

And my failure as a parent had spread through me like a black poison, obliterating every other thought and feeling. *We weren't there for him. This was our fault. My fault.* Later, I wondered if I would have acted differently if he hadn't said that. But it was too late by then.

W e'd sat in silence for a while, the only sound the ticking of the clock like the heartbeat of the house. Then I'd done what I always do, asked endless questions.

"Who else knows you kept quiet about Rosie's death, Jake?"

"No one. Well, Mama. But she won't say anything, obviously."

"Could anyone else have heard her telling you?"

"I don't know. She made a lot of noise, but Alex was drugged and out of it. So that leaves Jamie. Jamie Always in the Way," Jake had said to himself.

We'd talked on and on and round and round, but in the end, he'd persuaded me that nothing could be gained by speaking up. He'd held my hands and looked me in the eye as he'd summed up—my son the barrister . . .

"Rosie died and no one was to blame. Even if Jamie did hear Mama telling me, he's a murderer, isn't he? Who would believe him? We are talking about the rest of my life, Mum."

I'd felt so vulnerable. Like when I'd first held him when he was a baby. The all-consuming fear that I might do the wrong thing and harm my child had made me cry then. I'd been overwhelmed by the responsibility. I was out of my depth but I had to keep him safe, help him grow, do the right things. I'd carried the burden in the pit of my stomach, seeing danger everywhere. Steve had tried to help, explaining it all to me—postpartum hormones, maternal instinct, blah blah. But it was visceral, all-consuming. I'd thought it was over when our son got big enough to look after himself, when we waved him off to university. But it is never over. Here I was again, holding his future in my hands.

And I'd gone along with it.

SEVENTY-ONE

The Detective

FRIDAY, SEPTEMBER 19, 2014

Jake didn't speak in the car. He watched the other vehicles through his window until they pulled up at the police station. He hadn't had time to do up his laces before he'd been led to the car, and his feet slid in and out of his old trainers, making him stumble.

Salmond steadied him. "Through here." She guided him into the custody suite, presenting him to the grumpy-looking sergeant at the desk. Sparkes watched the ritual, ticking off the steps before they could talk to him.

Jake was silent unless spoken to. *He's retreated into his head,* Sparkes thought. *Is he rehearsing his story? Has he told Kate what he's done?*

His only words were, "This is better than Klong Prem."

"Can you give your name for the record?" Salmond said when they were all sitting in the cramped interview room. Jake looked even younger than before with his schoolboy glasses and bitten fingernails.

"Now, then," Sparkes began. "Why don't we start with your relationship with Rosie Shaw."

"I didn't have one. I hardly knew her," Jake said.

"Alex said she was flirting with you."

"Alex?" He looked completely confused.

"In e-mails she sent to her friend Mags. She said Rosie was trying to steal you from her."

"I don't know what Alex said in her e-mails. How could I?" His voice remained steady and reasonable, and Sparkes reminded himself that Jake had been a law student.

"But you do remember going to Rosie Shaw's bedroom on the evening of August the thirteenth?" he asked, matching Jake's tone.

"Er, I'm not sure. I don't think so."

He was beginning to hesitate, to trip over his words. Sparkes pressed on.

"We have two witnesses who say you did. That you went to her room and had sex with her."

"They're wrong. It sounds like supposition to me. Did they say they actually saw us having sex?" Jake shifted back in his chair and Sparkes wondered for a second if he was actually enjoying himself. He'd soon stop that.

"It's not supposition, Jake. Your DNA was detected in traces of semen found on Rosie's body."

Jake's head went down. His solicitor put his hand up. "I'd like a minute with my client, please."

The detectives filed out and leaned against the wall in the corridor.

"He'll tell us the truth when we go back, boss," Salmond said.

"Nearly there," he agreed.

Jake's face was blank when they went back in.

"My client has a statement he would like to make regarding his relations with Rosie Shaw," the lawyer said and sat back to give the floor to Jake.

"I had sex with Rosie Shaw—that's all," he said, his voice flat. "I didn't hurt her. She wanted me to have sex with her, to get back at Alex. But she died after I left her. The owner of the guesthouse told me later that she found her dead. "

"So you had sex against your will?" Sparkes said deadpan.

"I was drunk and she egged me on."

"I see. The witnesses say there was a row. You were heard shouting."

"I was angry because I felt so guilty—I liked Alex and I had done something incredibly stupid. Slept with her friend. What a fuckwit!" He banged his hand against the side of his head.

"Was Rosie Shaw alive when you left her room?"

"Yes, I swear she was," he said, his voice higher and louder. "She was saying she was going to tell Alex about us."

"So why didn't she? Go and tell Alex straightaway?"

"Alex had been drugged by Jamie."

So he knew. Sparkes nodded to himself.

"He's a complete psycho—he put something in Alex's beer to make sure she didn't go out with me. Rosie told me. It was such a sick place."

"So she never got to tell Alex . . ."

Jake shook his head wearily. "No. She died in the night."

"Well, that was lucky for you, wasn't it? Your little secret could stay that way," Sparkes said, writing a note on his pad.

Jake pushed his chair back and stood, shaking. "You are joking! I didn't hurt her. It was horrible when she died. Mama came and woke me up and told me. I was so shocked, I was like a zombie. I didn't know what to say or do."

"Sit down, Jake. So what *did* you do?"

The younger man hesitated and retook his seat but clung onto the chair as if it were bucking underneath him. "It felt like a dream, like nothing was real for a while. I lay there in my bed and tried to get a grip on what was going on. I must have fallen asleep again. When I woke up, Mama was acting as though nothing had happened."

"You went back to sleep after being told that a young woman you had had sex with hours before had been found dead in her bed?" Sparkes said incredulously.

"I'd had a lot to drink, Inspector. I told you. I know it sounds like I didn't care. But I did. I was in shock and didn't know what to do so

I went along with Mama's story that Rosie had gone off with the two Dutch boys."

"But you knew she hadn't, didn't you, Jake?"

He nodded miserably.

"I was going to tell Alex but I was arrested before I could."

"That was nearly two days later. You had plenty of opportunities."

"Don't you think I beat myself up every day that I didn't? But I couldn't. You don't understand. I was so scared, I didn't know what to do. Scared of what would happen if I did tell. Look, I'd slept with her. People might have blamed me for her death."

"So you didn't tell the police when they arrested you?"

"No. I hadn't told them who I really was. I was already in a world of trouble," he said and closed his eyes.

"Jamie says you were there when Rosie died."

Jake looked up and almost smiled. "Well, he would, wouldn't he? He hates me because Alex wanted to be with me, not him. He killed her rather than let her choose anyone but him. And he'd say anything to get his revenge. I bet he slipped something in Rosie's drink, too. She was going to tell Alex about him and his little roofie habit. Maybe he decided to stop her. He is capable of anything."

When they got Jamie Lawrence back in, he'd stopped the flirting. He sat down and put his bandaged hands on the table.

"I was having a sleep," he said. "I've answered your questions."

"There are a couple more we need to ask," Sparkes said, leaning forward to get the younger man's full attention.

"Did you drug Rosie Shaw?" he said.

Jamie sat up straighter. "She was doing that herself."

"But did you give Rosie anything? To stop her telling Alex about the Rohypnol? Mama has told us she knew about it. Was Rosie going to reveal the sort of man you really were?"

Jamie pressed his lips together tightly and shook his head as if he didn't trust himself to speak.

"We're doing tests on Rosie's blood, Jamie. So we'll know if you did," Sparkes said. He was pretty sure the toxicology tests couldn't produce evidence of Rohypnol at this late stage, but the suspect was at the tipping point in his confession and needed just a nudge to reveal the truth.

The silence grew, filling the room, but Sparkes waited it out. He sat completely still, offering no distraction to the boy opposite. Jamie's fingers twitched on the table and his eyes closed in apparent concentration.

"I only gave her a little bit," he muttered finally, almost under his breath, and Sparkes had to lean forward to hear. "Just to shut her up until I could figure out what to do next. I put it in her tequila and she went to sleep."

"Except she didn't go to sleep," Sparkes snapped back. "She was unconscious and full of drink, and you left her there to choke. That poor girl."

"She should have shut up," Jamie said quietly. "Anyway, it was her own fault. Nobody forced her to drink herself stupid."

Sparkes looked at him without speaking for a long minute. Letting the poisonous words drip down the walls.

"Did you put her body in the cold store, Jamie?"

"No. I woke up the next day and she'd gone."

"But you are the one who heard and saw everything going on in that guesthouse," Sparkes went on. "The lad no one noticed."

Jamie shrugged. "I had nothing to do with it."

"You told us this morning, 'All that stuff I'd done to make her take me.' Was this the stuff you meant? Disposing of a dead body? Hiding it from the police?"

Jamie banged one of his hands on the table, making his solicitor jump. "No!"

"But you knew she was dead, didn't you? And you helped to cover up Rosie's death. Mama told us that it was you who suggested making up messages from her," Salmond pressed on. "To keep everyone quiet about her disappearance. You seem to have been controlling that situation, too."

"I didn't care about Rosie, but Alex was upset about her going without a word. I thought it would help her make up her mind to come with me."

"But she didn't, did she?"

He shook his head wearily. "No, it all went wrong, like I told you."

SEVENTY-TWO

The Reporter

FRIDAY, DECEMBER 19, 2014

I've had a card from one of my ghosts of Christmas past—Glen Taylor's widow, Jean. The office forwarded it in a big brown envelope with my expenses statements and some union stuff.

In it she writes about our shared trauma of having the press on our doorsteps. As if I'm interested. I suppose I was so much a part of that time in her life, my presence interlocked in her memories of when her husband was accused of taking little Bella Elliott, that she thinks she knows me. I was there with her as the story unfolded, in her kitchen, her sitting room, in the hotel where we took her for the interview. And in her head, where, I suppose, I still am.

But I hadn't heard a peep from her since the last appeal in the Bella Elliott case, although she still appears in an occasional story, when she's written to the parents of missing children or befriended notorious criminals in prison.

Now it is my turn to be pitied.

She's heard about "my trouble" and obviously wants to rub my nose in it. She doesn't say that. Not her style, really. Little Jeanie Taylor wants to tell me how sorry she is to hear about Jake. I don't want her to use my son's name. I don't want her to touch anything of mine.

I won't reply. I tear the smiling snowman in half and put it in the bin.

. . .

Jake won't know. He's gone skiing with Steve and Freddie. A boys-only trip to take his mind off things. Steve said he needed it. Jamie Lawrence's trial is coming up in the New Year and we've all been on edge, waiting for the whole thing to be churned over in the press. For a while I thought Jamie might be sent back to Thailand and face the death penalty for murder. "By lethal injection," Joe, my new best contact, reported to me. "They haven't executed a foreigner or anyone else since 2009. But we won't want to send a Brit to death row. It'll be dealt with here—you can be tried in the British courts for killing a Brit anywhere in the world."

That won't please the families. Lesley rang me after Jamie Lawrence was charged with Alex's murder and told me they were writing to the home secretary demanding he be sent back to Bangkok for trial. "He killed her in Thailand; he should face their penalty.

"We're having a bake sale at school to kick-start fund-raising for our legal costs—we want our voices heard," she'd added, and I pictured rosy-cheeked juniors munching on Hang Jamie Lawrence cupcakes.

The venom in her voice had shocked me. She wasn't the same woman I'd last seen at the girls' memorial service. I'd stood near the back, unsure of my welcome, and watched Lesley, a quietly dignified presence at the heart of the service, Jenny a pale shadow beside her. The church was full of young people, the girls weeping freely and hugging one another while the boys stood awkwardly in groups, not knowing where to look or put their hands. Jake had talked about going but I'd persuaded him to stay at home. He'd have been a photo opportunity for the waiting press, a jarring distraction on the girls' day. I'd gone alone and mouthed the words of "Amazing Grace" as the kids around sang their grief and held hands. I left before the final notes ended.

I would never have thought of Lesley as an advocate for capital punishment. More of a campaigner for road safety. But I know now that protecting our children changes who we are. Who we seem to be.

Their battle for justice—and the death sentence—has had Louise Butler heaving and pushing from the rear. My editor didn't want to take it on, according to Joe—"Bit down-market for our readers," he'd told the news desk. "And it won't happen, so it will look like our failure . . ."

The O'Connors had always presented a united front, but I wondered how the Shaws would cope in their opposite corners. It was Joe who told me that Mike had moved back in with Jenny. "Wife number two kicked him into touch over his fumble-at-work habit," he'd said. "Jenny took him back. They're like newlyweds, apparently. I give it six months . . ."

That will be long enough for the crusade to die its own death and be forgotten.

Joe says Jamie's still claiming Alex's death was an accident—a loving embrace that went wrong because of his history of rejection. My office son has tracked down all the mothers, including the sad woman who gave birth to Jamie. It won't make for happy reading when the case finishes and the full background can be revealed. I feel my fingers itching to write the story, but I can't this time. I am part of the story. And I am back with Jake and his "loving" embrace with Rosie.

I wonder how my boy will fare if he comes under cross-examination. It would be only as a witness to Rosie's claim that Jamie drugged Alex. Not as a defendant. He wasn't charged with anything in the end.

"There is no evidence or reliable witness to report that anything untoward happened while Jake was with Rosie," our lawyer told us confidently. "He's admitted not telling anyone about Rosie's death but he was not a witness to it and he didn't see her body. It really astonishes me that the CPS is even considering a case of perverting the course of justice," he'd said each time we met to spend another five hundred pounds of our money. But we had to wait another nail-biting month before the decision was relayed to us by phone.

"Sensible decision. There just isn't any evidence to go with," the lawyer said. Bob Sparkes hadn't delivered the news himself.

"We can put it all behind us," Steve said after the lawyer's phone call. "Make a fresh start."

Jake is definitely looking to the future. When he gets back from skiing, he's going to look into returning to his law degree—"I'll be a mature student, Mum. I'll do it properly this time."

He will, I tell myself in the small hours of sleepless nights. He'll be a better person.

But there are days when I find it hard to look at my eldest son without choking on the guilt I feel for hiding his. I study that face that I gave birth to and search for his remorse, but he seems to have managed to put up a shield to "what happened in Thailand," as it is now referred to in our house.

Steve smiles optimistically and calls it the resilience of youth. And I let him think that.

I decided not to tell him the truth, because he would want to do the right thing—ring Bob Sparkes, have Jake own up and take the consequences. Because he sees things so simply—they're either right or they're wrong. I see beyond, into the gray, blurred margins where the consequences wait. Steve didn't see our son in prison. I did. I saw the old-man face of our boy, felt his despair. I can't be responsible for that happening to him again.

I distract myself with thoughts of my own future. I'm still on gardening leave—"You can sort out your geraniums," Joe said, trying to cheer me up. And I'm in with a chance of a payoff in the next cycle of redundancies. Steve wants me to take it, but I can't bear the thought. I need an anchor to my existence. Especially now.

I ring Bob Sparkes, just to hear his voice, really. He'd been in his usual pew—the one nearest the door—at the girls' service, and we'd managed a few vanilla words. But nothing since.

"DI Sparkes," he answers.

"Hello, Bob, it's Kate."

"Well, how are you doing?" He sounds unsure but not hostile, so I plow on.

"Not bad—you?"

"Same. Back at work full-time now."

"Good for you. I'm ringing because guess who I've heard from."

"Go on . . ." And I can hear the smile in his voice.

"Jean Taylor."

"Bloody hell! What did she have to say?"

And we are back on common ground, picking up the threads of a former life. Perhaps I ought to write and thank Jean Taylor for her intervention.

Today, I feel I've turned a corner.

I've done my stable cleansing. I've finally thrown the trousers away. The trousers I brought home in my overnight bag. The trousers with their telltale stain that could expose my son's lie.

"He came round in a bit of a state and wanted a smoke," his friend Ross had said when he'd given them to me. "He'd got some sick or something on his trousers."

And I'd forgotten them in the head-spinning events that followed. But I'd known as soon as I'd found them in my bag, thrown into a cupboard after I got home the first time without Jake. I'd known that they could undo everything. He was there in that bedroom with

Rosie's body, just like bloody Jamie Lawrence said. He'd hidden her. He'd perverted the course of justice.

I was going to confront him with the trousers a hundred times. But I always held back.

I suppose I hoped he would tell me himself. That he'd take responsibility for his actions.

But he didn't, and whenever I allowed myself to think about him being sent to prison, his life permanently blighted, I told myself I owed him this second chance.

The girls won't get another one, but I can't change that or make amends. Lesley and Jenny would like everyone involved to be publicly executed because they want them to suffer as they have. But pushing Jake back into the dock won't give them closure. This is what I tell myself as I bundle the trousers up with a couple of old jumpers in a plastic bag, and walk to the recycling bins up by the Co-op. I stand there unable to move, indecision clamping my arms by my sides until Bet from next door calls to me from the pavement. "Hello, Kate. How's that lovely boy of yours doing?" And I shove the bag in the dark maw of the bin. Gone.

"He's doing fine, Bet. How are you?" I call back as if our lives are unaltered.

I've had calls from reporters asking me to tell my story in time for Jamie's trial. I'm sure the words "dogged," "devoted," "brave," and "inspirational" will be scattered freely across their articles. To them I am the Good Mother who stood by her son, solved the case, and won his freedom.

I suppose I am in a way. I'm waiting for the first one to arrive. She'll be here soon. I wonder if she'll bring flowers. I would if it were me, knocking at the door. I've put out a plate of mince pies, and my favorite family photos are sitting among the fake holly on the mantelpiece. I sit quietly. I have my story ready.

ACKNOWLEDGMENTS

I want to thank so many people who have been vital to the writing of *The Suspect*, but let me begin with the wonderfully generous Louise Butler. Louise made the winning bid to be a character in *The Suspect* in CLIC Sargent's Get in Character auction. She is now immortalized as a scheming tabloid journalist (sorry, Louise . . .) and has helped raise a fantastic £10,696 for the fight for young lives against cancer.

My specialists: the brilliant retired Murder Squad detective Colin Sutton, who took time out of his own successful writing career to patiently guide me on police matters, and Home Office forensic pathologist Dr. Debbie Cook, who put down her scalpel to talk me through autopsies on embalmed bodies. I am so grateful to both of them.

The foreign correspondents and officials who expertly guided me through Bangkok's murky back streets and tourist scams— Marc Lavine, Andrew Drummond, Jonathan Head, Lindsay Murdoch, and Daniel Fieller at the British embassy. You were fantastic advisers.

Once again, huge thanks to my inspirational editors at Transworld and Berkley/Penguin Random House, Frankie Gray and Danielle Perez, for believing in me.

As always, love and thanks to my husband, Gary; children, Tom and Lucy; their partners, Orlanda and Martin; my brother, Jon; and my parents, David and Jeanne, for their encouragement and support. And to my lovely sister, Jo Wright, and my friends Rachael Bletchly and Jane McGuinn, who have listened, read, and cheered me on.

Finally, I would also like to raise a glass to, ahem, Literary Agent of the Year 2018 Madeleine Milburn. As the British Book Awards judges said: "The care of her authors is exemplary. It's clear she goes the extra mile for them." It is and she has. I cannot thank you enough.

THE SUSPECT

FIONA BARTON

QUESTIONS FOR DISCUSSION

1. Alex's thoughts often contradict what she says on Facebook and in e-mails to her parents. Why do you think this is? Do you think the author is making a statement about social media culture? Why or why not?

2. Discuss the relationship between Kate and the families in Part One of the book. How does this relationship change after Kate learns who the possible survivor is?

3. Examine Kate's relationship with her fellow journalists before and after she learns about the possible survivor and suspect. Do you think she is unfair to them? Do you think they are unfair to her? Why or why not?

4. It is a common perception that journalists often need to detach themselves from a situation in order to do their jobs. At one point, when learning details about the case, Kate thinks, "But this is us. Not some story to be picked over for the best quote." Do you think the events of the novel will impact Kate's career in the future? How?

5. A major theme in the novel is that parents might not know their children as well as they think they do. Discuss the ways this idea is explored in the novel. Do you think that this is inherent in parent-child relationships?

6. Similarly, Alex and Jake both end up in trouble because of their unwillingness to tell their parents about the trouble they're in. Discuss the relationship they each have with their parents. Did their actions surprise you? Why or why not?

7. What role does the media play in the book? As in *The Widow* and *The Child*, the media is inextricably linked with the police investigation. Do you think the author is conveying a broader message about the role of journalism and news organizations? If you have read *The Widow* and/or *The Child*, do you think that Kate's being a core part of the story in *The Suspect* dramatically changes the perception of the media in this novel when compared to the two other novels?

8. Discuss the character of Lesley. What did you think of her at the beginning of the story? Did your opinion change over the course of the novel? Were you surprised by her desired punishment for the person responsible for her daughter's death? Why or why not?

9. Discuss Kate's actions at the very end of the novel. Why do you think she chose not to confront her son? Do you agree with her decision?

Emma

TUESDAY, MARCH 20, 2012

My computer is winking at me knowingly when I sit down at my desk. I touch the keyboard, and a photo of Paul appears on my screen. It's the one I took of him in Rome on our honeymoon, eyes full of love across a table in the Campo dei Fiori. I try to smile back at him but as I lean in, I catch a glimpse of my reflection in the screen and stop. I hate seeing myself without warning. Don't recognize myself sometimes. You think you know what you look like and there is this stranger looking at you. It can frighten me.

But today I study the stranger's face. The brown hair half pulled up on top of the head in a frantic work bun, naked skin, shadows and lines creeping towards the eyes like cracks in pavement.

"Christ, you look awful," I tell the woman on the screen. The movement of her mouth mesmerizes me and I make her speak some more.

"Come on, Emma, get some work done," she says. I smile palely at her and she smiles back.

"This is mad behavior," she tells me in my own voice, and I stop. *Thank God Paul can't see me now,* I think.

When Paul gets home tonight, he's tired and a bit grumpy after a day of "boneheaded" undergraduates and another row with his department head over the timetable.

Maybe it's an age thing, but it seems to really shake Paul to be challenged at work these days. I think he must be starting to doubt himself, see threats to his position everywhere. University departments are like prides of lions, really. Lots of males preening and screwing around and hanging on to their superiority by their dewclaws. I say all the right things and make him a gin and tonic.

When I move his briefcase off the sofa, I see he's brought home a copy of the *Evening Standard*. He must've picked it up on the tube.

I sit and read it while he showers away the cares of the day, and it's then I see the paragraph about the baby.

"Baby's Body Found," it says. Just a few lines about how an infant's skeleton has been discovered on a building site in Woolwich and police are investigating. I keep reading it over and over. I can't take it in properly, as if it's in a foreign language.

But I know what it says and terror is coiling around me. Squeezing the air out of my lungs. Making it hard to breathe.

I am still sitting here when Paul comes down, all damp and pink, and shouting that something is burning.

The pork chops are black. Incinerated. I throw them in the bin and open the window to let out the smoke. I fetch a frozen pizza out of the freezer and put it in the microwave while Paul sits quietly at the table.

"We ought to get a smoke alarm," he says instead of shouting at me for almost setting the house on fire. "Easy to forget things when you're reading." He is such a lovely man. I don't deserve him.

Standing in front of the microwave, watching the pizza revolve and bubble, I wonder for the millionth time if he'll leave me. He should have done years ago. I would have if I'd been in his place, having to deal with my stuff, my worries, on a daily basis. But he shows no sign of packing his bags. Instead he hovers over me like an anxious parent, protecting me from harm. He talks me down when I get in a state, invents reasons to be cheerful, holds me close to calm me when I cry, and tells me I am a brilliant, funny, wonderful woman.

It is the illness making you like this, he says. *This isn't you.*

Except it is. He doesn't know me really. I've made sure. And he respects my privacy when I shy at the mention of my past. "You don't have to tell me," he says. "I love you just the way you are."

Saint Paul—I call him that when he's pretending I'm not a burden to him, but he usually shushes me.

"Hardly," he says.

Well, not a saint, then. But who is? Anyway, his sins are my sins. What do old couples say? *What's yours is mine.* But my sins . . . well, they're my own.

"Why aren't you eating, Em?" he says when I put his plate on the table.

"I had a late lunch, busy with work. I'm not hungry now, but I'll have something later," I lie. I know I would choke if I put anything in my mouth.

I give my brightest smile—the one I use for photos. "I'm fine, Paul. Now eat up."

On my side of the table, I nurse a glass of wine and pretend to listen to his account of the day. His voice rises and falls, pauses while he chews the disgusting meal I've served, and resumes.

I nod periodically but I hear nothing. I wonder if Jude has seen the article.

Kate

Kate Waters was bored. It wasn't a word she normally associated with her job, but today she was stuck in the office under the nose of her boss with nothing to do but rewrites.

"Put it through your golden typewriter," Terry, the news editor, had shouted across, waving someone else's badly written story at her. "Sprinkle a bit of fairy dust on it."

And so she did.

"It's like an assembly line in here," she complained to the Crime Man, sitting opposite. "Churning out the same old rubbish with a few frills. What are you working on?"

Gordon Willis, whom the Editor always referred to by his job title—as in "Get the Crime Man on this story"—lifted his head from a newspaper and shrugged.

"Going down to the Old Bailey this afternoon—want to have a chat with the detective chief inspector in the crossbow murder. Nothing doing yet but hoping I might get a talk with the victim's sister when it finishes. Looks like she was sleeping with the killer.

"It'll be a great multi-deck headline: 'The Wife, the Sister and the Killer They Both Loved,'" he said and grinned at the thought. "Why? What have you got on?"

"Nothing. Unpicking a story one of the online slaves has done." Kate indicated a pubescent nymph typing furiously at a desk across the room. "Straight out of school."

She realized how bitter—and old—she must sound and stopped herself. The tsunami of online news had washed her and those like her to a distant shore. The reporters who once sat on the Top Table—the newspaper equivalent of the winner's podium—now perched at the edge of the newsroom, pushed farther and farther towards the exit by the growing ranks of online operatives who wrote twenty-four/seven to fill the hungry maw of rolling news.

New media stopped being new a long time ago, the Editor had lectured his staff at the Christmas party. It was the norm. It was the future. And she knew she had to stop bitching about it.

Hard, she told herself, *when the most viewed stories on the paper's slick website are about Madonna's hands being veiny or an* EastEnders *star putting on weight. "Hate a Celebrity" dressed as news. Horror.*

"Anyway," she said out loud, "it can wait. I'll go and get us a coffee."

Also gone were the days of the CQ—the conference quickie—once enjoyed by Fleet Street's finest in the nearest pubs while the executives were in the Editor's morning meeting. The CQ was traditionally followed by red-faced, drunken rows with the news editor, one of which, legend had it, ended with a reporter, too drunk to stand, biting his boss's ankle and another throwing a typewriter through a window into the street below.

The newsroom, now in offices above a shopping mall, had windows hermetically sealed by double glazing, and alcohol was banned. Coffee was the new addiction of choice.

"What do you want?" she asked.

"Double macchiato with hazelnut syrup, please," he said. "Or some brown liquid. Whichever comes first."

Kate took the lift down, pinching a first edition of the *Evening*

Standard from the security desk in the marble lobby. As she waited for the barista to work his magic with the steamer, she flicked idly through the pages, checking for the bylines of friends.

The paper was wall-to-wall preparations for the London Olympics and she almost missed the paragraph at the bottom of the News in Brief column.

Headlined "Baby's Body Found," two sentences told how an infant's skeleton had been unearthed on a building site in Woolwich, not a million miles from Kate's east London home. Police were investigating. No other details. She tore it out of the paper for later. The bottom of her bag was lined with crumpled scraps of newspaper—"it's like a budgie cage," her eldest son, Jake, had teased about the shreds of paper waiting for life to be breathed into them. Sometimes whole stories to be followed up on or, more often, just a line or a quote that made her ask, "What's the story?"

Kate reread the thirty words and wondered about the person missing from the story: the mother. As she walked back with the cups, she ticked off her questions: *Who is the baby? How did it die? Who would bury a baby?*

"Poor little thing," she said out loud. Her head was suddenly full of her own babies—Jake and Freddie; born two years apart but known as "the boys" in family shorthand. Them as sturdy toddlers, schoolboys in football gear, surly teenagers, and now adults—*well, almost.* She smiled to herself. Kate could remember the moment she saw each of them for the first time: red, slippery bodies; crumpled, too-big skin; blinking eyes staring up from her chest; and the feeling that she had known their faces forever. *How could anyone kill a baby?* she thought.

When she got back to the newsroom, she put the cups down and walked over to the news desk.

"Do you mind if I have a look at this?" she asked Terry, waving the tiny cutting in front of him as he tried to make sense of a feature on foreign royals. He didn't look up so she assumed he didn't.

Her first call was to the Scotland Yard press office. When she'd started in journalism, as a trainee on a local paper in East Anglia, she used to call in at the local police station every day to lean on the front desk and look at the logbook while the sergeant chatted her up. Now, if she contacted the police, she rarely spoke to a human being. And if she did, it was likely to be a fleeting experience.

"Have you listened to the tape?" a civilian press officer would ask, in the full knowledge that she hadn't, and she would find herself quickly rerouted to a tinny recorded message that took her through every stolen lawnmower and pub punch-up in the area.

But, this time, she hit the jackpot. It was not only a real person; it was someone she knew. The voice on the other end of the phone belonged to a former colleague from her first job on a national newspaper. He was one of the poachers turned gamekeepers who'd recently joined the safer, some said saner, world of public relations.

"Hello, Kate. How are you? Long time . . ."

Colin Stubbs wanted to chat. He'd done well as a reporter, but his wife, Sue, had grown tired of his rackety life on the road and he'd given in to the war of attrition at home. But he was hungry for details about the world he'd left, asking for gossip about other reporters and telling her—and himself—over and over that leaving newspapers was the best thing he'd ever done.

"That's great. Lucky you," Kate said, determinedly upbeat. "I'm still slogging along at the *Post*. Look, Colin, I saw something in the *Standard* about a baby's body being found in Woolwich. Any idea how long it'd been there?"

"Oh, that. Hang on, I'll pull up the details on the computer . . . Here we are. Not much to go on and a bit grim, really. A workman was clearing a demolition site and moved an old urn and underneath was this tiny skeleton. Newborn, they say. Forensics are having a look but it says here that early indications are it's been there awhile—could be historic, even. It's a road in student land, towards Greenwich, I think. Don't you live round that area?"

"North of the river and a bit farther east, actually. Hackney. And still waiting for the gentrification train to stop. What else have you got on your computer? Any leads on identification?"

"No, newborns are tricky when it comes to DNA, says here. Especially if they've been underground for years. And the area is a warren of rented flats and bedsits. Tenants changing every five minutes so the copper in charge isn't optimistic about it. We've all got our hands full with the Olympics stuff . . ."

"Yeah, of course," Kate said. "The security must be a nightmare—I hear you're having to bus in officers from other forces to cope. And this baby story sounds like a needle-in-a-haystack job. Look, thanks, Colin. It's been good to catch up. Give my love to Sue. And, Colin, will you give me a call if anything else comes up on this?"

She smiled as she put down the phone. Kate Waters loved a needle-in-a-haystack job. The glint of something in the dark. Something to absorb her totally. Something to sink her teeth into. Something to get her out of the office.

She put on her coat and started the long walk to the lift. She didn't get far.

"Kate, are you off somewhere?" Terry shouted. "Before you go, you couldn't untangle this stuff about the Norwegian royals, could you? It's making my eyes bleed."

Angela

S he knew she was going to cry. She could feel it welling up, thickening her throat so she couldn't speak, and went to sit on the bed for a minute to postpone it. Angela needed to be on her own when it came. She'd tried to fight it over the years—she never cried, normally. She wasn't the sentimental sort—nursing and living the army life had trained that out of her a long time ago.

But March 20 every year was the exception. It was Alice's birthday, and she would cry. A private moment. She wouldn't dream of doing it in front of anyone, like the people who stood there and wept in front of cameras. She couldn't imagine what it felt like, to be on show like that. And the television people kept on filming as though it was some sort of entertainment.

"They should turn off the camera," she'd said to Nick, but he'd just grunted and kept on watching.

It made her feel uncomfortable but apparently lots of people liked it. The sort of people who tried to be part of everything in the news.

Anyway, she didn't think anyone would understand why she was still crying all these years later. Decades later. They'd probably say she'd hardly known the baby. She'd had less than twenty-four hours with her.

"But she was part of me. Flesh of my flesh," she told the skeptics in her head. "I've tried to let go but . . ."

The dread would begin in the days before the baby's birthday and she'd get flashbacks to the silence. That bone-chilling silence in the empty room.

Then, on the day, she would usually wake up with a headache, would make breakfast, and try to act normally until she was alone. This year, she was talking to Nick in the kitchen about the day ahead. He'd been complaining about the mountain of paperwork he had to deal with and about one of the new lads in the stores who kept taking days off sick.

He ought to retire. He could have done it two or three years ago. But he can't let go of the business. Neither of us can let go of things, I suppose. He says he needs a purpose, a routine. He doesn't give any sign that he knows what day this is.

Nick used to remember—in the early days. Of course he did. It was never far from anyone's thoughts.

People in the street used to ask about their baby. People they didn't know from Adam would come up to them, squeeze their hands, and look tearful. But that was then. Nick was hopeless with dates—deliberately, Angela thought. He couldn't even remember their other children's birthdays, let alone Alice's. And she'd stopped reminding him. She couldn't bear the flash of panic in his eyes as he was forced to revisit that day. It was kinder if she did the remembering on her own.

Nick kissed her on the top of her head as he left for work. And, when the door closed behind him, Angela sat on the sofa and let herself cry.

She'd tried to train herself to put the memories away. There wasn't much help at the beginning. Just the family doctor—poor old Dr. Earnley—who'd patted her shoulder or knee and said: "You will get through this, my dear."

Then, later, support groups, but she'd got tired of hearing her own and other people's misery. She felt they were just circling the pain, prodding at it, inflaming it, and then crying together. She upset the group when she announced that she'd discovered it didn't help to know other people hurt, too. It didn't take away her own grief, just added layers to it, somehow. She'd felt guilty, because when she'd been a nurse and someone had died, she used to give the grieving family a leaflet on bereavement.

I hope it helped them more than it did me, she said to herself as she got off the sofa. *Mustn't be bitter. Everyone did what they could.*

In the kitchen, she filled the sink with water and started preparing vegetables for a casserole. The water was too cold and numbed her hands so she found it hard to hold the knife, but she continued to scrape mechanically at the carrots.

She tried to summon up an image of what Alice would be like now but it was too hard. She had only one photograph of the baby. Of her and Alice. Nick had taken it with his little Instamatic but it was blurry. He'd taken it too quickly. Angela braced herself against the kitchen counter, as if physical effort could help her see her lost baby's little face. But it wouldn't come.

She knew from the photo that Alice had a fuzz of dark hair, like her brother, Patrick, but Angela had lost a lot of blood during the delivery and she was still high as a kite from the drugs when they put her baby in her arms. She'd asked Nick afterwards—after Alice was gone—but he couldn't tell her much more. He hadn't studied her as Angela would've done, memorizing every feature of that face. He'd said she looked lovely but had no details.

Angela didn't think Alice looked like Patrick. He'd been a big baby and Alice had been so fragile. Barely five pounds in weight. But she'd still studied Paddy's baby photos and the pictures they took when their second daughter, Louise, came along, ten years later. "Our surprise bonus baby, I call her," Angela told people—willing herself to see Alice in them. But she wasn't there. Louise was blond—she took after Nick's side.

Angela felt the familiar dull ache of grief round her ribs and in her chest and she tried to think happy thoughts like the self-help books had told her. She thought about Louise and Patrick.

"At least I have them," she said to the carrot tops bobbing in the dirty water. She wondered if Lou would ring her that night, when she got in from work. Her youngest knew the story—of course she did—but she didn't talk about it.

And she hates it when I cry, Angela said to herself, wiping her eyes with a piece of paper towel. *They all do,* she thought. *They like to pretend that everything is fine. I understand that. I should stop now. Put Alice away.*

"Happy birthday, my darling girl," she murmured under her breath.

Photo by Jenny Lewis

FIONA BARTON, the *New York Times* bestselling author of *The Widow* and *The Child*, has trained and worked with journalists all over the world. Previously, she was a senior writer at the *Daily Mail*, news editor at the *Daily Telegraph*, and chief reporter at the *Mail on Sunday*, where she won Reporter of the Year at the British Press Awards. Born in Cambridge, England, she currently lives in Sussex.

CONNECT ONLINE

fionabartonauthor.com

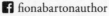 fionabartonauthor

 figbarton

NATIONAL BESTSELLING AUTHOR

FIONA BARTON

"Barton's writing is compelling and top-notch."
—The Associated Press

For a complete list of titles, please visit
www.penguinrandomhouse.ca